Guest of a Sinner

Guest of a Sinner

A NOVEL BY

James Wilcox

HarperPerennial

A Division of HarperCollins*Publishers*

Although this novel is set in New York, with references to Florida, none of its characters represents or is based on persons living in either of these states, or indeed anywhere. All events and personalities are imaginary.

A hardcover edition of this book was published in 1993 by HarperCollins Publishers.

HarperCollins books may be purchased for educational, business, or sales promotional use. For information please write: Special Markets Department, HarperCollins Publishers, Inc., 10 East 53rd Street, New York, NY 10022.

First HarperPerennial edition published 1995.

Designed by George J. McKeon

The Library of Congress has catalogued the hardcover edition as follows:

Wilcox, James.
    Guest of a sinner / James Wilcox.
        p.   cm.
    ISBN 0-06-016875-7
    I.Title.
  PS357.I396G83   1993
  813′.54—dc20   92-53324

ISBN 0-06-092646-5 (pbk.)

95 96 97 98 99 ❖/RRD 10 9 8 7 6 5 4 3 2 1

To Will Swift

"*I may always feel looking back on any past sin that in the very heart of my evil passion there was something that God approves and wants me to feel not less but more.*"

—*They Stand Together: The Letters of C. S. Lewis to Arthur Greeves*

"*. . . they all murmured, saying, That he was gone to be guest with a man that is a sinner.*"

—Luke 19:7

One

The dull ache was not helped by the hymns. As he reached for his wallet at the approach of a portly female usher, Eric diagnosed the ache: common loneliness aggravated by a strain of free-floating anxiety. But during the hymns the ache seemed to sharpen into pinpricks of plain and simple irritation. If he were pope, Eric would make any enthusiastic bleating of sappy modern lyrics a mortal sin.

"Let's give the choir a hand," the celebrant urged just before the final hymn.

The scattered applause drove Eric from the chill, modest nave of beige and tan bricks to the dank spring air of the East Village.

"Mr. Thorsen," a voice called out several times, while he calculated whether there was enough distance to pretend he did not hear. With a crowd on the sidewalk, a babble of voices, this might have seemed plausible. But there was no one besides him and the woman he had caught a glimpse of on the stairs of the church.

Eric was a firm believer in the fellowship of Christian anonymity, which Catholics seemed to respect more than any other denomination does. Of course, there were the exceptions. Recently he had fled from a parish on West End Avenue that had aggressively recruited him to enjoy a cup of coffee in the Lady Chapel after Mass—and it was a church whose choir, for some reason, did not sing through their noses. Uneasy, he wondered if he was going to be forced to pull up stakes again. It would be a shame, for he liked the way the priests here at St. Sofya never spent more than ten minutes, at most, on a homily.

"Hi." She was upon him now, a woman around his own age, early forties. He vaguely recalled chatting about the weather with her—or someone who looked like her—after the nine-thirty Mass last week. But had he given her his name?

Somewhat apprehensive, he returned the greeting: "Hi." She had the fresh, scrubbed look of the laity who devise tithing payment plans.

"I was just wondering—" she began but was drowned out by a truck, loaded with blue police barricades, passing in low gear. Greek-Americans were scheduled to parade up Fifth Avenue that afternoon, Eric had learned from a flier lying in the gutter, face up, as he had waited to cross Second Avenue on his way to Mass.

"I was just wondering," she resumed once the noise had subsided, "uh, if you happened to . . . I mean there's this book I just read, a really great novel. It's about a woman who turns sixty and discovers she's a lesbian."

A damp wind plastered the hem of Eric's alpaca coat to his jeans. With a look of polite expectation he waited for her to go on. "That's nice," he commented when she didn't.

"It occurred to me that you might like it."

"Well, I—" He shrugged and consulted his watch. "Thanks, I'll look for it."

As he started to walk away her hand groped in the pocket of her mauve parka, which she wore with a tweed skirt and expensive-looking cowboy boots. "Wait," she said, extracting a dog-eared quality paperback. "Here."

He took a step backward, as if it were a snake in her hand. "No. No, thanks."

"Take it, please. I won't need it back right away."

"But I don't read novels. Honest."

"It's so well written."

"I'm sure, but I don't like them."

Behind her he saw a corseted Ukrainian grandmother emerge from the gloom of the church and, clutching the rail firmly, begin to descend the steps with wobbly deliberation. Somehow the book was now in his hands, which made his protests sound much feebler. Apparently satisfied, his benefactress turned to help the old woman. Eric took this opportunity to drift away without another word.

The long walk back to his sister's apartment on the Upper West Side helped dissipate his annoyance. Of course, he would have to find himself a new church, for he had given the novel, along with a pocketful of change, to a menacing beggar across the street from the UN. Rather than brood on the injustice of having quality fiction thrust upon him, Eric forgot about the woman as he cut diagonally across Central Park. Past a grove of flowering dogwood he came upon a Norwegian maple that ruined his steady aerobic pace. A sign on the tree informed him that this species' leaves started out red in spring and turned green in autumn. Were it not for a nearby pretzel vendor, who glanced worriedly in his direction, he would have pondered this quirk a little longer.

"She's got a court reserved," Eric was told when he walked in the door and saw Kaye wasn't there.

"I thought you were going with her," Eric commented to their father.

"I was," Lamar Thorsen said. "But then I decided not to."

Eric himself had good reason to be staying with his sister. He had been driven from his Murray Hill apartment by the stench of twenty-two cats in the apartment below his. The move, of course, was temporary, since he had no intention of giving up his rent-controlled one bedroom. Once the cats were evicted, he would be back where he belonged. His father, though, was another matter. He had a perfectly nice apartment in Tallahassee, complete with an adjoining health club. There was no real reason for him to be in New York now. "I need to get away," was what Kaye had reported his saying over the phone a few days ago. "I need a change from this crummy town."

Though he would have liked to shut himself up in Kaye's study with a new score he had bought of the K.415 concerto, Eric was afraid his father might take this as a slight. All his life Eric had tried his best to be a good son. After his father had swerved into a tree to avoid hitting a squirrel, Eric had never once, in the fifteen years since, questioned if the squirrel's life was worth his mother's. Not out loud, at least. Mrs. Thorsen had been killed, while Lamar, properly buckled up, had survived without a scratch. Eric's mother

3

always refused on principle to wear a seat belt, mainly because she thought it was the liberals who made its use a law, but also because it wrinkled her clothes.

"What are you doing?" Mr. Thorsen asked as his son shut a window that afforded a truncated view of an occasional pair of legs. Though it was a basement apartment, Kaye's place was spacious by New York standards, especially for what she paid. And it was only three blocks from Central Park.

"Well, I—"

"It's stuffy in here."

"OK, Dad." Eric raised the sash a compromising inch or two. The problem was the sweetish odor from the garbage cans to the left of the window. Normally, this wouldn't have bothered him. No one in New York can afford to be too fastidious. But the experience with the twenty-two cats had made his nostrils ethically sensitive. Any disagreeable odor now seemed an invasion of his rights.

Lamar Thorsen squashed out a cigarette in a Buddha ashtray—actually, an incense bowl that he had turned into an ashtray. Eric worried about his smoking, especially since his father was overweight. But any warning or advice would be brushed off with a remark about the fact that normally in Tallahassee he didn't smoke at all.

"I don't know how Kaye stands it here," Mr. Thorsen said, while Eric sprayed a mist of germicidal air freshener in his father's general direction. "No light at all, like living in a cave." After a brief meditative pause, he gave the Travel section of the Sunday *Times* a startling whack. "I've got it!"

Now what? his son thought.

"I'll fix you an omelet."

Eric mentioned that he had already grabbed a Danish on his way home from church, but his father was not to be deterred.

Three different knives were produced, a cutting board, a sauce pan, colander, and skillet, green peppers fresh and half rotten, goat cheese, pimientos, herring, celery, cumin, mushrooms, and Benedictine, before Mr. Thorsen realized there were no eggs. Handing his son a fifty-dollar bill, he told him to run out and buy a couple dozen of the finest brown—free range, no mass-produced junk. Eric reminded him that he wasn't hungry.

"Fine, I'll go myself," he said, pulling off his daughter's apron with unnecessary force.

"All right, Dad, I'll go."

"No, you got more important things to do, I'm sure. Don't let me be in the way."

"Dad."

As Eric went to the door his father called after him, "The money."

"I've got some."

"Take it, Son. I insist."

The mound of chopped mushrooms Eric returned to was enough for an entire morning's worth of omelets at the Carnegie Deli. He said nothing, though, except to point out that part of a stem had found its way into the beard his father was growing. Hemingway, if he had lived a little longer and drunk slightly less, might have gone on to resemble Lamar Thorsen, who was built like a bull.

"Got 'em?" Mr. Thorsen asked as he combed his thick fingers through the salt-and-pepper bristles. "Hey, wait. I want you to hear something." The fingers now sought the dial on the radio, hung with space-saving efficiency beneath the spice rack.

As the volume increased Eric made a face, part mock, part real, of displeasure.

"All right, so it isn't Beethoven. But this girl really has something going for her. Janice Jackson."

"Janet."

"You know her?"

"I've heard of her."

The father's knife kept time on the counter for a couple of bars. "Great, huh? You know what I would do if I were you? I'd spend a lot more time listening to artists like this. They've got their finger on the pulse of the time. Folks are paying attention. You never know—you just might pick up something that will get you out of this rut you're in."

Eric did not appreciate having his career called a rut. Granted, he had to work hard for what little money he earned, but he was respected. His piano students stuck with him year after year, and the *Village Voice* had said his performance of Ravel's *Gaspard de la Nuit* was everything the dancing he accompanied was not:

haunting, elegant, thoroughly professional. This was sweet revenge, for the Mani Light Dance Ensemble had forced him to perform the Ravel onstage in a bathing suit. Eric had vigorously protested, but knowing from bitter experience how easily he could be replaced, he had given in and donned the gold Speedo.

"You got the training to be able to take this stuff apart note by note, analyze just what makes it tick."

As his father went on, Eric listened patiently. This was certainly an improvement over the days when Eric, as a teenager, was forced to take a boxing lesson before every piano lesson. Lamar Thorsen had always thought music was fine for a girl, but it was Eric, not Kaye, who turned out to have the real talent. Eric's mother had fought many a battle with her husband over her son's career. Only after she died did he throw in the towel and seem to accept a pianist for a son.

"And what you want to avoid is getting out of touch with the basic human emotions—that's where I fault your long-haired classical stuff. They're out of touch, your modern composers. No one wants to listen."

"Well, I—oh, before I forget, your change."

"What change?"

"The eggs."

"Keep it, Son. Use it to buy yourself a nice shirt. That thing you got on now. . . ."

Like the non-toiling, non-spinning lilies, Eric was somewhat unconcerned about his attire. Although he did not think much of his looks, he had long since resigned himself to the unwanted attention his chiseled features attracted. How many times had someone asked if he was a model—a real put-down, as far as he was concerned. To him there was nothing more pathetic than a man cashing in on his appearance. In a way, Eric was looking forward to the ravages of age, when he would no longer have to fear being asked to undress in order to ply his trade.

"Dad, you paid for dinner last night."

"Don't nickel-and-dime me." The crumpled bills Eric had set down on the counter were swept aside by Mr. Thorsen's knife. "Now, where was I? Modern stuff, right. You've got to get in touch with the pain of the man on the street, the boredom, the love gone wrong."

"You're talking as if I were trying to be a composer."

"Well, you honestly don't expect to get anywhere as a pianist, do you?" Mr. Thorsen put on the offended look that Eric thought he himself was entitled to. "Sit down a minute, Son. Let me explain."

Eric leaned against a counter, which made him more or less his father's height. Apparently satisfied, Mr. Thorsen went on.

"I was just around your age, forty, forty-one, when I realized what a rut I was in. There I was, a grown man with a wife, two kids, taping ankles on a bunch of college ballplayers. Sure, you could call it something fancy, physiotherapist, but what did it really amount to? Rubbing Ben-Gay on a bunch of knuckleheads, that's what. Now I could have gone along that way, comfortable enough. But what do you think I did?" The father paused, as if the answer were going to be a surprise. Then, as the knife came down on a pepper, he said, "I'll tell you what I did. I went out and got myself a doctor's degree in kinesthesiology."

"Those rinds, Dad—don't stuff them down the drain."

"Huh?"

"It's not a garbage disposal."

"Oh. Well, anyway. The point is clear, I take it."

Eric shrugged. "I'm not sure the analogy really works. You weren't happy as a trainer. I am—as a pianist."

"You calling your sister a liar?"

"What?"

"Kaye said to me just this morning, 'Dad, I'm worried about Rickie. He's in a terrible depression,' she said. 'Can't hardly get up in the morning.'"

Eric had told his sister he was feeling a little down because of the cat situation. Leave it to his father to turn it into a full-blown despondency. "It's my apartment. Once that's straightened out—"

"Sure, blame it on the bossa nova." The father began to crack eggs, one in each hand, simultaneously. "Let me give it to you straight, Son. I'm going to tell you exactly what I told your sister. There's something in you that's scared of success. You've been running away from it all your life. Lord knows how many women have thrown themselves at you, yet here you are living with your own sister like a couple of old maids."

"I'm not—"

"Hear me out. There was that chance you had to go around the world with that tenor, accompanying him. A first-class star he was, too. Even I had heard of the guy."

"Dad, he kept on—" Eric couldn't bring himself to say *grabbing me* to his father, so he substituted—"bossing me around."

"What are you, six two, one seventy-five? You telling me you couldn't handle that runt?"

"That's not the point."

"No, the point is everything's got to be perfect, or you won't touch it. Whatever happened to that gal you were so hot and heavy with last Christmas? I liked her."

"That wasn't last Christmas. That was five years ago."

"Nancy, that was her name—right? Now what was wrong with her: too short, too tall, too smart? Never mind, I don't want to know. It's none of my business, right? Hey, cheer up, boy. You're about to eat the best goddam omelet you ever tasted in your life. What do you think of that?"

Eric shrugged. "Can't wait."

"How long is he planning to stay?" Eric asked his sister first thing, as she walked in the door.

Kaye set down her gym bag, from which a racket and a loaf of French bread protruded. "Where is he?"

"Went to check the temperature," he said from the sink, where he was finishing up the dishes.

"Huh?"

"In the park. There's a weather station, he said, next to where they do Shakespeare."

The sister raised an eyebrow. Though her hair was gray, it seemed almost prematurely so. Nine years older than her brother, she had a remarkably fresh complexion and striking green eyes. Like her father's, her heftiness suggested an ex-athlete, which indeed she was. Eric could remember how she used to throw up before diving meets at Florida State. As a senior, she was allowed to switch to the university's circus arts program, which was a little less competitive. There she got an A minus in trapeze and a C in high wire. Now she sold espresso machines in Macy's Cellar.

"Is he bugging you?"

"No, not really. It's just that three's maybe too much for this place."

"I wonder if he would mind the cat smell," Kaye suggested as she retied the girlish ribbon that held her ponytail.

"What? You mean put him in my apartment?"

"Why not?"

Eric concealed his annoyance with a fresh assault on the egg-crusted iron skillet. For Kaye to say such a thing meant that she still did not appreciate the severity of the problem. When he had first told her about it, she asked if his nose wouldn't just get used to it. Perhaps it might if he stayed in his apartment day and night, he had replied. But whenever he stepped out, the contrast was too great. And it was impossible to have friends over. They noticed. Besides, in the past few weeks the smell had intensified, getting worse than ever. Air fresheners were no use, though he had experimented with every brand on the market. And Kaye had never been there in those pre-dawn hours when the heating ducts sent up an unbelievable stench, along with a mewling that sounded almost human, like babies.

"You know, I never did get a copy of the letter Sol sent," Eric said when all the dishes were neatly stacked in the drainer.

His sister pinched a yellow leaf from a three-hundred-dollar bonsai that her boyfriend had given her for her birthday. Eric repeated himself, knowing the tree gave her so much anxiety that she often couldn't think of anything else when she was around it.

"Yes, Eric, I heard."

"Well, don't you think I should?"

Sol Levy was the father of Kaye's long-deceased husband. Semi-retired in Queens, Sol had agreed to write a letter to Eric's landlord as a favor to his daughter-in-law. This was only after Eric had made countless attempts to settle the problem himself with friendly chats and civil notes to the tenant. He once, in desperation, had even taken the offending party to dinner at La Colombe d'Or. Fifty-three dollars that had cost him, and his downstairs neighbor had obliged him by going out and acquiring three more strays the next day.

"How am I going to know what he said to the landlord?"

"Relax, Eric. Sol's probably settled the whole thing by now. He knows how to schmooze."

"Why haven't I heard anything then?"

"You *are* anxious to get out of here, aren't you?" She glanced at the instruction manual that had come with the bonsai. "I hope this isn't too much light," she added distractedly. "Dad didn't water it or anything?"

Eric shook his head. "It's not fair to you, having your space invaded like this."

"I'm happy as a clam—my two favorite men." She frowned as she said this, her mind obviously still on the tree.

"What about Joel?"

Joel was her boyfriend. Since he was married, they could only rendezvous at her apartment.

"It's just as well for now."

A few minutes later, when Eric was scouring the bathroom sink, getting up desiccated dabs of his father's tricolored toothpaste, his sister stuck her head inside the door. "You didn't say anything to Dad about Joel, did you?"

"No, of course not. And Kaye, I wish you wouldn't talk to Dad about me."

"I didn't."

"You said something about my being depressed. You know how he blows things all out of proportion."

Their eyes met in the medicine-cabinet mirror. "He only wants you to be happy, Eric. He'd do anything for you."

"I'm not a child."

"Be good to him, please."

"I am. No one could be nicer."

"I know." She reached for a tissue and blew her nose. "But you could be a little more natural about it. You always seem so—I don't know, stiff."

"Thanks."

"I think that's him now," she said as the front door rattled. "I bought a ton of lox and cream cheese for brunch. And I got French bread for you, since you don't like bagels."

"I just ate an eighteen-egg omelet."

"Come sit with us anyway. I've got the most wonderful Bulgarian coffee. You'll just die."

Two

At the last minute she changed her mind and decided that this time she would not wear the cowboy boots to Mass. Though they made her feel young, she remembered the look he had given them the Sunday before. It was still cool, but she had changed her mind about the parka too. The extra bulk was not a plus. She would have to risk appearing a little staid in the tweed jacket that fit her so well.

Sitting in the last pew, Wanda discreetly surveyed all the late arrivals. But when someone entered her pew during a reading from Paul, she did not look, afraid her joy would be too obvious. Only later, after the homily, did she glance over and see it wasn't him at all. Clutching the ragged vest of a filthy brown suit, the man had begun to jiggle the kneeler with his laceless polished wingtips. Disheartened, she worried about the stench, which was becoming more and more apparent. Would it cling to her after Mass?

At communion, though, her hopes revived. Taking the chalice from Mrs. Ossomov, who, AIDS-conscious, always wiped the rim extra hard with her lace hanky, Wanda had the feeling that when she turned back to face the congregation, she would spy an obscure corner of the church—and there he would be, his golden head bowed. But as she well knew, St. Sofya had no such corners. Built in the early seventies, it was as foursquare as a Friends meetinghouse.

Not in the mood to stop and chat with anyone after Mass, Wanda headed for a nearby coffee shop. There, in a booth beneath an aggressively cheerful mural of the Aegean, she pondered what could have gone wrong. The book had been so carefully chosen, one that would give him doubts about her sexuality. Of course, she wasn't gay, but it was just as well he thought so at first. A man that attractive was probably wary of come-ons—and Wanda was anxious to make it clear that friendship was all she had in mind. She wasn't crazy enough to think a man that gorgeous could ever fall for someone like herself. Friends chided her about being a mouse, afraid to speak up for herself. Now, ironically enough, he probably saw her as being too bold, a brazen hussy.

Her fair skin went red as she reviewed every detail of the encounter last week, how he had surprised her by slipping out before the final hymn was over, forcing her to rush out and call his name. Had she no shame? And then to thrust the book on him like that, when it was obvious that all he wanted to do was escape. It was like a bad dream; she was not herself at all. Imagine what he must have thought when he found her name, address, and phone number printed at the bottom of Chapter Two. . . . She must have been mad, temporarily insane.

Too distressed to finish her jelly doughnut, Wanda wiped the powder from her lips and signaled for the check. Normally, she would have gone back to her apartment to get her clothes in order for the coming week. Wanda liked to have all five workdays planned in advance so she wouldn't have to think what to wear when she dragged herself out of bed in the morning. But once outside the coffee shop, she found herself drifting north.

Sitting directly behind him the Sunday before, Wanda could hardly be blamed for noticing the check he had dropped into the collection basket. Though he had folded it, the address was visible for a moment as the usher dipped the basket toward her. What surprised Wanda was that, after all this time, without her ever writing it down, the address was as easy to remember as her own. Of course, she wouldn't dream of taking advantage of it in any way. The fact that she had blurted out his name last week—this she had also learned from the check—could not be held against her. She had done it in desperation, without thinking. After all, what other alternative was there? Could she have called out, "Hey, you"?

Crossing 14th Street, Wanda realized where she was going. For years she had heard what a nice store Altman's was. Her mother's birthday was coming up. Why not look for a vase there? Just because she had a Macy's credit card, it didn't mean she had to go there for everything—though that was what she tended to do. Wanda realized that if she happened to bump into Mr. Thorsen in the neighborhood—he lived only a block or two from Altman's—she could do it with impunity. Cheered by this thought, her pace quickened.

My mother has a thing for vases.

Well, Altman's has a fine selection.

Yes, Mr. Thorsen, that's what I heard.

Stop with the Mr. Thorsen. Eric's my name.

I'm Wanda Skopinski.

Polish, huh? You know, my mother was Polish.

I thought there was something about you. . . . By the way, what did you think of the book?

Oh, I meant to bring it back today, but I wasn't feeling too well. Anyway, it was a great book, Wanda, very soul-searching.

I knew you'd like it. But really, do you think you ought to be out like this? You do look a little pale.

A man's got to eat, sick or not.

But you're in no condition to shop for anything—

"Can you give me a dollar?" Startled from her daydream, Wanda looked down at the man she had nearly tripped over. He was lying in front of the McDonald's directly across the street from the Empire State Building. For a homeless person, he looked sort of clean.

"I'm sorry, sir."

"That's all right, honey. Don't let it get you down."

"Oh, uh, thanks."

On the other side of 34th Street, Wanda discovered that Altman's was closed—for good. For a few moments she stood there wondering how this could have happened without her knowing the first thing about it. She read the papers, listened to the news. A distant rumble made her look apprehensively at the sky. She had not brought her umbrella, so she should probably look for a bus to take her back downtown. She was tired anyway and too hungry to walk all the way home.

Seeing nothing coming on Fifth, she decided to try Lexington—which would mean crossing Madison first. The address was only a block away now. What harm would a casual glance at his building do? She was a taxpayer, wasn't she? There was no law that said she couldn't walk on Madison Avenue. Nevertheless, she looked apprehensively about her as the numbers got higher. Then it occurred to her—the Morgan Library was in this neighborhood. A perfect excuse if he should happen to appear. Her stride became more confident—241, 245, 247. And there it was, 251. A bank.

It was the bank's address she had remembered, not his. Feeling somewhat foolish, she walked to the end of the block. Then it occurred to her that she could use a little cash. Returning to the red brick building, she noted that her bank card would be compatible with their machines. It was some compensation—her card was going into the same slot his did.

Twenty dollars richer, Wanda boarded the bus on Lexington.

Eric peered out at the rain. He had just finished giving a make-up lesson to a student who had been ill, and now it looked as if he would get soaked. It occurred to him that Omar, the porter, might have an extra umbrella. But where was Omar?

The halls of the settlement house where Eric taught piano to disadvantaged youths were dark and chill on Sundays, thanks to Omar's economies. After wandering from floor to floor, worrying all the time that he had not gotten in enough practice that week, Eric came across the porter stacking wooden folding chairs in the gym.

"Say, Omar, you don't happen to have an extra umbrella lying around, do you?"

"What do I look like, a department store?"

Eric gave a tentative smile. Omar was a prickly old man, easily offended. He slept in a storage closet in the basement and boasted from time to time of having killed a man with his bare hands.

"So you come without your umbrella. Best stay here, Miller, and eat with me."

"I'd love to, but I'm meeting my sister and father." Eric, who had long ago given up trying to explain that his name wasn't Miller, sometimes shared an egg-salad sandwich with the porter.

"You watch yourself, hear?"

"Don't worry, Omar. I'll be careful."

"Crime don't take no holidays."

Fortunately, the rain had turned into a light drizzle, and he could jog the few blocks to the 14th Street subway entrance without getting too wet. The wait for a train was long, but even so he arrived at the 77th Street entrance of the Museum of Natural History with plenty of time to spare. Rather than just hang around waiting for his family to arrive, he made a fifty-cent donation and went in for a quick look around.

Finding the Pacific Northwest gallery almost empty, he lingered there, trying his best to appreciate the animal masks and totems. Most seemed childish and inept, and the accompanying texts with their references to slavery and warfare were of little help. How odd that people so close to nature distorted the animals they revered, demonizing them with human emotions of rage or fright. Obviously there was a price to be paid for feeling at one with the earth; a bear was never just a bear. Perhaps, he mused, city dwellers like himself were in some ways closer to reality. And just as he came to this conclusion, he remembered the cat that had talked to him in his dream the night before. He had been trying to reason with her, to get her to move. And the cat had promised to, while sweeping aside a bloody feather with her paw.

Kaye and Mr. Thorsen were waiting for him when he emerged—as was Joel, Kaye's boyfriend. Beside Joel, Kaye seemed more compact. The man seemed to apologize for his bulk—and the excess natural resources required for its upkeep—with a slouching, melancholy deference. After a brief debate on the steps about where they should go for brunch, they set off with Joel and Lamar Thorsen in the lead to search for a restaurant Mr. Thorsen had passed earlier in the week.

"I thought you weren't going to tell Dad about Joel," Eric commented as they threaded their way through a flock of waist-high schoolboys in blazers and disheveled ties.

"I didn't," Kaye said. "He just showed up at the apartment."

"So Dad knows?"

"He knew I was seeing someone."

"Does he know Joel's married, that we might run into his wife and three kids any minute?"

"Relax."

15

"Kaye, I don't want to be in the middle of some horrible public scene."

"Well, it wasn't me who asked him along. It was Dad."

"And you didn't say anything?"

"I tried."

The restaurant the father had in mind was not on Columbus, as he had imagined, but on Amsterdam. And it was not as nice as he remembered it. His children, tired of wandering first north, then south, on one side of the street, then the other, tried to convince him that the place was nice enough. Humbly, courteously, Joel sided with the father, then with Kaye, then with the father again, until Eric took matters into his own hands and walked inside. Kaye followed, and they were soon seated at a table mapped by various ridges of bread crumbs and lakes of brackish water.

"Dad," Eric warned as his father reached up to finger the lime-green Boogie board on the shiny black wall.

"What?" The thick bare arm, frosted with hair, drooped.

Though they were the only customers, the waiter remained chatting with the female bartender, both, in their white T-shirts, looking as frail and young as amorphous larvae. Eric signaled once, twice, yet again, while Joel's pained, lovesick gaze strayed from Kaye to include the table as a whole.

"Hey, you think you could wipe this table off?" Eric finally called out. The waiter's head turned slightly, but there was no other response.

Mr. Thorsen nodded sagely. "Told you this place was no good."

"Let me," Kaye said apprehensively as her brother rose from his chair.

"Let you what? I'm going to the bathroom."

On the way Eric repeated his request to the waiter with the slow, patient menace of exaggerated politeness. It left him feeling a little ashamed, but the waiter, when Eric returned, did not betray any resentment. His face, as he set the menus on the crumb-free table, was the same—pale and blank as a Fifties beatnik's.

"Your father tells me you're having trouble with your apartment," Joel said when it was his turn to order.

Eric shrugged. The waiter kept his pen poised; Joel's was the final order.

"I told him I'd be glad to help out," Joel went on. "I devote a lot of time to Greenpeace, you know."

"Are you eating or not?" Kaye said, fanning herself with a menu. Though it was cool out, the restaurant was stuffy.

"What, darling?"

"I'm starving, come on."

"Sorry, dear. Let's see, is there a menu?"

"You were just looking at one, Joel."

Mr. Thorsen came to the rescue by suggesting Joel order the octopus soufflé.

"Sounds good," Joel said with a tentative pat to the crop of auburn hair that had been surgically implanted on his generous dome. Eric knew from his sister that this operation had not been Joel's idea, but his wife's. She had also made him color all the gray.

"Sounds good?" Kaye shook her head. "I thought you didn't like seafood."

With an almost bashful smile, Joel said, "Not as a rule."

Eric found it hard to imagine the man getting anywhere in court, though Kaye had assured him that Joel was very successful at keeping his clients out of jail. He was formidable looking, Eric had to admit—someone you wouldn't want to see get angry. According to Kaye, as soon as Joel got his son through Bennington and his twin daughters through Brearley, and finished paying off the mortgage on his Park Avenue apartment, he was going to devote most of his time to Greenpeace. He worried a lot about the earth.

"Order what you want, Joel."

"Fish would be good for me. I eat too much meat."

"Ease up, Kaye," Mr. Thorsen put in.

"Dad, he never eats fish, I'm telling you."

"There's always a first time." To the waiter Mr. Thorsen said, "Let's have that octopus, and throw in a few orders of the fried clams to begin with—and a round of Rob Roys."

"Rob Roys? Father dear, no one here drinks Rob Roys except you. We'll have some white wine."

The hurt look on his father's face was too much for Eric. "I'll have a Rob Roy," he said.

* * *

When they got back to the apartment, Kaye headed straight to the bathroom for a good soak in the tub. Eric went to the cupboard by the refrigerator, where Kaye kept the linens.

"Don't bother with that, honey," Mr. Thorsen said as his son walked into the living room with fresh sheets for the convertible sofa.

"You've slept on the same sheets all week, Dad."

"Why make more bother for your sister? Here." He patted the worn cushion beside him. "Sit. Let's you and me have a nice man-to-man." Five Rob Roys made him speak with the careful exaggeration some parents use when reading a story aloud to a child.

"I've got a score to study."

"Come on, when do we ever get to talk?"

"Dad, we've been talking all week."

"Not alone. Your sister's always been hanging around."

Perching tentatively on a Windsor chair opposite the sofa, the sheets on his lap, Eric listened as his father went on.

"So, Rickie, give it to me straight. What do you think of Kaye's chances with this fella? You realize he's married, don't you?"

"I don't like to interfere in Kaye's—"

"He told me so himself—first thing, as we were walking over. What a jerk, I thought. I wanted to give him a good belt in the nose. But then he starts to explain about his wife, what a tyrant she is. She's been in and out of institutions for the past ten years. Doctors don't know what to make of her, this temper she's got. She threw an iron at him once for not rinsing a glass properly. Now don't get me wrong." He fumbled for matches, then lit a cigarette. "I'm all for the institution of marriage. You won't find a bigger supporter. That's not to say your mother and I didn't have our differences. But we stuck by each other. You can't deny that, honey, can you?"

"Please don't call me honey."

"Huh? Anyway, this Joel seems like a pretty decent fellow to me. Worries me, though, how your sister treats him. If she's not careful with her criticism—I mean, did you hear what she said to him when he borrowed a cigarette from me?"

"Kaye's been trying to get him to stop smoking."

"Well, an exception every now and then—that never hurt any-one. Me, that's when I don't mind lighting up, for a celebration, like seeing you kids. In any case, she's got to learn how to treat a man. No man likes to be belittled by his woman."

"Between you and me, Dad, I'd be happy to see them split."

"What?"

"All this sneaking around, what possible good can it do her?"

"Hey, your sister's no spring chicken." He reached out and tapped his ash into an almost empty glass of chocolate milk. "She doesn't strike while the iron is hot, she just might find herself selling coffee machines for the rest of her life. Macy's." The contempt in his voice was familiar to his son, the same tone he used when referring to the piano.

"What's wrong with Macy's? It's a perfectly respectable job."

Mr. Thorsen smiled, with a rueful shake of his head. "You sound more like your mother every day, you know? Same lack of common sense."

This refrain had cropped up often during the visit, usually when Eric happened to disagree with his father. That morning, for instance, before setting off for a Park Avenue church he hadn't tried before, Eric was accused of being as superstitious as his mother, who used to go to Mass every day before breakfast.

"What's wrong with Macy's? You think I raised you kids to be store clerks? Is that why I slaved to give you both the very finest education? Tell me, Son, is this it? Is this how I'm going to have to leave this earth, seeing the pride and joy of my life, my two dearest possessions in all the world, living like a couple of old maids in some crummy basement? By God, it makes me want to puke!"

The sudden eruption seemed to disconcert the father almost as much as the son, for in the silence that followed—even the traffic outside seemed to have stilled—Lamar Thorsen looked lost. This was a reversion to the old days, before Eric's mother's death, when Mr. Thorsen would start in on the children over some minor offense, and then, before they quite realized what was happening, food would be flying, a plate tossed, as Mr. Thorsen screamed at the top of his lungs. The mother's lips would go tight with disgust while Eric would flee from the Sunday dinner table to the bathroom, locking himself in with tears of shame and fear.

"Eric," his father said now, with a sheepish smile, "you got to understand, you two are everything to me. There's not a day goes by I don't worry about you."

19

"That's not right, Dad." He had risen, leaving the sheets behind, and drifted toward the hall. "We're grown up now. And besides," he added angrily, "I'm not living here."

Mr. Thorsen winced as a thread of smoke teared his eyes. "Face it, you are, unless you get your act together. Why don't you let Joel help you out? That man knows what he's talking about."

"I don't want him to get involved. Besides, he's blowing it all out of proportion. The landlord's not behind all this. He's not trying to throw me out."

"You're rent controlled, aren't you? The landlord could get five times what he's getting if you left."

"I know, but it's illegal to. . . . They're not that way."

"Boy, you *are* naive."

"I don't care what the story is, I don't want Joel meddling."

Mr. Thorsen shrugged. "Have it your way. Your mother, you know, she was always right too. I couldn't tell her a thing."

"Leave her out of this, please."

The look in the son's eyes, deadly serious, made any further conversation impossible. Eric took the glass with the butt in it to the sink, while his father, with a faintly martyred air about him, pulled out the bed from the sofa to change the sheets.

Three

$\mathcal{W}$anda was trapped. If she pleaded illness, she wouldn't be able to go to work the next day. And she didn't want to use up one of her sick days when she felt perfectly well. As for other excuses, she had already let Mrs. Fogarty know that her afternoon was free. Unless she invented a relative in sudden distress, Wanda would have to go.

Mrs. Fogarty ran the newsstand in the lobby of the building on lower Broadway where Wanda worked. One day when Wanda was suffering from cramps—which she called "a headache"—Mrs. Fogarty had urged upon her a pill that really seemed to help. After that Wanda always made a point of stopping for the *Times* on the way to the elevator, and Mrs. Fogarty and she would exchange a few words about the weather or the city's going to pot. Then one day Mrs. Fogarty had asked what Wanda did with herself on Sundays. Wanda replied that after Mass she usually did her laundry and talked to her parents in Connecticut. Mrs. Fogarty suggested, in a generic way, that maybe Wanda would like to drop over for a cup of coffee one Sunday. Wanda hid her surprise and unease with a pleasant, "Yes, that might be nice someday." She had no idea that Mrs. Fogarty would lower the boom so suddenly: "Well, how about this Sunday, doll?" And before Wanda had a chance to invent a proper excuse, Mrs. Fogarty was handing over an elaborate, hand-drawn map giving directions to her house in Canarsie.

"Isn't that sort of far?" Wanda had asked.

"What's the matter? Brooklyn not good enough for you?" Mrs. Fogarty had waited a beat before tacking on a smile that showed her crooked front teeth.

Wanda decided to look casual, down-to-earth, that Sunday. From the chats she had had with Mrs. Fogarty in the lobby, she gathered that the woman was sensitive to any hint of snobbery. "It's all your college degrees that's running this city into the ground," Mrs. Fogarty would say, while Wanda politely refrained from mentioning that she herself was a "college degree." Wanda had matriculated at Albertus Magnus, a Catholic college for women in New Haven, right up the street from Yale. In fact, she had met Louis, her ex-husband, at a Yale mixer. He had told her he was a junior in Davenport, one of the nicest colleges at Yale. It was only after she lost her virginity that Louis admitted he wasn't a Yalie at all. He was enrolled at the C.I.A., the Culinary Institute of America, two blocks away from Albertus. Louis wanted to be a pastry chef.

The ride on the L train, which Wanda picked up on 14th and Third, got off to a bad start when a thin, pleasant-looking young white man who was reading *Vanity Fair* suddenly let out a hair-raising scream. A few people glanced over, but no one did anything, and when the young man went back to reading, everything seemed normal again. Wanda was glad she had sat down next to a conductor's box. When the conductor—a woman, it turned out—moved to another car after they had gone under the East River, Wanda followed, with an occasional nervous glance over her shoulder.

After two stops in Brooklyn the train emerged onto an elevated track. The children who were getting on and off were in one sense medieval, Wanda fancied. At Albertus she had learned that in Thomas Aquinas's time, there was no real concept of children. They were just small adults, which seemed to be the case here too, in these desperate, blighted neighborhoods. The children's eyes, without any illusions whatsoever, no sense of magic, of possibility, seemed so at odds with their lithe, graceful bodies. Whenever they caught her staring, Wanda looked down, anxious not so much about being harassed or mugged as about being exposed, of having her own precious illusions stripped away.

At the Bushwick stop, right next to the cemetery that stretched all the way to Forest Hills, two sisters got on. One maybe thirteen, the other perhaps nine, they wore identical white organdy dresses with ruffled collars. In their gloved hands were hefty white Bibles inscribed in gold. Neither spoke as the train lurched south through Brownsville. Their veils, bobbypinned to their strictly plaited hair, and their patent leather shoes were exactly what Wanda had worn to her first communion in the early Fifties. With some apprehension Wanda kept an eye on the sisters as the others—girls and boys in knee-length T-shirts, monstrous gold chains, and freshly laundered hightops, the laces trailing—bickered and flirted. The trip had already seemed long, but with the sisters aboard, the desolation seemed endless, block after block of sooty brick, barricaded doors, weeds shivering in the discarded Styrofoam of vacant lots. She was glad when the sisters finally got off. Only then did Wanda notice the pockets of decency: a few green awnings, a lawn chair on a cramped terrace, a clean gray four-door sedan.

Canarsie was the end of the line. After consulting Mrs. Fogarty's map, Wanda plowed through the turnstile and turned left on Rockaway Parkway. "It's perfectly safe," Mrs. Fogarty had assured her, "we don't have any coloreds." Wanda had not been referring to black people at all, and she resented the racist twist Mrs. Fogarty had given to her question. Nevertheless, Wanda was relieved that on this street of pizzerias, dim novelty shops, and bakeries she did not stand out quite as much as she did on the train. But her confidence was undermined when she stopped to ask the price of some lilies from a sidewalk vendor. "Suck my dick and they're yours for a buck," the young man replied. Sickened though she was by the insult, she felt some satisfaction that he was white. It made her feel less racist as, hurrying on with clenched fists, she imagined braining him with one of his vulgar ceramic vases.

An X on the map marked the Catholic church on the corner of Flatbush. Waiting for the light to change, Wanda said a prayer, asking Our Lady to forgive her evil thoughts. Her revenge fantasy had gotten entirely out of hand in those few blocks, the lilies by now red with blood. If only she could learn to say a few forceful, appropriate words at the right time. . . .

On the other side of the avenue she found herself in a residential neighborhood with a strangely deserted feel. Though the sun was out and a refreshing breeze blew from Jamaica Bay, no one else was using the sidewalks. The narrow houses reminded her of her own cramped neighborhood in Waterbury, Connecticut—except that here people were a bit more adventurous. Pastel doors, elaborate grillwork, flamingoes and Virgins in the tiny yards, all this would have been frowned on by Wanda's mother, whose favorite color was beige. Mrs. Fogarty's, which she came upon sooner than she expected, turned out to be the top half of a two-family dwelling. A steep flight of blue concrete stairs led to the front door. Wanda was breathing too hard to do anything but smile when she was asked to come in after ringing the chimes. They were still playing a Carpenters theme when she stepped inside, the longest doorbell she had ever heard.

The contrast between the gloom of the living room, whose curtains were drawn, and the bright spring day was so great that Wanda seemed at first to have entered a world of black and white. But as her eyes adjusted, the scene was colorized: Gray walls turned mauve, the ceiling—so low it was almost within reach—a spackled gold. As she was introduced in quick succession to Mrs. Lamarca, Mrs. Monastere, Mrs. Daiglish, Mrs. Spandos, Mrs. Moody, Mrs. Dante, Mrs. Veneroso, Mrs. Neely, Mrs. DiSalvatore, and Mrs. Monastere (no relation to the Mrs. Monastere by the ottoman), Wanda suffered the unease of a recent dream. In it she had gone to Mass in her best slip from Macy's, nothing else. Confronted now with lace collars, brooches, ivory cameos, earrings, and even a couple of feathered toques, Wanda could not help feeling almost naked in her whale T-shirt from the Museum of Natural History. A jean skirt and sandals did not help matters, either.

Suppressing a wave of resentment—the main reason she had finally decided to come was because she thought Mrs. Fogarty, a widow, might be lonely, in need of someone to cheer her up—Wanda settled in the only available spot, on a stool next to the elderly Mrs. Daiglish. All the other women in the room were closer to Mrs. Fogarty's age, in their late fifties, Wanda imagined.

"It's so nice out today," Wanda said as she selected a macaroon from a nearby plate of store-bought cookies.

The old woman's carmine lips gave a perfunctory smile.

After a discreet bite or two, Wanda inquired how Mrs. Daiglish happened to know Mrs. Fogarty.

"Who's Mrs. Fogarty?"

With a nod Wanda indicated the hostess by the velvet drapes. Mrs. Fogarty's pinkish blond hair was arranged vertically in a style new to Wanda, with little terraces like those of the Trump Tower. Precariously overburdened, the woman's petite, birdlike frame seemed to sway slightly atop her spike heels.

"Oh, her. I come with Loretta. Loretta is my niece—she's the one knows everyone."

"Is this some sort of club or something?"

"Search me. Loretta says I got to go, I go. Never mind it's my vacation."

"How nice, a vacation. Where are you from?"

The old woman twisted a diamond ring about her plump finger. "Perth Amboy."

"Oh, I had an uncle who used to live there."

Mrs. Daiglish nodded but didn't express any interest in this coincidence.

"He was a plumber, like my father. It runs in the family, I guess."

"A plumber, huh?"

For the first time the old woman looked directly at her. Wanda wasn't sure, but there seemed to be a glimmer of hostility in the watery blue eyes.

"He's retired now, my father." Wanda brushed a crumb from the corner of her mouth. "His lodge had this raffle, and he won a time share in a deer hunters' camp. It made him feel better about retiring, except that my mother made him sell it. She doesn't believe in killing anything."

"She Jewish?"

Wanda blinked. "No, why?"

"Sounds like something a Jew would say. You know how they are."

With that the old woman turned away to her neighbor on her right. Wanda sat a moment brooding. Yes, one should respect one's elders, but at the same time one had a duty, as a Christian, to stand up to prejudice, no matter how uncomfortable it might make one feel.

"Excuse me," she said, after waiting respectfully for a pause in the old woman's other conversation. "I happen to know a lot of Jews who believe in war and capital punishment and things like that."

Mrs. Daiglish's powdered face was a blank.

"There's even a lot of Jewish gangsters," Wanda added.

"Of course, dear," the old woman finally said in a hushed voice. "But you don't want to say that so loud. Loretta, you know, she's married to one." Leaning closer, she gave Wanda's hand a friendly pat. "Sam, that's Loretta's husband, Sam says to me just before me and Loretta go out to Mass this morning, 'Hey, Rita, what's with the hat? Don't you know it isn't a sin no more to go without a hat?' Now I ask you, I been going to church all my life, and this man has the gall to instruct me on canon law. All I can say is what I said to myself before I left Perth Amboy. 'Rita,' I said, 'you're making a big mistake. You know you and Sam are never going to see eye to eye. He's going to ruin your vacation. Why not be smart and go to the Poconos with Father Reed's group?' But no, I got to go to New York."

Pleased that the woman was confiding in her, yet worried that it was for the wrong reason, Wanda tried to steer the conversation onto safer ground. "Oh, but Mrs. Daiglish, there's so many wonderful things to see in New York. Have you been to *Les Miserables*?"

"You won't catch me setting foot in Manhattan."

"Why? It's safe, really. Nothing's ever happened to me."

The old woman sniffed. "Safe, huh? Last time I was there a plane ran smack into the Empire State Building. Me and my late husband had just gone to Mass at St. Pat's, and the next thing I know, it's like the end of the world. You don't believe me, huh?"

"No, no, it's just. . . . I mean I didn't see anything in the papers about it."

"Front page all over the world. Of course, this was a little before your time, dear, during the war. It sticks in my mind, though, like it happened just yesterday. I never was so scared in my life. Cried for days afterward, let me tell you. That's when I woke up and realized what life really is."

Wanda pondered this a moment while Mrs. Daiglish repaired her face with a delicate mother-of-pearl compact. For some reason the story reminded her of Mr. Thorsen. In some obscure way she now felt grateful to Mrs. Fogarty, as if by inviting her to Canarsie she had saved Wanda from a terrible disaster. Wandering about Murray Hill Sunday after Sunday, what sort of life would that be? As far as she was concerned, Mr. Thorsen didn't exist anymore. Wanda, after all, was a realist. Facts were facts—Mr. Thorsen was not coming back to St. Sofya. She had scared him away. And the sooner she forgot him, the better.

This feeling turned into a conviction when Wanda learned from the lady who was pouring coffee—was it Mrs. Monastere of the ottoman or the other Mrs. Monastere?—that everyone there, except for Mrs. Daiglish and herself, was a member of the Rosary Altar Society of San Lorenzo's. Wanda was sure then that Our Lady was taking special care of her and felt much less self-conscious about her T-shirt. Of course, it did hurt when she caught Mrs. Fogarty giving her a pitying look. But Wanda managed to stare right back at her, for a brief moment, as boldly as any child on the L.

Though he didn't like coming into the settlement house on Sundays, Eric made an exception for Tiburcia. A senior in high school with two children and a job at Woolworth's, Tiburcia often had no free time during the week. Before the lesson began she would always present her teacher with cookies or a pie her mother had made. Eric would have objected to this little ritual had he not realized that it was her way of not feeling like a charity case. Tiburcia did not have to pay for her lessons. Eric was paid with funds from the settlement house endowment, largely underwritten by a grant from a chemical company that had once manufactured Agent Orange.

"Good, good!" Eric exclaimed after Tiburcia finished playing the D-minor Rhapsody of Brahms. It was a little beyond her technically, but Tiburcia was only interested in pieces that sounded grand and passionate. Her will to learn was fierce. Despite her job, her children, and school, she always came to her lessons prepared. Of course, there was that one stretch of six weeks when her mother had to return to the Dominican Republic for a funeral. No progress was made then. But with her mother's return, Tiburcia was playing again as well as ever.

"Is it really good?" she demanded, her dark eyes ablaze with pride.

"Yes, of course. One or two spots are a little rough, maybe. You know where they are."

"But it is good? I am good?"

The urgency in her voice, the raw need, disturbed Eric. He had never seen her quite like this before.

"You see, teacher, my mother she is saying to me every day now, it is coming time soon. I say, Mamacita, an artist must work, work, work." Her laugh was unconvincing. Eric could see the strain beneath it—and to his dismay, the exhaustion that somehow he had overlooked before. Her plump, sturdy body, her round face, had misled him. She was perhaps not as sound and healthy as she seemed.

"You've shown remarkable progress."

"So, teacher"—as she turned away from the keyboard, he heard an eighteen-year-old's voice, her age, not the thirty-five she looked—"for my mother's sake, because she keep asking, tell me how long. Me, I don't care. I work months more, years. But Mamacita is getting tired. The children she watches, they are not so easy now."

A dim idea of what was going on caused Eric to glance at his watch. He didn't want to have to hear what was coming next. "I'm not sure I understand."

"You know, teacher. When will I be good enough for the people to pay? You say I'm good. You always say I'm good."

It was as he feared. "Yes, but you've got to understand, this is a very competitive business."

"No one work harder than me. And I feel the music all through me. When I play for the neighbors, they can't believe what they hear. Everyone can't wait for me to go on tour, to make the records they can buy. Then I can hire the babysitter, and Mamacita won't have to stay at home all day. I can quit my job at the Woolworth's, too. Oh, teacher, if you know how bad that job is, how I hate it so much, my feet hurt so bad. I don't know if I can stand it anymore. I go to sleep there twice, right at the register. They going to fire me if I do it again."

Tiburcia was light-years away from being a concert artist. It was even doubtful that she was qualified to be a piano major at a state university. Where in the world could she have got this mad idea from—her mother, her neighbors? Certainly not from him. Though Eric had encouraged her, praised her even, he had never, not once, held forth any hope of a serious career, even as a teacher. The most she could do with her playing was to enjoy it as a hobby, something to enrich her own and her children's lives.

"Tiburcia, let me say something that you might not like to hear." The distress that immediately registered upon her weary, round face made him swerve a bit. "It's good news, of course—you *are* talented. The fact that you didn't start playing until you were ten years old. . . . You know, most artists, they start at three, four, five. By your age they're already tackling the biggest pieces in the repertoire. It's a whole different league when you talk about playing for money. But that doesn't mean that music can't enrich your life in a big way."

"Yes, I will be rich, teacher. I just know it."

"No, no, honey, not in the way you think. Not money. But in your soul, in experience, in everything that really matters in this world. You have a precious gift, something you'll be able to pass on to your children."

"They will grow up better than me, yes?"

Though there was a flicker of doubt in her eyes, he still wasn't sure she grasped what he was saying. Something in her did not want to hear. Her hand strayed to the yellow ivory of the Chickering and played a tentative chord. Perhaps it would be best to go on with the lesson for now, he thought—but those shadows. . . . Behind the frosted glass door of his office he had been aware of someone hovering. Getting up from the chair beside the bench, he decided to see who this could be. It was a little distracting, after all.

"Oh, Omar."

The porter looked surprised. Beside him was another black man, younger, in a jacket and tie.

"Sorry, Miller. I told him to wait till your lesson was completed."

"It's all right." Eric looked curiously at Omar's companion.

"You Eric Thorsen?" the young man asked.

Eric nodded.

"Here," the man said, handing Eric a folded piece of paper.

"What . . . ?"

With a polite nod the young man said, "Sorry to interrupt you, mister. You can go on with your lesson now. Thanks."

"Sorry, Miller," the porter echoed as he disappeared around the corner with the man.

Glancing at the paper in his hands, Eric let out a little bark that some might have interpreted as amusement. Others, knowing him better, would realize it meant outrage, disbelief.

Tiburcia left after another five minutes of Brahms. Brooding making him even more upset, Eric went straight to Macy's in a cab. There he found his sister in the Cellar with a customer. It was one of the two Sundays a month that Kaye worked.

"A man could use robin's-egg blue, you think?" the customer asked Kaye, whose hair was knotted in a bun that made her look older. There had been no hot water in the apartment for the last two days.

"Oh, sure," Kaye replied, one eye on her brother. He was standing not far away with a look on his face that he hoped read in bold capitals CUT IT SHORT.

"But do men write thank-you notes?" the woman persisted, giving Eric an apprehensive glance.

"I suppose some might think it's effeminate," Kaye said.

"To be thankful?"

"In writing, yes. Maybe you should consider another gift for your cousin—hardware, perhaps."

With a baffled look the woman left the stationery department empty-handed. Eric was immediately upon his sister, thrusting the paper into her hands.

"What's this?"

"Can't you read?"

"Not without my glasses." With a vaguely offended look she went over to the register, where she fumbled about in a pile of receipts. "Do you see my glasses, Eric?"

"No."

"They were right here."

Kaye began searching by laying her large, shapely hands first on one stack of expensive stationery, then another, as if she were a medium, reading the vibrations. Urging her to think, Eric followed her about the displays until she remembered they were in her pocket. "I always get bollixed up when I'm not where I belong," she explained. Selling espresso makers was her regular post, but on Sundays she was sometimes shifted around.

The document once again in her hands, she perused it with raised eyebrows. It was a summons for appearance in criminal court, taken out by Mrs. Una Merton, alleging that Eric had committed the offenses of harassment and excessive noise. After a thoughtful pause Kaye said, "Do you know she was the only customer here in the last half hour? I don't understand how we stay in business."

"Kaye?"

"Yes?"

"I'm about to be thrown in jail, and you start talking about some stranger buying stationery."

"Calm down. You're overreacting." She glanced doubtfully at the summons. "What can this mean? Harassment, excessive noise—you're not even there."

"The woman's insane. She has twenty-two cats."

"Well, I'd ignore it if I were you."

"What?" Eric snatched the paper from her hands. "'If you fail to appear at the above designated time and place,'" he read aloud, "'a Criminal Action Against You may be commenced without your first having an opportunity to be heard.'"

"It says that?"

"Yes, it says that."

Whether it was the lighting or the general aura of the store, Kaye seemed a slightly different person there, her green eyes somewhat duller, her complexion not as fresh. She even seemed to move differently, with a certain constraint, as if she were more conscious of her size. Going to the register she said, "I wish Dad were here."

Lamar Thorsen had taken off earlier in the week to visit a relative in Newark.

"Are you crazy? What good would he do?"

"Well, he did talk to Sol."

"Yes, and he tried to drag Joel into this whole mess. I knew we shouldn't have let him get involved."

"Joel?"

"No, Dad." Eric cleared his throat. "There's no reason for Joel to get involved, right?"

Kaye had recently decided that if Joel was not serious about eventually leaving his wife and getting a divorce, she would stop seeing him. He had promised this from the very beginning, but he hadn't shown the slightest sign of doing anything about it. She had reached her limit, Eric had been told.

"We could always get Sol to explain this," Kaye said, avoiding her brother's eyes. "He could come to court with you."

"Sol?"

Eric did not have to say more. That one word expressed all his dismay. Kaye's father-in-law had been no help at all. When Eric had called him in Queens to find out what was going on, Sol had had to be reminded in some detail who Eric was and what his problem was. As if that wasn't bad enough, he had billed Eric an exorbitant amount. And this was after Lamar Thorsen had bought Sol a dinner—just the two of them—at an Upper East Side steakhouse where a side of French fries cost eight dollars.

"I suppose I could ask Joel."

"No, no, don't do that. I couldn't possibly let you."

"But Eric—"

"No, no, I'll find someone on my own."

There were pauses in this exchange, during which each hoped that the other would offer a stronger, more plausible contradiction. As they talked a young man approached, his staid gray suit making Eric feel, in his jeans and running shoes, if not younger, somehow irresponsible. When he was almost upon them, Kaye's tone brightened. "Yes, it'll be just right for you."

Eric caught on. The young man was obviously a store supervisor making the rounds.

"This is nice," Eric said, picking up a box of cotton-fiber paper with feigned interest. It hurt him that his sister had to kowtow to someone young enough to be her son.

"Mrs. Levy," the young man said, "have you any extra six-nine-ones?"

"Six-nine-ones? What are they?"

The stern, smooth face betrayed a flicker of a smile. "Right here," he said, grabbing a few receipts by the register. His designer tortoiseshell glasses were so clear, so thin, with so little distortion to the icy blue eyes behind them, that it seemed the lenses were not really lenses at all, just plain glass.

"He didn't need any six-nine-ones," Kaye observed as the boy walked away. "He was just checking you out."

"What?"

"He was on the make."

"What's that supposed to mean?" Eric said, fooling no one, not even himself.

Four

*I*t was 3:32, then 4:07, 5:36. Eric rose ten minutes after the last reading of the phosphorescent dial. They did not have to be in court until nine, but he was too agitated to remain in bed. Careful not to disturb his sister, he showered, dressed, and made himself a cup of tea. The tea was set aside when he realized his blue shirt was wrinkled. Rather than get out Kaye's ironing board, he laid a couple of dish towels on the Formica counter. The iron did not pass smoothly over the cotton, the towels beneath lumping the material. By the time he finished, he was not sure if the shirt looked less wrinkled or not. In any case, Kaye was up by that time. She noticed an old egg stain on his tie and suggested he put on another. When he told her he didn't have another with him, she went to the antique breakfront in the living room and, after pawing through some cherished Norwegian crockery, came up with a tie that had been left behind by their father.

On the way to the subway Kaye paused to give some change to a homeless man. She didn't seem to realize at first that he was in the process of relieving himself on the sidewalk. When she did, she apologized, her gaze averted, and went to catch up with her brother.

"Did you turn off the iron?" he asked as, at his prompting, they crossed Broadway against the light.

"Eric, you checked it three times before we left."

"One of my students, her mother left the iron plugged in once and—"

"Oh, would you relax!" Kaye snapped as she swerved to an island to avoid being sideswiped by a bus.

She was right, he realized. He was far too tense. Perhaps if Joel had been along to advise him, Eric might have felt less anxious. But his conscience wouldn't allow him this luxury. If Kaye had asked this favor of Joel, it would have made it harder for her to break off with him. Eric knew this was the only right course for her. Joel was never going to get a divorce. In any case, Joel or no Joel, what did he, Eric, have to worry about? He was the victim, not the perpetrator, of gross injustice. He should be glad that he finally had a chance to air his grievances.

"You know, I've been thinking lately, Joel is really a good man." This she blurted out, apropos of nothing, on the platform at Times Square, while they waited for the shuttle to Grand Central. They had been silent for the most part on the Number One from 86th Street.

"What do you mean by that?"

"He has his points. I sometimes wonder if, like Dad says, I'm not being a little too judgmental."

"He's married."

"Technically, yes. Maybe I shouldn't rush him too much. There's the children, after all. He has to take them into consideration. It's the main reason he stays with his wife, you know." She kicked aside a candy wrapper with the Italian pumps she was trying out for the first time. Somewhat higher than she was used to, the heels made her wobble and clutch at her brother's arm from time to time.

"What about his Mafia stuff?"

Kaye frowned. "What are you talking about? The people he defends have nothing to do with the Mafia. They're mostly Jewish, I think." Tossing her gray ponytail with girlish pique, she added, "It's hard to find a good Jewish man these days. If I throw Joel away—"

"Why must you have a Jew?"

It was a stupid question, Eric realized. Kaye's husband had been Jewish, the only Jew on the FSU swim team, and she had loved him with a passion. Her own Catholic stock she considered to be virtually indistinguishable nowadays from the WASP gene pool. In an ecumenical way she merged them both into a single cold, unfeeling, and bigoted respectability.

"Anyway, why are you bringing up Joel's good points now? It's too late."

"Too late?"

The train was pulling in. "It won't do any good to call him now, will it? He couldn't make it to court on time—could he?"

"I don't know, Eric. But maybe later, if things don't work out today."

The doors of the train opened. Brother and sister became obstacles, briefly, for the passengers getting off. "Forget it, Kaye. I'm not going to let you."

She followed him in. "It's not just you I'm thinking of."

"Sit here."

"I miss him."

"Sit."

"No, you sit, Eric. I don't want to smush my dress."

Emerging from the Number Three train on the fringe of Chinatown, Eric and his sister passed a video store specializing in Mandarin movies before turning up Broadway, where the sights were more mundane. There was something reassuring about turn-of-the-century buildings, Kaye thought aloud with a vague gesture toward a defunct wholesale needle company. Eric agreed that granite and stone seemed more real than glass and then waited while she took a tissue from her purse and applied it to some reddish clay that had somehow gotten onto her pumps. Wondering aloud where it could have come from, this clay that reminded her of Tallahassee, she was urged on by her brother.

A building that seemed very much like the wholesale needle's turned out to be Criminal Court, which they had walked past at first, Eric expecting more in the way of columns and blindfolded statues. Once through the brass doors, he peered belligerently into the gloom, angry at himself for the guilt he should not be feeling. It was the same anger he had had at his mother's funeral while his father indulged his grief.

The men who seemed to know where they were going all had shoulder holsters, the guns as big as Saturday matinee six-shooters. Unarmed men lingered on benches in the hall, waiting with corn chips, girlfriends, or coffee for their hearings. When Eric and Kaye came to Room 114, they found it was locked. Kaye said she knew all along they were going to be too early.

With time on their hands they wandered farther down the ill-lit hall, which at one point, near a cluster of vending machines, opened up into an unused, barricaded expanse of ruined grandeur. Gazing up at an intricately carved oak ceiling thirty or forty feet above, Eric noticed a net of chicken wire just beneath. Probably there to catch any loose pieces from one of the vaults, he speculated, as his sister extracted a cup of bubbly coffee from a machine that had stolen the change due her.

By the time a clerk opened up Room 114, Eric had endured enough boring anxiety to make this seem a welcome event. While Kaye chose their seats in what resembled a large inner-city classroom, Eric presented his summons to an attractive black woman sitting behind a long scarred table in front. After recording his name and case number on a tally sheet, she then drew a line through both. Eric thought this was odd but figured it must be some sort of bureaucratic regulation.

"This is Queens," the woman said, pointing to a sign behind her. "Your complaint is Manhattan, don't you know?"

"I didn't see the sign."

A plump Hispanic woman at an adjacent table registered him with calm efficiency. She even gave him a wan smile when he thanked her.

Kaye had picked a spot off to one side, by a window. Sitting down beside her, he told her Una Merton had not yet arrived. When she did, they would be assigned an arbiter, who would hear their case in another room. "I found out," he added, "that the arbiter isn't a judge or anything. That lady at the table told me it may not even be a lawyer. Could be a housewife or something."

"See, Eric?" she said, giving him a pat. "I told you there was nothing to get so worked up about."

"Then why do they have to say Criminal Court on the summons?"

"Look." She snatched the summons from his hand. "Right here, below, it says 'IMCR Dispute Resolution Center.'"

"I don't care. We're still in Criminal Court, and everyone seems to have a gun except us."

"Not to worry." She opened her purse and tilted it toward her brother. Clearly visible was a snub-nosed revolver.

"Kaye!"

"Joel gave it to me a few months ago. He doesn't think it's safe for me to walk around without one."

"Are you nuts?" He lowered his voice as a sallow man with a limp settled down directly in front of them. "You need a license, you know. This could mean a year in jail, mandatory."

"Why do you always have to look on the dark side?"

"Do you mind closing this?" Eric asked, snapping the purse shut himself.

Kaye shook her head and sighed. "Am I allowed to get some gum, sir?"

"No."

Furtively, she unclasped the purse and reached inside. "Want some?" she asked, holding out a stick of sugarless.

Not bothering to reply, he took it from her in an absentminded way, his eyes on the windows, wondering if they could be opened.

Though they had never met before, Mrs. Una Merton drew the face toward her with both hands and planted an audible kiss on one cheek and then on the other. Wanda, worried about getting back to work as soon as possible, brightened. The old woman was really charming, so different from what she had imagined. As the ambulette that had deposited Mrs. Merton on the sidewalk drove off, they entered the Criminal Court building hand in hand.

Eighty-three years old, Una Merton had a surprisingly fierce grip for someone with so mild, so sweet, a countenance. Though she was well nourished, a widow's hump enforced a stoop that made her no taller than a fifth grader. Wanda felt a surge of motherly concern as she steered her out of the path of an oncoming dolly. It seemed the soft-drink man propelling it would have run them both over without a second thought.

"Jerk," Wanda muttered, looking over her shoulder.

"What's that, dear?"

"Nothing."

"Come along, then. There's no time to gawk."

It had been Mrs. Fogarty who prevailed upon Wanda to accompany the old woman to court. Una Merton wasn't a friend of Mrs. Fogarty's but, rather, was the former mother-in-law of one of the Mrs. Monasteres that Wanda had met at the Sunday afternoon coffee in Canarsie. Wanting to be of service to Mrs. Monastere, who was president of the Rosary Altar Society, Mrs. Fogarty had volunteered to escort the mother-in-law to the hearing. It would be no problem at all, Mrs. Fogarty had reassured Mrs. Monastere, since her newsstand was only two blocks away from the courthouse. But then it turned out that Mrs. Fogarty had to be home that day because Castro Convertibles was finally delivering the new settee they had promised months ago. Hearing all this the day before on her way out of the office, Wanda had asked why Mrs. Monastere's husband could not look after his own mother. He was dead, that was why. "Besides, Wanda," Mrs. Fogarty had gone on, "you seem to have a real way with the elderly. Why, your ears would be burning if you could hear what Mrs. Daiglish said about you. Hardly anyone can get her to talk, and there you two were chatting away like two peas in a pod."

Though she was not taken in by this flattery, a chord was rung. Wanda did consider herself something of an expert with the elderly. At St. Sofya she had helped out at a senior citizen drop-in center for three years until she was falsely accused by a lady who used to be a butcher in Kiev of stealing her 3.2-oz. bottle of Elizabeth Taylor's Passion. The experience had been so painful that Wanda could not bear to return to the center. Nevertheless, the urge to be of service to others was as strong as ever. And it was this, not Castro, that finally decided her. In any case, the courthouse was not far away, and Mrs. Fogarty had assured her that she would be back in her office in an hour at most.

"It wasn't my idea to go to court," Mrs. Merton was saying as she took a breather, as she called it, in her progress down the hall. "I'm not litigious—live and let live, that's my motto. But the gentleman who lives next door, a dear man I've known for thirty-three years, he told me I got to fight this or I'll find myself out on the streets, a bag lady. So he went with me to the East Side Tenants Council and—"

"What exactly is the problem, Mrs. Merton? Mrs. Fogarty didn't really explain much to me."

"My rent is ninety-six dollars a month, that's the problem. The landlord could easily get two thousand if I left. He's been looking for a way to get rid of me for years, hoping I'll die. Now it's my poor cats. He's threatening to kill them if I don't move."

A wave of indignation made Wanda exclaim, "Oh, how awful!"

"He knows it would kill me. I'm all alone. They're all I have." She paused to adjust the patterned ultramarine scarf tied about her neck. Wanda noticed, with a pang of sympathy and repulsion, that the woman's ankles were dirty, swollen, and scabbed.

"They've been phoning me," Una Merton went on in a tenuous voice, almost a whisper. "Sending me registered letters. One of them even came to my door. He had this awful beard. My heart, dear, it was in my mouth, literally. He was so ugly to me."

By now Wanda had forgotten all about getting back to work. "Mrs. Merton, don't you worry. I'll be with you. I'll see that they stop harassing you. It's a real crime, just horrible. I can't begin to imagine what sort of people— Oh, here we are."

Wanda steered her charge to the nearest seat, in the last row, before going to the table in front to find out what they were supposed to do. Being white and well-dressed, she couldn't help feeling a little conspicuous, almost as if she were onstage. It made her uneasy; she preferred observing others from as dim a background as possible. But for the old woman's sake she girded her loins and braved the frowns of the clerks, her voice quavering a little as she spoke. And she had to ask the Puerto Rican woman to repeat herself on a couple of points. Wanda wanted to make sure she had heard correctly and would do the right thing.

As she was going back to her seat something barely glimpsed from the corner of her eye made her pause, look again. There it was—the golden head bowed. Yet could it be him, the very same him? Her heart pounding with a violence that dismayed her—for she thought she had squashed all hope completely—she told the old woman they would have to wait until an arbiter was free. It might take fifteen or twenty minutes.

"In the meantime, I might go freshen up," Wanda added. "I won't be long."

* * *

40

"Hi."

Eric had been perusing a Mideastern take-out menu he had picked up off the floor. Looking up at the vaguely familiar face, he returned the greeting. "Hi."

Wanda was about to ask in an offhand way about the book she had lent him, but then it occurred to her that this might seem forward. An alternative came to mind, saying something about church. But since he had stopped coming to St. Sofya, she might sound as if she were trying to get him to return. If there was one thing she couldn't stand, it was people who couldn't let other people be.

An awkward silence, during which first Wanda, then Eric seemed about to say something, was finally broken by Kaye. Extending a hand, she said, "I'm Kaye Levy, Eric's sister."

"Wanda Skopinski."

"Oh, so *you're* Wanda. I've heard so many nice things about you."

Eric gave his sister a look. How could she have heard anything about her when he wasn't even sure who she was?

"Eric was just saying the other day," Kaye went on, "what a good time you and he had at the recital the other night. Merkin Hall, wasn't it?"

"That was Susan I was with," Eric corrected.

"Oh." She clapped a hand over her mouth. "How stupid of me. Actually, Eric didn't say many nice things about Susan at all. He doesn't seem to like her very much."

"Kaye."

"What? Won't you sit down, Wanda? That's the nicest sweater. I bet it's handmade."

A little flustered, Wanda remained standing. "Yes, I like to knit."

Groaning inwardly, he suddenly placed her, the woman with the novel he had given away. Instinctively, he got up and excused himself, saying something about a rest room.

"So where do you and Eric know each other from?"

Wanda followed his retreat with her eyes. He didn't seem to be quite as spectacularly handsome as she remembered, and his hair was not as thick and lustrous as it had seemed in church. Indeed, there was gray in evidence. "Uh, church."

41

"Are you a nun?"

"No."

"Well, hallelujah. My poor brother, you see, he has a tendency to get involved with religious. There's all this passion of the soul and heartbreak. But I don't suppose I have to tell you this, do I? Eric's probably given you the blow-by-blow."

Wanda blushed, both too ashamed and too fascinated to reply.

"I've been trying for years to wean him from church—no offense, of course. I mean, religion can be a very meaningful thing, if you're a certain type. It's the last thing my brother needs, though. He's so conscientious as it is, wouldn't hurt a fly. A real saint, if you ask me. But he has such a low self-image—all that original sin business, you know."

"Oh, right," Wanda ventured. "But you know, the Church is much more upbeat these days. We don't emphasize sin anymore."

Kaye waved her hand impatiently. "Frankly, I think you'd all do a lot better if you did. It seems hypocritical to me, taking back everything you used to say. I mean, either you're going to hell for eating meat on Friday or you're not."

"Well, I—"

"I'm sorry, Wanda. I shouldn't get started on this topic. Eric and I, we've had so many scraps we can't even discuss it. Anyway, what brings you here? You here to help Eric?"

"No, I'm just giving a hand to this lady who's about to be evicted."

"You a lawyer? Sit, Wanda." Kaye patted the seat beside her, obviously eager for someone to help pass the time. But Wanda remained standing, her gaze straying to the door. The last thing she wanted was for him to think she was pushy, trying to insinuate herself into his life.

"So you're a social worker?" Kaye persisted.

"I'm a clerical worker—at a company that buys up scrap iron and brass and stuff. The Thais own it."

"How interesting. Do you speak Thai?"

"No, most of the people in the office are Laotian." Wanda glanced over her shoulder at the old woman, several rows behind them. Her face, her bearing were as serene as a Buddha's. Wanda could not help admiring such fortitude in the face of tribulation.

Her duty, she knew, was by her side. Much as she would like to stay and chat with Mr. Thorsen's wonderful sister—her eyes were so striking, so full of life—Wanda excused herself and, after going out in the hall and not finding a women's room anywhere in the vicinity, returned to her post.

Five

On her way back to the office, Wanda picked up a plain yogurt to eat at her desk for lunch. She wasn't hungry, but she hoped putting something in her stomach might help settle the confusion that made her pause from time to time in the middle of the sidewalk. The shock of learning who Mrs. Merton's persecutor was had still not worn off. And those looks he had aimed at her when she had said a few hesitant words on the old woman's behalf. . . . How was she supposed to have known that a whole roomful of cats was involved, half of them fully sexed toms? Mrs. Merton had talked as if there were only two or three. Of course, she could see now that Eric Thorsen wasn't the beast she had imagined at first while the old woman described her plight to the arbiter. But then again, was it right for his father to have made that visit to Mrs. Merton's, scaring her half to death? Mr. Thorsen claimed he knew nothing about this, or the dreadfully harsh letters his lawyer had been sending her, but some doubt lingered in Wanda's mind.

"Hey, you!"

Looking over her shoulder as she headed for the elevator bank, Wanda saw Mrs. Fogarty motioning to her from behind the newsstand's glass counter.

"Isn't that funny?" the woman commented as Wanda approached. "I forgot your name just now. Went clean out of my head."

"It's—"

"I know, Wanda, I know. Good news, doll."

"Pardon?"

"My settee came. And can you believe—it's the right fabric. I was able to open up here a half hour ago."

"Great."

"So tell me—hold on." Her attention was diverted by an elderly messenger who brought an Arabic newspaper to the counter but then seemed to change his mind about buying it. He just walked off.

"They're all nuts," Mrs. Fogarty said as she refolded the paper and stashed it behind her. Her hair, which had seemed so towering in Canarsie, lay flat, dull, and neat about her prominent ears. "Anyway, how did it go?"

"OK, I guess. She can keep the cats."

"And they say there's no God."

"Well, actually—"

Mrs. Fogarty's fine, sharp nose gave a little twitch as she confided, "Since I couldn't be there myself, I said a prayer for you both this A.M."

"That's nice—but do you realize she has twenty-two cats?"

"No. Well, imagine that."

"They're probably a health nuisance."

"I wouldn't worry about that, Wanda. The judge must know what he's doing."

Wanda was not so sure of this. For one thing the judge was only an arbiter, an extremely nice woman who had complimented Wanda for looking so fresh and natural. Flattered though she was, Wanda couldn't help feeling it was unfair to single out one side like that. And then when Mrs. Cusak, the arbiter, started going on about free speech and the First Amendment, Wanda couldn't help feeling her uneasiness mount. Mrs. Cusak seemed to think that the cats were an expression of Una Merton's affection and that any curtailment of that expression would be a violation of her constitutional rights. When Mr. Thorsen suggested that perhaps the cats themselves might be entitled to some rights—space, a clean environment—Mrs. Cusak had winked at Wanda. Then, with the singsong voice of a first-grade teacher, Mrs. Cusak had wondered aloud if Mr. Thorsen were one of those misguided activists who were always raising a stink about the rights of animals when millions of children were starving all over the world. It was perhaps a mistake at this point for Mr. Thorsen to threaten to report Mrs. Cusak to the ASPCA—and to demand to know her credentials for arbitrating a case like this. He was lucky to escape with a reprimand.

"I've really got to get back to work," Wanda said, after answering a few more questions about the proceedings for Mrs. Fogarty.

"Here's your *Times*."

As Wanda opened her change purse, Mrs. Fogarty said, "This one's on me."

"Thank you," Wanda said, putting the correct change on the counter, "but I think I'll pay."

"God will reward you, doll," Mrs. Fogarty called out after her.

Once at her desk, Wanda was so bombarded with requests for petty cash that she forgot all about the yogurt. Her boss, Mr. Ko, had told her shortly after she was hired that she was the only person in the entire office he trusted with the combination to the safe. Not even his secretary knew it. Wanda was flattered, but it made her feel somehow obligated to Mr. Ko, as if he were doing her a favor. The truth was, she regarded this job as only a make-do arrangement until she came across an opening in a personnel department, preferably in some large corporation with Ivy League types. Wanda felt that she would be good at interviewing intelligent men and women and placing them in satisfactory jobs. But even with her degree it wasn't easy to get such a position, though she had come very close at Philip Morris, where one of the vice presidents was a Catholic and chatted with her about Thomas Aquinas. K-Yok, Inc., where she had ended up for the moment, had its advantages. It wasn't far from her apartment in the East Village, and everyone went home at five on the dot. But she didn't feel challenged here. And she found it hard to make friends. English was a second language at K-Yok, and most of her colleagues had to exert some effort to make themselves understood. Among themselves they spoke Lao or, in the shipping department, something called Shan.

"Wanda, you sick in morning?" Phyllis asked as Wanda handed her seven dollars and thirty-one cents. Phyllis was a lovely, lithe Laotian who had her heart set on being an actress. Wanda often covered for her when she had to rush out for an audition.

"No, I had to help a friend."

"I tell Mr. Ko you sick."

"Thanks," Wanda said, wishing Phyllis hadn't lied for her. It bothered her, even small untruths. She would have to speak to Phyllis about this someday. She couldn't go on expecting Wanda to make up stories when she was out auditioning. Of course, Wanda would like to continue being kind and helpful, but no longer in a dishonest way.

"Hi."

"Hi."

This was what they said, Eric first, at the holy water fount. He had lingered there during the final hymn and, when he saw her coming down the aisle, dipped his hand in and crossed himself, as if he were just passing by. Whether this attempt to feign a mild surprise at seeing her at St. Sofya worked or not, he could not tell. They were in a small crowd of exiting parishioners, and Wanda seemed distracted by hellos and how-are-you-doing's.

Once outside Eric still wasn't sure what tack to take. The more honest course was simply to admit that he needed her help, that he was even willing to pay her. But being so blunt sounded crude and mercenary. She was bound to be offended and might even retaliate in some way, perhaps by urging the old woman to sue him.

Without settling this issue he found himself strolling toward First Avenue with her. She was saying something about a cheese shop in the neighborhood, what a wonderful selection it had. When they got to the corner, they both stood uncertainly for a moment.

"A cheese store?" he said finally.

"Yes. But it's closed on Sundays."

"Oh." He glanced at her plain, unassuming face. "How about a cup of coffee?"

"I don't know." Consulting her watch, she added, "I suppose."

The color visibly rose in her neck, flushing her face. He realized he must be honest soon, right away. He must not let her think he was interested in anything but his apartment. As his sister had reminded him that morning before he left for Mass, he might have a low opinion of himself, but it was unfair to assume that everyone else shared it. Besides, some women found male worthlessness irresistible.

The diner they wandered into was not the one she had intended. But it was closer than the nice one, she informed him as the rain began to fall. Neither of them had thought umbrellas would be necessary when they had left for Mass.

The scarred wooden booths had a certain charm, one appealing to the eye rather than the rear end. Eric was not sure at first if this was an authentically run-down establishment or one of the gentrified hangouts purposely designed to seem down-and-out. The waiter's filthy apron, though, helped decide him, even before he saw the prices.

"Have you gotten a chance to look at that book I gave you?" she said after they had ordered coffee and toast.

"Well, I . . ." Shifting on the painted wood, Eric wondered what sort of lie he was going to come up with. "I guess I gave it away."

Amazed at himself, he waited for her reaction.

"Oh. Well, that was nice, sharing it with someone else," she said, without much enthusiasm.

"No—see, I didn't read it. I just wanted to get rid of it. It's like, I don't even check books out of the library—you know, the thought that you have to return them. . . . I don't like to get tangled up in obligations. And I told you, too, I don't like novels."

Avoiding his, her eyes, pale yet intense, searched the tabletop. "It was stupid of me to force it on you like that."

Eric smiled. "This is interesting. We're both being honest."

Her smile was wan. "Look, I know why you came to church, why we're here. Before you get your hopes up, let me tell you, I hardly know her. I was just doing it as a favor for this lady I know, barely know."

"But Mrs. Merton seems to like you a lot."

"Listen, Mr. Thorsen—"

"Eric."

"—I don't feel it's right for her to have that many cats, even if they are strays without a home. At the same time, I couldn't have it on my conscience if she were evicted."

"That isn't what I want. I just want her to clean up her act. Couldn't she be happy with six cats?"

"Why don't you talk with the landlord?"

"You think I haven't?"

"Well?"

"They've talked to her, but they can't enforce a pet clause because she's been there forever—and doesn't even have a lease. She's a statutory tenant, and they're afraid of harassing her too much because it will look like they're trying to throw her out to raise the rent. The city's pretty strict about those things. They could get fined, even go to jail."

Wanda took a bite of toast, which had been set down before her with a clatter. "Then go to the ASPCA, the Department of Health."

"I will—but then I'm going to look like a real villain. She does seem to love the cats. It could kill her, I suppose. At least that's what she says."

"So what am I supposed to do?"

"If you could somehow talk to her, get her to listen to reason, tell her what this is doing to me—"

"What's this?"

Eric had taken a ten-dollar bill out of his wallet and put it by her saucer of toast. "For the novel you gave me."

"Don't be ridiculous." She shoved the money toward his plate.

"Please."

"No, absolutely not."

It was a stalemate. Neither one would touch the crumpled, dirty bill.

"Would you mind telling me why you thought I'd be interested in a novel about a lesbian?" he asked, after the waiter had given his cup of coffee a refill.

"Because I didn't want you to think I was after you. I hate aggressive women."

"Oh."

"I'm not gay, but I thought if you thought I was, it'd be easier for us to be friends." She looked him in the eye for the first time. "That was dumb, wasn't it?"

"Why did you want to be friends with me?"

49

"Because I could see"—her courage almost failed her, but she forged ahead—"you look sort of lonely."

This time it was he who blushed, glancing away in confusion.

"Your face is very open, you know."

"I have to go."

"Why are you angry?" she asked as he slid out of the booth.

"I'm not."

He had taken the ten and used it to pay at the register. Wanda left a generous tip herself.

"I'm sorry if I offended you," she said as they stood outside under the awning. It was still raining.

"You didn't offend me. I just think it was pretty stupid of me to . . . "

"To what? Ask for help?"

"You can't help me. I'm sorry—I'm late."

With a friendly wave of the hand, which didn't seem to connect at all with the expression on his face, he took off across the street, jumping over a pothole brimming with water.

When he got back to his sister's, Eric closed the three-dollar umbrella he had bought off the street and went to the study to change. His jeans were damp, his sneakers soaked.

Standing nude, undecided, before the desk where he had stashed his underwear in a drawerful of appliance warranties, he heard the door open behind him and Kaye's voice. Had he seen her contact lens solution?

"No," he replied. As she began to rummage around the room, he covered his rear end with a Laura Ashley catalog. "Kaye?"

"What?"

"Do you mind?"

"Mind what?"

"I'm dressing."

"No, go ahead." The imitation leather armchair gave a sigh as she settled into it. "Well, did you see her? What's wrong? I'm not looking."

Eric stepped into some baggy shorts, yellow with age. "She can't do anything. She hardly knows Merton. They're not relatives or anything."

"Well, I guess this means I should talk to Joel."

"No, I'm going to call the ASPCA."

"But I have to talk to him anyway."

"Why?"

"About the gun."

Eric paused as he buttoned a faded blue work shirt. "You haven't gotten rid of it yet?"

"It's his. I can't just toss it in the garbage."

"Give it back, then."

"I will."

"I can't stand having it around the house." He tugged on a sock. "I'm afraid I might use it."

"On me?"

"No, on me."

She adjusted her legs into a lotus position, holding her bare feet in her hands. "You shouldn't let that woman get you down."

She was referring to the arbiter, Mrs. Cusak, whom Eric was in the habit of denouncing whenever normal conversation lagged.

"It's not her, Kaye. It's me. Here the Berlin Wall is coming down, all of Eastern Europe is throwing off its shackles, and I can't feel anything but a—well, I guess I'm happy, but in a theoretical way. I don't feel it in my gut."

"If you were back in your apartment, then you would? I mean, is it just the cats, Eric? Are you maybe using them as an excuse?"

"Oh, sure, they're all in my mind."

His sarcasm had no effect on her. "Sometimes, you know, we create our own reality. I've been wondering lately—maybe you're not being driven from that apartment. Maybe you are driving yourself from it."

"Are you nuts? It's real, Kaye, the noise, the stench."

She breathed deeply, holding first one nostril closed, then the other. "You're not practicing like you used to."

"Right—you think I like that? At home, with the piano there, I could play whenever I liked. Now I have to trudge over to my office and have Omar grumble."

"Maybe you want to get away from the piano."

"What? I'm always worried because I'm *not* practicing. Why would I—? Kaye, you've got everything backwards. I wish you'd stop. This logic of yours really annoys me." Finally dressed, he looked around at her and saw her eyes were closed. Only Kaye would try to meditate in the middle of a conversation. "What if I told you you really, deep down, wanted to be a clerk at Macy's?"

"I do, my child."

"That this is the be-all and end-all of your existence."

"So it is."

"Oh, come off it," he said, picking up the phone, which had been ringing while he finished tying his laces.

When he put it down, after a brief conversation, Kaye still had her eyes shut. "Russell Monteith?" she asked.

"How did you know?"

"I can tell by your voice—very apologetic, and sweet, and irritated."

A member of the board of the settlement house, Russell looked older than Eric though they were the same age, only months apart. They had been close friends for years, Eric often spending weeks as a guest at Russell and his wife Audrey's summer house on Fishers Island. But when Russell got divorced and took up with a sanitation engineer, Eric and Russell drifted apart. Sylvester, the garbageman, was extremely jealous of Eric's looks and would accuse Russell of having a "thing" for Eric. This was fine with Eric, since it gave him an excuse not to see Russell. Of course, Eric did not consider himself prudish or homophobic, but nonetheless it had been something of a shock to discover that his friend liked men. Russell's three children all seemed to take it in stride, and his wife admitted that she had had doubts about him from the very beginning. The divorce was not rancorous, since Audrey was involved with a widower with the most wonderful sense of humor. Everyone seemed to remain good friends—except for Eric. He couldn't help feeling a tinge of resentment. Had Russell really liked him for who he was all those years? Or had he held out secret hopes? Of course, Russell had never made a pass at him, nothing overt. But there had been some searching looks from time to time.

"What did he want?"

"Sylvester's at his mother's. He wanted me to come over for dinner tonight."

"So?"

"I'm busy."

"You're busy?"

"Yes, I got to practice. The Mani's doing Prokofiev next, the Third Sonata. It ain't easy."

Kaye frowned, unconvinced.

"Plus I've got a gig with the Opera Forum. I'm accompanying two operas, and rehearsals begin next week."

As he gathered his music together, Kaye suddenly let out a little scream. Vexed with her, he turned and saw that she had been startled by the appearance of their father.

"Dad, please don't creep up like that, not when I'm meditating." She reached for his hand and gave it a kiss. "How are you?"

"Fine."

"How did you get in?" Eric asked.

"Well, great to see you too, boy."

Kaye got up and gave her father a proper hug. "I'm so glad you're back, dear." Then to Eric she added, "I gave him a set of keys."

Sunburned, his nose peeling, Lamar Thorsen tossed his plastic John Deere cap on the desk and began to tell them about a wonderful creek he had found in Newark, loaded with brim.

"I hope you didn't eat them," Kaye said.

"Are you kidding? Vivian and I ate nothing else. They were the finest-tasting fish I ever caught, I kid you not. And you won't believe, Vivian told me that Shelley's grandfather used to fish in that same creek."

"Shelley who?"

"Never heard of Percy Bysshe? His grandfather was from Newark. What do you think of that?"

This last question was directed at Eric, who was going out the study door loaded down with music. "I don't believe it."

"It's true. I'll bet you a hundred dollars, boy."

"Maybe there's a Newark, England."

"Hundred bucks says it's New Jersey."

Mr. Thorsen trailed his son to the front door, daring him to make the bet. Eric did his best to contain his annoyance, but when his father wouldn't let up, he finally said, "I hope you're satisfied."

"What?"

"You got me dragged to court, you know."

He yanked open the door and strode out past the garbage cans to the steps leading to street level. Mr. Thorsen followed closely behind, expressing his innocence, his surprise.

"Why did you have to go and threaten Mrs. Merton like that? You knew I didn't want you to meddle. It's my affair."

"Now, Son, be reasonable. You don't think I would threaten an old lady, do you?"

"Yes, I do."

"I simply tried to talk some sense into her." The anger in his father's voice did not surprise Eric. But the fear in his eyes did. It suddenly occurred to Eric, in a visceral way, how much power he had over this man, who had always intimidated him.

"What right has she to ruin your life?" Mr. Thorsen went on, striking the iron railing with his fist. "I'll be damned if any son of mine is going to let some old hag chase him out of his own home. You're darned right I laid down the law to her."

"Laid down the law"—this was the expression Mr. Thorsen had always used after a skirmish with Eric's mother over their son's piano lessons. Eric felt a little sick that history kept on repeating itself. Had there been fear back then, too? Or was it just the rage and hatred that had made Eric want to leave home for good?

"Where are you going?" Mr. Thorsen demanded in such a loud voice that a jogger looked over her shoulder as she passed them on the sidewalk. "Just where do you think you're going?"

"To practice."

"So when do we eat? I'm fixing brim tonight, you know."

"You and Kaye can eat anytime you like, Dad. I've got a dinner engagement."

"What? My first night home and—"

"Sorry, Dad."

"That's just great," Mr. Thorsen muttered, his pace slackening as his boy, with a burst of speed, crossed the street against the light.

Six

*M*aking sure that his father did not try to help him anymore took its toll on Eric. Ever vigilant, he would question Lamar's comings and goings and linger in the vicinity of phone conversations. Kaye spoke to her brother from time to time, urging him to lighten up. He tried. But his workload, heavier than ever, made it difficult for him to relax at Kaye's. There was never a moment when he didn't feel he should be practicing. The Prokofiev was turning out to be much thornier than he had anticipated, and the Mozart he played for the Opera Forum was so unfriendly for a pianist, all repeated notes at top speed. Because of this he didn't really have the energy to deal with the ASPCA or the Department of Health. His father, of course, did, and wanted more than ever to make personal calls upon these agencies. Mr. Thorsen just didn't feel right about going back to Tallahassee until he had settled his son's apartment problem. As a result, all this chronic tension and anxiety made Eric ripe for Wanda's suggestion.

According to Kaye, who had taken the call while Eric was giving a lesson to Tiburcia, Wanda was hoping to find someone to look after her apartment while she house-sat in an apartment uptown on Beekman Place. Wanda was afraid her own place would be broken into because no one was there. She wasn't asking for rent. All Eric would have to do was water the plants. And, Kaye added, Wanda's East Village apartment was not far from the settlement house. "Besides," she urged, when her brother remained impassive in the face of this wonderful news, "it would give us a little room here."

"You don't seriously think I would take her up on this, do you?"

"Why not?"

"I don't know her at all."

"What's there to know? You're doing her a favor. You won't even have to see her."

"Sure."

"My dear deluded brother, if it's your precious body you're worried about, take it from me, the woman is safe."

"How do you know?"

"Trust me." Kaye took a drag on a cigarette she had filched from Lamar. Years ago, when she was married, she used to smoke. Eric worried now about the occasional puff she took, wondering just how occasional it was. "All I know, you got to get out of here. Dad will drive you bonkers."

"Look, he has a perfectly decent place to go to. I don't know why it's me that has to leave."

With her free hand Kaye pumped a Heavy Hand weight that she used walking to and from work. "Didn't Dad tell you?"

"Tell me what?"

"You remember Dr. Davidson, he used to be head of Health and Phys. Ed. at FSU?"

"Right. Dad always hated him."

"Never mind that. He had a stroke a couple of months ago, in the same building Dad lives in. They didn't discover his body till a week later."

Eric waved smoke from his eyes. "Well? I'm sorry, but—"

"Can't you see? Dad's terrified that's going to happen to him. He's afraid of being alone when he. . . . All these excuses he's making to hang around here, like your apartment and seeing Aunt Vivian—he just doesn't want to go back alone."

"Doesn't he have any friends? A lot of men his age, they're chasing girls, having a ball."

"You know Dad. He's like those geese."

"What geese?"

"The ones who mate for life."

"What a crock—it's probably because no woman can stand being bossed around these days."

"Well, whatever the case—"

"Doesn't he have any men friends?"

"Used to, I suppose. But they moved away; some died."

Kaye brought up the subject of Wanda's apartment again in the morning, and once again Eric said no, he would not even consider it. But that evening, after Tiburcia informed him that she was stopping her lessons, he found himself walking from the settlement house all the way to Beekman Place. His intention had not been to see Wanda, but rather to walk off his disappointment and frustration with Tiburcia. He genuinely liked the Dominican girl and wondered how much he was to blame for her quitting. Block after block he concluded guilty, then not guilty, guilty, not guilty, while his body dodged traffic with the automatic skill with which the liver or the spleen conducts its business. He did not actually see anything, anything that consciously registered, until he was there in front of the building, which looked more like it belonged on Third Avenue than Beekman Place. The white brick facade did not harmonize with the more sedate sooty red brick of its neighbors. Although there was no Gristede's or A&P on the ground floor, it felt as if there could be. With a look of suspicion and distaste, the doorman announced him. Wanda's voice—"Who?"—pierced through the intercom a few times before Eric's identity was established.

When the door on the eighteenth floor opened, Eric expressed surprise that she was home. He had been in the neighborhood, he explained, and thought that she was probably still at work, since it was early yet.

"No, I'm here, I guess." For a moment, as she stood there in a pair of baggy shorts that made her legs seem thin, girlish, it seemed as if she might not ask him in. But then the door opened wider, and she stood aside.

"It belongs to my boss's brother," she was saying as they stood uncertainly in the foyer. Perhaps she had been napping, for a tuft of hair, like a large cowlick, jutted from her left temple. She applied a hand to it, trying to flatten it. "My boss, Mr. Ko, he asked me one day if I'd like to live in a fancy apartment for a while. I thought, Why not?"

Basically two-toned, in silver and white, the art deco duplex was not vast, but the mirrors, the wrap-around terrace, made it as airy and expansive as anything he had ever seen. After he commented on the view of the Queensboro Bridge, she asked him if he wouldn't mind taking off his shoes.

"The carpet," she added apologetically with a gesture toward the cream wall-to-wall. "Mr. Ko doesn't allow shoes in the house."

Eric removed his sneakers and discovered he had on brown dress socks with a hole in the right toe. But she didn't seem to notice as she slid a tape into a video machine. "This is the only bad part," she said, scrutinizing the controls with a worried look. "I've got to make sure these things are running all the time. There's two more upstairs, taping just about everything on TV. I can't ever turn them off. That's really why I'm here."

Wandering in the direction of a sleek bar, Eric stubbed a toe on the teeth of a polar bear rug, a ridiculously painful accident that contorted his face for a few moments. Wanda offered to go look for something in the medicine cabinet upstairs, but, feeling rather foolish, he told her not to bother.

"Let me fix you a drink."

"Yes, vodka; that would be nice. You wouldn't happen to have any chilled? Look in that little refrigerator there. Yes, that's it. Oh, good."

She had found a bottle of Russian, the best, frosted with a coating of ice. It was bound to help his still-throbbing toe.

Ivory draperies billowed in a brisk, pungent breeze as he settled onto an armless chair that faced the wall of sliding glass doors. The lamp beside him was a stylized nude, a silver female of grim fascist perfection. Beside Wanda, who had angled her chair so they could talk more easily, was an equally grim male.

"This place isn't me at all," she said, after taking a sip of her screwdriver. "I worry about spilling things."

"How long do you have it?" His crystal glass was heavy and curiously fluted. It took a little effort to raise it to his lips.

"At first I thought a couple of weeks; that's what my boss led me to believe. His brother's got some business in Arkansas. But then it was stretched out to a couple of months, maybe more." She sighed. "I'm homesick for the Village."

"And your boss thinks he's doing you a favor."

"Exactly. It was dumb of me to say yes. I didn't realize how much I liked my apartment until now." She dug her bare toes into the carpet. "It used to take me seven minutes to walk to work. Now I've got to take the subway twice a day, and I worry all the time that something's gone wrong at home—a leak, someone breaking in, my plants."

"A lot of people would die to be here."

"I know. At first I thought it was heaven, like one of those movies with Myrna Loy, a black-and-white where everything looks so slick and clean."

The gray in her hair, Eric noted, seemed at odds with the girlish voice and small, delicate hands. She went on talking, somewhat nervously and more and more irrelevantly, about old movies, beggars (via *My Man Godfrey*), and Thomas Aquinas (via a connection Eric, absorbed in the pleasure of his drink, did not catch), until he finally interrupted. "I just came to thank you for your offer. And to say I'm sorry I can't accept."

"Pardon?"

"Your offer."

"What offer? Oh, my apartment?"

Eric frowned. "You did ask, didn't you?"

"Well, actually . . . I mean, yes."

She was holding something back; it was obvious. "Miss Skopinski," he said with mock severity.

"It was your sister's idea, really. She called me to see if there was anything I could do about Mrs. Merton. And I guess we got to talking and I told her about moving and how I had this friend of mine, Phyllis—I had promised her she could move into my apartment because she was tired of living with her parents—and your sister said to please give you a chance at it, how your father's been getting on your nerves and all. So I called Phyllis and explained and she said she understands, but you know the Laotians are so polite you never know if they really mean it."

In his agitation Eric had stood up and gone to the white baby grand, where he tried out a few notes. It was out of tune, but the tone was really nice. "Well, you can call your friend now."

"You don't mind?"

"I can't believe Kaye did this to me."

"Your sister's very kind. I like her a lot." She regarded him curiously as he sank onto the piano bench. "You play, don't you?"

"What else?"

Wanda looked puzzled.

"I mean, she told you I played, right? What else? The nun—did she tell you about the nun I used to date?" He smiled in a way that did not put Wanda at ease. "OK, so I value my privacy. But it's not because I've got anything to hide. It's just that facts by themselves don't mean a thing. I don't understand people who can blather on and on about themselves. They even go on TV and let the whole world know that they used to drink a quart of after-shave lotion every day or had an affair with their dog. My sister just eats that stuff up, like she's learned something."

"Why don't you want anyone to know you?" This she said sometime later, as a non sequitur, after a reversion to Mrs. Merton. Wanda had been going on about how she had met the old woman, saying something about the Empire State Building blowing up, when Eric, wearied by the interminable explanation, asked for another vodka. He got it himself, which was when Wanda posed the question.

"Why pretend that anyone can?" he replied as he headed back to the piano bench. "Look how long it took you to explain one simple thing, how you ended up in court with Una Merton. I'm sure you left out a lot, but even then you came very close to boring me to tears." There it was again, he thought—this rude honesty. What was it about this woman that compelled him to tell the truth, even when he knew better?

"Well, I'm sorry if I—"

"Never mind," he said, thankful for the anger that flashed in her eyes, an improvement over the wounded looks he had been treated to in their previous encounter in the East Village diner. "The point is, this whole Merton business is just a tiny fraction of your life. I mean, what difference does it make to you that twenty-two cats are wandering around some apartment in Murray Hill you've never seen? And yet for me to understand how you got involved—I mean, I still don't understand—would take a good hour or two. Even then, I'd only have the bare essentials. I'd know nothing about who you really are. Imagine if you tried to tell me something really important about yourself, like why you never got married or—"

"I did get married, once."

"Fine. So let's say you tried to explain why it didn't work out, why you've ended up the way you are now. First of all, you'd have to give me a sketch of what he was like, how your personalities clashed. Then I'd have to know the details of what your life was like back then, all the sociological and financial facts. But even that wouldn't be enough. To really know what was happening, I'd have to let you explain as best you could what was going on inside—your psychology. And of course, as we all know, that would only be what you *think* you thought. What you *actually* thought and wished I'd have to find out from your analyst."

"I never was in therapy."

"This is all hypothetical," he said, a little impatient with her literalness. "But what you said in therapy would be selective too, wouldn't it? So what I'd be getting from your analyst would be an interpretation of you and your neuroses minus many significant details about your life that you had forgotten or thought unimportant. Furthermore, the only way you could be completely honest with your analyst would be to tell everything. And it would take you as long, longer, to tell everything as to actually live everything. But let's say you managed to do it, and I managed to have the time to listen. That's just the beginning. I'd have to—in order to really know you—listen to your ex-husband's side of things. And to judge the truth or accuracy of what he was saying, I should probably hear what *his* analyst has to say about him. Then again, what about these analysts? Are they as detached and scientific as they like to think they are? What are they holding back? What problems and frustrations do they have that color their interpretations? Or if you and he never saw analysts—"

"He did a few times, after he threw a spoon at me."

"Anyway"—again, that damn literalness—"let's say he didn't. So I'd have to go to his friends, your friends, your parents, your enemies—only then could I really work up some composite model that was getting close to the reality of who you are."

"The spoon stuck in the wall. I'm not kidding. We were having breakfast one morning, Louis and me, and he's acting real moody, not talking, and I ask him if maybe, since I never get to go out, if maybe he would mind skipping his hula class that evening and take me to a movie, and the next thing I know this like grated spoon we used for grapefruit is coming at me and I swear to God it stuck in the wall and—

"You're glaring at me, do you know? You're glaring at me just like Louis used to. I think I need another drink."

In the morning Wanda's hangover kept her focused on the immediate problem of where to find the strength or energy to rise from the satin sheets and make herself presentable for work. Nothing was automatic. Each part of her daily routine—brushing her teeth, showering, the touch of lipstick—was an effort of the will. Downstairs in the lobby she realized she had put on the wrong blouse, the one she had worn to work the day before. But she felt it would completely drain her to go back up and change.

At her desk in K-Yok's ill-lit offices, while reviewing a petty cash projection for the next quarter, Wanda suffered a mild panic when she tried to remember if she had turned on the upstairs video machines on her way out. This concern was still on her mind when Phyllis appeared, late and breathless as usual. With a worried look Wanda gave her the good news. She, Phyllis, would be able to stay in her apartment. Phyllis thanked her profusely. But she wasn't sure she would be able to now. Her parents had never thought it was a good idea, especially since the apartment was in a bad neighborhood. Wanda said something about Tompkins Square becoming more fashionable, but without much conviction. There had been a riot just two nights before when the police had tried to eject some street musicians.

On her way out to grab a sandwich for lunch, Wanda was hailed by Mrs. Fogarty as she hurried past the newsstand looking straight ahead. Mrs. Fogarty wondered if Wanda would mind bringing back a coffee soda for her. And also, if it wasn't too much trouble, a bag of pork skins. "The lite kind," Mrs. Fogarty added. "Low fat, you know."

"I've never seen any like that."

"They got them at the Eagle Deli."

Wanda did not like that deli, two blocks west of Broadway. It smelled, and the Pakistani clerk always tried to flirt with her. "I'll try."

"And if you got time, doll, you might throw in a ham sandwich. But only if you have time, if there isn't a line. No mayo, butter on both slices, ketchup, and—

"Two thirty-five is your change," she said to the man who had brought a muscle-car magazine to the counter.

Turning to leave, the man did a double-take, as if Wanda were a celebrity.

"I'll be dipped!" he exclaimed.

"Arnold? Arnold Murtaugh?"

His face was beaming. "Wanda!"

"Arnold!"

"What the hell are you doing here?"

"I work here," she replied, a few decibels softer. Arnold had always had a certain tendency to shout when he was excited. Wanda had met him years ago at Albertus Magnus, on a blind date. Sister Mary Patrick, his aunt, had thought they would make a good match. He was a good two inches shorter than she and had a crew cut at a time when long hair was in. Wanda had been embarrassed to be seen with him on campus—he had worn a pink-striped seersucker jacket in the fall—but nonetheless accepted two more dates after the blind date. This was mainly because she liked Sister Mary Patrick and didn't want to hurt her feelings.

"You can't work here!" he spluttered merrily. "*I* work here!" Though he had a reddish mustache now and was going bald—the little hair remaining was long, far too long—he sounded exactly like the sophomore from St. Joseph College she had known. Luckily, St. Joseph was in West Hartford, and he couldn't always manage to hitch a ride down to New Haven. So the relationship had died a painless, natural death.

"You really work here?"

Wanda nodded.

"How long? I've been here for years and never seen you. Third floor, that's where I am. Bear, O'Toole and Myrick, CPAs."

"I'm on eleven."

"Well, you better hop right on up to eleven and cancel any plans you have for this evening. You and I have some serious celebrating to do."

"Oh, Arnold, I'd like to, but I really can't."

"Why not?" Mrs. Fogarty demanded from the counter, where she had been arranging a display of cigarette lighters.

63

Arnold looked over, surprised, but then gave her a wink. "Yeah, why not?"

"To tell the truth, I'm exhausted."

"No good. Won't do. Am I right or am I right?" he added, to Mrs. Fogarty. "See you here at five sharp."

"Arnold, please," she called as he strutted toward the elevators.

"No excuses," he said with a huge smile, looking over his shoulder.

Mrs. Fogarty, in her agitation, reached over and plucked Wanda's sleeve. "What's wrong with you, girl?"

"I'm tired."

"He likes you. No ring. What's the problem? Too short? You don't like freckles?"

"Mrs. Fogarty, please," Wanda said, genuinely shocked by the woman's crudity.

"Pumpernickel," Mrs. Fogarty called after her as she headed for the revolving doors. "No mayo!"

The coffee seemed to help the hangover, and Wanda began to talk with more animation. Arnold had persuaded her to join him for a light supper at a falafel establishment not far from the subway she would take uptown. He had gone on a mile a minute ever since taking her arm, in an old-fashioned way, in the lobby of their building and walking her to Delancey. By the time her tofu burger was served, she already seemed to know his whole life story, how he had become a priest, worked in a mission in Luzon, fallen in love with a German, left the priesthood, gotten a degree in accounting from Pace, and joined Bear, O'Toole.

"Now, what about you?" he asked, after winding up his account.

"Nothing so glamorous or exciting."

"You seeing anyone?"

The question seemed a little bold to her, especially since it was accompanied with such a solemn, searching look.

"I'm divorced."

"Are you seeing anyone?"

"I go out occasionally." She looked down at her plate, wondering if she had told a lie. The month before she had been asked to a Knights of Columbus supper in Waterbury by a policeman who was her father's godson. That should count as a date, even if it turned out that the policeman was gay and made her promise not to tell anyone. And she had been listening to personal ads from men on a 900 line. Though some of them sounded nice, she wasn't quite brave enough yet to respond.

"Last night," she went on, avoiding his intent stare, "I saw someone."

"Your boyfriend?"

"No, nothing like that. Just this guy I know. He's sort of different, real closed off."

"So are you dating anyone?"

"Not really, but I think you'd like him. He's very handsome, and Kenny Rogers almost came to his wedding." A twinge of conscience gave Wanda pause. Perhaps it wasn't right to repeat what Eric had told her after he had switched to wine the night before. But it was so interesting she couldn't help it. "See, he was engaged to this Lebanese girl whose father owned all these record companies. The wedding was going to be this big *Gone With the Wind* thing in Atlanta, on a plantation. Eric's mother and father were coming up from Florida for it. And all Eric's friends in New York and Baltimore, where he went to graduate school, everyone was going to be flown down at the father-in-law's expense. But then at the last minute, after all the invitations were sent out and there had been articles in all the Atlanta papers, Eric realized he couldn't go through with it. He was going to get his own solo album, too; the father-in-law wanted him to do all these popular classical pieces in a jazzed-up way."

"Singing?"

"No, he's a real good piano player. But he felt funny, he said, because he knew there were people much better than him who never would get a chance to record. It all began to seem wrong, phony. He couldn't stand the thought of having to dress up like Rhett Butler for the wedding. His fiancée, she was older than him, she stopped being so sweet and became a bitch on wheels, spending all her time at fittings and parties and bossing him around, and then when he backed out—well, the father threatened to shoot him and his own father thought he had lost his mind and everyone was telling him he had ruined his life for good. Only one friend stuck by him, this rich guy called Russell. He helped Eric find a job teaching at a settlement house and even got him an apartment, a good cheap place in Murray Hill. Actually, that's how I met him, through the apartment. It's a long story, though. I won't bore you with that."

"You could never bore me, Wanda."

He said this so simply, without a trace of guile, that she couldn't help feeling pleased. "Now Arnold, that doesn't sound like something a priest should say. I swear, it's really hard for me to imagine you that way."

"I'm not a priest."

"I know. That's even harder, seeing you as a priest and then not. You never struck me as being very radical. Remember what you used to say about the Vietnam War, how it was our duty to contain communism and how horrible the Yale students were, how immoral?"

He smiled as he took a sip of mint tea. "You know, I really liked you back then. It hurt."

"Hurt?"

"It hurts to like someone when you know they really don't care."

"But I did like you," she said reflexively, worried that his feelings were still hurt.

"You were so pretty then. I used to have dreams about us, that we were running together, in slow motion, through a field of daisies. You were in that white dress you used to wear all the time, the one with the tiny lace border."

Wanda raised her eyes, amazed. She had forgotten all about the dress. But he was right. She had worn it all the time, and it did have a lace collar, delicate, almost unnoticeable. "Arnold."

"What?"

"That's a very beautiful thing to say."

Now it was he who looked down at his plate, his pita virtually untouched. "I knew I was too short."

"Arnold, don't."

"And now I got a potbelly."

"Stop. I won't let you put yourself down like that. You're a very attractive man, and you have the most wonderful smile."

"You mean it?" he asked, suddenly looking up, eager as a boy.

In a general, impersonal way, yes, she had meant it. "Of course. Any woman would be proud to be seen with you. Can we get the check? I really have to be going."

"This is mine."

"No, Arnold. I want to pay for myself."

"Forget it. I asked you, remember?"

He was so forceful about it, his voice growing loud enough to attract stares from other customers, that she finally gave in and let him have his way.

Seven

At his last dinner with Russell Monteith, Eric realized, he had spent too much time talking about Mrs. Cusak and Una Merton. Russell had listened politely, with the pained expression of someone trying to look interested and sympathetic. But he had not, as Eric had hoped, come up with any suggestions or referrals to high-powered friends in city agencies. As a matter of fact, Russell had muddied the waters himself with a piece of information that had been withheld from Eric for years. It seemed that in order to get Eric into Russell's cousin's apartment, Russell had had to pass Eric off as his cousin's brother. A rent-controlled apartment could only be inherited by someone in the immediate family. Russell explained that he knew Eric was too moral to lie, so he had let the cousin and the cousin's lawyers do the lying for him.

Having learned that he was illegal and had been for years, Eric was much more reluctant to press his case with the landlord. This meant concentrating on the ASPCA. For some reason they thought his particular case would fare better with the Animal League Society. Eric followed up with a personal visit to their offices, where he urged them to be as kind and gentle as possible with Mrs. Merton. He explained how attached she was to her toms and how too violent a separation might affect her health. Weeks went by after that visit, during which he heard conflicting reports of a case worker being assigned to Una Merton, of this case worker then going on a pregnancy leave (even though Eric had been told he was a man), of the case worker being reassigned. In the meantime, Eric was reaching his limit at Kaye's. His father had managed to put in his two cents with the Animal League, which only added to the confusion. Something had to be done.

It was Arnold Murtaugh who decided him. Seeing the looks Arnold gave Wanda, filled with adoration, and hearing from Wanda herself that they went out on weekends—in fact, every single weekend—Eric realized he had nothing to worry about and it was foolish to let Wanda's apartment go to waste. Besides, he would be doing her a big favor. Every other day she had to stop by the Tompkins Square apartment to make sure the plants were all right and nothing was stolen. If he was there, she could go straight to Beekman Place, her mind at ease.

The relief of being in a place of his own again was immense. Not having to worry if a sister or father was going to burst in on him, naked, went a long way toward calming his frazzled nerves. And being so close to the settlement house meant it was much easier to practice. His anxiety about the Prokofiev and the Mozart lessened as, after hours of hard work, the notes flowed easily, naturally, becoming deeply embedded in his muscle memory. As for the apartment itself, though he could have done without a few of its decorative flourishes, such as the oil painting of some kittens in a basket that was hung over the mantelpiece, it was more than satisfactory. Wanda's furniture was solid hand-me-downs, comfortable, well arranged. A locust tree just outside the living room window gave a greenish cast to the light, almost as if one were in the suburbs. Eric enjoyed reading by this bay window, with its old-fashioned lace curtains and the locust pods, like giant snowpeas, brushing against the wavy, imperfect glass.

"Don't you feel guilty about not paying any rent?" Russell Monteith asked one afternoon after admiring the pods. He had shown up early, curious to see what Eric's new place was like. Kaye and Lamar would be along in a half hour or so, giving them plenty of time to eat before heading off to the opera.

"I do pay rent, for an apartment I can't use," Eric said with a touch of irritation. Didn't Russell realize that he barely made ends meet as it was, with just one apartment? In fact, because the Mani Light was late again in paying, he had had to dip into his very meager savings.

"Who is this woman, anyway?"

"No one, really, just someone I happened to run into. You want a mimosa?"

"Better not. I fall asleep if I drink during the day." Russell wandered over to the mantelpiece, where he looked for a moment at a framed color photo. "Who's this?"

"Wanda's brother. He was killed in Vietnam. Fragged."

"Haven't heard that word in years." Russell peered closely at the lieutenant, giving a little sniff like a dog checking out new territory. "His own men killed him, huh? Must have been tough on the family."

Wanda, when she had shown him around the apartment, had mentioned that the shock had done something strange to her mother. The woman began to check the garbage two or three times a day, afraid that Wanda or her father had thrown something valuable away. Mr. Skopinski had taken to drink, and Wanda herself had gotten married to Louis, the cook.

"Coffee, tea?"

"Coffee would be nice," Russell said, moving on to inspect a clay candlestick hand-painted with daisies.

At forty-two, Russell was, as he put it, legally bald, which seemed to go well with the comfortable paunch of a family man. He dressed like a father, too, in washable polyesters that could not be permanently ruined by drooling or spilled food. Nonetheless, a stain was usually in evidence somewhere on this millionaire's apparel.

"You told him?"

"What's wrong with that?" Russell asked.

While the coffee brewed, Russell had mentioned that Sylvester knew he was seeing Eric that afternoon. It made Eric uneasy, almost as if Russell were using him to make his lover jealous. If there was one thing Eric wanted, it was to stay clear of anything going on between those two.

"What have I got to be guilty about, Eric? It's not as if we're going to be alone. Besides, I don't like sneaking around. Like that dinner we had when Sylvester was at his mother's. I finally came clean. I told Sylvester. So he blows a gasket. I tell him it's completely innocent, and he says if it's so innocent, why did I hide it from him? The man's completely irrational."

Getting more and more uncomfortable, Eric changed the subject. He asked Russell how much he knew about *Die Walküre,* which was what they were going to see at six that evening. Kaye had gotten the tickets from a friend—and, incidentally, had extended the invitation to Russell without consulting Eric first. Scratching his chest in an abstracted way, Russell said he thought it was fascinating that the supreme being, Wotan, was hoping someone would disobey him, that this was the only way he himself could be saved. Luckily, he had Siegmund for a son, not Jesus. Maybe it's the same for all of us, he said. The only way we can be saved is to be thwarted. "It's funny," he added after a pause, "but he can't seem to get it into his head—Sylvester can't—that two men can be friends, period."

Eric adjusted to the non sequitur with a little cough. "He knows I'm not gay, doesn't he?"

With a shrug came the reply. "Sylvester's the type who's convinced every man, underneath it all, is gay. If he sees a married man, he thinks it's a cover. If a man's single and screwing every woman in sight, he's just trying to prove to himself that he likes women. And if he's an old-fashioned confirmed bachelor—well, all that means is he hasn't the guts to admit who he really is."

"Did I tell you Ida Grossman came over the other night?" Eric said, almost before Russell had a chance to finish. The garbageman's opinions did not interest him.

"What can you do with a man like that?" Russell said with a bemused smile, taking his coffee into the living room. "Ida Grossman, you said? Poor woman."

Eric settled into a wing chair, complete with antimacassar, by the bay window. "You saw the *Times?*"

Russell nodded.

Eric had met Ida when they were both students at the Peabody Institute in Baltimore. Ida had gone on to join the faculty at Indiana University, while concertizing as much as her schedule would allow. Her recent recital at Merkin Hall had left Eric weak with admiration. As far as he was concerned, no one played Scriabin better—and her Schumann, the *Kreisleriana,* was the most intense emotional experience he had had in years. When the second-string *Times* critic called her originality "feckless and perverse," he was even more outraged than Ida herself. She had tried to numb the pain with her flask of Russian vodka. But Eric could see it was doing her no good. That was why he had set the flask aside and made love to her, tenderly, quickly, before her cab arrived.

"Did you console her?" Russell asked.

Eric smiled, happy to have been found out.

All the warmth and friendly concern that had meant so much to Eric in the past were still evident in Russell's voice, his regard, as he said, "Was this wise, leaping into bed with a two-hundred-pound woman?"

"She's lost a lot of weight."

"Never mind about that. It's your nun that bothers me. Did you tell her?"

"Ancient history, Russell. Nancy and I haven't seen each other in years. Joy Foxe is the most recent."

"Well, then, sir, did you hide this from Miss Foxe? And who is she, anyway?"

"An aerobics instructor—my sister's, actually. She's the one who introduced us. What a body—you wouldn't believe."

Russell, who had been hovering near the mantelpiece, finally sat down on a bench cushioned with tasseled pillows. "You know, it always used to concern me, how you seemed to be obsessed with women's minds. Your girlfriends were always so earnest, so accomplished. Now I see you've come to your senses. A blond bimbo. May I offer my congratulations? Welcome to the real world."

"Well, she's not blond. And she does have a degree in anthropology from Columbia."

"I should have known."

"And we've broken up."

Russell sat there a moment, seemingly absorbed by the jiggling of one of his Topsiders. "You're still on that grail quest, I see. The perfect woman."

"No," Eric protested, as he had in the past over and over again, when one of his relationships didn't work out. "I know there's no such thing."

"What are you waiting for, then?"

"Joy came close, real close. But she was too young. Our minds—I mean, how can you live with someone who was born during the Vietnam War? She inhabits a totally different world."

"We all do, don't we? That's what makes it so interesting, such a challenge. It's a struggle, Eric, to make anything work. Even our friendship, yours and mine, something as simple as that, something we both took for granted for so long. . . . It's sad."

"What?"

"It's practically dead, isn't it? We're both so self-conscious now. Everything I say to you, I'm afraid you're misinterpreting. It never was like that before. Before, we could say anything and we knew it was safe, we knew there was no doubt how much we cared for each other. I can't tell you how much I miss that. OK, so I have Sylvester. I love him with all my heart. But maybe it's a little bit like your Joy—there's parts of me he'll never understand. He's pretty literal, too. I can hardly make a joke without being cross-examined." Suddenly he was on his feet, his cup set roughly aside, almost spilling.

"What's wrong?"

"I better go."

"But—"

"If you could only see yourself, the panic in your eyes. Goddammit, you are one conceited son of a bitch."

"Russell."

"Can't you get it through your head? I'm not after you!"

"I didn't think—"

"You're lying. You lie all the time, Eric. I can't take it anymore. I'm too old for this fucking moronic purity of yours. I'll just—"

"Knock, knock."

It was Kaye, standing uncertainly in the foyer. Eric had seen the door open—she had her own key, for emergencies—but Russell seemed surprised, turning around so suddenly that his Topsiders gave a squeak.

"The buzzer isn't working," she said. "I rang and rang."

"Three?" Eric asked.

"No, four. This is three? Oh, well—how are you, Russell? Am I late? These heels nearly killed me. I could barely make it up the subway stairs."

By the innocent look on her face, Eric figured she had overheard a good deal of the conversation. She and Russell shook hands, and Russell complimented her on her mink stole.

"You'll stand up for me, then," she said, draping it over the back of the couch. "Joel is going to fuss at me for wearing fur, but it doesn't seem fair to me. My husband bought this for me twenty-some years ago, before we knew it was wrong. Eric, aren't you going to wear a tie? This is the Met, you know."

He was planning to put one on after they had eaten. "Joel's not coming, is he?"

"Yes, it looks like he'll be able to make it. He'll be by with Dad in a few minutes. I asked them to pick up some Philadelphia Cream Cheese."

Eric realized now that the "friend" Kaye had gotten the tickets from was Joel himself. He should have known that Kaye's reticence on the subject of Joel meant that, despite all her resolutions, she was seeing him again. It had all probably started up anew when she had gone to return his gun.

"Look, if your friend is coming, I'll let him have my ticket," Russell volunteered.

"Don't be silly," Kaye said. "Just tell me why you men aren't wearing ties."

"Life's too short," Russell explained as he followed her into the kitchen, where she and Eric began putting the meal together. "I really don't mind missing this."

"Too late for that," Eric said, pouring champagne into an earthenware pitcher of orange juice. "Can't escape now."

Russell regarded him sternly for a moment, then said, "Maybe I'll have one of those mimosas, after all—without the juice."

Since there was no table large enough for them all, they balanced their plates on their laps. Though Lamar Thorsen volunteered to supplement the bagels and lox with an omelet, no one took him up on the offer. There was brie, as well, from the cheese shop Wanda had recommended, and exquisite raspberry tarts, courtesy of Joel. These he did not touch himself, having just lost nineteen pounds on a macaroni diet recommended by Kaye. Perhaps it was this deprivation that made him seem more like a criminal attorney, for the lovesick look Eric associated with him was now replaced by frowns and raised eyebrows, particularly when Kaye ventured an opinion that was at odds with his own. It was to Joel's credit, though, that he refrained from turning the mink stole into a moral issue; he simply commented that it looked a little warm for this time of year.

As for Eric's father, he seemed almost beside himself with pleasure at the sight of Russell and was keenly disappointed when he turned down an omelet. Russell used to include him in the dinner parties at his Park Avenue apartment whenever Mr. Thorsen visited New York, and these, Mr. Thorsen declared now, had always been the high point of his trips up north. After asking about Russell's children, Mr. Thorsen went on to give him a rundown on the state of the world. Russell listened patiently, with what seemed real interest, though even he betrayed some confusion when Mr. Thorsen accused the right-to-lifers of being a bunch of closet queens. Kaye, apparently, had not informed her father of Russell's recent history. In any case, Eric could not be too surprised by anything his father said about politics.

Back in the Dark Ages, when he was a trainer for the Florida State Seminoles, Lamar Thorsen had drilled into his children the fairness of the separate-but-equal doctrine and had even signed a petition to impeach Earl Warren. But over the years, as first his daughter and then his son took up residence in New York, these views gradually eroded under a steady stream of criticism. Kaye, determined to make her father accept and like her Jewish husband, used every opportunity to convince her father that he was a racist pig. Watergate proved to be the turning point—not the crime itself but the language Nixon used on the tapes. Shaken by this, Mr. Thorsen began to listen to what his daughter and son were telling him and even tried to convince his wife, who always left the room during these discussions, that the children might have a point. Nonetheless, his liberalism was always suspect in his son's eyes, running as it did, as turgid and muddy as it was shallow, over a bedrock of conservatism.

Feeling like a third wheel in both conversations—his father and Russell's, Kaye and Joel's—Eric washed up a few dishes in the kitchen and then went into the narrow bedroom that must have been, in the days when one did not have to be a millionaire to live in middle-class comfort, a pantry. Wanda still had much of her wardrobe here, and in his search for a pair of socks he might encounter a garter, panties, a Cross-Your-Heart bra. The next time he spoke to Wanda he would have to ask her if it would be all right to pile her things in one or two drawers.

The tie he was looking for turned out to be draped over a woolen shawl. As he knotted it beneath his raised collar, he wondered why he had bought something with pink whales on it. Then he remembered it wasn't his tie but his father's, urged upon him as an improvement in his wardrobe.

"You got an extra?"

In the mirror beneath the crucifix Eric caught a glimpse of Russell. There was a hesitancy in his voice that made Eric want to reassure him, in some way, that all was well between them. The anger and confusion they had experienced earlier now seemed so childish.

"Kaye really wants me to put one on," Russell said as he took the only other tie, one of Eric's that had a small, almost unnoticeable grease stain on it. Eric had offered him the one he had on, but Russell had insisted the other was fine.

As Russell knotted the tie and then, when it turned out to be far too short, undid it and reknotted it, he seemed on the verge of saying something, perhaps an apology for his outburst earlier. In a way Eric hoped he wouldn't. Some things did not need to be said, particularly between men. And the role Eric found himself cast in, as some sort of vain homophobe, was not the most appealing. It seemed that every time he tried to extricate himself from this position, he wound up more firmly typecast.

"Eric, listen, there's something I got to tell you," Russell said finally, once the tie was on and Eric had straightened the collar.

"It's all right. I know."

"You do?"

Eric nodded.

"Well, that's a relief. I felt sort of awkward, having this a secret from you. Kaye made me promise not to tell."

"Kaye?"

"Yes, I'm going to lend your father a few thousand dollars, you know, and I don't want you thinking it's because of you."

In the dim light of a shaded bulb, Eric saw his own puzzled face in the mirror balanced atop the dresser. "Lend him what?"

"You *don't* know, huh? Why did you say you did?" Russell's irritation was infectious, but Eric held his peace. "This is not about you, understand? I happen to like your father a great deal, and I think he deserves a chance. He hasn't had an easy life and he's getting on now, and the thought of him having no place to go—"

"What do you mean no place to go? He's got a damn nice apartment in Tallahassee, much better than anything I've ever lived in."

Russell's smile did not improve Eric's mood; it was the least bit patronizing. "He was evicted. That's right, he—"

"I don't believe—"

"—he owes four months' rent and he begged Kaye not to tell you, and she didn't."

After sinking onto the narrow bed, Eric sat there a moment, angry, humiliated, saddened, before saying, "Why? Why keep it from me?"

"Well, you do tend to be a bit judgmental."

"Me?"

"Yes, you." Russell had strayed from the door to the dresser, where he idly picked up a bottle of holy water, examining the reflection of the cut glass in the yellow light. "You think your dad doesn't know how you feel about the accident, your mother? So now he has to admit this to you? Frankly, I don't blame him one bit."

"But he'd have plenty to live on if he just watched his budget. He's got a pension from FSU, his Social Security."

"He bought a boat."

"A boat?"

"He said he's always wanted a boat of his own. When you were kids, he said, he never could afford anything *he* wanted. He was always buying you clothes, food, seeing you through college, helping you out in grad school. Now he feels it's time he did something for himself, and he—well, he just told me out there—" Russell nodded in the direction of the living room, past the kitchen— "he said he literally fell in love with a boat in a showroom, and the salesman convinced him he could afford it with a finance plan—"

"Hold on. Did he just ask you now for money?"

"No, no, nothing like that. It was Kaye. Yesterday I was in Macy's getting a present for Sylvester, his birthday—and she was free for lunch, so we talked."

"Well, he can just give up that damn boat."

"He won't. That's the problem. He'd rather be without an apartment. And of course it isn't big enough to live on. It's just a Whaler, nothing fancy—though the motor is sort of powerful."

"Listen, Russell, last year it was a car; he had to have a Nissan or he couldn't live. Before that it was a stereo VCR and then a Jacuzzi. He's really nuts, can't you see?"

"Is it crazy to want a few nice things in life?"

"Yes, if you can't afford to pay your rent." Suddenly Eric was on his feet. "Look, I'm afraid I'm going to have to put a stop to this. You are not to give him a nickel."

"Excuse me?"

"If you're really his friend, Russell—"

"You don't have to talk down to me."

"I'm sorry. I just meant—"

"This is not your decision anyway."

"What? He's *my* father. I'm the one stuck with him, not you. And—Who the hell is that?"

Behind Russell, who had drifted to the bedroom door again, Eric had caught sight of someone bustling about in the kitchen, a stranger, it seemed.

"Just what does he think he's doing?" Eric muttered as a second, closer look helped him tag the intruder with a name, Arnold Murtaugh, that dispelled some of the strangeness, if not quite all.

"Buddy, you seen the grater?" Arnold called out as he plowed through a drawer. Not so much as a sorry-to-disturb-you or may-I-come-in.

"Ko has everything in his kitchen but a grater. Wanda wants a grater. What Wanda wants, Wanda gets." He said all this as he started in on the cabinets, opening them with such energy that they banged against one another. And he didn't even bother to shut them—or the drawers.

Eric was about to say something he knew he might regret when the ex-priest suddenly startled him with a "Hooray!" A little leap accompanied the cheer.

"Look!" Arnold said, waving the grater in Eric's face. "And she said I'd never find it."

"Perhaps you might—"

"Eric! Russell!" came his sister's voice, raised to an unnatural pitch. "You guys hurry. Joel's got a cab waiting. Come on!"

"Better go," Arnold advised as Russell obediently squeezed past them into the living room.

"Eric, honey, please," Kaye urged, sticking her head through the archway. "The meter's going."

"Don't worry about me, folks," Arnold said in answer to the look Eric gave him. "I'll lock up when I go." He jiggled a set of keys he had pulled out of his vest pocket.

"We'll wait for you," Eric said stoically while his sister protested about the time.

"Let's see," Arnold mused, "grater, tweezers, toenail clippers . . . I suppose those would be in the bathroom."

"Mine are. Hers are in—" Eric found himself finishing the sentence in his head as his sister's powerful grip propelled him out of the kitchen toward the waiting cab.

Eight

"I could have killed him."

"Who?"

"Your boyfriend. He was playing with death, whether he knew it or not."

Wanda assured Eric that she would speak to Arnold about the incident. And she promised to take the keys back to prevent any future surprise visits. They were in a booth, she and Eric, in the diner she preferred, which was a little farther away from St. Sofya than the cheap diner they had once had coffee in. Eric, of course, had only gone to Mass at St. Sofya in order to see her about the violation of his privacy. That was clear to her now.

With a thoughtful expression on her face, Wanda took a bite of her jelly doughnut. She was wondering if she should object to Arnold's being called her boyfriend. But she supposed if two people of the opposite sex slept together, then that was what he was. After so many years of celibacy, she was still trying to adjust to the fact that she had given in to Arnold after only two or three dates. She supposed it had something to do with his having been a priest. And he did seem to worship her in a way no man ever had before. The poems he faxed her at work were so lovely they brought tears to her eyes. The Godiva chocolates, the orchids, the little heart-shaped balloons—it was everything she had always wanted in a romance. If Louis could only see the way Arnold held the door open for her, the expensive restaurants he took her to, the kimono he had bought her, pure silk, that made her seem truly the mistress of Mr. Ko's apartment. . . .

"You know, it's funny," she said, after the waiter brought her a second jelly doughnut and Eric another Danish, "this place used to have red booths, and now everything's pink and gray. And it's not just here. Have you noticed that almost every Greek diner in town, they've all turned pink like this? Do you think it means something?"

"Is that all you got to say?"

"What? Well, I told you I'd talk to Arnold. What more do you want?"

She glanced self-consciously at her reflection in the side of the napkin dispenser. Arnold had talked her into a new hairdo, a very fashionable and expensive perm—and rinse—that covered her head with tight ringlets, which, if they had been blue, would have made her look like a retired grade-school teacher. Why Arnold found this sexy she would never know. Eric himself hadn't made any comment yet. All the trouble and expense she had gone to, and he couldn't even say something like, Hey, you look different.

"I'm sorry, Wanda. I don't mean to sound so impatient. It's just that it happened at a bad time. See, I had a few people over. You don't mind if I have people over, do you?"

"Don't be silly."

"One was this guy I think I mentioned before, Russell Monteith. Well, Dad starts monopolizing him and saying these idiotic things about closet queens. He's gay, you know. I told you that."

Wanda nodded, though she didn't really remember. Indeed, she was rather startled to learn Eric's father was gay. But, fearful of offending Eric, she betrayed no unseemly curiosity. After all, he was in no mood for any further violation of his precious privacy.

"The next thing I know, Russell is trying to make it seem like I'm some sort of homophobic bigot because I won't let him lend Dad some money—a lot, actually. Can you believe it?"

"Why don't you?"

"Because it's not right. Dad should realize you can't just have everything you want in life. It's wrong, immoral."

Wanda felt a pang of sympathy for the father, as well as for herself. Why couldn't Eric at least have asked her to the party? Was she not good enough for his fancy friends?

"Well?"

"Well what? You do sound narrow-minded, Eric. I'm sorry."

"Great. You're saying Dad should keep his boat even though he can't afford to pay the rent. I like that."

"What boat?"

"What I was telling you about on the way over."

"Oh."

Wanda had been so happy to see Eric at Mass, then to be invited out afterward, that she really hadn't attended to everything he said. It was enough to be walking beside him on a glorious, brisk, late-September morning, to see the wren chirping officiously from its nook atop a streetlamp. But now it was not enough; now she realized she was unhappy that he hadn't asked her, as a common courtesy, to his party. She wouldn't have accepted, of course. But it would have been nice to have been asked.

The mild resentment lingered, and caused Arnold, later that day, to ask if anything was wrong.

"No, nothing."

They were stretched out on the lawn directly outside the sloping glass walls of the Metropolitan's Temple of Dendur. After brunch, Arnold and she had rented cassettes to guide them through a Velázquez exhibition. Despite all the praise lavished on the paintings, and knowing she should be more appreciative, Wanda had still thought Philip and his Iberian courtiers were physically repulsive specimens. She was glad when they could finally escape to the fresh air outside.

"Something's the matter," he said, tracing her hairline with his finger, over her ear, down the nape of her neck.

Stirred, she gave his free hand a squeeze. "I don't like the Spanish. They nearly ruined the Church with their Inquisition."

"The Italians were no slouches, kid. And Avignon—when I heard what they used to do there, in those dungeons, that was it for me."

"I sometimes wonder why I go to Mass."

"You'd really wonder if you saw the instruments they used to bless."

"What instruments?"

"Tongs to pull a Jew's tongue out with, iron pincers, rods to

82

break a midwife's legs, sulfur shirts to help a university student burn."

"But that was only for a little while, back when everyone was cruel."

"Yeah, that was what I was told too." Arnold was leaning back on his elbows, his freckled arms pale, bluish, against the grass. "If the Church hadn't lost the Papal States, you can believe it'd still be going on. What gets me is that there hasn't ever been any official or unofficial repentance—only the mildest gestures, tokens, for what they did to the Jews. But what about the thousands of women they snuffed out, the students who had valid doubts? Not even a token word. And they call her Mother Church. What if a mother actually behaved that way? What if she tortured and burned the children who didn't agree with her—and then, when she lost her power, acted as if she had always been sweetness and light, claiming everything she had done in the past was justified by the times, by how cruel everyone else was. And besides, it wasn't her fault at all. It was the state who did the killing. She herself never shed a drop of blood. Well, I tell you, Wanda, you'd call her the worst sort of hypocrite, a loathsome child abuser without the slightest hint of a conscience. Oh, but all she was trying to do was protect the deposit of faith entrusted to her. She had to." The vehemence in Arnold's voice surprised Wanda. She had never known how strong his feelings were against the Church. "Tell me this, Wanda, what kind of word is 'deposit'? It's money in the bank, which is what they've turned their faith into. It's also what dogs leave behind when they take a squat."

"Oh, but Arnold, all the good people, the saints—"

"You ever hear what some of these saints had to say about Jews, about women, Protestants? Saint Thomas More was glad to see Protestants burn. Saint Thomas Aquinas thought women were defective men, caused by a moist south wind blowing during conception." He had turned to face her now, the anger in his eyes so personal, as if she herself were the Church. "What really gets me, though, is how the Church has the gall to claim natural law is behind her, uses natural law as the stick to beat birth control with, homosexuality, abortion. As if the Church hadn't done her damnedest to suppress and deny natural law from day one. Where is natural law when it comes to Galileo, Darwin? Hell, it wasn't until the nineteenth century that it was finally OK to believe the sun wasn't going around the earth."

The tears in Wanda's eyes overflowed. She had never known Arnold to be so mean.

"Baby, darling, what's the matter?" he crooned, taking her head in his arm and cradling it with a gentle rocking motion.

"You were yelling at me."

"Not at *you*."

"Yes, you were. You were saying how stupid and horrible I am to go to Mass every Sunday." Of course, Wanda was aware it was she herself who had been thinking this, how she still couldn't get out of the habit of looking for him, that golden hair. Blaming Arnold made it so much easier.

"No, no, I think you are a good, good woman. I mean it. And church is right for you."

"For me, you mean for stupid people like me? I studied Aquinas too, you know. I never saw anything about moist winds. It's awful of you to make me feel unwanted by my own church. And to say those terrible things about a child abuser—"

"Hush," he said, still rocking her.

Despite the tears, perhaps even because of them, she felt strangely at peace, content in his arms. "I won't go back."

"What?"

"If you think the Church is really so awful—"

"Hey, don't you have any backbone? You hear one tirade and that's it, you've lost your faith? Why not come back at me with Ephesians, where 'deposit' is used so beautifully? Or say something about the Vatican hiding Jews during—"

"Please, let's not argue."

Out of the corner of her eye Wanda could see a man, a middle-aged Japanese tourist, staring in the wrong direction, not at the Temple of Dendur but at her in Arnold's arms. A cloud reflected in the tinted glass made the Japanese seem airborne, exempt from the law of gravity. It was a delicious feeling, she discovered, to be watched, envied perhaps as someone who really belonged on this lawn, among so many smart, interesting-looking New Yorkers. Arnold really was wonderful, she decided. He was joyful, fearless. Even his irreverence seemed good somehow, because it was passionate and real. Compared to this, her own faith, what she had clung to after her brother had been killed, began to seem a little like her father's drinking, a crutch, a spurious solace. There had never been any real joy for her at Mass, only the dim hope that somehow the communion bread, the wine, would protect her from a cruel and violent world. Arnold had told her on their last date, at a lovely bistro in the Village, that she was using religion as magic, a way of warding off evil. She had shed a few tears then, as well. "I'm not a primitive savage," she had said. "I don't believe in magic." "But you are," he had said. "You're performing certain rituals in the hopes that this will appease God, save you from his wrath."

And Eric Thorsen, she wondered now, nestled in Arnold's arms, was he also a savage? What god was he trying to appease, the terrible god who had given him a gay father with a boat he couldn't afford?

"Arnold?" she whispered.

"What, darling?"

"I saw him today."

"Yes, I know."

"How? How did you know?"

"Because you looked so sad."

"Really?"

"Yes, my love. Your Greek god always makes you look that way."

"I'm that transparent?"

"Yes."

There was no man in the clouds when she glanced over. He was gone.

At first the stench was so unbearable that Wanda was afraid she would have to cut her visit short. But after twenty minutes she had adapted herself by breathing through her mouth, which made the odor somewhat less intense. As the old woman talked, Wanda became aware of brief lulls when the room smelled almost normal. While chatting amiably, holding up her end of the conversation, Wanda would anticipate the relief of the next lull, and with this hope in mind she was able to endure. Perhaps after a hundred or so generations, a noseless Wanda might evolve, perfectly adapted to Una Merton's apartment. It was a silly thought, she knew, that came from watching too much public television at Mr. Ko's.

A sense of duty had made her ask Mrs. Fogarty for Una Merton's address and telephone number. It had finally sunk into Wanda's thick skull, as she herself put it, that she had a chance at real happiness. And there was only one thing standing in her way, her foolish infatuation with Eric Thorsen. Once she got the man out of her apartment and back into his own, where he belonged, she was sure that the admiration and respect she felt for Arnold would blossom into a modest, quiet love. But this would never be possible with excuses always at hand to see Eric, to phone him about her fern or a can opener she might need. And he himself would sometimes take the initiative, wondering about a leak in the bathroom ceiling or—feeling guilty, no doubt—occasionally asking her over for a drink. The last time she had dropped over, she had brought up the matter of his father's sexuality—and been laughed at like a fool, almost as if she were crazy. He denied ever telling her that his father was gay. This, for Wanda, was the last straw. She stopped going to Mass and decided to call on Mrs. Merton. Eric Thorsen was not to be trusted. There was something weird about him, and she was not going to let herself be toyed with any longer.

"I hope you enjoy tea," Mrs. Merton said, as she watched Wanda take a dubious sip from the china cup.

Wanda feared, because of the stench, that the tea would taste awful. But it was fine. Indeed, minus the stench and with a little more light, the apartment would have been perfectly habitable. She had come expecting the worst sort of squalor and was pleasantly surprised by the almost suburban feel of the Danish modern furniture, a style that Wanda had admired in grade school, when it seemed the last word in elegance. Una Merton herself seemed much less decrepit than Wanda remembered, her step more determined, her speech steady, clear, and a merriment in her eyes that made the azure scarf about her neck seem appropriate. But as Wanda's eyes adjusted to the light, a shadow on the old woman's bosom became, quite clearly, a blob of half-dried stew meat—while other shadows, glimpsed from the corner of her eyes, began to stir. The cats, of course. She had not noticed them when she had come in. Even now, though, as she and the old woman discussed the weather, they did not seem so numerous—six or seven at most.

"Listen, sweetie," Mrs. Merton said as she refilled Wanda's cup. "You like cats, don't you?"

Wanda nodded. Ever since she could remember, her mother had kept a pair of cats around the house. Wanda probably would have had a cat herself now if it weren't for Louis. Back when she was married, Wanda had lavished almost all her affection, it seemed, on Cindy, a Siamese from one of her mother's cats' litters. Coming home one day from work, she found Louis out in the backyard with a shovel, putting the finishing touches on a small grave. Cindy had been mauled by the neighbor's dog, he had told her in a matter-of-fact way. Horrified, Wanda had run over to Mr. Genovese's next door. Mr. Genovese knew nothing about it. In fact, his dog had been at the vet's that afternoon. Louis claimed that Mr. Genovese was lying—and when Wanda dug up Cindy's grave and found no body, Louis insisted this was Mr. Genovese's handiwork as well. Sick with grief, Wanda realized she had married a mentally disturbed man. She never confronted Louis about any of his lies after that, so afraid she was for her own safety. It was only a matter of preparing a way out, back to her parents, with as much of her money and property as she could safely sneak away. Louis being edgy and suspicious, this had not been easy. Almost all the nicer wedding presents had been left behind. And Cindy never did turn up anywhere, dead or alive.

A clear, childlike joy danced in Una Merton's blue eyes. "Then it's settled." She gave Wanda's hand a powerful squeeze.

"I don't understand."

"'I don't understand,'" the old woman mimicked in a girlish way that was really quite charming. Wanda couldn't help smiling. "You don't understand," Mrs. Merton went on, "that you're an angel and a love? Well, my dear, understand it. My life was a misery before you came along, the threats, the torment."

"But it wasn't me who—"

Mrs. Merton put a finger to Wanda's lips. "Hush. You gave me the courage to go through with it. Alone, I couldn't have done it. And now, no more threats, no more phone calls or letters. That man upstairs, why he must weigh a ton, clomping up and back with no rugs on the floor, day and night. I can't tell you what a relief it is to have him out of there. And the way he banged that piano." Mrs. Merton raised her hands, palms outward, in a theatrical gesture of exasperation. "Day and night the same passages, over and over again, the same mistakes. I thought I would lose my mind."

"But it's his career, Mrs. Merton."

"Fine, let him get an office. This building isn't zoned for careers." Her frown was not convincing; it seemed as forced as most people's smiles. "So, darling girl, for saving this old biddy's life, for giving me the peace and quiet I've hungered for ever since that fat, ugly devil moved in, I want to give you something that's very dear to me."

"Oh, no, I couldn't possibly—" Wanda had a momentary vision of a diamond choker, stashed away in the old woman's bedroom, from which, at that very moment, came the sound of a child's wail.

"Don't mind her," Mrs. Merton said, glancing toward the bedroom door. "Lulu is sulking because Harry ate out of her dish this morning."

"Oh." The wail had caused the down to rise on Wanda's arms. Though it was warm out, hot even, she realized she felt chilly.

"Look, Wanda dear."

Mrs. Merton had drifted to the far end of the room. Stooping by the faded floor-length draperies, she appeared to be coaxing a cut-glass punch bowl on a blond lowboy. It was only when the old woman reached out with both hands to grasp the mottled dim light behind the glass that Wanda could see—even if she did not quite believe.

"I want you to have Charles," Mrs. Merton said, crossing the dim room with the fierce blue eyes glaring from her bosom.

"Oh, no, I can't." Wanda got up from the sofa as the old woman tried to lower the Siamese onto her lap.

"Oh, yes, you can. Take him, my darling, he's yours. My beauty is yours."

Going down in the elevator, Wanda realized she could have been more gracious about refusing the gift. The coincidence, though, that it was a Siamese, had flustered her. One of the marmalades, a tabby, would not have had the same effect. After that, of course, Wanda could hardly reveal what the real purpose of her visit had been. She had simply pretended to have stopped by as a friendly gesture, and Una Merton had seemed to find this completely plausible. She had told Wanda she was welcome any time, day or night.

Not long after this visit, Wanda asked her boss if it would be possible for her to move back into her own apartment. She didn't want to appear ungrateful, she explained, but she was getting a little tired of running the video machines. Just do as many tapes as you can, Mr. Ko said. If you miss some shows, don't worry. Perhaps since the apartment was so beautiful, Wanda then suggested, maybe someone else might like a turn living there. Phyllis, for instance. Mr. Ko's eyebrows shot up. Was Wanda losing her mind? Phyllis was a flighty chit. No one could trust that girl. The grumbling about Phyllis became more general, and Wanda soon found herself taking notes for a memo she was ordered to distribute that afternoon: (1) Fax machine for business use only; (2) no yogurt, Gummy Bears, or bananas to be consumed at desks; (3) personal phone calls subject to fines; (4) lying or prevarication in regard to illness carries the penalty of immediate dismissal.

It would have been easier to tell Eric he must leave because she had to move back in herself. Without this excuse she was afraid she might sound flighty and irresponsible. As she walked east toward Tompkins Square shortly after handing out the memo, she considered inventing a friend who needed the apartment—or, better yet, a relative. Perhaps she might have a cousin who was not well off, whose parents had died. Actually, she did have a cousin whose father had died, but Hulga lived in Pennsylvania and made good money answering questions on an 800 line about health insurance policies for the American Association of Retired Persons.

In khaki shorts and a T-shirt, Eric was more appropriately dressed for the inversion that had hung over the city for the past three days, making October seem like late August. Wanda, her eyes bloodshot with pollution, had on a sweater set to combat the air conditioner's blast in the office. Mr. Ko did not stint on electricity, believing that shivering workers were more efficient.

"I brought some plant food," Wanda said, having provided herself with a mundane excuse for the visit.

"How about a drink?"

"No, thanks. I don't have much time. Arnold is taking me out to dinner and if you have a tablespoon—"

"What?"

"I want to show you how much of this to put on the plants. You can't overdo it; the roots will get burned."

Wanda went to get a tablespoon in the kitchen, but the silverware was not in the drawer by the sink. Eric explained that Kaye had rearranged some of the things in the kitchen. "She says she's got it more logical now," he added as he handed over a spoon.

"What's more logical about that drawer?"

"You'll have to ask Kaye."

With the tablespoon Wanda went from plant to plant measuring out the correct amount of food. It made her feel practical, as if she knew what she was doing. "I'm not sure if you realize, Eric, but Arnold and I are becoming serious."

"Wonderful. Three tablespoons for this one?"

She had meant to measure out only one and a half for the fern. "Uh, it's a little anemic now. In general, I'd use only one or one and a half."

"By the way, did Arnold ever get the piano tuned like he said?" Eric asked from the embroidered footstool, where he had settled down with a beer.

She nodded. Every time Arnold came over he played "Moon River" for her on Mr. Ko's white Yamaha. He could also play the first three bars of "More," the theme from *Mondo Cane*.

"It's a fine piano."

Wanda shrugged. "The tuning cost eighty dollars. I told Arnold it wasn't worth it, and his feelings got hurt."

Eric drained the last of his beer and offered to get her one. Again she said no.

"The toilet is dripping and won't stop," he commented as she dusted the single leaf of her cherished moonwort.

"I'll take a look at it."

"Thanks." His long, muscular legs stretched out so that his dirty socks were almost in her face. The odor helped temper an alarming stab of lust. "How would Arnold like a lesson or two?"

"What? Oh, Eric, I don't think that would be a good idea."

"Why not? I'd like to come over one evening anyway and try out the piano."

Wanda shrugged. The next thing she knew she was saying she had to be on her way. Eric reminded her about the toilet, though, so before she left she went into the bathroom and removed the tank cover. It was a simple matter of realigning the rubber stopper. The leak was fixed in half a minute.

"Well, that's that," she said, feeling almost as if she had accomplished the purpose of her visit.

He thanked her, and she was on her way. Thwarted plans did not have quite the same effect on Wanda as they did on someone more ambitious, her brother Earl, for instance. When Earl used to make up his mind to do something, he did it. The photo on her mantel had reminded her again of how happy he had been in the army and how much he had hated the mess and clutter of civilian life. He had had his life planned to a T: lieutenant by age thirty (this he had accomplished), captain by thirty-three, major by thirty-seven, colonel at forty-two, general by forty-seven. As she walked down the stoop of her brownstone, Wanda found it was pretty much a full-time job just trying, at forty-two, to be herself.

Nine

The report from the Department of Health did concede that there was an odor—"displeasant" was the adjective—but no outstanding violations of city codes per Article 61H.929 could be cited. Only three cats were found on the premises. Kaye agreed with her brother that Mrs. Merton must have been tipped off about the inspection and had hustled the cats into a neighbor's apartment. For hadn't the old woman herself admitted in court that she had twenty-two? It was a real setback for Eric, yet he seemed to take it with surprising equanimity. "I think I'll kill myself," was all he had muttered, a line she had heard often enough in the past, usually when an out-of-service bus passed their stop after a twenty-minute wait or when a checkout line in the grocery store closed down just as it was his turn.

In a way Kaye was relieved that she did not have to spend a great deal of time discussing this latest development with him. Her heart was too full of her own troubles. Joel had just changed jobs and moved with his family to Los Angeles. Kaye's initial reaction had been relief. Finally there was an excuse to end the suspense. They could part on good terms with neither cast in the role of heavy. Yet the more she brooded on this, the less satisfactory it began to seem. Joel had not looked terribly upset when he had told her the news about his move. Indeed, ever since *Die Walküre* he had been a little aloof, not as attentive and flattering as she had grown accustomed to. Had it been wise, she asked herself during a lull between customers at Macy's, to have flaunted her mink stole at the opera? It had been a gratuitous insult to his beliefs. What could have gotten into her, making her behave that way?

"Miss!"

With a little cry Kaye gave such a violent start that her father, who had crept up and whispered in her ear, got a jab in the ribs with her elbow.

"Oh, Dad," she said with both reproach and apology, "are you all right? I've asked you not to sneak up on me like that. And look," she added, pointing to her tiny watch face, "you're early, forty minutes early."

"I got through sooner than I expected."

Mr. Thorsen had gone to the Delta office to pick up a ticket for Tallahassee. He was able to return now that Russell Monteith had lent him five thousand dollars interest free.

"You really jumped," he said, rubbing his side with evident satisfaction.

Annoyed though she was, Kaye couldn't help feeling a pang of regret. With Joel gone it was going to be especially hard to see her father leave. She had gotten used to having him around. "I can't come now, Dad."

"Why not? I'm here."

"I can't punch out yet."

"What is this, a factory? You let me speak to the manager. I'll explain. After all, I am your father, and I won't be around much longer, you know."

"Dad, please."

It took an inordinate amount of time to convince him to browse around the store until her shift was over, and this he did only grudgingly. Then when it was time for her to leave, he was, of course, nowhere in sight. At her locker in the dimly lit Employees Only quarters, as grim as the backstage of a Broadway theater, she repaired her face and changed into her more elegant, uncomfortable shoes. A quick inspection of the finger food she had made revealed that the salmon on toast squares had gotten jumbled up, but the chicken squares were still nicely stacked. Where was he?

she thought crossly as she set down the boxes and bags to punch the time clock.

"You said here," Mr. Thorsen insisted when she finally came across him on the main floor near the information desk.

"Did I really?"

"Yes."

Kaye knew she had told him to meet her in the Cellar near her register, but she wasn't going to press the point. For a man his age he had, all in all, a very fine memory. In any case, the important thing was to get over to Beekman Place as soon as possible.

"We're running a little late, Dad. Do you mind?" She held out three boxes for him to take. "My arms are breaking."

Once outside on Broadway they debated the merits of taking a cab across town. Traffic at Herald Square seemed almost at a standstill because of the rain. Surely a subway, Kaye thought aloud, would be much quicker. But the trouble was, she didn't know for certain which train would get them nearest to 52nd and First. That settled it for Mr. Thorsen, who didn't even wait for a taxi to pull over but, rather, plunged right into the stalled traffic and yanked open a door.

"I don't know why a little rain always causes such a panic," Kaye said as she clambered in behind him with her boxes and bags. A van behind them had begun to honk furiously, as if she were the one personally responsible for the gridlock. Rolling down her window, she shook her extended middle finger in the air for the benefit of the honking driver.

"Kaye."

"I'm sorry, Dad. I just couldn't help it."

Lamar Thorsen scratched his scraggly, iron-gray beard. "And you wonder why Joel has moved to Los Angeles."

"What?"

"This city has had a bad effect on you, Daughter. It's made you very unladylike."

"Dad, Joel left because he's joining a firm out there that's doing wonderful work for the environment."

"I see. That explains everything."

Tears welled up in her eyes. It was unkind of him to even talk about Joel, much less blame his leaving on her. Surely he must know how vulnerable she was feeling these days. And to start up again with that old song and dance about being a lady—it was really too much. Ever since she had won the division championship in high school for diving, he had subtly undermined her athletic ability. No wonder she had not been as good in college, with his constant warnings about becoming too much of a jock. As if diving were going to change her into a lesbian, she thought bitterly. Well, now she almost wished it had. Surely no woman would be as difficult to figure out as Joel. Oh, if only she could yearn for a woman's body the way she did for Joel's, life would be solved.

"Now, now, Kaye."

"You're really mean."

He smiled and shook his head, obviously well aware of how much she loved him. She did, of course, to the degree that she could almost be glad, in a perverse way, that he was sometimes thoughtless and cruel. It made it that much easier to see him go. Of course, they must all live their own lives, but how nice it had been having him around. On her own she would barely have the energy to heat up a microwave dinner after work, but now she was coming home to gourmet meals Lamar had spent the entire day preparing. Always the freshest ingredients were used, and the wines he chose were the result of an in-depth study of a forty-dollar book from Shakespeare & Co. She did not even mind the twelve pounds she had gained.

"Just do me a favor, Dad. Don't mention Joel to me again. I don't think it's something we can discuss." Kaye realized her father deserved a severe lecture about the whole notion of referring to women as ladies, but experience had taught her it would do little good. He had married a lady, a beautiful lady who would not have been caught dead going shopping without her gloves. This was reality for him, and no matter how much he might agree with Kaye's feminist ideas in the abstract, such as when they were enjoying an after-dinner drink, he would always revert the minute a real issue came up.

"Peace?" he said, holding up his hand like an Indian chief.

"You got a cigarette?"

Reaching in his vest pocket, he said, "You shouldn't, really."

"I know, but I'm a little upset. What? You too?" she added as he helped himself to one from the pack.

"I'm having my quota now. I don't want any lectures from Eric."

Both cigarettes were finished—in fact, there had been time for two apiece—before they finally pulled up in front of the awning on Beekman Place. Lamar Thorsen tipped the driver far too much and then kept his daughter waiting while he got into a discussion about the Yankees with the doorman.

"Come on, already," she finally called out.

"Why is he having it here?" Mr. Thorsen asked as they walked past the fountain in the lobby. Rust scored the basin into which the water trickled at a measly rate. "Didn't Russell volunteer his own place on Park Avenue? Now that's real class for you. I can't for the life of me understand why Eric has to turn up his nose at that. You have a very strange brother, you know."

"This place is nice too."

"You've seen it?"

"No. Please don't tilt those boxes. The sandwiches will get smushed."

In the elevator, the boxes held properly in his arms, Mr. Thorsen shook his head ruefully.

"What is it, Dad?"

"Nothing."

"Come on, tell me." She was admiring the new suit he had bought himself at Barney's. Of course, she could have got him one at Macy's with an employee's discount, but Aunt Vivian in Newark had told him Barney's was *the* place for men's clothes. Even Eric would have to admit how handsome he looked, though of course neither Lamar nor Kaye would dare admit how much it had cost. Over seven hundred dollars! Even Kaye, at her most tolerant, found that hard to stomach. But then she had relented, thinking of all he had done years ago so that her mother would have those fancy hats to wear to Mass. Those silly things her mother insisted on were so expensive. Kaye would never forget the summer he had tried to hold down three jobs at once: teaching in the morning, supervising the Hollins Avenue recreation center in the afternoon, then acting as night watchman at the Jitney Jungle warehouse. Was it really a mystery why he blew his stack so often around the house back then? He must have been exhausted, just plain worn out.

"I know I'm not supposed to have any opinions about this, but Kaye, maybe you can tell me what Eric sees in this girl."

"What girl?"

"This Wanda character. You know how I thought that nun of his was pretty lean pickings, but this one sets the all-time record."

"Dad, she—"

"Hear me out. Now I know I've only run into her once or twice, but Lord help me if a son of mine can't do any better than that. A plain Jane if I ever saw one, no sense of style at all. And that accent of hers. Eric says it's just the way some people talk in Connecticut, but it sounds to me like her father was a ditchdigger. I wouldn't be surprised if she never finished high school."

"Are you through?" Kaye said crossly, relieving him of the boxes, which had begun to tilt again. "Wanda just happens to be a very sweet, intelligent woman, and for you to be talking this way when she's doing Eric such a big favor—"

"I don't deny—"

"She's not his girlfriend anyway."

Mr. Thorsen looked visibly relieved as he straightened his tie in the elevator's convex mirror. "Oh. Well, what is she, then?"

"She's his friend."

"Friend? What's that supposed to mean?"

"Never mind. We're here now, Dad," she added. It was sometimes necessary to state the obvious with him. "You can get off."

A threadbare carpet, unworthy of a Beekman Place address, led them past a spindly hall table on which a bowl of patchouli gave off its pleasant scent. As they stood before the apartment door, Kaye's arms aching with the effort of holding the boxes correctly, she was required to ask her father to ring the bell. He just stood there, as if Wanda should somehow know they were there.

It was not Wanda, however, who answered the door. A diminutive woman—her mother?—with a sharp nose and very red lips stood aside for them while announcing, "The eats are here!"

Not quite sure if she had been mistaken for a caterer, Kaye peered over the boxes to say to the top of the tall mound of pinkish hair, "I'm Eric's brother."

"His sister, actually," Mr. Thorsen corrected.

"Yeah, well, I'm Mrs. Herman Fogarty. Eric isn't here yet. Did you wipe your feet? Wanda's worried about this white carpet, and

I don't blame her one bit. I can't imagine who would be dumb enough to put white all over his entire house. This isn't Wanda's place, you know. She's just house-sitting. And be careful, don't touch no one. You'll get a awful shock." This information was imparted as she led Kaye past the fanciful art deco bar to the kitchen. Holding open the swinging door for Kaye, Mrs. Fogarty said with a touch of vehemence, "What is that man up to?"

Kaye looked around and saw her father had opened one of the sliding glass doors to go out onto the terrace. "That's my father."

"I don't care if he's the Duke of Windsor. We can't have a thirty-mile-an-hour wind blowing through here." With determined strides the woman crossed the room in her open-toed black pumps, and yelled out, "You—yes, you! Come help me set up the folding chairs. Let's give a hand here. They'll be here any minute, and Wanda's not half ready."

Going into the kitchen, her face lit up with a mild amusement, Kaye apologized to Wanda for being late.

"You're wet," Wanda said, looking around from the counter, where she was painstakingly inserting colored plastic toothpicks into boiled shrimp. "Do you want to use my hair dryer upstairs?"

"I'll be fine. I better help you here." Kaye set down the boxes and bags, which Wanda began to inspect.

"Oh, they're lovely, Kaye. Salmon and chicken, my favorite things, really."

"I was up all night, practically. Everything homemade." Kaye grabbed a dish towel and gave her gray hair a vigorous rub. "Not a cloud in the sky this morning, so I didn't bring my umbrella. Next thing I know it's cats and dogs."

"What? Oh . . . is it still raining?"

"No, it's let up. I swear, this has been the craziest October. Remember that hot spell we had a couple of weeks ago, then last week freezing? Now it's like spring, really nice since the rain let up. I wish that woman would let us keep the doors open a little. Who is she by the way?"

Wanda murmured something.

"What?"

"Uh, this woman I know from work. I think it was probably a mistake to invite her."

"She is a little bossy," Kaye said with a smile while she arranged the salmon squares on a platter.

Wanda remained silent, unsure of how she was going to explain her dilemma. Right from the very beginning Wanda had had a funny feeling about inviting the newsstand vendor to Eric's students' recital. Something warned her that it wouldn't be such a great idea. Yet at the same time she was anxious to make up for the terrible impression she must have given Mrs. Fogarty when she arrived at her home in Canarsie wearing the whale T-shirt. Mr. Ko's apartment was bound to impress the woman, as would Eric and his fancy friends. Wanda could not help feeling patronized by Mrs. Fogarty, almost as if the woman felt sorry for her. Seeing what sort of social circles Wanda was accustomed to, Mrs. Fogarty would be forced to change her tune.

Noticing that Wanda had stopped putting toothpicks in and was just standing there, Kaye said, "I wouldn't worry about Mrs. Whosit, dear. She's good for my dad." The shimmering green cocktail dress Wanda had on looked just a bit large for her slight frame. Touched by all the trouble the girl must have gone to—Kaye did not look dressed up at all, in comparison—Kaye added, "You look stunning. And this place—well, it's really something. Eric told me about it, how much fun he thinks it is."

"She didn't tell me," Wanda said, not responding to any of the compliments. "Mrs. Fogarty didn't ask or anything. I just opened the door, and there she was."

"Mrs. Fogarty?"

"Yes, with Mrs. Merton." Kaye's face was a pleasant blank until Wanda added, in a toneless voice, "Una Merton."

"Not the cat lady?" Kaye said, frowning at a salmon square she was about to put down on the platter.

Alarmed by the look on Eric's sister's face, Wanda hastened to explain, barely pausing for breath. "She said she knew how much Mrs. Merton likes me and how Mrs. Merton is always talking about how nice I am and so she figured it would be a good chance for Mrs. Merton to get out of the house—that's what she told Mrs. Monastere, who wasn't able to check up on her this week, so that's why Mrs. Fogarty volunteered, she wants to be in good with the Rosary Altar Society, so she said she tried to phone me first to see if it would be all right but all she could get was my machine and Mrs. Fogarty says she doesn't talk to machines and so there she was and Mrs. Merton was kissing me and I couldn't just throw her out, could I?"

Kaye spent a moment trying to digest all this.

Her eyes brimming with tears, Wanda added, "I just know Eric is going to think I brought her here to ruin his recital."

"Don't be silly. Eric will understand," Kaye said, without a great deal of conviction. It was Wanda's tears, more than the cat lady's presence, that was giving Kaye pause. For some reason Kaye had been so confident that Wanda had a level head on her shoulders where Eric was concerned. Several times Eric himself had assured Kaye that there was nothing to worry about. Wanda had her boyfriend and only saw Eric occasionally. Yet it was evident now that Wanda's feelings were engaged on a somewhat deeper level than was advisable. And if so, the blame was all hers, Kaye's, for having been so anxious to get Eric out of her own apartment. Life there had been getting harder and harder for the old man. Lamar was even forced to peel the prices off the Dijon mustard and virgin olive oil he bought, knowing how his son could be upset by anything costing more than 98 cents.

Her nose running, Wanda accepted the cocktail napkin Kaye held out to her. "I tried to take her back home myself," Wanda said after blowing.

"The cat lady? Where is she now?"

"Upstairs in the loo. Mrs. Fogarty thought it was rude of me to send her away after only five minutes. I don't know what to do now." With a sigh she wilted onto the counter, resting on her elbows.

Kaye gave the prominent spine of the bare, delicate back a reassuring pat. "You leave this to me. I'll make sure they don't see each other."

"How?" Wanda said without raising her head. The tightly permed brown ringlets seemed to quiver.

"Don't worry. I've been through much worse. Now come on, dear, there's lots to be done. You finish putting out these squares while I go talk to her."

"What are you going to say?"

"Never mind."

Somewhat encouraged, though still anxious, Wanda got busy again as the door swung shut behind Kaye. It was clear to her now that her big mistake had not been inviting Mrs. Fogarty. No, the real mistake had been volunteering Mr. Ko's for the recital in the first place. At the time, when Eric had come by to try out the newly tuned Yamaha and mentioned the difficulty he was in, it had seemed only natural to make the offer. Eric usually had the recital at his own Murray Hill apartment rather than the settlement house, which had a bleak, bare-bones atmosphere. Kaye, he had told Wanda, had persuaded Russell Monteith to have the recital at his place—without consulting Eric first. Russell's Steinway was nice, but Eric was afraid the action of the keys was going to present difficulties for some of his less advanced students. Mr. Ko's Yamaha had a lighter touch and—and before he could say anything more, Wanda had made the offer.

How this offer squared with her resolve never to see Eric again was puzzling. In her attempts to reason her way out, she always came up against Mrs. Merton, whom Wanda was continuing to visit for no other reason than that she liked the old woman—though at times, when the stench in her apartment was especially awful, Wanda herself would find mere liking a weak if not implausible motivation. Vague thoughts of being saintlike didn't quite fill the bill either, since most saints weren't divorced and didn't sleep with their boyfriends. In any case, she never mentioned these visits to Eric, especially after Mrs. Merton had somehow drawn out of her the date of the Health Department's surprise inspection. Wanda wished Eric hadn't mentioned the date to her in the first place. There were some things she would rather not know. But she supposed she must have felt a little guilty about letting the date slip out and so, to make up for it, she had offered Mr. Ko's apartment to Eric.

"Princess," she heard him whisper in her ear, and then she felt him cup her derrière. Though it could be annoying, Wanda did not discourage Arnold from these displays of affection whenever they had a moment alone in the kitchen. He was being so good about the recital, never complaining about the errands she sent him on for cheese or fresh lemons. Yes, that was what she liked about him, almost loved: He was good, deeply selfless. Any other man would have been resentful of so much effort being lavished on a male friend of his girlfriend. But Arnold did not have an ounce of pettiness in him.

"Would you mind taking this platter out?" Wanda asked as she extricated herself from his arms.

"Madam," he said with a playful bow. But she did not smile, for it had suddenly occurred to her: Why couldn't he be at least a tiny bit jealous? Was it so completely farfetched that Eric might be aware that she was a member of the opposite sex?

"Go on, Arnold. We haven't got all day."

From the second-floor walkway overlooking the living room, Kaye listened to the Dominican girl tackle the Brahms rhapsody with vigor and conviction. For Eric this would be the high point of the recital. It had been a real coup, persuading Tiburcia to resume her lessons after she had given up in despair. Kaye had heard all the details from her brother, how he had talked to her at Woolworth's for so long that Tiburcia was reprimanded by her floor supervisor, how he had made an appointment to see her homeroom teacher at Washington Irving High, how he had phoned Tiburcia's mother to plead his case. Russell was on the bench beside the perspiring girl, who had been too nervous to play from memory as Eric had hoped. Turning the pages, Russell seemed almost as nervous as the pianist herself; both had grim expressions, one step removed from panic.

In the front row of folding chairs that Omar had carted in from the settlement house sat Tiburcia's mother, Wanda, Omar himself, and Arnold, who from time to time would look up and give Kaye a wink. Lamar Thorsen had staked out a prime spot for himself on the sofa, while Mrs. Fogarty, perched upon a sleek upholstered chair, surveyed the roomful of students and their families with the patronizing smile of a grand duchess. Earlier she had taken Kaye aside to remark upon the number of "colored friends" that Wanda seemed to have. "Not that I'm prejudiced myself, mind you," she had hastily added when Kaye treated her to an icy stare.

Eric himself was farthest away from the piano, at the other end of the room, where the crystal goblets hanging in front of the tinted bar mirror reflected the luster of his unkempt golden hair. In such an exuberant setting Kaye thought that even in his worn gray tweed jacket, with the same old tie, he looked like a movie star. Totally absorbed in Tiburcia's performance, he seemed unaware of his sister's worried gaze. Could he not listen to the girl's playing without such evident anxiety? He seemed so dogged by perpetual anxiety—if it wasn't Tiburcia, it was an erroneous bank statement, a sonata he didn't have time to learn properly, a bad review, smelly cats, a rumor he had heard about himself, starving Ethiopians—that sometimes it was all she could do to keep from grabbing him by the shoulders and giving him a good hard shake. Wake up! she would have liked to shout. You've got everything going for you, Eric Thorsen—looks, brains, talent! What is your problem?

Two years ago, when she was dating a cognitive therapist, Kaye thought she had known what the problem was. Gordon, the therapist, had listened patiently as she described all the symptoms she could come up with: how Eric had been so worried about commercial rent tax forms concerning his Murray Hill apartment; how he would go back to make sure his door was locked two, three, or four times; how he had begun to pay bills using expensive and unnecessary Certified Mail forms because one of his American Express payments was lost; how he sometimes opened his wallet while visiting her to make sure his credit cards were still there; how he went to Mass every Sunday even though he seemed to hate the homilies. Gordon said it was a clear case of an obsessive-compulsive personality and urged her to get him into therapy as soon as possible. Eric was incensed when the diagnosis was relayed to him and called Gordon a quack of the first magnitude. Kaye had vigorously defended her boyfriend until she discovered he was having a simultaneous affair with a former patient, a woman he had supposedly cured only two months before.

While recovering from Gordon, Kaye had entertained a second theory about what was wrong with her brother. This came from watching a talk show one day when she had stayed home from work with a cold. The guests were people who had had happy short-term affairs with either a cousin, brother, sister, or a step-mother. A clip from Louis Malle's *Murmur of the Heart* was shown as supporting evidence that such a relationship need not be traumatic. Though the thought seemed strange to her, Kaye could not help wondering if Eric could be suffering because of sup-pressed erotic feelings for her. After all, he had been the one to ask if he could move in with her. To tell the truth, she did think he was making a mountain out of a molehill as far as the cat lady was concerned. Of course, she would never breathe a word of her doubts to him. He was quite neurotic on the subject of the cats beneath him, just like the princess with the pea. She went along with him, helping out where she could, but always a little concerned about the way this particular pea had become an obsession. Perhaps he was too frightened to admit that the pea was just a cover for his incestuous longings. How sad that would be. Kaye was prepared to do just about anything for her little brother, including dying. This, however, was another matter. She had to draw the line somewhere, didn't she? Of course, as they had said on television, the main problem with incest was genetic. If children were no longer a possibility, what was the real objection? But would she be helping Eric? Wouldn't she just be making him more neurotic and unhappy? So all right, he was a beautiful man, and—and it was perhaps best for all concerned if he didn't live with her. She had been able to think so much more clearly ever since he had moved to Wanda's. And there weren't so many crazy dreams at night.

"My tea, where is my tea?"

"Shhh," Kaye gently hushed the old woman, who had opened the bedroom door.

Before Tiburcia had begun to play, Kaye had brought up a pot of hot tea for Mrs. Merton. Apparently, the old woman hadn't been informed that a recital was part of the festivities. If she had known, she had said to Kaye, she wouldn't have come. As it was, she was only here because Mrs. Fogarty seemed afraid to go anywhere alone. What nerve that woman had bringing her to a recital when she knew full well how bad the piano was for her nerves. In any case, Mrs. Merton was appeased when Kaye suggested that she wait out the piano playing upstairs, where she could block out the sound with the bedroom door. Kaye would have preferred to get her out of the apartment altogether, but Eric had already been spotted coming down the hall from the elevators.

"I put it by your chair here," Kaye pointed out after she had closed the door behind them—and locked it, just in case Eric got curious and came to see what she was up to. It wouldn't do to have him burst in on them without his being fully briefed first about Wanda's complete innocence. And as long as Mrs. Merton was kept out of sight, there wasn't any necessity for such a tedious briefing, which was bound to do Wanda little good. How much could she protest her innocence without arousing his suspicion? It was a no-win situation.

"You had dozed off, and I didn't want to disturb you," Kaye explained as she poured out a cup. "Sugar?"

"And cream, please."

Since Mrs. Merton had said nothing about recognizing Kaye from Criminal Court, Kaye decided to sidestep the issue as best she could. There was no sense in making the old woman feel she was in enemy territory. Much more could be accomplished by friendly persuasion, as far as the cats were concerned. Indeed, Kaye already had a mental picture of herself accepting Eric's boundless gratitude for removing this pea from beneath his mattresses. Where strife and threats had failed, a little simple kindness and understanding would win the day.

"You look familiar," Kaye said after she had set the creamer back on the tray.

"Indeed?" The old woman's manner was gentle, refined, but somewhat distant as well. Thick, flesh-colored hose sagged about her swollen ankles while the surprisingly delicate lips, as sweet as a young girl's, blew cautiously on the by-now tepid tea.

"I sometimes see people on the street who look so familiar," Kaye improvised, not quite sure what she was leading up to, perhaps some white lie about having seen the old woman in a grocery store or park. "For the life of me, though, I can't place them. Most of the time it turns out to be someone who works at the post office or behind a deli counter. When you see them out of context, it's jarring." She gave a little laugh as applause broke out downstairs.

"Perhaps I can refresh your memory," Mrs. Merton proposed with a deferential smile. "You're the Jew who tried to intimidate me with a gun."

Kaye's dismay made it hard to reply.

"In court, dear," the old woman prompted. "A couple of months ago. It just came to me, why you look so familiar."

"Oh, Mrs. Merton, wherever did you get the idea that—"

"You deny that you were armed?"

"Yes, indeed I do. And I'm not really Jewish either."

"I thought—"

"My husband, late husband—oh, what difference does it make?"

"And you deny that you were carrying a sidearm that day?"

"Of course," Kaye said just before she remembered that sometime during the summer Joel had given her a revolver to carry in her purse. She could very well have taken it to court—but how would Una Merton have known about that?

"Dear, if you don't mind, would you help me up?" Mrs. Merton extended a plump hand garnished with a lovely aquamarine.

Kaye was surprised by the strength of the grip as the woman rose from the armless lacquer chair by the round bed.

"Thanks ever so much for the tea."

"Where are you going? Wait, Mrs. Merton," Kaye added as she placed her considerable bulk between the old woman and the door.

"Please don't hurt me."

Baffled by the role she seemed to be playing, Kaye could only sigh.

"I must get to a phone."

"Hurt you? I was just—there, there's a phone by the bed, see?"

With some relief Kaye watched the old woman turn and shuffle calmly, with an observation about how beautiful the weather was, toward the bed. Physically restraining the woman would have been inconceivable, of course.

"It doesn't seem to be hooked up, dear."

"Here." Kaye went over and demonstrated how the antenna could be pulled up from the cordless phone. "There."

Settling onto the bed, Mrs. Merton got through after a short wait. "Darling, this is Mrs. Una Merton speaking. How are you? . . . Oh. Well, I'm a widow, white, four feet eleven inches, and I'm not going to give you my weight. My first husband was a Mr. John Monastere, and then I met Mr. Merton, such a cut-up he was. . . . Oh, yes. . . . No, no, don't. . . . Well, I'm not sure how it all happened, but my landlord. . . . Yes, this *is* urgent. Let's see." Cupping her hand over the receiver, the old woman turned to ask, "Kaye, dear, could you tell me the address?"

"Here? I believe it's Forty-five—no, Forty-seven Beekman Place."

"Thank you." To the phone again, after smoothing her dress: "Forty-seven Beekman Place. And I've. . . . Yes, yes, I'm locked inside. . . . Well, I'm not really sure what you'd call it. I suppose it's something like a kidnapping, though it's not really what I imagined a kidnapping would be. I mean, they've given me tea—and this lovely counterpane, and you mustn't be too rough on them. . . . No, they've been so courteous—but I do have to get back home. My cats—oh, help!"

Kaye, who had been by the door straining to hear the little speech Eric was giving downstairs, suddenly realized what the old woman was up to. Hurrying across the room, she wrenched the phone from her powerful grip, but not without a slight, embarrassing struggle.

"I'm so sorry, Mrs. Merton, but who in heaven's name was that? You shouldn't be saying such nonsense."

"Please give it back, dear. That was nine-one-one, and I didn't get a chance to thank the young lady. She was very sweet."

"She's not sending the police, is she?"

"Well, I most certainly hope so. All the taxes I've paid."

"Look, you're free to go any time you like. I'll take you in a taxi myself, right this minute."

"Calm down, dear. Don't get yourself in such a dither."

The tears that had pooled in Kaye's eyes suddenly overflowed as all she had been through that day—the rain without an umbrella, Joel, her father, poor Eric, poor Wanda, and now this, 911—seemed to engulf her. How could she ever explain to Eric if the cops burst in on his recital? How could she explain to the cops themselves? All right, so she might be able to sneak Mrs. Merton out of the apartment. But it still wouldn't do anything about the cops.

"Blow," the old woman said, handing Kaye a delicate lace handkerchief.

"Oh, I hate to ruin it," Kaye said from the bed, where she had lain down at the old woman's gentle, soothing prompting.

"Use it, dear. That's what it's for."

Kaye blew—and felt better. "I'll just die if the cops come, Mrs. Merton."

"You didn't give me a chance to give the apartment number."

"Really?" Kaye's face brightened.

"What do you think I wanted the phone back for? And the address you gave me, it didn't seem right to me. I wanted to check it out. I seem to remember we were in the Fifties, like Fifty-something."

"Fifty-seven, that's it."

Mrs. Merton sighed and shook her head. "Forty-seven, that's what you told me."

"Oh, I'm sorry. I wasn't thinking. Eric was talking, and I was trying to listen and talk to you at the same time. Is that mink?"

"What?"

"Your collar."

"Mr. Merton bought this for me. It attaches to some sweaters I have."

"It's lovely." With the cops no longer a problem, Kaye was able to relax a little. Mrs. Merton had sunk down onto the chair by the bed. From outside the door they could hear the four-hand arrangement of Beethoven's Fifth Symphony that Eric and Tiburcia were playing to bring the recital to a rousing finale. "I have a stole, you know."

Mrs. Merton eyed her suspiciously before saying, "How nice."

"Ranch mink. Someone told me they treat them very kindly on ranches. There's no traps or anything. That's what my husband gave me years ago, for our first anniversary, a ranch mink stole. He couldn't afford it—we barely had enough to pay the rent. I guess that's why I got mad at him. It seemed so extravagant, I wanted him to take it back. When he wouldn't, I took it to Macy's myself, but I found out it was on sale and couldn't be returned. There were so many things Joey needed himself, a decent suit, some good dress shoes—Am I talking too much?"

"Go on, dear."

"I wanted him to have something nice. All I had gotten him was a tie for our anniversary. I was so ashamed of myself. And then, let's see—well, that was it. That was our last anniversary. He was twenty-nine when they discovered the tumor. Brain tumor. I was twenty-six."

"Blow."

Kaye blew. "Of course, there are some people who claim ranch minks aren't treated very nicely. I've heard they're electrocuted and crammed into small pens and—you know." Kaye saw the aquamarine glisten as the old woman reached for the phone. Quickly but gently, Kaye shifted the receiver so that it was out of reach, all the while talking. "Who are you to believe? I've never seen one of the ranches myself. You want to go home, Mrs. Merton? Wouldn't it be better to wait a few minutes? They're still playing, and we can't interrupt them now, can we? Anyway, like I was saying, I was twenty-six. . . . "

Ten

"She had a gun?"

"Yes, dear."

"Yesterday, in my bedroom?" Wanda interrupted herself to give Charles, the Siamese in her lap, a kiss. Usually Charles did not tolerate overt signs of affection, but this evening he was letting Wanda have her way.

Wanda was tired, her legs ached, and her throat was scratchy, yet she was happier than she had been in months, years even. Just before he had left the party yesterday with Tiburcia and her mother, Eric had taken her aside in the kitchen and told her how much he appreciated all she was doing for him. He had even squeezed her hand and given her a peck on the cheek. "I've never really had a woman friend before," he had gone on to say. "Girlfriends are always mad at you for not being more in love with them, for not making a commitment. It always seems as if there's this sword hanging over me—and when the pressure gets too much, I run away." Don't worry, Wanda had said, I promise not to like you very much. "That's why I was afraid of you at first, I thought you might—"

"You *are* vain, aren't you? I don't like your type anyway. Guys like you have these humongous egos. You probably think I did all this for you. I bet it never occurred to you that I might enjoy having underprivileged children over and sharing this apartment with them."

One lie after another had flowed so naturally that Wanda almost began to believe them. By the time Eric had left, after giving her another peck, she had revised her opinion of herself. No longer was she a plain, foolish woman letting herself be used by a devastatingly handsome man. Instead, she was a competent New York hostess with all sorts of interesting friends, a patroness of the arts. Indeed, she could even smile at Eric's impossible male ego. Not once during the party had he asked where his sister was, and there was poor Kaye holed up in the bedroom with Mrs. Merton all that time. When Kaye had finally emerged shortly after her brother's departure, Mrs. Merton had refused to go home with Mrs. Fogarty. Not even Wanda was allowed to escort her downstairs to the lobby. It all became clear, though, when Kaye described what had gone on in the bedroom, how Mrs. Merton thought that everyone was conspiring to restrain her.

"You actually saw the gun?" Wanda asked patiently while stroking the cat. She had hurried over to Mrs. Merton's the day after the recital to reassure the old woman that nothing was amiss. Though greeted at the door with some reserve, Wanda was soon back in her good graces when she explained that she hadn't known Kaye Levy was going to be a guest at the party. Wanda's task now was to convince Mrs. Merton that even if she had known, it wouldn't have made any difference, since Kaye Levy was a wonderful, good woman who hadn't the slightest intention of harming her.

"It was in her purse, I imagine, dear."

"But did you actually see it?"

"No, there was no need for her to brandish it. I was quite docile." The old woman swallowed the bite of oatmeal cookie she had just taken before adding, "Besides, she seemed depressed, not really up to the job. It was all very confusing. I started feeling sorry for her. When she dozed off, I suppose I should have run away, but I was afraid it would hurt her feelings. She's very sensitive."

"See!" Wanda said a little more forcefully than necessary; the Siamese had startled her by leaping up suddenly from her lap and jumping off the sofa. "I told you she was a nice lady. How could you ever suspect her of having a gun?"

"I saw it with my own eyes."

"You just said—"

"In court, when we were all in court."

Wanda put a scented handkerchief to her nose, the one she used when a particularly horrible wave of stench wafted over from the bedroom. Mrs. Merton, as usual, was totally oblivious.

"I got mixed up," she went on, "and started looking for a breath mint in her purse."

"In *her* purse?" Wanda said nasally, breathing through her mouth.

"She had left it right next to me when she went out for some water. I thought it was my purse. You can imagine how shocked I was when I saw the gun there. That's when I asked for a recess."

Wanda did remember that in the middle of the hearing Mrs. Merton had had a private conference with the arbiter.

"I told the judge about the gun—"

"Arbiter," Wanda inserted.

"—and asked if it would be all right if I pressed charges. But the judge told me it might not be a good idea since I'd have to explain how I knew Kaye had a gun. Boys, boys," she added, "stop that!"

A portly Maine coon had taken a swipe at the Siamese, and in the disturbance that followed five or six cats fled the dimly lit room. On a previous visit Wanda had surreptitiously counted thirty-one cats, though this evening the number had seemed to dwindle to twenty-nine. Most of them stayed in the bedroom or the kitchen during Wanda's visits.

"Just how did Kaye happen to be at your party?" the old woman asked after Wanda had put the coon in the bedroom, away from the Siamese.

"Like I told you, someone brought her along. I didn't know she'd be there. Just one of those coincidences, I suppose." Lying about this once was bad enough, but twice? Wanda could not help wondering what she was doing. She had always thought of herself—until recently—of being as honest as she was plain. "It's like I was telling you about Charles."

"Charles?"

"What a coincidence it was. I had a Siamese once that was lost and I was thinking about her when you offered to let me keep Charles."

"Charles isn't a girl."

"I know, but still it felt weird."

The old woman's hand, which had been resting lightly on Wanda's arm, now clutched it. "My dear child," she said, leaning close enough for Wanda to smell her sweet breath, "do you really think it was a coincidence?"

Wanda's heart pounded dully, as a possum's might when it was playing dead. Louis used to have this effect on her when he would reach for her in the middle of the night as she pretended to be asleep. She used to be so uncertain then, in the first few months of her marriage, whether Louis was a normal American husband, somewhat inconsiderate and withdrawn, or a horrible psychopath who might actually kill her someday. Oddly enough, after the Cindy episode, when she had not found her Siamese in the grave, it was easier to know what to do, how to act.

"Well, I really didn't know you were coming," Wanda stammered.

"What? I'm talking about Charles."

"Oh."

"You must not be afraid."

Wanda bit her lip.

"Girl, look at me, look right into my baby blue eyes. There. That's it. No, I'm not going to bite. Now tell me, why are you so afraid? Why are you hiding?"

"Hiding?"

"Your beauty, dear. You know, of course, that you are a beautiful girl."

There was no doubt about it now, Wanda thought. The old woman was indeed crazy, just plain nuts. First accusing Kaye of toting a gun—and now this, calling her beautiful.

"Are you sure you shouldn't see a doctor?" Arnold asked as he escorted Wanda past the newsstand (Mrs. Fogarty had her back turned, so they didn't have to stop and chat) to the revolving doors. Wanda had phoned him to say she was leaving work early because she didn't feel well. Though she had protested, he insisted on accompanying her downstairs.

"It's probably something you got in that old lady's apartment yesterday," Arnold commented as he held a hand to her forehead.

113

"No, I was feeling funny before."

"Well, it couldn't have done any good. Here." He crammed a twenty-dollar bill into her sweaty palm.

"No, Arnold."

"Cab fare. I insist."

"The subway will be quicker." A woman had been stabbed on the platform of her stop just the week before, in broad daylight. Arnold had forbidden Wanda to ride that line ever again.

"Don't be difficult, Wanda. Just take it. Or would you rather I came with you?"

"No, no, I. . . . 'Bye."

After waiting in vain on the curb for an unoccupied taxi, Wanda began to walk. The sun seemed low for midafternoon, the slanting rays often blinding her as she turned a corner. Powerful as they could be head on, at an angle they radiated a gentle light that made the cranberry and violet daisies by Gandhi's statue in Union Square seem illuminated by a rare part of the spectrum. Though she now spotted a free taxi or two, Wanda was so entranced by the light that despite her aching head, her heavy limbs, she trudged on.

Farther north at Gramercy Park she peered through the wrought-iron fence at the labeled trees and counted five yellow roses in a well-tended bed, only a few of the petals withered and brown. Ten minutes later, at Madison Square, she had to take a rest beneath a bronze Chester Alan Arthur. Her arms and legs had begun to ache as badly as her head. Shivering, feverish, she looked up and saw two bare-chested youths, one strangely feminine, gazing down from the roof of the courthouse across the avenue. Life-sized or larger, they lolled on either side of another marble figure, a woman draped like the Statue of Liberty in a modest toga. Flanking this threesome were two disagreeable old men, one of them looking mandarin with his voluminous robes and Fu Manchu mustache. Five, Wanda counted, the same as the number of roses. Wondering if this could mean anything, she got up and walked on through the shadow of a relatively new skyscraper, forty glass stories that blocked the sun from the shapely marble bosoms.

"I don't know why you don't just tell the woman that her apartment stinks," Arnold commented when he showed up after work to check on her.

Propped up in Mr. Ko's round bed with a damp cloth on her forehead, Wanda said weakly, "You think I haven't tried? No," she added as he urged her to finish the instant chicken soup he had heated up in the microwave, "I can't."

"Well, what does the old lady say?"

"I've got to be very careful, Arnold. If I come on too strong she'll think I'm on their side. To her, anyone who smells anything is conspiring to get her thrown out. She thinks Eric and Kaye are in league with her landlord, that they're being paid by him to harass her until she leaves. You know she's rent controlled, and the landlord could make a mint on her apartment. It's roomy and in a great location. So I'm trying to show her, as an independent objective observer who really likes her, that her place doesn't smell very nice. She won't believe me if she doesn't trust me first. And this incident with Kaye hasn't helped at all. That Mrs. Fogarty always manages to bollix everything up with—What's wrong?"

Arnold was staring at the half-empty bowl on the tray he was carrying back to the kitchen. It was unlike him to be lost in thought, unmindful of what he was doing. "You don't really mind that smell, do you, Wanda?"

"Huh?"

"I told you the only agency that can do you any good is the Environmental Control Board, not the Department of Health. It's their jurisdiction, sanitation and stuff like that. Have you called them? Did you ever give Eric the information?"

"Careful," she murmured as the tray seemed to tilt. "And I don't know what you mean by not minding the smell. It nearly killed me yesterday. But I'm not going to get involved with any bureaucracy. It's a personal matter."

"I see."

Wishing he would go, she closed her eyes and turned toward the wall. The NyQuil she had swallowed just before the soup was beginning to work. Although she did not hear him leave the room, after a few moments she did hear the faucet running downstairs in the kitchen. And then there was the hum of the dishwasher. Yes, there were dirty dishes in it, but not a full load. It was wasteful, all that hot water, the electricity, going for a few cups and saucers.

"Wanda, Wanda. Darling?"

Curled up in a fetal position, she pretended not to hear.

But then there was a hand on her shoulder, shaking her gently.

"What?" she said crossly, not bothering to open her eyes.

"Where is the spot remover?"

"What spot remover? Oh, Arnold, please, I'm so tired."

He was rubbing her neck now; she squirmed out of reach.

"Isn't there anything for the carpet, princess?"

Wanda's eyes opened. "What happened?"

"The soup." He smiled like a mischievous kid. "I guess I sort of spilled it downstairs, in the living room. And the tea you didn't drink." His eyes were sparkling, as if he expected a hug as he sprawled on the bed. "It's sort of funny, huh? Here you were so worried about the party, how someone might spill something, and then nothing happens until—"

"Get off this bed."

"—now."

"Get your filthy shoes off this bed."

The smile on his round, freckled face did not disappear right away, as if he thought she might be joking. But there was doubt etched on his brow.

"You know what you are, Arnold? You're an ass. That tea will never come out of the carpet. What am I supposed to tell Mr. Ko now? Huh? Tell me."

"I was checking the video machine for you."

"Don't do me any more favors, please."

"Wanda," he pleaded, the silly smile finally gone, "don't get so upset. It's just a little spot, no big deal."

"No, I suppose my job is no big deal, is it?" Wanda stared hard at him. Never before did he seem to be such an ugly little man: coarse, reddish skin, a little snub nose, razor bumps on his neck. Did he realize how close she was to telling him the truth, the whole truth, and nothing but the truth?

"I'll manage," he said, retreating from the bed.

"Don't bother. There's no spot remover. Go, please."

"Princess, you're really sick, aren't you? Let me—"

"For God's sake, leave me alone! Go!"

The stricken look on his face did not have its full effect until half an hour later, when her confusion and anger finally gave way to remorse. At the time it seemed that if a spoon had been handy, she could have made it stick in the wall beside him, easily.

"Wanda and I are completely honest with each other," Eric assured his sister as they watched the New Jersey Transit bus pull away from the curb. Because of the reflection of overhead lights in the terminal's exposed girdings, Lamar Thorsen was not visible through the bus windows. Kaye waved nonetheless to the bus at large as it began its journey to Newark Airport.

"It was her idea to have the recital there," he said as they turned back to the elevator that had carried them up from the main floor of the Port Authority building.

Kaye seemed preoccupied, even though she was the one who had brought up Wanda almost as soon as Mr. Thorsen had boarded. "I hope Dad remembered to pack his lures," she mused aloud, as if she hadn't even heard Eric.

"You think I'm taking advantage of her, is that it?" he suggested.

After a pensive moment or two, during which Eric couldn't decide if it was Wanda or lures that were furrowing his sister's brow, Kaye said, "She *is* a woman."

Maybe so, his shrug seemed to say, before he actually said, "She's no fool."

"Oh, I suppose any woman would have to be a fool to think she was even in the running."

"That's not what I meant," he said hastily as the elevator disgorged a load of customers for the next airport bus.

They were silent on the way down, Eric not caring to explain himself in front of the other passenger, a dazed-looking young man from, according to his canvas-and-straw suitcase, Eritrea. Once on the main floor Kaye walked slightly ahead, in the wrong direction, until Eric overtook her and pointed to an overhead sign. He himself stumbled over a bag of empty soda cans when he took the lead. It belonged to one of the homeless women propped up against the newly renovated tile wall in misshapen lumps of tattered rags and swollen sooty flesh. Like the victims of a recent blast, the women seemed in shock, unable to acknowledge the twenty Eric stuffed into one limp hand, the five into another, while his sister looked on with barely concealed exasperation.

"Talk about foolish," she muttered as they resumed their trek to the subway entrance.

"Don't you care?" he snapped, to cover the shame he always felt whenever he helped someone on the street.

"Sure, give a Band-Aid to someone who's lost her legs."

"What's eating you, Kaye?"

She had been behaving strangely all day. Eric could understand that seeing Lamar off involved a certain amount of stress and strain. But Kaye usually handled these occasions well, remaining calm and even amused while Eric and Lamar worked themselves into a lather of mutual irritation. Today, however, Kaye had been so officious that Eric and his father had exchanged sarcastic comments, like two teenagers with a bossy, slightly absurd mother. And it was Kaye, not Eric, who had insisted her father take the bus to the airport. Eric had even offered to chip in for a cab but was overruled.

"Is it your stomach?" he persisted as they threaded their way through a herd of commuters, who, with the brisk trot of wildebeests, kept a wary collective eye on the sleek, muscular youths lounging, with sated good humor, on either side.

"My stomach?"

"Well, you *were* in the bathroom all afternoon." As she was about to protest, he added, "At the recital. I'm talking about the recital." As if she needed to be reminded about missing his students' performance. Eric forgave her, of course. It wasn't her fault if she had gotten a case of the runs, as she had put it. But she certainly had managed to recover quickly enough. Lamar and she had eaten at a Thai restaurant immediately after the recital, he had been told.

"My stomach is fine," she said as they advanced upon the turnstiles, "but I'm afraid I don't feel like eating."

The logic of this statement was a fitting conclusion to the day. Knowing she might be feeling lonely this evening, he had offered to take her out to dinner. And this was the thanks he got.

"It's up to you," he said noncommittally, fearing that too many protests on his part might make her change her mind. In the mood she was in, it was probably best to keep his distance.

"Well?" she said as she descended to yet a lower level for the uptown IRT.

"Well what?"

"Are you coming or not?"

"I thought you said you didn't want to eat. Why should I come uptown?"

"Don't be coy with me, Eric."

"What?"

"If you could have seen the expression on your face. I'm not going to disappoint you. If you must eat, we eat. Now hurry, I hear it coming. And don't look so worried. I'll pay for myself, OK?"

Between 50th and 59th the door to the adjoining car burst open, and a black man, tall enough to play center for the Knicks, shouted out over the clatter and screech of the iron wheels, "Don't be alarmed, folks! I'm not here to ask for your money."

Kaye, who was sitting directly beneath him, took the handbag that was wedged between her and Eric and clung to it grimly with both hands. Eric retracted his stretched-out legs so the man could pass by. But he remained standing where he was, balancing himself by extending his amazingly long, leather-clad legs across the aisle to the conductor's box, while gesticulating with his huge, beringed hands. The stale, slightly fetid smell that had oppressed the passengers was replaced now with a pungent cologne that made Eric think of the chinaberry tree outside the old family home in Tallahassee.

"Relax, folks," the man went on with a menacing look in his narrowed eyes as he smoothed a palm over his shaven head, "don't go hugging your purses and feeling those nice gold chains round your necks. My name's J.T., Social Security number one-two-three, four-five, six-seven-eight-nine. I'm not here to take anything away from you. I'm here to complain about ugly people. Ugly people are everywhere nowadays. You can't get away from them. Just look around you. It's a crime. They shouldn't be allowed to have children. Just cut it out. I have a mother-in-law so ugly, she hurts my feelings. That's right, there ought to be a law. . . . "

It finally dawned on Eric, whose heart had been thumping violently during the spiel, that the man was a stand-up comedian. Indeed, Kaye even smiled when the man brought Eric into the act. ("Take this spook here, he's so pale and ugly I wouldn't waste government cheese on him.") And she actually gave him fifty cents from her purse when he went around after "the act." ("If you appreciate what you just heard, folks, please help me get bus fare to the Scarsdale Comedy Club. I be opening there in the kitchen, cracking up eggs.")

"At least he was trying to do something with his life," Kaye defended herself in the middle of the Chinese dinner, when Eric brought up the incident.

"You didn't have to smile."

"That cheese thing was sort of funny."

"It made no sense."

"Sure it did. He was implying you were a mouse."

"What?"

"You know the surplus cheese they give to the homeless? That's what he meant. Baiting a trap with it."

Eric held his peace. Before Lamar's so-called visit (over six months he had "visited"), Eric had felt so close to his sister. She could always be relied upon to understand him, often in an unspoken, almost telepathic way—or so he had assumed. When he had found out that she had been deceiving him about the reason for Lamar's visit—or, if not deceiving outright, withholding vital information—he had been saddened and hurt. It aggravated the loneliness that was plaguing him.

"I don't think it had anything to do with a mouse," Eric couldn't help commenting after they had divided up the bill.

"What? Are we back to him again?"

"I think you smiled and gave him money because you were afraid of him. There was something extremely hostile and threatening about the whole thing."

"That's what made it funny. He was playing on the white man's neurosis, this knee-jerk fear of any black man with a sense of dignity."

Well, Eric thought in near despair as they parted ways in front of the restaurant on upper Broadway, if this was her idea of funny, there was little hope of any real communication between them. Maybe, though, she was only enjoying the fact that he had been called ugly (and a mouse?) in front of a carful of strangers. But why should Kaye resent him? What had he ever done to her? Earlier that day while they were packing, Lamar had suggested sotto voce to Eric that she was upset about Joel. Women did have a tendency to complain about men, Eric reasoned, when they meant man, singular.

As he walked down Broadway on the lookout for an M5 bus, Eric passed a familiar face in a Nike sweatshirt. It was only much later, when he was on the bus, going by the Empire State Building, that he placed the mild, contented face in a pulpit—or, rather, down among the congregation, trailing a long mike cord like a nightclub comedian as he delivered his chummy homily. The latest church Eric had found was off Broadway, a long haul from Tompkins Square. He wasn't quite sure why he was going there now, since there was no longer any real reason to avoid seeing Wanda. Except that he wouldn't want to feel he had to sit by Wanda if he did go back to St. Sofya. Mass didn't feel right to him unless he was alone. That was one thing he didn't like about this Nike priest, the way he made everyone hold hands during the Lord's Prayer. It was embarrassing. And furthermore, what kind of priest would walk around with an ad on his shirt? Didn't he realize how shameful it was to be a walking advertisement for a sneaker company? At one time men wore sandwich boards out of desperation, but at least they were paid for the indignity. Now it was getting almost impossible to find reasonably priced clothes that didn't have words on them. When he shopped, Eric couldn't help feeling that *Invasion of the Body Snatchers* had been all too real. And Reagan, Bush, and Quayle, all laughable B-movie fictions, had come to life, or a reasonable facsimile thereof. . . .

Becoming more embittered as he mused, Eric determined that he would not set foot in the Nike church again. He would go back to St. Sofya. Wanda would just have to get used to his sitting in a different pew.

Eleven

During the homily that Sunday, Eric's gaze roamed over a clump of stout old women who might be blocking his view of Wanda. But later, as he was returning to his seat with the sweet wine on his breath and a crumb lodged in his windpipe (a cough and a discreet growl cleared it away), he could see that she wasn't there. Good. He wouldn't have to make excuses about not going out to get a cup of coffee with her afterward. Though come to think of it, rarely had he seen such a brilliant fall day. The wind was brisk and the sun warm, a perfect combination for a walk, maybe along the East River.

He could have done this on his own, of course, but during the final hymn he began to wonder if he had locked the front door on his way out. The fact that it wasn't his own apartment made him feel doubly responsible, which was why he had developed a system of tapping lightly three times on the door after he had locked it. This was his way of confirming that it was locked. The trouble was, he couldn't remember tapping. Had he tapped and forgotten, or had he locked it and forgotten to tap, or had he not locked it and not tapped? Or, worst of all, had he not locked it and tapped anyway—and then forgotten he had tapped? Get a grip, he told himself, knowing this sort of worry was crazy. Nevertheless, his pace was brisk as he made a beeline for the apartment after Mass; and he was definitely relieved when he was able to confirm that all three locks on the front door were secured.

Checking his answering machine, he was upset by a message from Rosa, the director of the Mani Light: *We mailed your check two weeks ago, Eric. You should have it by now.* It was the second time this had happened, he fumed. Then: *Honey, do you have my whale tie? I need it ASAP.* His father.

Damn that whale tie, Eric thought. He didn't want to have to deal with wrapping paper and tape and post office clerks. It would make more sense to just send him the money for a new tie. Then it dawned on Eric that somehow the machine was playing back old messages. It wasn't even time for his Mani Light check yet. And his father hadn't called from Florida; this was a call he had made from Kaye's two weeks ago.

Eric Thorsen, came a voice from the machine just as he was about to turn it off, *could you give me a buzz at your earliest convenience? This is Arnold Murtaugh, 555-1213. I'd like to have dinner with you, buddy. Let me know when you're free.* And then, before Eric had time to think about this, the next message was playing:

Hi, look, Dad thinks he left his alligator belt at your place. Do you mind sending it back to him? He said to Federal Express it, but first class should do, I think. 'Bye. . . . Oh, and listen, I'm sorry I was such a grouch the other day. Joel called from L.A. this morning, and we had a good talk. It's now at a definite end, Eric, but at least I know why. He says he was really offended by my attitude toward the earth. I didn't realize how much he kept bottled up inside, but he went on and on about all these things I did wrong. Like I never bundled up the Times, *just threw it in the trash, and I used too much plastic, and once I laughed at this ad Lauren Bacall did on TV for the rain forests. Then, of course, there was my mink stole. That was the last straw. I never realized how deadly serious Joel was about all this. He says he's working now to stop space shuttle launches. Each launch sends up tons of chlorine from the liquid fuel, equivalent to a year of factory emissions, and it destroys ten percent of the ozone, I think he said, or it will by the year 2000. And did you realize that the average American is one point five billion pounds overweight? We consume, each of us, two hundred and fifty thousand calories a day, if you calculate according to the energy used up by our wasteful farming methods and all the beef and stuff we eat. All this is a huge insult to Gaia. You've heard of Gaia? She symbolizes the concept of the earth, the entire planet, as a single living organism. See, Christianity has man somehow separate from his environment, like he was better than it. This whole false hierarchy, with man at the top, exploiting all the creatures and things beneath—well, this is the legacy of your wonderful Church. But I'm not going to get started on that. I've got to work today. Now be good and mail off that belt. Dad really needs it.*

Eric let out a theatrical sigh. At least she was back to her old self again. But why in the hell did Arnold want to have dinner with him? It made him uneasy.

"I can't talk now," Wanda said after Eric finally got through to her. It had taken seven or eight rings. "I'll call you back later."

"How later?"

"I don't know. I'm on the other line."

"You OK?"

"Yes, I'm fine, Eric. But I got to go."

After pressing the disconnect button, Wanda was back on the line. Mr. Ko had call waiting, which was how Eric had broken in on her conversation. She had tried to ignore the clicks, but it was making it hard to talk.

"I'm sorry," she said. "It was just a friend. Anyway, like I was saying, I enjoy being by myself. What I love more than anything is reading. I got sort of addicted to it when I was married."

"You were married?"

"Years ago. My husband was never around, so I filled up the time with books. This nun who used to teach literature in college, she would send me a list of things I should read. So I went through all the classics, Dostoevsky and guys like that. They were good as long as they didn't try to be funny. I had to skip any of Sister's books that were funny."

"Why's that, Tanya?"

"Well, sad things made me feel better about my own situation. If I read about people being happy and all, I'd start feeling sorry for myself. I guess I could read something that was funny now, if I wanted, but I prefer serious writers. After all, real life is no joke."

"I wanted to read *The Brothers Karamazov*—"

"Oh, Chad, that's what I read on my honeymoon."

"Yeah, well, I made the mistake of seeing the movie first. It came on about four in the morning, and the guy from *Star Trek,* Captain Kirk, was one of the brothers, and when I picked up the book I couldn't get spaceships out of my mind."

"You ought to try Jean Rhys."

"Huh?"

"You wouldn't think about outer space at all."

"I don't really mind outer space, per se. Like I read this book once about some space explorers who somehow went back in time and one of them got eaten by a prehistoric whale—whales lived on land back then—and then when they came back to the twentieth century they didn't even feel sad about the guy who was eaten because he had never existed—or something like that. . . . Listen, Tanya. There's something I have to tell you. My name's not Chad. It's Lenny."

"Oh."

"You mind?"

It was disturbing, a false name. "No, not really."

"You're not anti-Semitic or anything?"

"No, why?"

"Well, Lenny is sort of—"

"There was a Lenny I knew once that was Italian."

"Yeah. Well, anyway, you think I could have your number?"

"Well, I—"

"You've got mine."

"I know, but—"

"Will you call me? Will you promise to call me? Tanya, I've never had such a great conversation with a woman. Believe me."

"I'm really not a bombshell or anything."

"What do you mean? You fat or something?"

"No. I'm actually on the thin side."

"Oh, that's great. I knew it. I knew you couldn't be fat. If there's one thing that turns me off, it's—"

"Listen, I'm hanging up."

"You promise you'll call?"

"Right. I'll . . . goodbye."

Well, she thought after she had hung up, she had finally done it. She had actually talked to someone on a singles connection, a 900 line that cost 99 cents a minute, two dollars for the initial minute. Her mother, of course, would die if she ever found out. Wanda would never have had the nerve to actually talk to someone if she hadn't been fortified by a Bloody Mary on top of a healthy dose of NyQuil. She had meant to knock herself out completely, the best remedy for the chronic ache of the flu. But instead of falling asleep, she had lapsed into a strange euphoria, as if she were not quite in her body—double-exposed. In this state she had begun to vacuum Mr. Ko's endless carpet; when she got to the tea stain near the video machine, she realized with sudden clarity that there was only one logical solution. Switching off the machine (oh, wouldn't it be nice if they made riding vacuum cleaners, like riding mowers?), she consulted an ad in the *Voice* and dialed.

Telling herself she was just going to listen in, she was still a little nervous when she heard how ungrammatical the first two men on the Elite Singles Connexion sounded. But then Chad—or Lenny—had come on, his voice hesitant, even shy, and every subject and verb in agreement. Before she could think about it, she spoke. Where Tanya came from, she didn't know, but she had to say something to one of the cruder men who asked her name. Then Chad had asked the Elite operator to put them on a private line so they wouldn't be interrupted.

Yes, she had begun to feel a little creepy when Chad turned into Lenny and started talking about what didn't turn him on. But everything before that had been wonderful. To finally meet a man who read was such a pleasure. It made her regret all the time she had wasted at Mr. Ko's looking at television. Back in her own apartment, where there hadn't been a set, reading and knitting had kept her occupied. But now with three sets going day and night, she had begun to watch the programs Eric sometimes mentioned. He had installed his portable black-and-white in her bedroom on Tompkins Square so he wouldn't miss reruns of *The Honeymooners*. Wanda tried her best to appreciate this show, but she couldn't get over the feeling that it was basically crude and ugly—and violent. How could someone as sensitive and cultured as Eric find this funny? It was like Earl watching *The Three Stooges*. Her brother, who was so neat, so conscientious, would hole up in his room when the Stooges came on. And he never laughed. His face would be drawn and intent, and if anyone interrupted his show he would threaten to beat the living shit out of them.

"I thought you said you were going to call back," Wanda heard, after groping for the phone.

"Lenny?" she croaked, wondering how he had managed to get her number.

"It's Eric."

"Oh."

Curled up on the sofa with one of her homemade afghans twisted around her feet, Wanda realized that the Bloody Mary she had fixed herself after talking to Lenny had knocked her out cold. The vacuum cleaner was still plugged into the wall, and what seemed to be a home movie gone haywire danced upon the drawn ivory curtains of the sliding glass doors. Another look told her this was just the reflection of the television near the bar. It had turned dark, and she hadn't switched on any lights.

Sitting up, she smoothed back her hair and realized she was drenched in sweat, every joint and muscle defined by an ache.

"You weren't at Mass this morning, Wanda."

"Huh?"

"Don't you usually go to the nine-thirty at—oh, wait. I just remembered. Didn't you say something once about the Inquisition? You don't go to church anymore, do you?"

"Hold on a minute."

After hauling herself up from the sofa, she aimed for the kitchen. Water would make her feel human again.

"Wanda, you OK?"

"Flu," she said from the kitchen extension, a mug of lukewarm tap water in her hand. The sympathy he went on to offer sounded rote, as sincere as a greeting card. Perhaps, she thought, if the virus had a longer, more forbidding name, it would command the respect it deserved. After all, people used to die from this.

"Look, I was wondering, why would Arnold want to have dinner with me? I got a message on my machine this morning, and he called back twice this afternoon."

"Did you make a date?"

"No, I've been hiding behind the machine."

"Well, don't worry about it. Just tell him you're busy."

"You don't think he's jealous or anything like that?"

"Don't be stupid."

"I got enough to deal with as it is. I mean, you've made it clear to him we're just—you know—"

"Acquaintances, casual acquaintances," Wanda supplied, almost more annoyed at Eric than at Arnold for bothering His Majesty. Wanda, after all, hadn't spoken to Arnold since the incident with the carpet stain. She had returned none of his phone calls. So why was Eric making it sound as if it were her fault Arnold was calling him? And why was Eric so worried about such a man? Arnold wouldn't stand a chance in a fair fight.

"I swear, Eric Thorsen," Wanda said, just before hanging up, "you're really something else. Here I am nearly dying, and you haven't called once to ask how I am. But the minute it's about you, you pick up that phone soon enough. And furthermore, I think Ralph Kramden is stupid and fat and ugly, and anyone who likes him is a real dope. Now someone's trying to get me, so goodbye."

Before he had a chance to say anything, she pressed the receiver button. The call-waiting signal had been clicking all through her final speech, which she couldn't help feeling proud of. Let him hate her for speaking the truth. See what she cared.

"Yes, Mom, it's me."

"It doesn't sound like you."

"I've got the flu."

"You've got the flu? How can you have the flu?"

Wanda had learned long ago that it was a waste of time trying to answer many of her mother's questions.

"Listen, Wanda, do you have your brother's birth certificate?"

"Why would I have Earl's birth certificate, Mother?"

"I've been through every drawer in the house and turned the attic upside down."

And probably the garbage as well, Wanda thought sadly. Her mother had a mania about documents, often spending an entire weekend looking for a warranty or a ten-year-old bank statement. After all, you never knew when the toaster oven might go on the fritz, or when you might be audited.

"OK, Mother, now listen. You're hyperventilating, aren't you? I want you to take a couple of deep breaths. Yes, that's it. Good. Now stop worrying about that birth certificate."

"But what if they ask me to prove he—"

"To prove what—that he was alive? Yes, Mother, you made up

128

the whole thing. He's a dependent you invented as a tax deduction."

"Oh my," came the breathy, girlish voice over the wire. "I do seem to worry too much, don't I, Wanda?"

"Have you read that book I sent you?"

"The one on how to live in the moment? Well, your father took it into the tub with him and it swelled up. I don't know how many times I've asked him not to read in the tub."

Read, in this case, was a euphemism for *drink*. Wanda's father often passed out in the tub, reviving occasionally to add more hot water as the evening wore on. Though Wanda lived in constant anxiety about his drinking, her mother accepted it with equanimity and refused to seek the help that Wanda urged upon them time and time again. After all, her mother would say, who could bring Earl back, their pride and joy? And who could restore Earl Senior's faith in his country when no one, not a single drug-crazed hippie soldier, had been prosecuted for Earl Junior's cold-blooded murder? Wanda simply had no idea what her father had suffered when he resigned from the American Legion post he loved with all his heart. And besides, Earl Senior could hold his liquor. He never got nutty or out of control. He was no alcoholic.

"Well, I've got to get Father's supper now. Give my love to Arnold, will you, Wanda?"

"Arnold?"

Wanda had never told her family about Arnold. Being strict Catholics, they had never really accepted Wanda's divorce from Louis, not after the beautiful church wedding they had given her. Indeed, one uncle, her Uncle Joe, went so far as to tell Wanda that her divorce, coming so soon after her brother's death, had crushed the one spark of hope her parents had left in them. "You might as well have taken your father's gun and shot them both through the heart," Uncle Joe informed her.

After that, Wanda could not stand Waterbury any longer. It was bad enough that she had to fear running into Louis at the mall or the post office—though he had calmed down somewhat after Earl Senior had threatened to put a bullet up his ass if he ever laid a hand on his daughter. But to feel that she herself was a painful disappointment to her parents, whose house she had fled to after six weeks of married life, was too much. Though they both made the expected fuss about a daughter living alone in New York City, their objections were as tepid as Earl Senior's bathwater. No real feeling went into their invitation for her to stay. Indeed, Wanda's mother was rummaging through a trunk in the attic while she tried to talk her out of New York.

"Arnold, Mother?"

"Isn't that his name, the young man you're seeing?"

Wanda hesitated.

"I've never known anyone to be so secretive," her mother went on before Wanda could explain. "You never tell us anything."

"There's nothing to say."

"No? Well, apparently this young man thinks differently."

"Mom, he's forty-five years old, and I'm not seeing him anymore."

"Wanda, let's not fib to your mother, please. I just spoke with him a couple of hours ago."

"What?"

"He called and introduced himself, and we had a nice long chat. I was so pleased to hear that his aunt is that Sister you liked so much in college—Sister Mary Louis, wasn't it?"

"Patrick. Sister Mary Patrick."

"The one who used to give you those reading lists, right? Arnold said she had a vision in the nursing home before she died. She saw a rose."

"Yes, I know—and I think Arnold has a lot of nerve calling you. He and I aren't getting along, and I'm thinking it's all been a big mistake. So you don't have to worry. I'm not going to disgrace you by getting married again. And by the way, you don't have to worry about me being in mortal sin anymore. I've stopped going to communion."

"Oh, Wanda, please don't blaspheme."

"Didn't you tell me it's a mortal sin for a divorced person to receive the host?"

"That was a long time ago. You know how strict Uncle Joe was about those things." Uncle Joe used to be a parish priest. Just after Vatican II he had what was called in the family a nervous breakdown and was forced into early retirement. "And furthermore, I don't think it's wrong for you to go out with a nice young man. I've been talking to our new pastor about you and Louis, and he thinks it wouldn't be impossible for you to start thinking about an annulment."

"Mother, I'm not—"

"Arnold agrees. I was telling him how from the very beginning, when I first met Louis, I knew he was a bad egg. You just don't walk into someone's house and sit down without being asked. And that mustache he had, like he was Charlie Chan. I tried my best to warn you, but no, you had made up your mind he was it, the cat's meow."

Wanda had never told her mother that she had missed two periods and that it was a false alarm that had made up her mind about Louis. And then there was her fear of hurting him. He loved her so much, he used to say. And he actually threatened to kill himself if she didn't marry him.

"I've got to go, Mother. I'm really not feeling well."

"Yes, dear, you get plenty of rest. Oh, by the way, I almost forgot. Uncle Joe is going into town next month for the Feast of the Immaculate Conception. You know how he *has* to hear Mass at St. Pat's on that day. I've already told him I won't be able to take him this year. Your father has an appointment with the urologist that day. So Wanda, you'll just have to grin and bear it. I'll send you the exact time he's due at Grand Central, and then you and he can—"

"No, it's impossible."

"So little I ask of you, one tiny favor. Well, I must go feed your father—and there's that downstairs closet I've been meaning to organize. Now that's one place I haven't looked. Maybe Earl's birth certificate is there behind those plastic tumblers your cousin Hulga gave us. They're so ugly, I really should throw them out."

Wanda had left behind seven or eight half-empty bottles of shampoo and conditioner. Eric had offered to take them over to Mr. Ko's, but she said she couldn't use them. Now that her hair was tinted she had to buy a special brand. So when Eric showered in her tub, he set aside the 99-cent shampoo he had bought at a discount drugstore to give one of her exorbitantly priced brands a try. Was Wanda really taken in by these labels? he wondered. Full-bodied, silky hair was not all that was promised. With the electrolytes balanced and the roots nourished by the amino acids found in the closely guarded herbal folk wisdom of the Finns, the purchaser was guaranteed hair so irresistible that the manufacturers could not be held responsible for the consequences. As he lathered his head, Eric could not help smiling as he thought of how gullible Wanda, who seemed so sensible, really was. The Middle Ages' alchemy was only minor league compared to our own.

On the back of Wanda's bathroom door, the full-length mirror was something he was still not used to. In his own apartment there was only the medicine-cabinet mirror. Catching a glimpse of his body as he dried himself, he couldn't help thinking of his near-nude Ravel for the Mani Light Dance Ensemble. What a nightmare that had been, like one of those dreams he often had of going to physics class or church stark naked. Ida Grossman had laughed when, in September after her Merkin Hall recital, he had told her about these dreams. "Freud would say it's a wish fulfillment," she had told Eric as they lay on Wanda's bed, half dressed. Her flask of Russian vodka had already been set aside, out of her reach.

"But it was an awful feeling."

"You wouldn't be dreaming about it or doing it, my dear, if it were so awful. Admit it, you got a charge out of that Ravel."

"I hated every minute of it. I felt like a whore."

"But that's just the point, dear boy. You are."

"What!"

"You probably want to be. You're just too ashamed to admit it."

"You're nuts, Ida."

"Think so? Look at you now, a gorgeous hunk who never ages—no wrinkles, not an ounce of fat, oh, I do hate you—and you're in bed with a broad like me. Explain that one to me, mister."

"You're beautiful, you're really a beautiful woman."

"God, you could make a fortune, Eric. I almost believe you."

His back to the mirror, he was drying himself when he heard the phone ring. If it was Arnold again, he was going to answer it this time. He would be polite but firm. No, he didn't have time for dinner. He had a terribly busy schedule and so much practicing to catch up on.

"Hello?"

"Fish market? I'd like to order two dozen fish heads and an eye of newt."

"Give me a break," Eric said, relieved that it wasn't Arnold. Russell was reverting back to the childish greetings they had used on each other years ago.

"Not very good, was it?"

"Not one of your best. What can I do for you, sir?"

Russell said he just wanted to find out if Lamar had gotten off all right.

"Gotten off?" Eric repeated, somewhat childish himself. He didn't want to sound formal or businesslike, which could easily lead to charges of being remote and homophobic.

"Ha ha."

"Dad was fine, actually. I think he was sort of glad to get out from beneath Kaye. She was acting pretty—"

"*Beneath* Kaye?"

"—pretty weird. You should have seen her ordering us around when we packed." Realizing that he had an appreciative audience, Eric unloaded some details. He told Russell about the large comedian on the subway, the Chinese dinner afterward, the priest with the Nike sweatshirt, Arnold calling, the alligator belt. As Russell chuckled and commented sympathetically, Eric began to feel that life was maybe not so impossible after all.

"By the way," Russell interjected just as Eric was about to tell him his thoughts about the insanity of shampoo advertising, "I forgot to mention the other day that I have a friend on the Environmental Control Board. He says they might be able to look into this cat thing for you."

Suddenly realizing that he was standing in front of Wanda's bay window without a stitch on, not even a towel, Eric eased down into her wing chair. The curtains were open, and someone could easily have been out there in the dark, peering at him.

"Eric?"

"Yeah?"

"Spacing out?"

"No, I just. . . . You sure they would be able to do something?"

"Why not? Got to run now; Sylvester just came in."

"Give me your friend's number."

"I'll call you later. Tomorrow."

After hanging up, Eric used one of Wanda's embroidered cushions as a fig leaf while he pulled the curtains to. "Sorry, folks," he commented to the dark, "the show's over."

Twelve

When Wanda opened her eyes, she thought at first it was the maid. Who else would be vacuuming downstairs? But then it occurred to her that she didn't have a maid. More curious than alarmed, she groped for her kimono, which was lying on top of the counterpane, and then headed for the door.

From the walkway overlooking the living room she could see the vacuum going up and back, as if it were self-propelled. A better perspective nearer the stairs afforded a glimpse of the arm that was making the machine move. It belonged to Mrs. Fogarty.

"Get back in bed," the news vendor said crossly when she saw Wanda standing in front of her. "What do you think I'm here for?"

"How did you get in?"

"What?" Mrs. Fogarty switched off the vacuum. "You look a wreck, young lady. Here, sit."

Her tone was so authoritative that Wanda couldn't help but comply. "Mrs. Fogarty, please don't vacuum."

"Not to worry. Am finished."

"Did the doorman let you in?" Wanda asked in vain as Mrs. Fogarty, in sandal heels and brown rayon slacks, disappeared into the kitchen. Angelo had no business letting people breeze in like this. It was a violation of Wanda's privacy. Besides, how did Angelo know that Mrs. Fogarty was trustworthy? And to think Angelo had had the gall to refuse the fifty cents she had given him for holding her dry cleaning. *Five dollars is the customary tip at this address.* Ha!

"Here, drink," Mrs. Fogarty ordered, returning with a glass of orange juice.

It was glorious—fresh-squeezed with the pulp left in but the seeds taken out. And cold.

"He should have buzzed me," Wanda said as Mrs. Fogarty held out a thermometer.

"Don't talk," Mrs. Fogarty said, inserting the glass tube herself.

"One hundred point nine," Mrs. Fogarty read after three minutes of silence had been observed. "Back to bed, young lady."

On the way upstairs Wanda paused to change the tape in the video machine next to the bar. Stooping over, she commented on hearing the dishwasher going in the kitchen. Mrs. Fogarty said she had tidied up a little. Though Wanda protested, she was already succumbing, in that part of the mind where words mean little or nothing, to these ministrations. How good it felt to have the apartment fresh, aired out, in order. Mrs. Fogarty had even done a load of laundry in Mr. Ko's combination washer-dryer.

"It wasn't the doorman," Mrs. Fogarty admitted when Wanda was finally settled on the bed with fresh satin sheets, which she had helped Mrs. Fogarty put on. "I got the keys from your friend. He said you were very ill and asked me to check up on you."

The maid service Wanda was just beginning to enjoy no longer seemed permissible. Nevertheless she remained where she was while Mrs. Fogarty hung up the kimono and straightened a row of shoes in the closet.

"Arnold shouldn't have done that. You have your own work to do, Mrs. Fogarty."

"A little holiday does me good every now and then. Besides, Arnold made it worth my while, if you catch my drift."

The nerve! Wanda thought with a flash of anger, aimed not entirely at Arnold. "I still think the doorman should have buzzed me."

"I told him you were sick, needed your rest," Mrs. Fogarty replied while smoothing the static cling from her slacks. "Said I was your sister."

Aunt would have been more probable, at least in Wanda's mind. But it was useless to protest now.

"Listen, I really appreciate all you've done, Mrs. Fogarty. Now if you don't mind, I think I'd like to rest. You can leave Arnold's keys here with me," she added, grateful that there wouldn't have to be a scene with him about returning them. If she had been in any doubt before about whether to drop Arnold as a boyfriend, Mrs. Fogarty's appearance had made up her mind. She saw clearly now that she was letting herself get railroaded into a relationship, possibly even a marriage, that her heart was rebelling against. Though Arnold was almost the complete opposite of Louis as far as looks and personality went, he was playing the same game, making her feel sorry for him, guilty about not loving him enough. Certainly she wasn't going to allow herself to make the same mistake twice.

"Arnold will want these back, won't he?" The keys dangled coyly from Mrs. Fogarty's little finger. As Wanda reached out for them, Mrs. Fogarty withdrew her hand. "No, I can't let you do this to yourself."

"Mrs. Fogarty, please."

"One little spot on the carpet, and you chop his head off. That's not right, Wanda."

"How dare you tell me what's not right? You come barging in here, prying into my most intimate, private affairs—"

Wanda had never spoken her mind to Mrs. Fogarty before. The exhilaration was heady but short-lived, for Mrs. Fogarty's thin, steely lips had crumpled like a child's. Wanda had no idea the woman could be so easily, and visibly, hurt. Tears pooling in her sharp, narrow eyes, she tossed the keys onto the bed.

"I'm sorry," Wanda murmured as Mrs. Fogarty tied a scarf over her limp hair. "I'm not myself today, I guess."

"It was Arnold who come up to *me*," Mrs. Fogarty said in a choked voice. "I didn't ask him nothing. He's the one who just started to pour it all out. What am I supposed to do, tell him to shut up?" Her back to Wanda, Mrs. Fogarty went on speaking to the invisible audience that so many New Yorkers resort to in times of injustice. "It's all my fault, right? I should've learned long ago you can't have a heart. 'Cause if you do, if you care about someone and try to help them a little, well, then, Gladys, you're a snoop and a busybody. You scrub their kitchen floor, you do up their dishes, and they call it prying." Picking up a hefty green vinyl handbag, Mrs. Fogarty pretended not to hear the mild protests from the bed. "Fine, Gladys, so you keep your trap shut about those videotapes," Mrs. Fogarty went on, gesturing toward the stack of tapes that Wanda planned to take to the office as soon as she got well. "You don't say a thing about them—and her living here in the lap of luxury, not paying a cent of rent. You keep that to yourself—"

"The videotapes?"

"Oh, no, doll, not me. I wouldn't dream of prying."

"What do you mean?"

"You're the one with a college degree. Figure it out yourself."

On that obscurely triumphant note, Mrs. Fogarty made her exit, her dignity, it seemed, fully restored.

Though still a little weak in the knees, her sinuses clogged, Wanda returned to work hoping that a change of scene might do her good. Seven days of lying in bed were plenty. Dozing fitfully rather than sleeping, she had lost her appetite and suffered so cruelly from hangovers that drinking was outlawed by her sterner self. If she could have read, the time might have passed less tediously. But her attention span was too short. It affected her knitting, as well, which was no longer automatic but tiring and willful.

At first she had blamed Arnold for her inability to focus on even a half-hour sitcom. But then, a day after Mrs. Fogarty's visit, Wanda had called him to clear the air. She told him that she thought it was sneaky of him to have talked to her mother, that this was an action not worthy of the Arnold she admired and respected. And though she could appreciate the thought behind having Mrs. Fogarty drop by, there was still something under-handed about it. Arnold could not have been sweeter, admitting that he had been wrong. This gave Wanda the courage to admit her own guilt.

"I've been worried all along, Arnold, that I might be leading you on. But it hasn't really been that. I've just been trying to see if my feelings could change, could grow. Because you know how I value your friendship. The trouble is, lately I've been feeling pushed. Things are going too fast. I need time to get things straightened out in my own head." She couldn't quite bring herself around to saying outright that there was no hope for him at all. That would have to come later.

In any case, Arnold did not scream or rant or rave as Louis might have. He said he could appreciate where she was coming from and respected her decision. Would it be all right if he phoned her occasionally to see how she was doing?

"No, I'd prefer to be really alone, Arnold."

Though he agreed not to phone, every time it rang, she expected it to be him, calling with second thoughts. "You whore, you bitch!" she imagined him saying. "After all I've done for you!" He kept his word, yet she had no peace, her mind beginning to doubt more and more her own treatment of him.

"The *Times*, please." Adding, "How are you this morning?" Wanda took the risk of being snubbed by Mrs. Fogarty, who handed over the paper without a word.

Wanda had the chance now to end this trying friendship by simply walking away from the newsstand. But something in her balked at this solution. True, she had never really wanted to be friends with Mrs. Fogarty in the first place. But at the same time she knew it would bother her to feel such enmity radiating from the newsstand every time she walked past.

Standing uncertainly by as another customer paid for a find-the-word booklet, Wanda decided to give it another try. "I'm going out to the deli around noon. Could I bring you something back?"

Without looking at her, Mrs. Fogarty shrugged.

"You like pork skins, don't you?"

"Not today."

"Oh."

As Wanda was about to walk on to the elevators, Mrs. Fogarty said, "I might want a Reuben."

"OK, I'll check with you on my way out."

Satisfied that Mrs. Fogarty would eventually relent—though it might take a little groveling on Wanda's part—Wanda picked up her shopping bag filled with videotapes and moved on. Her next task might not be as easy. As she waited in front of an elevator embossed with gilded brass lilies, she considered how best to inquire about the tapes. It had never occurred to Wanda that she was doing anything shady until Mrs. Fogarty had planted the seed of doubt. For days Wanda had fantasized about Mr. Ko's brother being involved in some international pirating ring. After all, she had been taping movies from HBO and Cinemax, as well as the endless game shows and sitcoms. Was there some law against this? Would the FBI get upset if they found out? Wanda knew that if Mr. Ko could not give her a satisfactory answer, her conscience would not allow her to remain at his brother's. Where she would go was another matter. But there was no way she could stay on at Beekman Place.

The quaint brass pointer above the elevator finally began to run counterclockwise as the cab descended toward the lobby. It wasn't until the doors opened with a *ping,* though, that she wondered about her job. The slightest hint of disloyalty would be enough to set Mr. Ko off. And if he thought she suspected his brother of being a crook? Well, it was going to be a very delicate matter. Perhaps now wasn't the best time to question him, after all these sick days she had taken. Mr. Ko never believed anyone was really sick. But Wanda did have a note signed by her doctor. Then again, maybe she shouldn't put it off any longer. She wanted a clear conscience.

"I wouldn't call her," Eric advised his sister. "She has the flu and needs her rest."

Kaye looked doubtfully at the limp stalk of the asparagus plant. "Are you sure you're not overfeeding it?"

"I'm doing what Wanda said."

"What's her number? You should have reported this to her long ago." Picking up the receiver, she dialed the number Eric gave her. But there was no answer.

Kaye had dropped by her brother's to pick up Lamar's alligator belt, which she would mail to Tallahassee herself. Eric claimed rather childishly that he didn't have the time to fuss with wrapping paper and the post office. And he even scolded Kaye for going through all the trouble herself. "It was irresponsible of Dad to leave it behind in the first place," he had informed her. "Anyway, Kaye, it's an old belt."

Plucking a few yellow leaves from the asparagus, Kaye suggested that he move it out of the kitchen to the living room. There would be more light.

Eric grunted. He was at the pine kitchen table marking up the score to *The Magic Flute*. The opera company he was working with in Brooklyn required a number of cuts because their Papageno was experiencing technical difficulties.

"Well, I suppose I should be going," Kaye said as she deposited the belt inside her handbag. "I have a date tonight."

Another grunt.

"Got to get all gussied up." With a sigh she settled into a wicker chair to change her shoes. She had come from Macy's in her good shoes without bothering to put on the Nikes in her handbag. But her feet ached, and it might be worth the trouble.

"God, Eric, we're living in a cruel world, you know. I'm old enough to be a grandmother and yet I have to be a teenager, all butterflies about whether I look attractive, how far I should let the man go. Ugh."

"Who is it?"

"The duck guy."

One of Eric's eyebrows arched. There had been a standing joke between them about the man who sold ducks and chickens in the Cellar's deli. Kaye had been making fun of him for so long that it was more than a little surprising she was accepting an actual date with him.

"OK," she said, reading his mind. "So he's not Cary Grant. What am I supposed to do, curl up and die of loneliness? He's taking me to a singles dinner at his church."

"You mean synagogue."

"Church, Our Lady of Pompeii on Carmine Street. I figured if you can't find a good Jew, then Italians come in second—real Italians, you know. There's supposed to be a lot of men there who barely speak English."

"Nice, Kaye. Using him to meet other men."

"He knows that. I made him promise to let me dance with anyone I want to."

"How romantic."

Her running shoes on, Kaye realized what was wrong with the kitchen, what had bothered her when she had first walked in. It wasn't just the sagging asparagus plant. It was the grease surrounding the burners on the stove, the fingermarks on the refrigerator, everything betraying what at first seemed passably neat and orderly. Yes, Eric had washed the dishes and put everything away.

But he had obviously done little else in all the time he had been at Wanda's. As she walked over to inspect the sink, her soles stuck to the unmopped linoleum. And the sink, as she feared, was coated with schmaltz. "How long do you plan on staying here?"

"Hmm?"

"Don't you think it's about time you did something about your own apartment?"

With a bemused smile he looked up from his score. "As a matter of fact, Russell has finally come around. He's got a buddy at the Environmental something, and he thinks it's curtains for the cat lady."

"I see."

Eric's smile wilted. "So what's the problem? Why are you looking at me like that?"

"I don't know," she said, hoping she looked more sad than angry. "It just seems weird that you're letting it happen again. The white knight to the rescue."

"Russell? Don't make me laugh." Though he managed a grin, Eric resented the implication that he was a damsel in distress. "And what do you mean by again? What has he ever done for me?"

"Oh, nothing much, I guess. Just got you an apartment that most people would kill for nowadays."

"It was no skin off his back. All he had to do was ask his cousin."

Kaye extricated a bit of pepper rind from the sink drain. "Sure, easy as pie."

"Wait a minute," Eric said as she started to go.

"Yes?"

"Look, I've leaned over backward to be friends again with Russell. Even after what he did, that latest stunt with Dad, I haven't held it against him. You should have heard us on the phone the other day. We were laughing and joking."

Ever since her days of ten-meter full-gainers, Eric had been for Kaye the very ideal of manhood—not just incredibly handsome but truly modest, gentle, and considerate. Hearing him speak like this, though, made her wonder if his ego was not just as large as the movie stars' he so despised.

"Oh, so you actually laughed and joked with the man who

shelled out six thousand dollars for you. Gee, that's big of you."

"Huh? What are you talking about?"

Kaye had promised never to tell a soul. She had kept the secret all these years—but enough was enough. It was time baby brother grew up. "You think it was that easy getting a rent-controlled apartment in Murray Hill?"

"Yeah, I know, Russell lied and said I was his cousin's brother. I know all about that."

"Well, didn't you ever wonder how you could be his cousin's brother when she obviously had a different last name?"

Eric shrugged. "I suppose she said her maiden name was Thorsen—something like that."

"You're right, something like that. Russell paid the landlord's lawyer six grand so he wouldn't look too hard at the proof she was your sister. And don't forget, this was back in 'seventy-five, when six grand meant something."

"I don't believe you," Eric said helplessly. "Who told you this?"

"Audrey."

"Yeah, right. As if she doesn't have an ax to grind herself."

"This was before the divorce." Audrey, Russell's wife at the time, had not meant to tell Kaye. It had slipped out as a minor part of a complicated story about a neighbor on Fishers Island who had made fun of Russell for resigning from the Knicker-bocker and Brook clubs, something about his being a tightwad when it came to dues. Audrey was simply defending her husband, explaining how generous he was, and was truly dismayed when she realized her slip. Russell had made her promise not to tell a soul.

"Don't look so upset," Kaye said, beginning to doubt the wis-dom of spilling these particular beans. The point was not to make him feel miserable and guilty. "You should be glad you have such a good friend."

"Six thousand dollars. My God."

"Now, Eric."

"How am I ever going to pay him back?"

Eric's distress was so evident that Kaye forgot about his ego. "You're not supposed to, that's the whole point."

"But—"

143

"But nothing. It was like a contribution to the arts for him. He believed in you as a pianist. He wanted to show his snotty friends, the ones who snubbed you after the broken engagement—he wanted to show them you'd make it, you'd be a . . . " Kaye's voice trailed off as she realized she was just getting in deeper.

"A what?"

"A success. And that's what you turned out to be," she said, a little too heartily.

"Yeah, right."

"Oh, Eric," she moaned, resisting the urge to run over and cradle him in her arms. How could she have done this to him? Didn't she know he had the world's most fragile ego? Well, was she satisfied now that she had crushed it entirely? Good going, Kaye. "Can't you understand what a compliment this is, to have someone believe in you so much? Besides, it's not a lot of money to Russell. He probably got a big tax write-off or something."

"I can't go back there now, to Murray Hill."

"What? Are you meshuga?"

"First of all, it's totally illegal. I can't live with that on my conscience."

"But you had nothing to do with it."

"Never mind. I couldn't live there anyway unless I paid him back every cent. I wouldn't feel right."

Kaye was old enough to realize that these were probably just words. Most of the time, if you let people have their say, make their grand moral pronouncements, they will eventually wind up doing what is sane and normal. Just look at Joel and all the fine words he had spouted to her over the past year and a half.

"Eric, I've got to get home and do my hair. Promise me you're not going to tell Russell I said anything. Eric? I don't want you acting silly over this. Now where's that belt? Did you see where I put Dad's belt?"

"In your thing."

"Oh."

"Arnold was the short guy at the recital. He used to be a priest."

"Yeah, now I remember. So he just barged into your apartment when you told him you didn't have time for dinner?"

"Right, just showed up on the doorstep and invited himself in.

Then he goes on and on about Wanda, wondering if there is anything he could do to get her back . . . make her 'come to her senses.'"

"Sounds strange, asking you. Isn't he jealous of you?"

"Why should he be?" Eric snapped. "Look, I don't know how we got on him. Let's stick to Bach for now, OK?"

Cracking his knuckles, Russell said, "Sorry, maestro," and resumed his struggle with a Menuet from the First Partita.

Russell had a good ear and had taught himself to improvise on show tunes. But he had never had any formal lessons or solid grounding in the classic piano literature. Eric had agreed to work with him on an ad hoc basis, whenever their schedules could mesh. It was Russell's solution to the problem of the $6,000. As soon as his sister left the apartment, Eric had wasted no time in tracking down Russell. Reaching him by phone at the settlement house, where Russell was reviewing applications for a new phys. ed. instructor, Eric had let him know that he didn't appreciate in the least being turned into a charity case. In fact, Eric had lost his temper, using a number of words that he later regretted. It was the first time in his adult life that he had lost control, and when, a week later, he had called Russell back to apologize—the priest in confession had made Eric promise to do this as his penance—Russell had made the task amazingly easy. "Tell you the truth, Eric, it did me good to hear you like that. At least it was real. I'd rather that than have you pretend you were grateful or some sort of bullshit like that. See, you really are a little redneck underneath it all. That's why you can't stand your father. Two peas in a pod."

Not exactly delighted with this explanation of his behavior, Eric had served up a more palatable excuse. "Kaye's been on my back about Wanda, the woman, you know, who—the apartment I'm in. She thinks I've been here long enough, that I'm taking advantage of her or something. I don't know. It's all crazy because Wanda's got Beekman Place for nothing, and I'm doing *her* a big favor here. I'm under a lot of pressure and I'd like to get back to Murray Hill, but then I find out I'm illegal and you're bribing lawyers and I think what if someone finds out and I'm thrown out of the place—where will I go then?"

"To jail, maybe."

"Yeah, it's funny to you. I'm the one left holding the bag."

It was then that Russell made his suggestion. He told Eric he had always wanted to take lessons from him, but he knew Eric would be uncomfortable about it and didn't bother to ask. "Look, I've checked with other teachers. The mediocre ones are sixty, seventy-five an hour. Good ones are a hundred bucks a crack. You give me a few lessons and that's it—we'll be even. Just don't charge me."

Having little choice in the matter, Eric had agreed, though not without many internal reservations. This first lesson, however, was turning out to be not quite as unpleasant as Eric had anticipated. Russell was in earnest about making his Bach sound a little less like Bobby Short. He listened to Eric; he stared hard at the notes. Nonetheless there were those digressions, such as when Russell found it necessary to ask, out of the blue, if Wanda was attractive. It was this that had led to the mention of Arnold. Eric couldn't think of the man now without seeing red. The nerve of that little twerp to assume he was gay. "No, Wanda never said you were," Arnold had admitted. "I just thought, your looks and all, living alone. . . . " If only Arnold had been bigger, Eric would have punched him out. Of course, he said nothing of all this to Russell.

"Well, have you called my buddy at the Environmental Protection Agency?" Russell asked as he stuffed the Bach into a plastic shopping bag filled with corn chips and root beer. "No, I bet not, huh?"

"Thanks to you I feel pretty weird about Murray Hill now. I'm really not legal, and if the landlord finds out, it's curtains for me."

"So the cats are going to win, after all. And—"

"You got a spot on your pants." Eric was holding his office door open for Russell, who was halfway through it. "In back. There."

"Ketchup. See you later, teach."

Thirteen

"What arch?"

"That big thing."

"You mean like a fence, that cast-iron fence?"

"What? I'm talking about that big stone thing they built for George Washington when he visited the Village or died or something."

"Oh, that." Eric realized now that she was talking about Washington Square Park, not Gramercy. It had sounded so unlikely to him, a big arch in Gramercy Park. He was folding his socks, though, and hadn't been listening very carefully. Three of his crew socks were unmatched, and he was wondering if he might have left their mates behind at the laundromat.

"So you're meeting under that," Eric said after a brief silence, during which Wanda stood on tiptoe to reach an irregular pane of the bay window. Dismayed to see how dirty the glass had become in her absence, she was cleaning as much as she could before going out on her date. It would be nice to come home to a clean apartment if Lenny turned out to be a disaster. And she was so fond of the bay window, the way its imperfect, wavy glass distorted the light.

"Yes, Eric, we're meeting under an arch, not a fence."

"How will you know who he is? There's bound to be more than one male under the arch."

"This male said he would have on pink sneakers."

Eric looked up from the faded carpet, where he had begun sorting his underwear. "You sure you want to go through with this?"

Wanda didn't. If she had her own apartment to herself, she would never have called Lenny back, at least not this soon. But she realized that with Arnold out of the picture now, it was necessary to develop some sort of romantic interest. Eric would feel uneasy if she never went out on any dates; it was evident from the way he had tried to hide his alarm when she told him that Arnold and she were history. Perhaps it had been a little unfair for her to have withheld this information until she had moved back into the Tompkins Square apartment—but then again, it was *her* apartment. And she had been in no state of mind to sort everything out then—not after that terrible scene with Mr. Ko.

Wanda still did not understand how things had gotten out of hand so quickly when, a week ago, she had given Mr. Ko the videotapes for his brother. In the nicest possible manner, she had asked if he had any idea what his brother did with them. Mr. Ko had said, in an equally nice way, that his brother enjoyed television programming. The "-ing" gave her pause. Smiling, she asked if he had meant to say programs. When Mr. Ko didn't reply, Wanda tried a new tack. "Your brother could get a lot of money for his place. I could understand someone house-sitting for a few days, maybe even a couple of weeks. But I've been there so long. It doesn't seem right to me, Mr. Ko. Even if I weren't taping those programs. . . . Can't you at least tell me what he does with them? I don't understand how he could watch so many tapes."

"What are you saying, Miss Skopinski? Come, speak plain. You think he is a crook, stealing the TV shows, huh?"

"No, I was just wondering—"

"Well, for your information, these tapes he gives free to the nursing homes he is building. I don't tell you this because my brother don't like to brag about his good heart."

"Oh, I see. I didn't know he built nursing homes."

"This is gratitude for you. He gives poor working girl a chance at luxurious home, and what does she say, huh? She thinks he is dishonest, a thief."

"No, no, I always was grateful, Mr. Ko. It's just hard to believe in this day and age someone can be so nice."

"And what do you do to people who are so nice, Miss Skopinski? Behind their back you have wild party and spill wine and liquor all over their white carpet. *Their* own personal wine and liquor, which you stole from their bar, my brother's personal bar!"

Wanda blanched. How had he found out about the recital? "You don't understand. It was just a few people, and I paid for the wine and drinks myself. I swear."

"So you did have a party, huh? No wonder you so sick."

"Not a party, really." Wanda realized she had no reason to feel guilty. After all, no one had ever forbidden her to have people over. And she did pay for the wine, she and Kaye had. Unfortunately, she remembered the vodka she had given Eric on a previous occasion—Mr. Ko's vodka. But that had only been a small amount. She had done it only to please Eric, not to seem stingy. She was planning to replace it before she left. "It was just some friends, Mr. Ko. And no one spilled a thing, I promise. I was very careful." Again, another inconvenient memory made her hesitate. "Well, later, there might have been some tea on the rug. I spilled— I mean this friend of mine—"

"Your lover? Yes, very nice, Miss Skopinski. I invite you to stay at my brother's because I think you have highest morals in office. Then you have men over, drinking, spilling. I am fooled by your looks. When I first see you, I think there is woman with high morals who go to Catholic church. But now I see you don't even go to Catholic church, huh?"

"Yes. I mean no. Well, I did, but you know, the Inqui—"

Wanda was asked to clean out her desk that very day. And of course, she would have to leave Beekman Place as soon as possible.

Mrs. Fogarty turned out to be a lifesaver. She closed down her stand in order to help Wanda lug several cardboard boxes filled with her ficus, philodendron, and fern, her thesaurus, coffee mug, and extra shoes. It wasn't until Wanda was back on Beekman Place, phoning Eric, in tears, sobbing like a baby at the injustice of it all, that she put two and two together. Mrs. Fogarty had gotten her revenge, after all. She knew what Mr. Ko looked like. On his way in, as he passed the newsstand, she could easily have stopped him and told him about the tea stain, the recital. Oh, it was hard to believe that anyone could be so evil. And then to have the gall to help carry those boxes out.

"Calm down," Eric had advised on the phone. "You don't have any proof she did it."

"Who else could it be?"

"It doesn't matter now."

"Arnold would have never done a thing so low."

"It's all right. You weren't happy in that job, anyway. And I'll be moving in a few days. Just give me a little time. Once I get the cats all straightened out, I'll be out of here."

Because of the pink sneakers and the rather shameful fact that she had met him on a 900 line, Wanda could not help thinking, as she waited under the arch for Lenny, that anything short of being raped would have to be considered a success. Twice she had seriously thought about walking away and lying to Eric later. But then she remembered her pledge. Before she moved back home, Eric had made her promise that she would be completely, one hundred percent honest with him. It was the only way for them to get along. If something he did annoyed her, she had to tell him right away and not let it fester. Little things like sharing a bathroom could cause a big explosion if they weren't handled just right. He would hang up the towels, and, by the way, he would let her have the bedroom and move out to the fold-out sofa in the living room. Wanda started out by telling him she really wasn't mad at him for letting the asparagus plant die. It was the truth. But then when he cross-examined her, explaining to her that it wasn't humanly possible for her not to be a tiny bit annoyed, she changed her mind and said that, yes, maybe he could have tried a little harder. This apparently satisfied him until, the next morning at breakfast, he admonished her for not being completely honest about the asparagus in the first place. "Don't make me work at making you honest, Wanda. Try to do it yourself, right off the bat. You have to get in touch with your feelings, see? It can't be all in the head, what you *think* is right."

How much easier it would have been to lie to him about Lenny, to say she had met him through a friend. But the pledge of total honesty was in effect, and she had admitted to phoning the 900 line under the influence of NyQuil. Eric had laughed when he heard this, and, in keeping with the pledge, Wanda let him know that this hurt her feelings. Eric had explained that, though normally he wouldn't have laughed aloud, under the conditions of the pledge, he had to. Wanda was not sure if this made her feel better or not. But she did remark, just before she poured ammonia into a plastic bucket to begin cleaning, that it was a shame Eric hadn't put some effort into keeping the apartment a little cleaner. Eric had muttered something about not being a maid—which, she supposed, was an honest statement of fact.

"Tanya?"

Wanda looked blankly at the pleasant face that had loomed upon her so suddenly as she stood shivering under the arch, lost in a fog of speculation. Glancing down and seeing a grayish pink, she ventured, "Lenny?"

"Sorry I'm late."

"That's OK."

"There's a girl with a green ribbon over by that statue. I was staring at her, getting sort of mad. I mean, we said the arch, and there you were next to Garibaldi, and you weren't at all thin like you said. I was planning to just walk away, and then I turned around."

Wanda's green ribbon fluttered in a sudden gust that urged them from the shadow of the arch.

"Well, I guess. . . . " In the sunlight it felt a little warmer. Wanda looked furtively at Lenny, who was staring at a squirrel. He was actually pretty good-looking. And he didn't seem anywhere near forty-five. He could pass for thirty-nine with that nice thick black hair.

"Would you like to get a cup of coffee or something?" she asked, after Lenny said he wished he had a peanut or something for the squirrel, which looked sort of weird, she noticed now. Almost white.

"I would, but I got to help this friend catalog his CDs. I forgot I told him I would do it this afternoon, and he's counting on me."

"Oh."

"See, I was thinking maybe it'd be better if we had more time together." His voice was warm, gentle, even more appealing than it sounded on the phone. "Maybe later this week we could grab a bite. I'll give you a call."

Wanda looked at him, but his eyes followed the albino squirrel up a maple. "That would be nice," she said.

It was only after she had lost sight of him, as she was strolling across Waverly, wondering if she was hungry enough to eat, that she realized he didn't have her number.

After Eric had stuffed his nylon laundry bag behind some hardcovers in Wanda's bookshelf, he phoned the number Russell had given him that morning during Russell's second bout with J. S. Bach. Eric had mentioned that he had left a message for Brown Johns, Russell's friend at the Environmental Protection Agency, but Johns had never returned the call. So Russell had given him the home number, which was what Eric tried now. A woman answered in primitive English. Switching into his primitive Spanish, Eric learned from her that Señor Johns was in some place that sounded like the Galápagos until next week. Eric left his name and home and office numbers, reiterating, "Uno amigo de Russell Monteith."

Under normal circumstances, Eric would have moved back to his sister's when Wanda let him know that she had to leave Beekman Place. But he was still stewing about the $6,000. It was so insulting that Kaye could have known about it all these years and not said a word. Did she think he was some sort of dimwit, a child needing protection from the "real" world? Mulling this over while Russell had struggled with the Menuet, Eric felt waves of anger batter against his growing awe that Russell could have been so generous, expecting nothing in return. Even if he were as wealthy as Russell, Eric knew he could never have been so generous with a friend. For a starving African, yes, Eric could see that. But an ordinary friend?

As for Kaye, he would be darned if he was going to listen to her anymore. Let her make a fuss about how terrible it was for him to share the apartment with Wanda. He now trusted Wanda far more than his sister. Wanda was a sensible woman without the slightest trace of guile. And she was so considerate and unobtrusive. In the few days they had been together she had kept to her room, reading, when she was at home. She even ate in her room, and did most of the cleaning while Eric was out working. With some relief he noticed that he didn't have to tap three times after he locked the door behind him. And furthermore, he was glad that

Arnold was nervous about this arrangement. Wanda was better off without him, in any case. He was a real jerk.

"You're back," he commented as Wanda passed through the kitchen on her way to her room. She didn't say anything, just nodded.

After finishing the bowl of cereal he was having for supper, he knocked on her door. "Want to watch *Sixty Minutes*?" he asked, letting himself in. His black-and-white portable had been moved into the living room.

"No, thanks."

"Did you eat?"

"I'm not hungry."

The tensor light clipped to the headboard of her bed left most of the room in shadow. Though it was narrow and windowless, Eric had never felt claustrophobic in there, but rather cozy and safe, as if it were a secret hideaway. Wanda too, sitting up in her terry-cloth robe on the bed, seemed to be enjoying the solitude it afforded. Because it jutted out as an afterthought to the building, there were never any neighbor's feet clomping above. This blessed silence Eric missed in the living room. But of course, even though Wanda had volunteered to use the sofa, Eric would never have permitted her to give up this sanctuary.

"You should eat something," he said, settling onto the edge of the mattress. "You look a little thin."

"I've had the flu."

"What about some chili? I found this new meatless kind. All you have to do is heat it up. No?" He glanced at his watch. From the living room a chorus sang lustily, "Oh, what a feeling—Toyota!"

"He was nice."

"I wasn't going to ask."

"Come on, Eric. You were dying to know, right?"

"Not dying," he said, honing his honesty. "Curious in a mild way."

"Well, I got shot down. He wasn't interested. Didn't even have time for coffee."

As she set her book, *1984,* face down on the bed he said, "You call that nice?"

"Well, he did try to soft-pedal it—said something about dinner maybe later in the week."

"That's being shot down?"

"He was just saying it. He didn't mean it."

"Are you a mind reader?"

"He didn't ask for my number."

"But you have his."

"Look, if he were really interested, he would have asked for my number."

"I think you're too used to Arnold. Most men are a little more diffident these days. They're afraid of being rejected themselves."

"I'm not going to call a man up and ask if he was serious about taking me to dinner. There's a limit." She bit her lip. "Well, thanks a lot, Eric. Here I was getting used to being completely rejected, and now you've got to give me hope."

"Isn't that nicer?"

"No, it's much harder. Now I'll be worrying about whether I misread him, if maybe I should call him. And then if I do, I'll feel so pushy and desperate. Don't you know men hate desperate women?"

The pronounced ticking in the other room distracted him. "It's on," he said, getting up. "Come watch," he added as he went out, shutting the door behind him.

In the morning Wanda lay abed for a good hour, savoring the smell of her furniture, the feel of her linen sheets and lumpy mattress. Mr. Ko's seemed like a dream now—or like something she had watched in a darkened cineplex. Being there in that slick apartment had somehow made her vulnerable to Arnold. She suspected that if she had been at home, here on Tompkins Square, she never would have gone to bed with him. It was on her conscience, something she would like to confess in the old-fashioned way, to an unknown priest behind a grill. But she was afraid her faith was not strong enough now for her to believe she really would be absolved of Arnold, ever. How nice it would be to have that child-like faith that the past, once repented of, no longer could be held against you.

Though she had taken a shower the night before, Wanda did not feel properly clean once she was dressed. It was her habit to shower in the mornings, but Eric tended to sleep late, and she didn't want to disturb him. They were getting along so well, better than Wanda had imagined possible. Unrequited love, she thought, was supposed to make one moody, depressed, and spiteful. Perhaps if she had been beautiful and rich, with nothing else to worry about, Wanda might have acted more normally, scheming for a way to get him into bed with her. But she was genuinely concerned about finding another job. Unemployment checks would stop soon enough. What a nightmare it would be if she had to go back to Waterbury and live with her parents.

"For you."

Wanda gave a start. She had been hovering over the pine dresser, unable to decide which earrings to wear, when Eric suddenly appeared.

"The phone," he urged grumpily.

His eyes half shut, he turned and headed back to the living room in his droopy boxer shorts. Wanda followed, trying not to notice how smooth and clear his skin was. More than once she had imagined that Eric's clothes hid some minor deformity, a livid birthmark, perhaps, or crooked toes. She had seen a man once, a waiter, who looked so handsome in profile. Full face had been such a shock. His right cheek was caved in and scored with purple streaks. Wanda had felt herself falling in love with him as the meal progressed, much the same way she had been attracted to Eric when she had first seen him at the nine-thirty Mass. But so far she hadn't discovered the flaw that made Eric so different from every other handsome man, the secret of his loneliness.

"Hello?" Wanda whispered, stretching the cord as far as it would go.

Eric had climbed back into the pull-out bed. With a groan he crammed a pillow over his golden, tousled hair.

"It wasn't Mrs. Fogarty."

"What? Oh, Arnold, I can't talk. Please don't call me—"

"You shouldn't be mad at Mrs. Fogarty. She didn't tell Mr. Ko about the recital."

"Good. I'm glad. Now I've got to go."

"It was the doorman, I talked to him myself. Mr. Ko checks in with him from time to time."

"Fine, but how did he know about the carpet stain?"

155

"Well, Mrs. Fogarty did admit she blabbed on you about that. But only to the doorman, Angelo, not to Mr. Ko."

"OK," she said with little feeling, "so I'm not mad at Mrs. Fogarty anymore."

"It wouldn't be fair."

"And like I've said before, Arnold, I'm not mad at you either."

"Then can I see you? Tonight? No, you won't let me. 'Cause you *are* still mad at me, Wanda. You still think it was my fault you lost your job, don't you? But I didn't mean for it to turn out that way. I only asked Mrs. Fogarty to go visit you—"

"Yes, I know, I know." Wanda was standing in the nook of the bay window, where the curtains lapped gently in a lazy, unaccountable draft. It was a strain, talking in a whisper. Arnold was wearing her out.

"No one will ever love you the way I do."

"Please don't talk to me that way, Arnold."

"I'm not giving up. I know you love me. I can't make myself believe that you don't love me anymore. I've tried, Wanda, but I know you. I've seen the way you looked at me. Why do you deny it? You know what your heart is telling you! We were meant for each other. Do you think it's just a coincidence that we ended up working in the same building after all those years? You don't think God didn't know what she was doing when she put us together like that? She gave me back my past, Wanda. She healed that wound."

"Arnold, it was all too fast. I still don't understand how it happened, how I let myself—You were lonely, and any woman who was kind to you—I mean, I never got the sense that it mattered to you who I was, as an individual. I was a generic-brand woman you didn't—"

"Oh, no, no, no. I know what you're hoping for, what you've always wanted. It's crazy, Wanda, you know that. If you had the slightest chance with him, believe me, I love you so much I'd let you go. But you're going to ruin your life, Wanda, waiting and hoping. He doesn't care at all. You know, at first I just assumed he was gay. That was great, I thought. My best friend in the seminary was gay. I love gay people. I think they're very dear to God. But after I talked to Eric—he and I had a long talk, Wanda, did you know? He's not gay, Wanda, he's simply unable to love anyone, man or woman. He's scared to death of life, of any sort of involvement with anyone. Wanda, you got to listen to me before it's too late. He told me he never even wanted a pet, that it would make him feel too much responsibility. This man is sick. You're living with a real monster. One day you're going to get too close, I just know. And he's going to hurt you terribly. Because there's nothing inside him but emptiness and rage and despair. Eric would make a great bishop, a great pope, but Wanda, I beg you, don't think he could ever be a friend. Goddammit, wake up, wake the fuck up!"

Wanda had to hold the phone away from her ear, he was shouting so loud. And then the next thing she knew, he had hung up on her, just slammed the phone down.

It took a moment for her to regain her composure. A beige leaf dangled from the shiny locust branch she stared at blindly through a gap in the curtains. She was hyperventilating, and her hands trembled as noticeably as her mother's when she was looking for a warranty.

On the other side of the room, Eric began to snore.

Fourteen

On the Feast of the Immaculate Conception Wanda had three interviews in the morning. Though the employment agency that was sending her out advised her to knock a few years off her age, Wanda insisted on telling the truth. She had also been coached to say that she had decided to leave her previous job in order to find a position more commensurate with her proven administrative abilities. But in each interview, after some hesitation, she found herself admitting she had been fired and then went on to explain about the carpet stain and Mr. Ko's high-strung personality. In one instance she even touched upon the videos before the interviewer interrupted her with a question about her salary expectations.

Aside from her earrings, which she decided weren't right for the taupe dress she had picked out, Wanda felt that she had made a good impression. At the end of each interview she was actually a little surprised when no offer was forthcoming. But she consoled herself with the thought that these were not jobs she really wanted in the first place. In fact, she didn't know how she had let Edith Professional Placement talk her into giving these companies a try. One firm made metal staircases, another gourmet popcorn, and the third was a herpes advice center.

Consulting her watch after pushing through the advice center's revolving door, Wanda realized she was running a little late. Mass would be over by the time she got to St. Patrick's. A cab wouldn't help that much, either. Midtown traffic wasn't moving any faster, it seemed, than she could walk. Luckily, the advice center wasn't too far from the cathedral, so her anxiety about Uncle Joe remained a low-grade buzz, not having time to mount into an actual panic. Of course, her mother expected her not only to meet her uncle at Grand Central but to actually attend Mass with him. As if her time counted for nothing. Just because the old man had wandered away from a halfway house years ago, it was no reason to suppose he couldn't function by himself now. After all, he had his own apartment in Waterbury, cooked for himself, did his own laundry.

"I told you in *front*," she said rather sharply after rounding him up from the north side, where he was shredding a vendor's pretzel for the benefit of some pigeons. One had alighted on the padded shoulder of his bright blue suit, so distracting the old man with delight that Wanda had to repeat herself in order to be heard. "Come on, Uncle Joe, we've got to hurry or you'll miss your train."

"What?" he said finally, when the bird had fluttered to the ground to compete for the last of the pretzel. "But Wanda, aren't we going to eat?"

His eyes, guileless and blue, would have registered the rejection so clearly that she would have probably ended up blushing. If only he didn't look so harmless and genial, with his white hair lifting in the breeze, his neat hand extended like a child's, ready to be led anywhere, how much easier it would be on her.

"Let's go to your apartment, Wanda. I'll make you a nice watercress sandwich."

"No, it's too far," she said, relenting. After all, she was finished with her appointments for the day. She had nothing else to do. "We'll find someplace closer."

Wanda hadn't told her mother yet about her new roommate, and certainly she had no desire to explain Eric to Uncle Joe. The old man still hadn't accepted the fact that she was divorced. His dearest wish was to see her reconciled with Louis, which was the only way, in his eyes, she would find eternal salvation. What was especially galling about this was that Uncle Joe had never once set eyes upon Louis. Wanda had been too embarrassed by Uncle Joe to introduce him to Louis when they were dating, and then when they were married, Uncle Joe was in the hospital with complications from hepatitis. By the time he got out, Wanda and Louis were separated.

"What's this?" Wanda asked as he stuffed a piece of paper into her jacket pocket. They were heading south on foot, passing slowly by Saks so Wanda could study the outfits on the lithe, severe mannequins, all very pale Asians.

"I've enrolled you, my dear, in the Cardinal Cooke Guild."

"Oh, Uncle Joe, really. I don't want—"

"Please, if you only knew how much this meant to Cardinal O'Connor. He's fighting against all odds, determined to make his predecessor a saint. You know, I've already given my own testimony. I wrote His Worship about thatMass I attended, right here at the cathedral on the Feast of the Immaculate Conception, when Cardinal Cooke's sleeve brushed my arm as he walked up the aisle. You remember, Wanda, how I got those bleeding hemorrhoids when your mother told me about your divorce? Well, after his sleeve—"

"Come along, Uncle Joe. You're in this man's way."

As she maneuvered him out of a sightless beggar's path, Uncle Joe inadvertently stepped on the beggar's supine dog. The German shepherd looked bleakly at them both but did not protest.

By the time they were in the neighborhood of Grand Central, Wanda knew that she would not be able to bear a lunch alone with her uncle. Louis had already cropped up twice as they headed west off Fifth Avenue, and her uncle's pointed references to the marriage at Cana made their route even more of a Via Dolorosa. It was no good trying to explain to him yet again how Louis had treated her. It would only lead to the response she had heard over and over again: "The Church has never taught that marriage is a bed of roses." If he said this one more time, she was afraid she might scream.

"What are you doing?" her uncle inquired as she stopped in front of a pay phone that was actually working. Three others she had tried had no dial tone, and one receiver was covered with bubble gum.

"Never mind." Wanda put in a quarter. Lunch was going to be worthwhile after all. She would kill two birds with one stone.

The restaurant they ended up in was halfway between Mrs. Merton's apartment and Grand Central and happened to be Spanish, a cuisine Wanda had always been meaning to try. Uncle Joe was usually on his best behavior with anyone outside the family, and Mrs. Merton proved to be no exception, particularly when he learned she was Catholic. For her part, she seemed suitably impressed that he was a priest, and even indulged in some mildly flirtatious banter when he gallantly proposed to interpret the rather complicated menu for her.

"Such a charming young man," Mrs. Merton commented after the uncle had been pointed in the direction of the door marked CABALLEROS. "But I do wish you would have come up to my place. The prices here!"

"It's all right. I said I'd pay. And Una," Wanda ventured, emboldened by the success she was enjoying so far, "you know I couldn't bring him into your apartment."

"I don't know why on earth not." The old woman's fingers groped toward the top button of her blue cloth coat, a spring coat that seemed suitable enough for this mild December day.

"Maybe you've noticed, Una, that every time I visit you—"

"Visit me? It's been ages, you naughty girl."

"Well, there's been a lot going on lately. I won't go into it now. But anyway, whenever I've visited you, maybe you've noticed I always bring a scented handkerchief with me."

"For heaven's sake, don't worry your pretty little head about that. I don't mind in the least, though I do think it bothers Charles. Cats are very sensitive to smell, you know, and that cologne you use is awfully pungent."

Mrs. Merton's blue eyes, unclouded by the slightest doubt or reflection, returned Wanda's wondering gaze with unsettling clarity.

"When Mrs. Fogarty visits, or Mrs. Monastere"—Wanda tried again, while the crooked fingers continued to twist the coat button—"don't they ever mention the horrible smell?"

"Oh, love, your handkerchief isn't *that* bad. Besides, they always wait for me in the lobby. Neither one seems to like cats."

"Una, I really can't believe that you don't know how awful—"

"Oh, I give up. Wanda, here, undo me. It's so warm with this on."

Halfway rising, Wanda leaned over a squat, flickering candle so she could unbutton the coat. "Careful," Mrs. Merton said as she reached for Wanda's scarf, which was dangling over the paella the waiter had brought just before Uncle Joe had excused himself. "There, dear, now let me do the rest."

Subsiding into her chair, Wanda said, "Una, I think it's time the truth about your—oh, wait. Don't."

Hastily, Wanda rose again to try to prevent Mrs. Merton from unbuttoning herself any further. Already it was evident that the old woman had forgotten to put on a dress underneath. Though the slip she was wearing was nice, it really wouldn't do in public, especially with her large, sagging breasts.

"Sit down, Wanda, let go," Mrs. Merton protested.

"Una, you don't have anything—"

"For heaven's sake! Father Joe, help!"

Returning from the rest room, the uncle hesitated a moment before coming to the old woman's rescue. Wanda was ordered to sit down, which she did after a brief, futile struggle with her elders. It was her, of course, that the waiter was eyeing from across the room. He had *her* pegged for the troublemaker. Well, she thought, let the stubborn fools find out for themselves. They wouldn't listen to her, wouldn't let her explain.

As button after button came undone in the uncle's fingers, Wanda waited for the realization to sink in. Leaning over Mrs. Merton, he was evidently apologizing for his niece's behavior in the low mutter of the confessional.

"Is everything all right?"

Wanda looked up and saw the waiter—a not very Spanish-looking man with a blond crew cut—hovering. "Yes, fine."

Still looking doubtfully at her, the waiter retreated to the kitchen. Wanda almost felt like restraining him, saying, Stay, look what I have to put up with. But by then Uncle Joe had begun to hastily button up the cloth coat. Though she couldn't see his face, Wanda could read his trembling fingers. He wasn't even able to finish the job.

"What is it?" Mrs. Merton asked as Uncle Joe returned to his seat. Bewildered, the old woman looked down and gazed for a moment, as if her almost naked bosom were a landscape as awesome and forbidding as the moon's. This time, Wanda's fingers were welcome. The coat was soon properly buttoned.

"I made you rush out," Wanda said, breaking the silence during which Mrs. Merton tried valiantly to eat. Uncle Joe crossed himself. "I'm always forgetting things when I rush out of my apartment."

Bright with tears, Mrs. Merton's eyes remained on the meager spoonful she had scooped up from the paella, a chicken tail. "I always eat the pope's nose," she said as she bit halfheartedly into the gristle and fat.

"I beg your pardon," Uncle Joe said, putting down his fork. His lips compressed, his brow furrowed, he regarded Mrs. Merton now with an expression Wanda was all too familiar with, as if the old woman were no longer company.

"That's what Mr. Merton used to call it," Mrs. Merton explained in an unsteady voice. "He was a Methodist, such a dear, funny man."

"And they ask what's wrong with mixed marriages," Uncle Joe commented bitterly before returning to his roast pig.

Eric had Mrs. Merton's paella for dinner that evening. It was a shame to let something so expensive go to waste, so Wanda had asked the waiter to pack it up for her. Uncle Joe, of course, had no interest in it, since he was allergic to shellfish.

"So you didn't say anything about the stench?"

"How could I? If you could have seen how upset she was about the slip. . . . It just about broke my heart."

"I don't see the connection," Eric said, using a nutcracker on a lobster claw.

"You really don't, do you? That's sad."

Wanda was transferring the silverware from the drawer Kaye had preferred to the one that made sense. There were also stray spices that had to be herded into the proper cupboard, and the pots and pans were a mess, jumbled together without any regard for size.

With a fistful of forks, Wanda drifted across the newly scrubbed lineoleum, her face abstracted with doubt. Maybe it was wrong for her to have mentioned the incident with Uncle Joe and the slip. Mrs. Merton had begged her not to say a word. The poor woman was so afraid that Mrs. Fogarty would find out and tell Mrs. Monastere, who might use this as grounds to ship her off to a nursing home. "They're getting tired of worrying about me,"

Mrs. Merton had confessed to Wanda after Uncle Joe had been dispatched to Grand Central. "They're afraid I might leave the stove on or fall down and not be able to get up. They bought me this gadget I'm supposed to wear around my neck all the time. You press it, and an ambulance comes and breaks down your door. I had to quit wearing it, though, because Charles would get on my lap and put his paw on it. They got real mad at me for false alarms."

Of course, the only reason Wanda had told Eric was because she had promised to be totally honest with him. He had asked her what she had done that day, and she wanted to show that she was doing her best to get him back into his own apartment. This should prove to him that she didn't need him, that he had no reason to fear her even if she wasn't dating. Yes, she had called Lenny about the dinner he had promised her. But she had slipped and said it was Wanda, not Tanya, calling—and he had used that against her, saying he didn't think it was very nice of her to go on using a false name after he had admitted his real name to her. He wasn't mean about it. He just sounded sad and disappointed and said he didn't want to get involved in a relationship that had started out with deception. Wanda said she thought she understood and thanked him for being honest; it was probably not easy for him to be that honest. Lenny had agreed. It wasn't. So that was that.

"Eric, listen, I hope you're not going to tell anyone what I said about the slip, you know, not wearing a dress." She waved the forks in a helpless gesture. "I wasn't supposed to tell anyone."

With his fingers he picked out a slice of sausage from the paella and set it aside. He hated ham or any flesh from intelligent or large creatures, Wanda had learned. "Why not?"

"Because Mrs. Merton is afraid of being forced to go into a home."

"But isn't that what we want?"

Wanda was indignant. "How can you say that?"

"She needs supervision. She obviously can't manage alone. Look at all the trouble she's caused."

"But not a nursing home, Eric. Have you any idea what they're like?"

"They can't all be so horrible. Maybe there's some nice ones."

"Nice or not, she's a woman who enjoys her independence. It's not fair to make her live like she was some sort of invalid. She's perfectly healthy and aware of her surroundings, bright as can be. So she may have occasional lapses. Who doesn't? I mean, tonight, Eric, I saw you look in your wallet three or four times. What if someone made a big deal about that? You were checking your credit card, right? Making sure it was still there?"

A pained expression on his face made her realize she had gone too far. As she sorted the forks according to size, she wondered just how she had ended up on the wrong side of the fence, as far as Mrs. Merton went. This had not been her intention at all. Ever since the old woman had accused Kaye of holding her hostage with a gun, Wanda had feared Mrs. Merton was losing her mind. Now here she was insisting to Eric that she was as capable and sane as anyone on the planet.

In her confusion Wanda happened to notice some writing on a ragged sheet from the roll of paper towels with the beige floral design. Reaching for it, she said, "What's this?" Eric's hand was virtually indecipherable.

"Some guy called."

"O'Malley? Does this say O'Malley?"

He grunted, still miffed, it seemed, by her comment about the wallet. Nevertheless, he did seem to be enjoying the paella.

"What did he want?"

He poured himself another glass of milk before answering. "He said you should drop by his office first thing in the morning. Bring a résumé."

Wanda had an image of herself leaping into the air, like the people did in the Japanese car commercial. Outwardly, though, she maintained her calm. She had left a message with Mr. O'Malley's secretary that morning before her interview at the metal stairway company. Three years ago, before signing on with K-Yok, Inc., she had come close to getting a job with Mr. O'Malley at Philip Morris. She wasn't even sure that Mr. O'Malley, who liked Thomas Aquinas, even remembered her. But apparently he did. And the fact that he wanted to see her first thing in the morning could only mean there was some hope for a good job there. Otherwise, he would have put her off or not wanted to see her at all.

"Well, I better get to work right away," she said to herself, more than to Eric, as she abandoned the silverware. "I wish you had told me sooner, Eric," she added cheerfully. "My résumé needs sprucing up."

"Don't tell me you're serious about this?" He swirled the milk around in his glass and sniffed it, as if it had become a dubious vintage.

"Of course I am," she said, opening the door to her room.

"You actually want to work for a cigarette company?"

"You don't understand." She had hoped that Mr. O'Malley had not identified his firm to Eric, but apparently he had. "We really hit it off, Mr. O'Malley and I. See, his wife went to Albertus Magnus, and I almost got a job there for forty grand a year."

"What's Albertus Magnus, some sort of institution?"

"It's the college I went to."

The glass paused on its way to his lips. "You went to college?"

Not deigning to reply, Wanda shut the door behind her with some vigor. Her anger gave her the energy to plow through the suitcases and cardboard boxes on the floor of her closet until she finally unearthed her old portable typewriter. Clearing the jewelry case and holy water from the top of her chest of drawers, she made a space for the machine. It was awkward having to stand up to type, but she certainly wasn't going to use the kitchen table. Before inserting a clean sheet of paper, she sprinkled a few drops of holy water onto the typewriter and then crossed herself.

"I think you misinterpreted what I said."

Wanda had seen the door open in the mirror but went right on typing. Now she said, to the image in the mirror, "Look, I know you think I'm dull, plain, and slightly retarded, but maybe it's not necessary to say it aloud while we're sharing quarters."

His face crinkled into one of the most charming smiles she had ever seen on a human being. "You're great."

"It's very difficult living with you," she went on, doing her utmost to disguise her delight at those words. Could he really mean it? "You look so nice and human that I've constantly got to remind myself that I'm living with a real beast."

On her bed now, he held up a bare foot and spread the toes in an idle, insouciant way. Wanda typed an unnecessary word or two, disgruntled at the perfection of the insole's gentle curve. What could he mean by draping himself over her bed like that?

"May the beast inquire why such a paragon of all that is humble and virtuous is so anxious to put herself in bondage to a merchant of death?"

"They don't just make cigarettes. They make cookies too," Wanda said with some passion, having a vague memory of a tobacco company that had gotten mixed up with Sara Lee or Pillsbury. "And they give millions to the arts. They have their own Whitney Museum downstairs, and besides you don't know how hard it is for a girl my age to get a decent job. I'm sick to death of working for crazy bosses. That's all I've had my entire life. Now for once I have a chance to work for someone who's cultured and appreciates me. He went to Yale, you know, and he goes to Mass almost every day."

"Well, if you like beasts, Wanda, then go right ahead. Because you know and I know that this man is a dragon. Smoke is pouring out of his mouth, he's devouring children alive, putting up billboards in all the ghettos to make smoking look hip and cool."

"I don't think I need rescuing, Mr. White Knight, so you can get off your high horse—and my bed too, if you don't mind."

Remaining where he was, Eric held up the other bare foot for inspection and, while frowning at it, said, "Seriously now, why don't you give that college another try?"

"What, Albertus?"

"You said they almost offered you a job for forty grand. Why not let them know you're free?"

Wanda turned from the mirror and looked directly at him. "I don't know what you're talking about. I graduated from there. They never offered me—"

"You just said, out in the kitchen—"

"I never. . . . Eric, you know you're either crazy, plain nuts, or you need a hearing aid." Troubled by the memory of a similar incident but unable to come up with the details, Wanda turned back to the typewriter.

And she was typing, in the midst of a dangling participle that later would be corrected, when she felt the hand upon her thigh, a touch so delicate, so gentle, that even as her entire body seemed to convert itsMass into pure, pulsing energy, the doubt was enough to prepare her for what she saw when she looked into the mirror: He was not there. He had left the room.

167

Separately, neither would call attention to herself or himself. Together they might draw a glance or two from a weary shopper—yet even that glance, she realized, might be imagined. People by now, especially in this city, had seen everything. If a near-naked young man, a silver Mercury posing stock-still in the middle of the crowded sidewalk, attracted no more attention than a litter basket one swerved to avoid, what was there for her to feel self-conscious about? She might be a little taller, a little heavier than the average American woman; he might be slightly shorter than the average American man. Beside him, though, she feared she dwarfed him, and as they paused at the corner of Greeley Square for a traffic light, she realized she was not standing up straight and was hunching her shoulders.

Arnold had acted surprised when he came across her in Macy's Cellar. But Kaye had a feeling this was no coincidence, that he knew exactly what he was doing. Nevertheless, she played along with him, as courtesy seemed to dictate. He complimented her on the hors d'oeuvres she had made for the recital and said something about how wonderful her brother was to work with all those underprivileged children. It was near closing time, and when he suggested they get a drink in the Cellar's bar, Kaye hedged. Even though she had often enjoyed a cup of coffee or a vodka and tonic there after work, she said she hated to be so close to her job when she was off-duty. Her real objection, though—and this she kept to herself—was her fear of being disloyal to Eric. Arnold was bound to ask questions, and her replies, conscientious and truthful as they might be, could possibly be open to misinterpretation.

Nevertheless, when Arnold said he knew a nice bar in the neighborhood, Kaye agreed to accompany him. After all, she reasoned, she had an obligation to help Wanda out of the mess she had gotten herself into. Kaye should never have talked Eric into looking after Wanda's apartment. It was her meddling that had landed him there, and now the poor woman was in danger of ruining her life by doting on Eric. The idea of those two living together was something Kaye just could not reconcile herself to. It was bound to put a strain on Wanda's relationship with Arnold. Hadn't Eric himself told her that Wanda was practically engaged to Arnold? She owed it to Wanda to listen to whatever her fiancé had to say—and to assure him that Wanda meant absolutely nothing to her brother. Kaye had consoled enough ex-girlfriends of Eric's to know there was no hope for Wanda. The sooner the girl woke up and came to her senses, the better.

"She refuses to see me," Arnold said, as soon as they had settled into a booth in the A&S mall, whose top floor offered a variety of attractive cafés. "Now she won't even return my calls."

"You mean you're no longer engaged?" Kaye asked with a sinking heart. It was happening much faster than she had predicted. Wanda was already jumping off the deep end.

"Engaged? We never were engaged. Who told you that?"

Loyalty, as well as the appearance of the waitress, made her hold her tongue. Arnold ordered a scotch on the rocks and guacamole. Kaye decided a vodka and tonic would be nice and let Arnold talk her into buffalo wings as well. Being new, the café they were in seemed spotless, and the chic neon lights and minimalist Mexican decor made Kaye feel young and trendy.

"You feel disloyal?" Arnold asked as the svelte, comely waitress strode off in a no-nonsense way.

"What?" she asked, worried that he might be one of those Irishmen who could read minds. That button nose of his, the mischievous grin, the ruddy, freckled face, they were all telltale signs. Her friend Ellen O'Toole, who had given up a good job to open a spiritualist parlor, had the same nose, the same coloring, and the same wide, thin-lipped grin.

"Being here, at a rival store."

"Oh," she said with a combination of relief and disappointment. It was exciting to be around mind readers, after all. "Doesn't bother me in the least, not with what they pay me. In fact, I was thinking how much more cheerful Abraham and Straus is. It's lighter, more airy. No one's buying, though—did you notice as we came up? This is going to be a rough Christmas. We're in a real depression."

"It wasn't Wanda, was it?" he said, after they had both deplored, in a perfunctory way, the commercialization of Christmas. "She didn't say anything about being engaged, or wanting to be engaged, did she?"

"It was me, I guess. I just assumed—you both seemed so close, so right for each other."

Undistorted by a grin, his face became legible to her. It was easy to misread a face like his, elfin and, despite the lines, boyish. "We are. It's your brother. What's the matter with him? Why is he doing this?"

"It's my fault, Arnold. I'm totally to blame. Like today I was just thinking," she said, emphasizing her point with a blue corn chip, "I had a perfect opportunity to talk to Mrs. Merton about her cats at the recital. I could have reasoned with her, explained how nice Eric is and all. But instead, what do I do? I start crying like a baby. Everything seemed hopeless to me. I didn't even feel like trying to help anyone anymore. My boyfriend had left me, and I was thinking how my husband and I had quarreled. I'm a widow, you know."

"No shitting, he died?"

Kaye didn't know quite how to take this. "Of course he's dead."

"Fuck, it must have been a real shock. He seemed so healthy to me."

Looking hard into his gray-green eyes, Kaye said, "Now look, you couldn't have possibly known my husband, could you?" The thought that Arnold might have been an obscure business associate made her tingle all over. Her husband had been an accountant too.

"Wasn't he at the recital? The guy you came with, huh?"

Kaye's face fell. She could hardly believe her ears. Just how old did Arnold think she was, anyway! "That was my *father.*"

"Oh. Well, I knew you two were connected somehow." He shrugged in the exaggerated way Kaye associated with Jewish comedians. His hands spread, palms up. "I mean, what am I to know from? Everyone keeps calling you Mrs., and you're sniping at him, pick pick pick."

"Oh, be quiet," she said with an involuntary laugh.

The conversation reverted soon enough to Eric and Wanda, but Arnold's mistake continued to trouble Kaye. The easy rapport that she had begun to enjoy now had a nick in it. How could he be so stupid as to think that? she wondered, while doing her best to display her genuine interest and sympathy. A tale of her own misery finally got her mind off the mix-up and even brought a real smile, not a grin, to Arnold's weary face. She told him, in somewhat exaggerated terms, of her date with the man who sold ducks at Macy's. Though he was of average height, Kaye made him shorter and more squat and introduced a waddle that hadn't been there before. Nothing, though, could exaggerate the misery of the church basement at Our Lady of Pompeii. She had drunk Gallo out of a plastic cup and dined upon cheese balls and potato-chip crumbs. But the worst part was that the duck man turned out to be a centerfold compared to the other men. "And what's more, he only danced with me once. I sat there like a great big fat wallflower while all the ladies waltzed around with him."

"Tell me about it," Arnold said, tapping his swizzle stick on the polyurethaned tabletop. "They're hell, aren't they, those church socials? I always felt that the only people who went to those things were rejects, people who only get invitations from God."

"Yeah, but at least you were a man. Women outnumbered men ten to one, right?"

"I was a priest."

"What? You're kidding."

Arnold shrugged with a stand-up comic's helplessness: *What can I say?* "I was also an idiot. I fell in love with a Sister of Mercy. We were working together in the Philippines, at a mission that I thought was going to be for starving natives and all that. But most of the Filipinos I saw were real middle class and complained about everything I did. They didn't like my red hair, thought it was funny."

"Was she a Filipina?"

"No, Sister was a Kraut, very intellectual and severe on herself. She had internalized a lot of self-hatred, even though she wasn't even alive during the war, World War Two. That's all she ever really thought about, what her people had done to the Jews. Her whole life was an expiation—is. She's the one who told me about Pius XII and the Church's history with the Jews. I guess I just assumed that since she hated the Church so much—well, we'd get married. She did love me. God, she loved me. And me, I couldn't think about anything else but her. So it was something of a shock—I had made all the plans to leave with her, and she tells me I've totally misunderstood her. That she wouldn't dream of leaving the Church in the hands of Pius's successors, that she was going to stay and fight. Well, it about ripped me in two."

Kaye was respectfully silent a moment before asking, "Had you made love?"

He nodded. "That's my problem. I'm a pretty passionate guy. I mean if I like someone. . . . I don't know how I ever thought I could be a priest. It's funny, when you're young, these abstract ideas seem so real. Everything got turned around in my head in the seminary—the Trinity was real, my body was not. There was no such thing as time, since everything good lasted forever. But after Sister Berthilde, I suddenly realized my body was real, that time was real. First thing I did back in the States was get the clap. Then herpes. Then I got torn up by three women in a row. Three!" His hand smacked the table in a parody of outrage, and Kaye smiled. "Three broads dumped me, one after the other, and all three led me on. Well, so I tried sleeping with a man, a friend of mine I really loved. But it was a disaster. He enjoyed it; I felt like an ass. He went on to other men, and I went on to nothing. I gave up completely, no dates, nothing. I made a vow never to let myself be hurt again. Then what happens? I run into Wanda in the lobby of the building I work in."

"And it was love at first sight."

"Second." Some guacamole dribbled onto Arnold's tweed overcoat, which he hadn't taken off. With a curse he dipped a napkin in his scotch and wiped at the stain. "I had dated Wanda back in college and really liked her. In fact, if things had worked out between us, I wouldn't have gone into the seminary. See, Kaye, back then I had no confidence at all, as a sex object, I mean. I had suffered too much at mixers and all. I mean you don't know what suffering is until you've picked what you think is the ugliest girl at a mixer, someone no one's been dancing with, and then get turned down by her—with a look of disgust, to boot."

"Oh, Arnold," Kaye said with a slightly hysterical giggle. "Stop it."

"I'm not kidding. Wanda, I knew, was beyond me. So I could resign myself philosophically. She was really pretty and could have done much better than me, and Yale was right next door."

"So what you're saying, Arnold, is that Sister Berthilde restored your confidence?"

"She really dug me, as a man. It gave me hope. If she could, why not someone else? That's how I got started on the road to ruin. I really wish I didn't find women so attractive. I'm really obsessed by them; it's like an addiction. I even went into therapy once, a hundred bucks a crack. I wanted to stop being so turned on, because all it brought was misery. I swear to you, Kaye, there's not a single woman I can't find something I really like about—physically. OK, so she may have an ugly mug, but God, her legs. Or her hands; that in itself might be enough. Or her perfume. So I say I gave up on women, yeah, I stopped dating. But Lord Jesus help me if I didn't whack myself off eight or nine times a day. That's what I wanted therapy to help me with. I went to a real psychiatrist, an M.D., hoping he could prescribe a drug that would cure me. I told him I thought I had satyriasis. But he laughed and had the gall to say I was pretty normal. God, how I was hoping I wasn't normal. It nearly killed me. And the older I get, it doesn't seem to go away. Even with Wanda—sleeping with her, I mean—I'd still have to masturbate alone. She's very uncomfortable with sex and won't let me do it more than once a night and never in the morning or afternoon. In fact, I think she really hates sex. She's said to me more than once that she wished people could be married and celibate. I kept on thinking that the more she trusted me, the more turned on she'd get to making love. Look, I don't like to brag or anything, but I know a thing or two about what turns a woman on. Wanda, though, no matter what I whispered, no matter how I stroked her, she would always interrupt and just want to get it over with. That was her idea of fun: Get it over with, Arnold. If you must, you must. Well, of course, she had that horrible marriage. You can't really blame her. She's got a lot to recover from. But I know I can help her, if only she'd let me. . . . "

Kaye was thankful that Arnold was not at all her type, for his talk was beginning to stir her. She had never met a man who spoke this freely, in a totally vulnerable way. Yes, men had tried to talk erotically to her, but it had never worked, for most of the time they were lying.

"You know," Arnold went on, "she was gray when I saw her the second time, when I ran into her in the lobby of our building. That's what gave me courage. Something told me I had a chance this time. If she had been as pretty as she'd been in college, I'd have been too afraid to start anything again. But I could see right away that life had caught up with her too—that she'd been put through the mill. And the funny thing is, instead of the crow's-feet and all being a turn-off, they did a number on me. It was like I could still see the Wanda I knew, the fresh, delicate girl beneath the gray, and whammo, I was a goner. See, the way I look at it"— the swizzle stick rode softly, up and back, between his fingers— "you can't really be in love without double vision. When kids say they fall in love, that's all chemical, nature's way of preserving the species. Everyone's beautiful then. But real love is seeing the beauty of the body's suffering. When youth has been transformed into a memory, then the body has a soul."

"Oh, Arnold, that's so profound," she heard herself say as, beneath the table, his stockinged foot began to stroke her calf.

Fifteen

Russell had obviously been practicing. The Menuet went off without a hint of the cocktail lounge. Indeed, it was even a little too stiff and correct. He could afford to add some personality to it now, a bit of life.

"First it sounds like you're praising me," Russell complained after Eric had told him this. "Then it ends up being a criticism."

Because of Russell's schedule, Eric had agreed to make a house call, though Russell's neighborhood was not one he was particularly fond of. As he left the Tompkins Square apartment that morning on his way to the lesson on Park Avenue, Eric noticed that two more tents had been set up in the park, pup tents where the homeless lived with all their possessions. At the time of *Die Walküre*, when Russell, Kaye, and Lamar had come by Eric's for lunch, the police had cleared Tompkins Square, forbidding any squatters. But soon after, the tents, blue and yellow, always soggy, had blossomed among the trees. Though the sight was distressing, it didn't suggest the abject despair of the cardboard tents of Russell's Upper East Side, where the homeless slept over sidewalk grates or in the foyers of banks beneath cash machines. Indeed, there was even a certain sense of community among the squatters in Tompkins Square, and it was not unusual for Eric to hear laughter as he walked by, bitter as it might be.

The hour was soon up. As Eric rose from the Empire chair beside the piano bench, he saw something that made him pause in the middle of a lukewarm commendation of Russell's efforts.

"What's this?" Eric said, reaching into the Steinway grand's innards. Tugging carefully, he eventually unearthed a toy tank.

Russell sighed. "So there it is. Sylvester's kid likes to play army here. He threw a fit when he couldn't find the tank yesterday." Sylvester and his son were at Disney World, Russell had told Eric. Russell was flying to Orlando right after the lesson, which was why he had asked Eric to come up to Park Avenue. It would save Russell a lot of time if he didn't have to trudge all the way down to Eric's office at the settlement house.

"You mean you let him play in the piano?" Eric asked with as much wonder as annoyance. The buzzing in the octave above middle C had obviously been caused by the tank.

Stooping to pick up a pair of underpants from the Aubusson carpet, Russell said, "I've asked Sylvester to speak to him." Red in the face, he straightened up. "About the piano. I can't interfere myself. Sylvester is very touchy about Richie. He's extremely concerned about raising him right."

"You should really keep him away," Eric said with a touch of sternness as he went to get his parka. "Pianos like yours shouldn't be fooled with," he added, just before knocking accidentally into a boxing glove that hung by its laces from a Sheraton breakfront. The statuettes inside—Mycenaean, 1400 B.C.—shivered. Both Eric and Russell winced.

"How about staying for lunch?" Russell asked, as if nothing had happened.

Eric was not so quick to recover. "Huh?" he said, imagining a broken fertility god, what it would cost to replace.

"Inez fixed the most wonderful duck last night. It wouldn't take a minute to heat up the leftovers. I had a little dinner party yesterday. It was Audrey's birthday."

Eric smiled dimly, trying to imagine an ex-wife's birthday party.

"She asked about you. You ought to give her a ring sometime, Eric. Audrey misses you a lot."

Russell had settled onto a couch strewn with G.I. Joes. The window directly behind him cast such a brilliant aureole that his head seemed dark, almost featureless. "She's got a lot of girlfriends, you know, some really intelligent women. I know you don't go for divorcées, but there's one or two who've never been married, I think."

"No setups, please." Eric moved to the side, to adjust the angle of light, but still remained standing. It was easier to look at Russell now.

"You're spoken for?"

Eric zipped his parka up, not bothering to reply.

"It's not that Wanda Kowalski, is it?"

"Skopinski. No, of course not."

"How do you have dates, with her around?"

"I'm giving myself a little breathing space for now—until I get back in my own apartment."

Russell was lining up the soldiers on the back of the couch as he talked. "So has Brown ever gotten back to you?"

"Not yet. He's in the Galápagos."

Russell's hand passed over the plastic figurines, knocking them all down, some onto the floor behind the couch. "Hate these things. Imagine, teaching innocent children to love war, to think it's fun. Sylvester and I had a real set-to about it. That's why I didn't go to Disney World with them. Then I got scared. I called him up in Orlando and said I was sorry. It was silly to make such a big deal about it, I said. And so here I am, about to fly down, shorn of all my principles, plucked naked as a silly goose." Smiling sadly, Russell shook his head. "Maybe you have the right idea after all, kid. Maybe it's better to forget about love altogether. I sometimes feel that every last ounce of my integrity has been drained away, one compromise after another. It's funny. After my break with Audrey, I thought from then on I was finally going to live a completely honest life. No more lies. But it's been just as difficult, just as complicated."

Eric found himself sitting down on the other end of the couch, awkwardly, for there was a bed pillow crammed against the arm. "Well, if it's any consolation, Rust, it's just as complicated being a cold fish."

The old nickname made Russell look up; quite visibly, the sour humor that had been written on his lined, somewhat paunchy face melted away. "What is it, Eric?" he asked with gentle seriousness. "What is it you want?"

Eric folded his arms across his chest, hugging himself.

177

"Obviously you must be doing something right," Russell said after a brief silence. "Look at you. I could be your father. No one would think there's only three months' difference between us."

Still hugging himself, Eric kept his eyes on the rug, which was lightly dusted with cracker crumbs.

"Maybe it's not such a great idea," Russell went on after they had both cleared their throats. "These lessons."

"No, I don't mind."

"They bother you, I can tell."

Eric shrugged.

"I think if you had suggested the idea, Eric, it would have been OK. The way it is now, it's like you're trying to pay back a debt."

"Well, aren't I?"

"No, I never meant that at all. I really wanted to learn and was using that stupid thousand bucks as an excuse."

"Six, Russell."

"Eric, not too long ago I gave a friend of mine, a female friend, a drawing for a wedding present. Would you like to know how much it would get at Sotheby's?" Russell leaned over and plucked a baked bean from the mahogany coffee table. Popping it into his mouth, he said, "You're making too big a fuss about this."

"Look, if I put aside a certain amount each week, I think I could eventually pay you back."

"If it makes you happy—"

"As a matter of fact," Eric said, turning to regard the complacent face, "it makes me angry that I have to be saddled with this. I've told you before."

"Why not forget about it then?"

"Because it wouldn't be right."

Russell sighed. "I suppose this means you don't want any duck."

Eric didn't. He had had no intention of staying for lunch. But now that Russell had voluntarily released him from his duties as an indentured servant, the memory of Inez, the cook, and what she could do with the simplest ingredients, swayed his better judgment. "I like duck."

"What?"

"I'm starving, Rust. Let's eat."

* * *

Although Russell was inclined to leave the dishes on the dining-room table, Eric thought it would be more considerate to take them into the kitchen. When he started to wash his plate, though, Russell stopped him by turning off the faucet. Inez, he explained, did not like anyone touching her dishes. She was very particular about how everything was cleaned and had her own system. Even the housekeeper was not allowed in the kitchen.

The bottle of wine Russell had opened was not quite finished. The kitchen, larger than many restaurant kitchens and certainly cleaner than most, seemed the logical place to kill it off. Eric was glad to escape from the crumbs and soldiers that littered Russell's study and wondered aloud how the housekeeper, Xavier, put up with Sylvester and his son. Russell told him, as he pulled up a chair to a refectory table, that Xavier was on sabbatical. He was spending the winter in Madrid with Russell's oldest daughter, she studying the fluctuation of the peseta, Xavier working out some arcane theory about the entablature of a certain section of the Escorial.

"I think they might be having an affair," Russell added after Eric refused the last of the wine. Two glasses were plenty for him, one over his usual limit.

"What? He's old enough to be her grandfather."

Russell smiled. "You're thinking of Ruiz. He's long gone."

"Oh, I'm sorry."

"Xavier's only twenty-six, a refugee from El Salvador. He's illegal, of course, because our wonderful government supports those fascist pigs down there. But I got Xavier fixed up with a few false documents. He really is quite brilliant. They tortured him, you know. They forced his head down into a latrine, a bucket of shit, actually. He nearly died."

Eric, who had wanted to ask who did the cleaning now, changed his question to a comment. "It's hard to believe, in this day and age. . . . It's like I was saying to Wanda the other day: What goes on today, the horrible torture by legitimate governments, makes Torquemada and his gang look like a bunch of Milquetoasts."

"Maybe . . . but you have to admit, there's something particularly horrifying about being tortured in the name of a man who gave his own life for love. You better believe in that man, love him, baby, or else you're going to get this red-hot poker up your ass." Russell gulped down the wine in his glass. "I think I'd rather be tortured for not believing in a corrupt dictator. It would be a little less confusing."

"Aren't you going to be late for your plane?"

Russell consulted his dime-store watch with the plastic band. "Hmm."

"Well?"

"Just like you to change the subject whenever I score a point."

"What about Disney World?"

"I'll get a later flight."

"So he took a later flight?" Wanda asked, after sitting quietly for some time while Eric talked. He had returned home in a mellow haze of benevolence. Two twenty-dollar bills had been handed out to a man lying in a blue pup tent in the park opposite Wanda's apartment. But he realized this didn't count as any real charity since he had told Wanda about it. The right hand, after all, was not supposed to know what the left hand was up to.

"Actually, he's going tomorrow."

"And you're not going to give him any more lessons?"

Eric shook his head.

She was at the stove heating up some leftovers for her supper. "I don't think that's very nice."

"Look, the guy can afford Horowitz for a teacher. He doesn't need me."

"Isn't Horowitz dead?"

With a modest portion of linguini on her plate, Wanda returned to the kitchen table, where he was devouring a huge slab of Inez's almond torte. Russell had told Eric he would have to throw it out if Eric didn't take it home with him.

"Any word from the dragon?"

She swallowed before replying. "Not yet."

"I can't believe you'd actually accept a job like that."

"Did you buy all that toilet paper?" Wanda asked, ignoring the comment. She had no stomach for arguing now.

"It was on sale."

"Oh."

"As a matter of fact, I think I'm going to start paying rent to you."

Instead of objecting, as he had expected, Wanda continued to neatly wind her pasta.

"See, before, when you weren't here, I was doing you a favor, looking after the place, you know—the plants. Keeping thieves out. But now that you're here, I'm just taking up room."

"OK."

"OK?"

"You can pay half if you like, Eric."

Half, he thought. And I'm the one sleeping on the sofa. Not to mention all the extra food I've bought. And those light bulbs and toilet paper, eight rolls. "Of course, as soon as Brown Johns gets back from the Galápagos, I'll be out of here."

"Yes, that'll be nice."

"Thanks."

"Well, I mean we'll both have our own space. I'm getting tired of not being able to take a shower in the morning."

"Who said you couldn't?"

"You're pretty grumpy if anyone wakes you up."

"It's your house. Do what you want."

"Gee, thanks."

Wanda returned to the book she had been reading, *The Insulted and the Injured,* while he picked at his torte. "Yes?" she said after a paragraph. "You want to say something?"

"No."

"Is it the rent? Is that why you're sulking?"

"I'm not sulking. I'm thinking." Eric had been sulking about the rent, but he had also been thinking at the same time about his recent lunch with Russell. The sulking was making Eric think that maybe he hadn't had as good a time as he thought he had had.

"I'm thinking about Russell," he went on as Wanda continued to eat and read, or at least appear to read. He knew she was listening. "He started baiting me about the Church. We used to have some great debates about religion. Back in the old days he used to accuse me of going to Mass just to annoy him."

"Did you?" Wanda asked, not looking up from the book.

"No, it was mainly to annoy my father."

"You're kidding?"

He was, of course. The fact that she had to ask, though, irritated him. "My dad always thought church was fine for women but sissy for men."

Wanda regarded him as he reached over and plucked a few strands of linguini from her plate. "You don't talk much about your father. How is he?"

"According to Russell," he said, pulling her plate a little nearer, "he's having a blast racing his boat all over the place. He's upgraded the engine so he can collect a few speeding violations."

"Would you like me to make you some?" she asked before he had finished his sentence. Her linguini was fast disappearing.

"No, I'm pretty stuffed."

"Don't touch!"

He had reached for her book with his greasy fingers.

"I just wanted to see who wrote it."

"Dostoevsky."

"Oh." For a moment he pondered the torte before him with glazed eyes, as if trying to decide if it should be eaten or read. Then he pinched some crumbs together and popped them into his mouth. "We talked about you."

Wanda shrugged, her eyes back on the page.

"He kept on asking all these questions about you. I think he might be a little jealous."

"Your friend must not be very bright."

"He was really curious why we're living together."

Turning a page, she said, "We're not living together."

"We're roommates."

"No, hardly. That implies people deciding to live together." Her fork began to wind the pasta. "I think we're more like people thrown together in a Red Cross shelter for a couple of days, like we've been driven from our homes by a fire or—"

"An act of God?"

"Yes, a flood, a deluge."

"Raining cats and dogs," he added, amused by her use of "deluge." Ever since taking up Dostoevsky, Wanda would occasionally let drop a slightly archaic word or turn of phrase. *1984,* her previous book, might have influenced her decision to buy glue traps for mice, which were not in evidence anywhere in the apartment, as far as Eric could tell. Books apparently had their effect upon her, in some strange way.

"You remember that novel you tried to make me read?" he asked later that evening, as he bumped into her on his way to the bathroom.

"*Little Dorrit?*"

"No, way back when I first met you. Something about a lesbian, a grandmother who becomes a lesbian."

Wanda pulled her faded yellow robe tighter about her. He was barefoot, in shorts only. "You mean atMass?"

"Right."

"Well, what about it?"

"Why did you . . . ?"

Eric was careful not to slur his words. He didn't want her to know he had been sipping vodka after his torte supper. She might think he had a problem with alcohol, which would be ironic, considering all the jibes he had taken from his father over the years. "Drinks like a real lady," Lamar would comment when Eric would refuse a second beer or glass of wine. Not once in his life had Eric ever gotten loaded. The closest he had come was the first time he had visited Wanda at Beekman Place. Strange, the effect she had on him.

"Why did you give me *that* book?"

"I already told you why, Eric."

"Yes, but it was so stupid, your reason. I don't think I believe you." He had ambled into the bathroom and was standing at the sink, where he had a good view of her in the medicine-cabinet mirror. "You wanted me to think you were gay? Give me a break."

"Look, I don't even remember the book. It was something I happened to admire and—"

"You know what I think?" He shook a toothbrush at her in mock anger. "I think you thought I was gay. That's it, isn't it?"

"Why would I chase a gay man?"

"Ah ha, so you admit you were after me?"

In the mirror her face was as expressionless as Orwell's heroine, forced to recant her love—or so Eric fancied.

"Yes, I was desperately in love with you, like every other woman on earth. And man. And I won't be happy until you have pledged yourself to me for all eternity. Now, if you don't mind,

Eric, I'd appreciate it if you would refrain from using my toothbrush."

"Huh?" He looked at his hand and realized he had picked up the wrong color.

"Don't take too long, sir," Wanda said as she walked off to her room. "I'm not finished in there."

The door closed behind her. Wanda padded to her dresser and sprinkled a few drops of holy water onto her right hand. Genuflecting, she crossed herself. Then she took off the flannel yellow robe and got in bed.

Under the bed was the bottle of Russian vodka that she had taken from Mr. Ko's. If she was going to be accused of stealing, she had thought she might as well get some benefit out of it. Of course, this pilfering had occurred at a time of high emotion when she was barely herself. She was ashamed of having done this now and often wondered if there was not some way of restoring the bottle, or its monetary equivalent, without being found out. In any case, she had decided to ease her conscience by not drinking a drop of the expensive liquor. Perhaps she might even donate it to a homeless shelter or something like that.

These were her plans before bumping into Eric outside the bathroom. They were revised after that encounter. She deserved a drink, after all. It had taken quite a toll on her, trying to remain cool and unflappable during supper. But with him walking around nearly naked afterward, and then finding herself forced to tell the truth beneath a very flimsy mask of irony, who could blame her for wanting a good belt, as her father would put it.

Her hand groped. No bottle. She peered over the side. It must have rolled deeper under the bed. More futile groping and still no bottle.

After getting up, she took the shade off a lamp and used the bare bulb as a flashlight to investigate under the bed. But aside from three glue traps, there was nothing to see. The traps, though, caused a pang of regret. She sincerely wished she had never read *1984*. The idea of rats gnawing on Winston's face, imprisoned in that masklike cage, had scarred her for life. And why did she have to tell Eric about this when they were arguing about the Inquisition a few days ago? She was sure he was wrong when he told her Orwell was talking about what cigarettes did to you. "Why do you think he called him Winston?" Eric had said, trying to make her feel guilty. Of course, they didn't have Winstons in England back then. He was just teasing her. It wasn't about cigarette smoking at all. It was about totalitarian institutions, what happens when popes start saying they're infallible. Vatican Newspeak, Arnold had told her when he had urged the book upon her, back when they had been dating.

Oh, Arnold was a good man. He was truthful, honest, loving, caring—everything Eric was not. And Arnold was so right about the way people corrupt language to suit their own needs. The gall of Eric to say Winston was a cigarette.

"Have you seen my . . . ?" Wanda said as she marched into the living room. Eric was stretched out on the pull-out bed looking at a sitcom.

"Your what?"

She had hesitated at the last moment. Did she want to admit that she had stolen the bottle from Mr. Ko's refrigerator? Well, she could say she had bought the bottle, couldn't she? But that would be a lie. Did she want to lie?

"Wanda?"

"My toothpaste."

"I bought my own, you know. You don't have to worry."

She stood uncertainly in the semidarkness. Footsteps above competed with the canned laughter and a badly played electric guitar blaring from the park across the street. Why couldn't she have a drink if she wanted one? Why did she even have to explain where the bottle came from? It was none of his business.

"Under my bed, Eric, I had a—" Now why would she hide vodka under her bed? he would wonder. Obviously there was something fishy about that. Probably he would think she was a secret drinker. Good Lord, she didn't want him to think that.

"I had four traps," she improvised, "and now there're only three."

Eric laughed in an uncharacteristic, raucous way. "You accusing me of stealing a trap? That's right, Wanda. While you were in the bathroom I crept into your room to see if there was anything under your bed I could steal. That mousetrap, how about that? I could sell it in the park tonight. And surely you wouldn't miss it. Not when you had three others there."

"Oh, be quiet," she said, hurling a cushion at him.

"Temper, temper."

"I hate you."

He adjusted the thrown cushion behind his head. "'Good night, sweet prince,'" he said as she marched out of the room.

Sixteen

On her day off Kaye eased her conscience by going through the apartment and collecting all the newspapers, magazines, and catalogs she knew she would never read and stacking them according to size. Then she discovered that the only twine she had was so thin it snapped as she tried to tie the first bundle. Over a third cup of Ethiopian coffee she pondered whether there might be another roll of string stashed away in some unlikely place. And she wondered, as well, why she had bought such flimsy twine to begin with.

"You don't happen to have any twine, do you?" Kaye asked later that day after a supper of microwaved lasagne.

The woman she had asked pressed down on the lid of the trash can with a puzzled expression.

"Twine, string," Kaye urged, anxious to get back inside. She had just finished taking her garbage to the cans outside her windows when her neighbor from the top floor of the brownstone had appeared with a soggy paper bag.

"Oh, twine," Betty said.

Years ago, when Kaye had first moved in, Betty Lovejoy had welcomed her with a plastic philodendron and an invitation to coffee upstairs. Kaye soon found herself on friendly terms, mainly out of gratitude for all the small services Betty seemed so anxious to provide. While Kaye was at work, Betty would accept packages from UPS, let in repairmen, and even pick up her dry cleaning. In return Kaye would submit to endless monologues about Betty's ex-husband. At first Kaye did not have to feign interest, for the injustices that Betty suffered at the hands of the ex-husband and his mother were truly remarkable. Unfortunately, Betty's repertoire was limited, and the same injustices kept cropping up with only minor alterations. Just when Kaye's yawns were beginning to penetrate Betty's cozy womb of misery, a young man moved in on the third floor. No unpleasant words ever passed between Kaye and Betty. The break was painless for both as Betty began seeing to the young man's dry cleaning and advising him about local restaurants. When Betty and Kaye did happen to run into each other, they always exchanged a greeting or, at least, a nod.

"What do you want twine for?" Betty asked, oblivious of the sleet that had begun to fall onto the concrete areaway. She was not a fastidious woman, often receiving her guests in nothing but a slip. This evening she had emerged in mules and a seersucker housecoat.

"Never mind," Kaye replied, more annoyed with herself than with her neighbor. She had put twine down on her shopping list that afternoon and then forgotten to consult the list as she went about her errands.

"Say, Kaye," Betty called out as Kaye opened the heavy vestibule door, "you know who I ran into the other day? Bet you can't guess."

"Who?" Kaye was shivering but could not help pausing to admire Betty's insensitivity to the elements. The bleached blond hair began to turn brassy as the sleet plastered it to her large, sturdy head.

"Guess."

"I can't. I've got to go inside."

"Ellen O'Toole."

"Oh."

"Yeah, she said to tell you don't be strangers. She says you never call her. Why doesn't she call me? she says, and I say—"

"Yeah, well, thanks. I'll. . . . 'Bye."

Back in her own apartment Kaye puttered around anxiously for a few moments, worried that there might be a knock on the door—Betty wanting to continue the chat. Ellen O'Toole used to work with

Kaye in lamps when Kaye was at Altman's shortly after her husband had died. Against Kaye's advice, Ellen had gone on to open up a little business of her own, reading palms and cards. Though Ellen was good at guessing which lamp Kaye had hidden her charge card under, she was less impressive when it came to personal matters. Reading Kaye's palm one afternoon, she said Kaye's husband was five feet six inches (he was six-three) and had red hair (it was black and he was dead to boot). Worried that Ellen might not get any customers, Kaye had induced Betty to accompany her on a trip to the newly opened spiritualist parlor on Second Avenue. For professional reasons Ellen, who had never been married, called herself Mrs. Karlovsky and used candles instead of electric bulbs. Otherwise, she was the same cheerful woman Kaye had known at Altman's. Right in front of Betty, Ellen read the cards Kaye had picked from a shuffled deck: "You're having trouble with an older man."

There was no older man in Kaye's life at that time. She hoped Ellen would reshuffle the cards and give herself another chance to save face. But Ellen kept on insisting there was big trouble with an older man, sexual complications. With Betty looking on, Kaye felt under some obligation to come up with an older man. So she invented a problem with a forty-year-old she had had one or two dates with. She lied and said he wanted to marry her, but she didn't feel she was ready so soon after her own husband's death. Betty was deeply impressed with Mrs. Karlovsky's powers and couldn't wait for her turn. Of course, all this happened before the young man moved in on the third floor.

Kaye heard the vestibule door open and Betty's mules slap on the tiles. Then for a moment there was no sound. Betty was apparently hovering right outside her door. Holding her breath, Kaye felt her heart throb like a cartoon mouse's. But she was spared. The mules shuffled on.

Kaye went back to wrapping the frayed cord of her pole lamp with electric tape.

Where does it hurt?

There.

Relax, girl. Take it easy. We'll have that charley horse right back in his stable.

* * *

189

"Yes, I was kneeling by the lamp with the wire in my hand, but there was no shock, no electric shock. I heard his voice first. Then I began to see."

"You've been drinking tonight?"

"No," Kaye snapped, offended. "Not a drop. All I had was some lasagne for supper. And non-lactose chocolate milk."

"Let me call you back," Joel offered.

"Doesn't she look at your phone bills?" Kaye did not want to get Joel in trouble with Rachel, his wife. Joel and Rachel were going to a marriage counselor in Los Angeles, a brilliant woman who had made Joel feel comfortable enough to confess his affair with Kaye. Rachel, in turn, had admitted to sleeping with three different men in the past five years. Though this wounded Joel and angered him, it also helped restore his sense of virtue. After all, he had told Kaye, he had not been promiscuous.

"Let her see," Joel said somewhat pompously. "I haven't got anything to hide now."

Long distance costing what it did, Kaye hung up and let Joel ring her back from Los Angeles. He gave her enough time to use the toilet and blow her nose.

"So you saw yourself stretched out on aMassage table, and Lamar was fixing you?"

"I must have been fifteen. It was right after a diving meet. I had pulled a muscle, and Dad was taking care of it. We were in the training room at the gym. Dad was being so nice and gentle. I was crying a little, not so much because of the pain but because I hadn't won. He was telling me it didn't matter, that he loved me anyway, even if I came in last the rest of my life. It was so sweet of him. I took his hand and kissed it, just a little chaste kiss. He smiled, but then all of a sudden this look came over him, like he was sick, ill. Get dressed, he said, and then just left me lying there while he walked out of the room. He didn't even wipe the liniment off my thigh, this professional-strength stuff that really penetrated. All my life, Joel, I'd never been able to figure it out, how he could change so suddenly. But tonight it all came back to me. It was the smell."

"What smell?"

"Well, I couldn't smell it at the time—because the odor of the liniment was so strong. But this evening there was no liniment smell. It was just like I was under a chinaberry tree; they have this strange smell, the berries. And then it hit me—she was always arranging those berries, mixing them in with black-eyed Susans and daisies and cheap things like that."

"She?"

"My mother. I was always embarrassed when my friends saw those stupid vases filled with junk flowers and twigs."

"So what's the point, Kaye?"

"Don't you see? She was there that night. My father must have looked up and seen her. That explains the sudden change, the look on his face. She was waiting in the car for us, but then she must have come inside the gym to see what was taking so long and caught him—I mean, seen him, me—and misinterpreted everything completely. When I finally got dressed and went to the car, they were both cold as ice, not even speaking to each other."

"Well, I suppose it could have happened that way. But . . . I better go now," he muttered after a pause.

"Is that Rachel?"

"Right." He hung up.

Kaye was putting away the electric tape, with hopes that the phone would ring again once the coast was clear, when she was startled by a knock at the door. Thinking it was Betty, she didn't answer until a man's voice called out, "I know you're in there!"

Going to the peephole, she recognized the balding head.

"'I know you're in there,'" she quoted as she let Arnold in. "What do you mean by barging in like gangbusters? The front door is supposed to be locked."

"This dame let me in. She said you were home."

"Why don't you sit down?" she said, gesturing to the rattan chair he had already appropriated.

"We're neighbors, you know." Unfazed by her irony, he surveyed the room with a critical eye. "I was out for a stroll and decided to just drop over. I'm seven blocks south, that's all."

"I'm glad, Arnold. But I don't think you should be here."

Though Arnold had not gotten any further than rubbing his foot against her leg at the A&S mall, Kaye still felt guilty about the drinks they had had at the Mexican café there. When they had parted, she had given him a brisk handshake and almost said that they should never see each other again. But at the time this had struck her as being overly dramatic and might have prompted an equally dramatic response from him. (*I've never met anyone so sensuous. I can feel your pent-up sexuality radiating from every pore* blah blah blah.) Kaye could not bear the thought of Arnold being unfaithful to Wanda, even if it was only in his mind.

"Why? Why shouldn't I?" he demanded as she leaned wearily against the wall, a safe distance from him. "I got to ask you something important about your brother. I mean, do you want to help me get Wanda back or not?"

So, Kaye thought, the game is denial. Nothing happened. Well, that suited her just fine. After all, she would rather not think about why she had let him rub against her leg. Why hadn't she told him off as he deserved?

"She called me today."

"Wanda called you?"

"Pretty exciting, huh?" he prompted. One hand toyed with the zipper of his parka, a phosphorescent orange that seemed incredibly effective against the sleet outside. Barely a drop adhered to the space-age fabric. Likewise his sneakers, the very latest in air-pump design, were as immaculate as a ghetto youth's.

"I had just about given up," he went on, the zipper going up, down, up again, "when I get this call at work. Fuck if it isn't her. I mean, after our talk, Kaye, I didn't hold out much hope. I figured I should just resign myself. I had struck out again. Wanda didn't give a hoot about me. But then there she is on the phone calling me!"

His all-too-evident joy had a curiously depressing effect on Kaye, who had drifted to the sofa and sat down. "That's wonderful, Arnold. I'm so glad."

"So she starts right in, asking me what she should do. She's upset because her Greek god filched her vodka."

"What?"

"She said she had some expensive vodka in her room, and he went in and ripped her off. She was looking for it the other night and couldn't find it, but the next morning she saw it by his bed, almost half empty. He was asleep, so she didn't say anything. But then when she comes home from an interview, she finds a full bottle in her room. The half-empty one is gone."

"So what's she complaining about? She's got her vodka."

"It's the principle of the thing, the fact that he's trying to deceive her. She asked me if she should confront him. I said no, it's not worth the trouble. He'd squirm out of it somehow."

"Listen here"—Kaye was roused—"my brother is the most honest man I ever met in my life. I'm not going to have you sitting here implying—"

"Who's implying? I'm saying it outright. The guy's a bum. You call it honest to encourage a woman to fall in love with you when you know there's not the slightest fucking chance in the world you're going to reciprocate?"

The disdain in his voice incensed Kaye to a convenient boil, in which all her own doubts about her brother's conduct were dissolved. "He's told her time and time again—"

"Yeah, people say a lot, don't they? It's what they do that counts."

"*You* say a lot, Arnold."

"Huh?"

"Oh, stop it."

"Stop what?"

Her courage failing her, she said somewhat lamely, "Stop playing with your zipper."

He complied. But then his foot began to jiggle, and as they went on to discuss his chances with Wanda, one of his air pumps was unlaced.

"I itch," he said in answer to her raised eyebrows. Scratching vigorously at a sock with the brand name sewn into the design, he added, "Athlete's foot."

Wanda was not home when Eric made himself a peanut-butter-and-banana sandwich after his four o'clock lesson with Tiburcia. This meant he could take the huge bites that such a sandwich invited—and that Wanda found so disgusting. In half an hour he was on his way to the Mani Light's rehearsal studio on Hudson Street. If Rosa, the director, kept him past nine, he was going to demand overtime. She had been taking advantage of his good nature too long now. Let her fire him, he resolved, if she didn't like it.

Shortly after eleven he was back at the apartment on Tompkins Square. "She's going to pay," he said as he bolted the door behind him. The lamp was on by the wing chair in the bay window's alcove. "Rosa kept me till ten-forty. You're a witness, Wanda."

"Going blind, are you?"

Eric frowned. It was Kaye, not Wanda, in the chair. He had just assumed it was his roommate when he had come in, not bothering to look directly at her. In such close quarters, he had learned, direct looks were not always advisable.

Setting down his knapsack stuffed with battered scores, he said, "Not so loud. You'll wake her."

"She's not here."

"Then how did you get in? Listen," he added, supplying the answer himself as he strode into the kitchen, "those keys are supposed to be for emergencies. You can't just barge in like this."

When he emerged from the kitchen with a bag of pretzels, she said calmly, "This *is* an emergency."

"What? Did something happen to her?"

His sister studied his face a moment before replying. "She's fine. She's at her parents' in Watersomething. It's on your machine."

"You played my messages?" A few pretzel crumbs spewed from his mouth as he said this with unnecessary urgency.

"'Course not," Kaye said, wiping a crumb off her jeans, which were a bit too tight for her. "I was here when she called and didn't know how to turn the volume down."

"Very complicated, I know. There's this knob that says VOLUME."

"Oh, shut up and get your poor sister a drink."

"I could use a beer myself. Might calm me down. Rosa wants the Prokofiev slowed down to a crawl. It's ludicrous. She has no idea what that sonata's all about. It's a youthful, joyous, almost barbaric free-for-all and she's trying to turn it into a minuet. Here."

She had followed him into the kitchen, where he found a couple of sleek cans of low-calorie beer beneath the sink.

"I can't drink warm beer. Give me some vodka."

Holding the can out at arm's length, he successfully avoided the foam that spurted out when he pulled the tab. "Don't got none."

"You sure?"

194

"Wanda might. But I'd rather not mess with that. She made a big fuss about it just this morning. I had borrowed some one evening and forgot to tell her about it, so she tries to make a big scene about it, like it was the climax of some Ibsonian tragedy. Ibsenian," he amended as he rummaged behind Wanda's box of hair coloring, which she kept in the refrigerator.

"Voilà," he said, handing over half a bottle of a fairly good sauvignon blanc. "This is hers, but she won't mind *you* having some."

Settling onto a high stool by the kitchen table, Kaye reached into the drainer for a tumbler. "You know you're really going to have to move out, Eric. This can't go on."

"I know. Just as soon as Brown Johns gets back from the Galápagos, I'll be all set. That's that friend of Russell's I was telling you about." He took a sip of warm beer and decided he didn't want any more. "So what's the big emergency?"

Kaye filled the tumbler, a jelly glass, with wine. "Be straight with me, Eric. Did Mother ever say anything to you about Dad and me?"

"Just that you're both nuts, that's all." Mrs. Thorsen had never reconciled herself to a daughter in a circus-arts program or a husband who could encourage such nonsense in a college education.

"Aside from that," Kaye said with an impatient wave of her hand. "Anything specific?"

Eric shrugged.

"The reason I ask—Eric, are you listening? Well, last night I had this weird experience. The lamp I had been meaning to get around to, there was a frayed cord, I finally decided to tape it up—and the next thing I know there's this tingling in my leg, my thigh. I've never felt anything so warm and comforting. And then there was the voice, so calm and reassuring. All the pain, all the heartache began to dissolve, and I was sinking deeper and deeper into this wonderful womblike darkness when—"

"It was Mom, wasn't it?" Eric's heart thumped dully, caution still tempering the joy her words had aroused.

"Yes, of course, I knew you'd understand. I tried to explain to this friend of mine, but it's so hard over the phone, you know."

Of all people to have had a mystical experience, Eric

thought—Kaye, the one who had spent her whole life debunking religion. "Well, go on."

"It was back when I was a teenager, around fifteen."

Yes, Eric thought, that sounded right. Their mother, in her mid-thirties, had been incredibly beautiful.

"See, Eric, Dad wasMassaging my thigh. I had a charley horse from a bad dive."

As his sister went on to describe the "weird experience," Eric felt his disappointment growing. There was nothing mystical about it at all. It was simply a confused memory.

"I doubt Mom was spying on you and Dad," Eric finally interrupted. "She never did like to go inside that gym."

"She was jealous of me, Eric, and you know it. She tried to make Dad feel like a pervert. Back then I never understood what was going on. I just thought we were the average American family, screwed up, of course, but in all the normal ways. But now I finally see what it was all about, how sick that woman really was."

"You know what you're doing, don't you?" Eric said patiently, trying to disguise his anger. "You're projecting your own guilt on her. Mom loved you, she loved Dad, she sacrificed her life for the family, and this is the thanks she gets." Mrs. Thorsen, it was true, had been stunning enough to be a movie star. She would turn heads, men's and women's, when she walked down the street. Store clerks would get nervous and blush when waiting on her. Eric had seen all this with his own eyes time and time again. And yet she was content to make oatmeal for the family every morning afterMass, to make the beds, sweep, clean, shop. She was completely without vanity, thinking nothing of scrubbing the bathroom tiles on her knees. All she ever insisted on for herself was a decent hat to wear to church.

"Can't you see?" Kaye said with some heat. "You'll never break out of your shell until you come to terms with her, what she really was. She's not a saint, Eric. She never was."

"I know that. But"—he backtracked—"what do you mean, shell?" The refrigerator door was open as he searched for cheese.

"Something inside you is fixated, frozen. You can't really love anyone, can you? You're terrified of intimacy."

"Look, I'm in no mood for psychobabble. I've got to get up early."

"You like to make people fall in love with you, don't you? Then, when you're sure of them, you drop them like a hot potato."

He took out a pasteurized cheese spread Wanda had bought. "Surely you can do better than 'hot potato.'"

Kaye finished her wine with an unnecessary flourish, a gesture out of an Errol Flynn movie. "I better go."

Concerned about her safety, Eric decided to see her into a cab. Once outside she walked a little ahead, miffed, no doubt, that he had not been impressed by her "experience." Eric wished he could have been more sympathetic, but he couldn't help resenting the way she tried to make a villain of their mother. Yes, perhaps she had been prim and disapproving at times. But couldn't Kaye see that she was just playing the role of perfect housewife, that their mother at times was even parodying herself? It was all part of her charm, this wicked, sly humor that was far too subtle for their father to perceive. Sometimes his mother would even wink at Eric as she despaired of the crumbs he or Lamar left in their beds.

"What are you doing?" Eric asked as he hurried to catch up. Kaye had crossed the street and seemed to be headed into the park itself. Even in broad daylight Eric would have had some misgivings about walking through the broad square. The squatters in their tents were back in force, more belligerent than ever, it seemed, from their most recent ousting by the police.

"I want to see the tepee," Kaye protested as her brother restrained her by the elbow.

Wafted over from a campfire beneath the bare limbs of a maple, smoke, acrid with rubber, teared his eyes. "What tepee?"

"I saw on the news that someone made a giant tepee out of mailbags to protest Wounded Knee and all displaced persons."

"Oh, that. It's not here. It's farther east, by the bridge." Steering her back onto the sidewalk, he maintained a grip on her elbow. "Let me give you money for a cab."

"I'll take the bus."

"I'd rather you didn't."

"Put that away. I'm not taking ten dollars from you."

"Look, here's one coming." He went out into the street and flagged it down.

"By the way," she said, after he had opened the door for her and she was settled on the thinly upholstered seat, "what would you think if Eric and I—Eric, are you listening?—if *Arnold* and I became an item?"

Eric was trying to urge the ten upon her again. She swatted his wrist. The driver looked anxiously in his rearview mirror.

"Did you hear?"

"You're joking, of course."

"It's a real possibility, Eric. Arnold came over last night, and we had a long talk. We didn't do anything, of course, but there's this charged atmosphere between us."

"Is this some sort of threat?"

"I think I could like him."

"You're twice as big as he is."

The driver, an Albanian, turned and said something unintelligible. Kaye's look of pity, mingled with disdain, was misdirected for a moment in the innocent man's direction. "A man's mind can be horribly attractive," she said, still looking at the driver.

"Where? Where you want?"

"Upper West Side, head up Broadway," Eric commanded through the window as he handed over the ten to Adil Shehu, who sported a FREE TIRANA sticker on his dash.

Seventeen

When Wanda returned from Waterbury the next evening, laden with boxes and bags, she offered her roommate no specifics about the visit. Eric asked if everything was all right at home. She nodded. Your mother fine? Another nod. Father? She walked into her room and shut the door.

"A new perfume?" he commented later when she emerged for supper. He was attempting to heat up leftover angel hair.

"What?"

"You smell nice."

"I don't have anything on. Why don't you sit down? You're doing this all wrong."

From the pine table he watched her take over with the calm, efficient skill of a professional. Knowing exactly what drawers to look in, what cupboards, she wasted no effort, each movement counting for something. All of this had a soothing effect on Eric, who had been floundering about with no-stick pots and pans that were sticking and burning and spattering oil into his face. As she minced garlic, he noticed even then the curious aura about her, shades of his favorite memories: a pungent whiff of squashed china-berries mingling with the rich promise of a yellow cake rising in the oven—and perhaps even a hint of ozone after a cloudburst.

"I told you I don't have any perfume on," she protested when he sniffed her arm as she set a butter dish down before him.

"You must."

"It's just me. Agggghh!"

Her scream was totally disproportionate to the playful bite he had administered. There weren't any teeth marks, after all.

"Are you crazy!" she demanded.

"Relax," he said, hugely gratified by the scream. It was so funny, seeing this rather prim and proper Catholic let loose like that. Or was it ex-Catholic?

"Eric Thorsen, I think you're certifiable," she commented later after her ruffled feathers had been smoothed by a few insincere apologies. Though he was no longer smiling, the grin seemed to linger as she tried to eat the delicious meal she had concocted from what was lying about in obscure corners of the refrigerator, odds and ends just about to turn brown or moldy.

Wanda admitted, "You were right all along."

"He *is* crazy, huh?"

"I don't know how I ever let him talk to me like that. Imagine the gall, Arnold, telling me I had a moral obligation to quit."

Wanda and Arnold were eating a take-out lunch in the plaza of a new skyscraper not far from Wanda's office. It was her first day on the job at Philip Morris, which had a nice place on the ground floor to eat in. But the homeless men and women who were using the cast-iron tables and chairs next to the art exhibits disturbed Wanda. She got enough of that at Tompkins Square. So she and Arnold had wandered across Park Avenue a couple of blocks south.

"Arnold, please," she said, removing his hand from her breast, which he had attempted to fondle. "People are looking."

"So?"

Though it was unseasonably mild out, an occasional gust of wind would send deli wrappers into the air and make it hard to hear. Wanda realized she should have brought a jacket. She was getting chilled despite the bright sun.

"Instead of sharing my joy," Wanda resumed, after taking a bite of Arnold's eel sushi, "he comes down on me like a ton of bricks. I waited to tell him about the job till after we had eaten. I figured he'd be in a better mood, see. And I wanted to show him some of the new outfits I had bought in Waterbury. There's a discount outlet there with the most amazing bargains. This Donna

Karan blouse was marked down ninety percent. I can't imagine how they do it, financially speaking."

"Maybe it's all fake."

"Arnold."

"Or stolen. Just joshing, princess." He held up both hands as if she were a cop making an arrest.

"Mr. O'Malley is taking me to lunch on Thursday. Isn't that nice? I'm sure it's going to be a real fancy place. You ought to see the way he dresses. All his shirts are tailor-made without buttons. He hates buttons. I saw him atMass this morning at St. Patrick's, and we walked to work afterward."

"Hey, hey," he said, almost before she had finished, "hold on a minute. You going toMass again? On a weekday?"

Wanda realized, too late, that she shouldn't have mentioned this. "Look, God was very good to me, getting me this job. I'm making thirty-two thousand. It's really a miracle as far as I'm concerned. Three weeks' vacation and the chance of a bonus at Christmas—next Christmas. You don't know what it means to me, this type of security. And the people I work with now—well, it just makes me wonder how I put up with K-Yok at all."

She looked boldly at him. He shrugged.

"So when are you giving His Majesty the boot?"

"You'll be proud of me. I'm going over to Mrs. Merton's tonight first thing after work. I've got this new type of kitty litter, scratch and sniff or something, the more you scratch the more pine scent it lets out. I'm going to be firm with her, tell her about the smell, make her put this stuff out."

"Don't waste your time."

"Don't discourage me, Arnold. I mean it. I'm determined now to get that place smelling right. Some of the cats are toilet trained, you know. They go right in the potty, but they don't flush. We'll have to retrain them and—"

"Are you nuts? What's all that got to do with you? Fuck the cats. Let him clean up their crap."

Wanda's lips compressed. "Fine language for a priest."

"Whoa—priest?" Arnold jerked his head about. "I see a priest somewhere? You see one? Hey, buddy, you see—" he began to say to a passing stranger, who pretended not to hear.

"Mr. O'Malley says once someone's ordained, that's it. He

believes a sacrament like that can't be revoked by—Arnold! Arnold, come back here."

She took a few steps after him but then returned to pick up the eel that was overturned from his lap onto the pink granite.

"They're all nuts, men," she muttered to herself, knowing he would not be gone for long.

After bolting the door, she looked apprehensively into the shadows. "You home?" she called out. He was probably at the Mani Light, though she started when she passed a mirror and saw the movement of her own reflection. Next to the phone, illuminated by a streetlamp shining through the bay window, she paused to admire the streamlined attaché case she had bought on Madison Avenue after the aborted lunch with Arnold. Then it occurred to her to close the curtains. Someone could be looking in.

"It's me," she said into the receiver after a good three minutes of ringing had revived her anxiety. "I just wanted to make sure that everything is all right. You're not mad, are you? . . . Good, good. I was worrying on the way home that I might have been too harsh. You don't think so, do you?"

Reassured, Wanda hung up. But a trace of anxiety still lingered. She gave the attaché case another look, wondering if she hadn't spent far too much at Crouch & Fitzgerald. But it had been on sale, after all.

She picked up the phone again. And once again the old woman took forever to answer. "Listen, Una, I don't really have to call the Animal League tomorrow. If you'd like some time, I could hold off. . . . OK, I just didn't want to bulldoze you into anything you might not be ready for."

Wanda still could not get over how easy it had all been. First thing after work that day she had taken the kitty litter over to Mrs. Merton's. Prepared for the old woman to protest about having some boxes put down, Wanda found herself being thanked instead. The next thing she knew, Wanda was telling Una Merton the plain, simple truth: The stench in her apartment was horrible. For the cats' sake, Wanda went on, she should do something about it. Cats had a keen sense of smell, and they could not really be happy living this way. Furthermore, the crowding must cause them terrible distress. Cats needed space, their own territory. Look at all the squabbles that were breaking out whenever she visited. Without ever having to raise her voice, Wanda convinced the old woman that the cats would be far better off in the hands of the proper authorities. She assured her—with crossed fingers—that each and every cat would find a new home and live a better life. The old woman had cried as Wanda spoke, but she apparently agreed with everything that was said. Wanda realized, as she came home on the bus, that Mrs. Merton's self-confidence must have been undermined by the incident of the slip in the restaurant. And Wanda herself must have gained a certain authority by keeping this incident a secret from Mrs. Monastere and Mrs. Fogarty. Of course, Wanda would never have threatened Mrs. Merton outright. But she did, in the course of her calm and rational lecture about the cats, drop a hint or two that it might be wise to listen to her if she, Mrs. Merton, wished to maintain her independence.

On the phone now the old woman assured Wanda that she did not feel bulldozed. But the voice sounded tired and thin. There was a quaver.

After hanging up, Wanda stood in the alcove a moment, undecided. It was the darkness that disturbed her. Usually, Eric was thoughtless enough to leave several lights on when he went out. And the sofa bed—most of the time it was pulled out, ready for him to lie down. But now it was folded up. Even the throw pillows were neatly arranged on the cushions.

She switched on the lamp by the sofa bed and saw, with mounting uneasiness, that there were no crumbs on the side table. None on the sofa. She tossed the pillows aside, then the cushions. It was as she feared: no sheets on the mattress when she pulled it out.

And no underwear in the maple side table, no socks in the pine. Wanda felt a surge of anger. So he had decided to move out without saying a word to her first. Her triumph was ruined. What a scene she had planned for him. She would have told him that she had solved the problem of the cats. And then she would have asked him to kindly pack up and leave.

In the kitchen Wanda made herself a sandwich and wolfed it down, untasted, somewhat as Louis, her ex, used to devour her carefully prepared suppers. When she washed up, she noticed several cigarette butts among the rinds and eggshells in the garbage.

Had he been entertaining someone here, some leggy blonde too dumb to read the Surgeon General's warnings?

Her initial plan had been to soak in the tub. But she decided to harness the energy of her anger and dismay by washing her delicate undies by hand. It was a job she had been putting off until she had some time when Eric was not around the apartment. In her bedroom she changed into a robe and gathered up seven silk panties. Her mother had raised her to always buy the finest quality underwear. Without it, no matter how expensive a dress you might be wearing, you couldn't help feeling tacky.

The fluorescent tube over the bathroom sink crackled like an outdoor bug trap electrocuting moths. She hoped she would remember to buy a new one before the current tube expired. Glancing up at the flickering light, she happened to notice in the mirror that the shower curtain was drawn. If there was one thing she thought she had taught him, it was the absolute necessity of keeping the curtain open when one was through. Otherwise the tiles would not dry properly. Mildew.

The whales on the curtain from the Museum of Natural History collapsed as the rings sped over the rod. She had given the curtain a good yank. The cry she let out, even as she yanked, was as tame as the yelp of surprise when a friend comes upon one unawares. It was only a few seconds later, when he didn't respond to his name, repeated sharply, that the horror of his inert nude body made her sink to her knees. A waterlogged cigarette butt was moored, it seemed, to a nipple. In a clump of suds another butt had foundered, staining the water brown. As she shook him, a filter tip floated out from behind his neck.

"Eric!" she moaned as the half pint of cheap vodka in the soap dish toppled over, dislodged by her vigorous shaking. "Eric, Eric, my love, my darling, Eric, please, don't, oh, please, I love you so much."

"Yes?" he replied, his eyes still shut. "What can I do for you?"

The relief that surged through her was ghastly.

"Oh, you beast," she murmured, enraged, joyous. "You filthy low-down—"

"What? Can't a guy take a little nap?"

"Get up. You're drunk. And what are all these—" She plucked one of the cigarettes from the suds and tossed it into the hall.

"I'm not drunk." He got to his feet in the tub steadily enough, but his eyes were glazed. "I just thought I'd play a little trick."

"How dare you—"

"How dare you barge in without knocking?"

"I hate you! I really do!"

"Then why are you staring?"

"I'm not staring."

"Haven't you ever seen a naked man before?"

"You're drunk, drunk as a coot. And where are all your clothes? There's nothing in your drawers to put on."

"That Brown man . . . "

"What brown man?"

"He's back from the Galápagos. I stuffed all my things into my bags and then got myself a little drink to celebrate. You're free, Wanda. The beast is finally going."

Taking him firmly in hand, she got him out of the tub without disaster. (How easily he could have slipped and cracked his head open!) In the cupboard she found a clean towel, scented with fabric softener, and began to dry him off in a no-nonsense manner. His arms dangled loosely as a child's, and when he squirmed, she scolded. The idea, him thinking he could go anywhere at all in *his* condition.

"Ow!"

"Hold still." She was running a brush over his tangled golden locks. "Hold still, I said. Do you want a whipping?"

He yanked free and escaped, still naked, into the kitchen.

"I warned you." The brush landed gently on his rear end. He did not budge.

"Now are you going to behave?"

He looked over his shoulder at her, his eyes betraying the secret terror of his growing delight. "No," he said in a hoarse croak.

"Well, then, you asked for it."

Resting his elbows on the sink, he submitted to the brush. At first the strokes were somewhat symbolic. But later, as she became more certain of the power welling up inside her, all the anger and frustration, her hand left red marks on his cheeks as he sprawled across her lap on the narrow bed in her own quiet sanctuary.

Eighteen

*P*ut that out."

Without waiting for him to comply, Kaye reached over and removed the cigarette from between her father's lips. She still hadn't recovered from the shock of seeing Eric, the day before, with a cigarette. Three he had smoked, right in front of her. Soon he would be back to his three packs a day, the habit he had renounced fifteen years ago without a single lapse. It was a tragedy. Kaye herself could occasionally take a puff without danger of addiction. The same went for Lamar. But now it wouldn't do at all for either one of them to light up. They must not give Eric the slightest excuse for his horrible lack of self-control.

"There can't be any ashes, no smell of smoke when he comes," Kaye said rather dogmatically while her father sulked.

"It must be some sort of male menopause," Lamar observed a few minutes later when Kaye brought him some stuffed grape leaves to tide him over until dinner.

"Whatever it is, Dad, be careful."

"Careful? What's that supposed to mean?"

"You can be bossy. At a time like this, that could be dangerous. He'd like nothing better than to make you blow up."

"Blow up? Who's going to blow up?"

Hands on hips, Kaye let him have a stare that shamed him out of any further protestation of innocence.

Whether it had been a good idea to have phoned her father the day before and told him the news was now a moot point. But Kaye couldn't help feeling that she might have made a mistake, letting him fly up from Tallahassee to try to reason with his son. Perhaps Lamar's input would have been more effective after Kaye had had a chance to work on Eric alone.

"Is *she* coming?"

"Tonight? No. I just asked Eric. He doesn't know you'll be here, of course. That's going to be a surprise."

"You're sure he's actually done it?"

"Yes."

"It's impossible. Asking a woman like that to marry him."

"Well, it's a fact."

Their mutual irritation made both of them look away for a moment.

"You sure he didn't say he was *thinking* of asking her someday? If that's the case, there's still some hope. A,"—here he bent a meaty index finger—"he may have said this just to give us a scare. B, he might have no intention of actually going through with it. And three, she might turn him down anyway."

Three was said with so little conviction that Kaye didn't bother to respond to it. As for A and B—a single point, really—she was sure Eric had already spoken to Wanda, though he hadn't given Kaye any details.

"Dad, please, enough," Kaye pleaded after he had cross-examined her at length about how much Wanda knew. "This isn't the issue. Now, one possibility we haven't considered, and that's maybe—well, maybe Wanda will end up being a good wife for him."

The blank stare this was greeted with made it hard to play devil's advocate with much conviction. But she went through the motions. "After all, who are we to judge—"

"Hold on, whoa. Is this the daughter who called me in tears the other day saying she wasn't going to stand by while her brother threw away his last chance at happiness?"

Her voice calm, measured, she replied, while wringing her hands, "I might have overreacted. It takes getting used to, the idea. But if you think about it, she does have *some* good qualities. She's not fat, she's not an alcoholic or a drug addict—I don't think. And she doesn't smoke."

"Fine, I hope you're satisfied." Rice from one of the grape leaves clung to his beard. She resisted the urge to pluck it out.

"Me?"

"Who was the one throwing them together every chance she got? I knew something was cockeyed the day we went to that fancy apartment of hers—the recital. But no, Dad is so old-fashioned, he doesn't understand how a man and woman can just be friends."

Kaye, too, could not help wondering at her own behavior in regard to Wanda. Why couldn't she have left well enough alone as far as Wanda's apartment went? And then to have told Eric that she was attracted to Wanda's ex-priest? Why, it must have seemed to Eric that she was clearing the way for him, absolving him of any guilt in regard to Wanda. But that wasn't what she had meant at all. If she had known what Eric was up to, well. . . .

"It's no use throwing blame around," Kaye said firmly, hoping to convince herself. "Eric is a grown man. He must know what he's doing."

"You really think so?"

"Yes, Dad, I do. I think he's doing this to punish you for something. He knows how this must hurt you. I think if you and he had had a better relationship, this never would have happened."

Lamar's face darkened. "I see. All my fault, huh?"

"Quite frankly, yes. I don't think you've been a good father to him—to *him*, not to me. You've been perfect for me. But you've always belittled Eric about his piano playing. You've made him feel he's not really a man because he doesn't make a lot of money and never got married. You should just be thankful that he didn't turn out gay after all that."

"Right," Lamar said, his voice barely audible. "After all that. Working my dang tail off day and night so you kids could have the best education. Paying through the nose to keep him not only in college but at that pansy conservatory. Either you know how to play the piano or you don't by that age. No degree is going to mean a damn thing except money down the drain, that's all. So I get my way, huh, missy? Did I want him to go there? Did anyone listen to a thing I had to say? No, it was always your mother who was right. *She's* the one who got her way with him. He turned out exactly made to order. I could have told her from day one. And you have the gall to say I don't care about him. Well, let me tell you something, I love that boy more than life itself. Right this minute I'd go outside and jump in front of a bus if it would do my son the slightest bit of good."

"Got any insurance?" This slipped out before Kaye had a chance to think. She was getting a bit weary of the bus routine, which he trotted out whenever he got angry. "Just joking, Dad. I'm sorry."

"Sure, make fun." He looked really hurt.

"I didn't mean it."

"You don't know, do you? You have no idea." Reaching in his vest pocket, he pulled out a pack of cigarettes and tapped one out. "All this time I've kept my mouth shut for him. Haven't said a word. Let him think his mother—ah, what's the use." He looked at the cigarette as if it had just materialized between his fingers and, with a grunt of disgust, tossed it to the floor.

"No, Dad, go on." Kaye's foot rolled the cigarette toward her, furtively. "What do you mean?"

"I can't tell you."

"It's about Mother. You must tell me." Under the skirt of the club chair went the cigarette, propelled by her heel. "I've had a feeling all day that we were going to talk about her."

He looked doubtfully at her from beneath a scraggly hedge of eyebrows, which inexplicably had not gone gray.

"Not long ago I was fixing a lamp. I saw it all then, what happened with you and her, Dad. It's odd how it came to me. I guess I was just ready for the information—all the bits and pieces were there in my head all along, but the picture didn't come together as a whole until I was mature enough, objective enough, to see it clearly, outside myself and my petty concerns."

A grain or two of rice fell from his beard as he stroked it. Like his eyebrows, it could use trimming, she thought. He had let himself get a little wild-looking since the last visit. There were stains on his shirt, and his broken nails were encrusted and bruised.

"You think it's been easy all these years, Kaye, taking the blame?"

Her heart seemed to swell in an unpleasant, nonmetaphorical way that made her short of breath. She was not sure now that she was brave enough to face the issue, though she knew she must.

"I did it for you kids. It wasn't something you had to know. Him especially. It would have ruined his life. Hell, you know how he idolized her. You got to promise me one thing. If I tell you, Daughter, you're not to breathe a word of it to him. You—well, I'm not surprised you finally put two and two together. Was it your Aunt Fern let it slip? I never could trust that woman to keep her mouth shut. Anyway, I wasn't in the car."

"Car? What car?"

"What the hell car do you think? The one she. . . . You were married then, had just moved up here. Eric was at Peabody."

"You're talking about the accident?"

"It wasn't me."

Kaye's confusion abated once she had adjusted herself to the fact that she wasn't reading her father's mind. Indeed, she hadn't the slightest idea what he was getting at.

"Who was she with, then?"

The wrinkles in his leathery face, darker now after all the time he had spent on the water, etched lines of resistance as his mouth tightened.

"Tell me, Dad, who was driving?"

"*She* was. She was all alone."

"But why did you tell us it was you?"

"We were staying in a motel just outside Pensacola, on our way to your Aunt Fern's in Texas. Your mother told me she had to have some shampoo, conditioning shampoo. I said it could wait but she went anyway, took the car out to look for a drugstore. Next thing I know there's a couple of state troopers knocking on the door. She had smashed into a tree."

His voice had become lifeless, as if he were reading the minutes of a tedious faculty meeting.

"There were no skid marks. The troopers said it was a little farm road, hardly any traffic on it. I didn't want to hear. They waited till later to say what I knew already. See, it was deliberate. Of course, they couldn't be a hundred percent certain. But all the evidence seemed to point to one thing. No mechanical problems with the brakes, nothing like that."

Kaye stopped clutching the arms of her chair. Stunned, she could no longer resist and felt herself drifting, helpless. This could not be the mother she had known, the staunch, priggish woman

210

who had tried to get the seven A.M. daily Mass rolled back to six.

Lamar's pale eyes seemed washed out, drained by too much harsh sunlight. "She didn't want to fight it out with me."

"Fight what?"

"Together we could have licked it. Her mouth. It would have been OK. A couple of operations."

"Cancer?"

His formidable head remained sunk on his chin. "The doctor said she might end up with her mouth a little crooked—the operations, you know. Her face. She was terrified: not about dying; it was the scars, a crooked mouth, living with that."

"Oh, God. Dad, you poor thing." She wanted to go over to the sofa and put her arms around him. But the effort of rising seemed too much at that moment. "Why did you have to blame yourself, though? Why did you tell us it was you driving?"

"I should have been. It's a man's duty, his responsibility. A real man wouldn't have let his wife out when she had been drinking like that."

"Mom? She never drank a drop, I thought."

"After you kids left home, she got in the habit of a couple of martinis before dinner. We started squabbling in the motel about the shampoo. I said it was a damn-fool thing to do. She could darn well use my shampoo, even if it didn't have any conditioner in it. I was hungry, wanted to eat. We were drinking more than our usual quota that day, and I thought we should eat. It frightened me, the way she was putting away those martinis. I lost my head. I blew up at her. She was in no condition to drive, but I let her go out. I said if she wanted shampoo she could damn well go out and get it herself. She said—"

"What's that? The buzzer? Doesn't he have a key?"

Lamar had started, looking almost frightened. Kaye glanced at her watch. If it was Eric, he was early.

"Go wash up, Dad. You look a little beat. Give me time to explain to Eric that you're here. I don't want it to be too much of a shock. Yes, that's right, straight down the hall. No, dear, the light's to your left. Left . . . that's it."

"What are you doing here?"

"We've got to talk."

211

"I can't now. It's impossible."

"This is an emergency. My life is over."

"Your life isn't over, Arnold. Wanda is not going to marry my brother. Get back, you can't come in."

"What do you mean he isn't? Did he change his mind?"

"Not yet."

Kaye stepped outside into the areaway and adjusted the lid of one of the garbage cans, clamping it down tightly.

"She's going to ruin her life if she marries that lunatic."

"Eric is not a lunatic. He's just temporarily . . . disoriented."

"Why is he doing this? Why does he hate me?"

Kaye wrenched her hand free from his moist grip. "It's not you he hates. It's his father. Eric knows this will kill him. He's doing it for the effect the announcement will have on him."

"On his dad? Why is it going to kill his dad?"

"Wanda is obviously not—" Kaye realized she couldn't pursue this line of reasoning with Arnold. "It's not important. The point is, Eric has no intention of going through with it—at least, he won't have any reason to once I get through with him."

It was so clear to her now. Once Eric found out that Lamar hadn't been responsible for their mother's death, Eric could stop all his Oedipal nonsense and find a sensible mate, the beautiful, talented woman he deserved. Oh, how foolish Lamar had been for lying to them all these years! She was so angry—and at the same time so relieved, so shocked, so sad. And so worried that Eric might happen along at any minute.

"Arnold, you must go. I promise I'll have everything straightened out in no time at all. You have nothing to worry about."

"Can I trust you, woman?" He had taken her by the hand again and was boring into her eyes with a far-too-earnest gaze. "Yes, I can. I know I can. I have faith in you. You won't let me down, no way you could. You see what I'm going through. You're not blind."

"If you don't leave right this instant, you'll ruin everything."

"I'm going, see? Now listen, you'll call me with the good news, won't you? I won't leave my apartment until I hear from you. I haven't been able to eat or sleep ever since I heard. You've got to save me, Kaye. Hey, don't push. I'm going."

"Hurry—get."

"What a nice shirt," Kaye commented when her brother arrived a few minutes later. The shirt was not him at all, a pinstripe button-down from someplace like Brooks Brothers. And instead of jeans he had on gray slacks. "Did Wanda pick it out?"

Without answering he handed over the bouquet of Peruvian lilies he had brought.

"For me?" she asked, trying to hide her concern. Eric never brought flowers. It was obviously that woman's doing.

"There's some wine here too," he said as he set a stylish carry-all on the foyer table. Where was his knapsack? she would like to know. And the wine wasn't Gallo, she noted with mounting anxiety. It looked quite expensive.

"I'm sorry I'm late, Kaye."

"Three minutes. I'll never forgive you."

"I had the slowest cab driver. He obeyed all the speed limits, stopped at stop signs—must be nuts, huh?"

"You took a cab?" Eric was usually so frugal. To him a bus was a luxury, walking the norm.

"Well, I was practicing and forgot the time, I guess, and . . . Dad!"

Against orders, Lamar had emerged from the bedroom. Kaye had asked him to please remain there until she had talked to Eric first. But Lamar obviously didn't trust her to keep her mouth shut about their mother's "accident." Of course, Lamar was right. She wasn't to be trusted. It was insane to keep Eric in the dark at a time like this, when he was on the verge of ruining his life with an irrevocable mistake.

"Dad, what are you doing here?" Eric asked after he had submitted to a painful squeeze on the shoulder from the old man.

"To tell the truth," Kaye answered with a bright smile, "this is sort of a mini-intervention. I told Dad about your engagement, and we both decided that the best thing was to confront this thing head on. We love you, Eric, you must understand that. We only have your best interests at heart. Anything we say, painful as it might seem, is simply for your own good."

"Mind if I smoke?" Eric said as he lit up.

"Son, you're not serious about that Polish gal. Now if you would listen to what I have to say for two minutes, you'd see—"

213

"Dad, please," Kaye interrupted. "He's not a child. Talk to him like he's a grown man. Eric, a drink?"

"Thanks. But listen, you two. I hate to throw a wrench into the works. I know you probably have many interesting things to tell me, but it's a little late. See, Wanda and I were married this morning. No real ceremony or anything—just a judge."

Lamar's face was ashen. His daughter burst into tears.

After three days in mourning, Kaye rallied enough to start worrying about her father's condition. He was not himself at all, sleeping till noon, staring blindly, hour after hour, at TV, meekly picking at the microwave dinners she heated up after she got home from work. The cruelty of her brother seemed so enormous, so thoughtless, that it was hard to believe he was the same person at all. To get married in secret, to refuse to share his joy (or whatever it was) with his family, and then to react the way he had to the news that should have changed his life. . . . Yes, Kaye had gone ahead and informed him of the manner of his mother's death. But the facts meant nothing to him. He didn't believe she really had cancer. Surely she would have let him know. And why had she taken up drinking, anyway? Wasn't Lamar to blame for that? If she had been properly appreciated, if Lamar had realized all that she had sacrificed for him. . . . There were rich men who had courted her, millionaires. There had even been a priest once who would have left the Church for her. Oh, the nonsense Eric believed. Kaye didn't stand a chance against all those fables he had been spoon-fed over the years.

One evening after Kaye had exerted herself to prepare a home-cooked dinner from fresh ingredients, she took the remote control from her father's lap and pressed MUTE. "Dad, something just occurred to me at work today. I want you to listen."

"Turn up the sound."

"In a minute. I've been going over this whole thing, all the reasons Eric might have done this. OK, so he's mad at you maybe. He adored Mom. I might have. . . . Anyway, the point is, nothing's new about all that. He's had these same reasons for years. Then it hit me. There's one person we've left out of the equation."

Lamar's bloodshot eyes hadn't overcome inertia yet; they were still on the set. "Yeah?"

"It's her. Dad, look, doesn't it seem strange to you that after all the trouble we went through with lawyers and the Animal League and going to court, isn't it odd that *she's* the one who manages to solve the problem? The smell is gone. Eric said she talked the old woman out of the cats. They're moving back into the Murray Hill apartment."

"So?"

"So naturally Eric's going to be grateful to her. It's a smart move, right?"

"I suppose. Turn up the sound."

Kaye passed him a dish of M&Ms instead.

"Wanda's sort of mousy, wouldn't you say, Dad? She's nothing to look at, never says much. It's been the perfect disguise. She's blended right into the woodwork like an innocent little wallflower."

He munched thoughtfully after picking out the reds from the dish.

"But she's known all along what she's been up to. Don't you see, Dad? Every step's been calculated. Look how she wormed herself into the middle of the cat business. Then the next thing we know she's got an apartment with a piano Eric likes. And that poor boyfriend of hers. Lord, when I think how she manipulated him, it's breathtaking. Playing one against the other, getting them both to hate each other. How could we have been so blind? The woman is a genius, a goddam witch. Do you realize how many women have been after Eric in the last twenty-five years? She's the only one who's been able to break the spell."

Lost in thought, Kaye was only half aware that her father had grabbed the remote and returned sound to the screen. She remained beside him on the sofa, staring blankly at the electrons that amused neither of them.

"Have you told Arnold yet?" he asked during a commercial.

She nodded.

"How'd he take it?"

"He'll live."

"Yeah?"

"I think he'll get over it once he—"

"Hey, that's a lie. I tried that stuff, and it didn't do my drains any good at all."

Nineteen

Though Wanda had given up her job at Philip Morris to placate Eric, a real sacrifice, she still couldn't persuade him to quit smoking. It bothered her, especially since she felt partly responsible for reviving his habit. But this worry was as minor as a leaky faucet while she eased herself into a bubble-bath of domestic bliss. Filled with an energy that made her start up conversations with lonely old widows in checkout lines, Wanda focused on getting the Murray Hill apartment in tiptop shape. Every square inch of floor was scrubbed on hands and knees. The filthy baseboard was repainted with the same off-white she used on the kitchen cupboards. A horsehair sofa that prickled and shed was carted away by the super and his paroled son and then replaced with the convertible sofa from Tompkins Square. Indeed, almost all of her furniture ended up being imported uptown. Eric had no end tables, no bookshelves, no decent armchairs or lamps. And he ate off cracked, mismatched plates with a Donald Duck fork.

While Eric was at the settlement house, Wanda would look in on Mrs. Merton from time to time. Three cats were left, and Wanda wanted to make sure the litter was changed. The old woman could be forgetful.

"Are you all right?" Mrs. Merton asked one afternoon, rapping on her bathroom door.

Wanda was inside hunched over the toilet bowl with a powerful cleanser that teared her eyes. She was determined to clean the encrusted porcelain, even though on a previous occasion she had been forbidden. "No guest of mine is going to clean my commode," Mrs. Merton had declared with quiet outrage. But she had never done anything about it herself, and there was a vent leading right upstairs to Eric's bathroom. What if he smelled something one day?

"Wanda?"

"I'll be right out."

"You come out now."

"Yes, just a minute."

"Now, or I'm coming in."

Wanda sighed. Mrs. Merton, if the truth be told, was becoming difficult. The sweet old lady with the twinkling, merry eyes was fast transforming herself into a suspicious crone. And this when Wanda had leaned over backward to be friendly and aboveboard with her. How easy it would have been to avoid seeing the old woman when Wanda moved in. Yet Wanda had made a point during the first week to come downstairs and tell her the wonderful news of her marriage. Yes, perhaps it was understandable that the old woman might have seemed a little dismayed at first. Wanda could appreciate this. But what bothered Wanda was that the dismay had not gone away. It had hardened into a resentment that made small talk difficult. So Wanda had to give up any hopes of patching things up between Mrs. Merton and Eric. Eric himself would have been glad to go downstairs for a cup of tea, but when Wanda suggested this to the old woman she said she would just as soon have Hitler over. "He gassed my babies," she declared once when Wanda was describing her husband's good qualities. Wanda hastily assured her that they were all enjoying wonderful new homes, perhaps in the suburbs, on farms. But it was getting harder and harder to convince the old woman of this. The bucolic pictures Wanda conjured up did not soften the frown on Mrs. Merton's face.

"Aha! Just as I thought."

With childish guilt Wanda tried to conceal the scrub brush behind her. The old woman had flung open the door with a violence that sent Wanda's heart racing.

"I was on the toilet."

"You were *in* the toilet, my dear. Here, give it to me." She wrenched the brush from Wanda's hand. "Didn't I tell you to leave that commode alone?" she demanded, shaking the brush at her.

Wanda winced as a few drops landed on her cheek and nose. This sort of asperges she could do without.

"Why won't you let me help?" Wanda pleaded, trying to wedge past the old woman, who was blocking the doorway.

"Help? You've helped enough, young woman. I should have known you were in cahoots with that monster, pretending to be my friend. The sneaky type, that's you. Oh, they'll all find homes, Una, dear—yes, and I was fool enough to believe you. Your so-called shelter, they gas them there, don't they? No one's going to adopt them, my poor toms. It's the kitties they want. The big cats get a couple of weeks and then—"

"Damn!"

Mrs. Merton raised an arm as if to ward off a blow. But Wanda was only interested in getting the scrub brush away. A drop or two had hit her in the eye, which seemed on fire from the ammonia in the cleanser. Blinded with pain, Wanda tugged at the wooden handle, but the woman's grip was fierce.

"Let go this instant, Una!"

"Don't hurt me!"

"Una!"

They danced about in a lumbering, aboriginal way for a moment or two before Wanda saw the puce through her one good eye.

"What's going on here?" Mrs. Fogarty demanded from the other side of the doorway. Her puce sweater set was comple-mented by a puce scarf draping a somewhat phallic mound of hair.

"She's trying to beat me up!"

"It's all right, Mrs. Merton. I'm here now. No one's going to hurt you."

The excruciating pain gave Wanda no chance to explain. She was on her knees by the tub, cold water from the faucet running directly onto her left eye. The sting gradually abated, though she felt the eye was swollen twice as large. When she looked in the mirror, she was relieved to see it was only bloodshot. Taking one of Mrs. Merton's none-too-clean towels, she attempted to dry the hair that was plastered to her face. Yes, she looked a fine sight.

And there was no brush or comb other than the ones she suspected Mrs. Merton used on her cats.

Emerging from the bathroom, Wanda found Mrs. Fogarty and Mrs. Merton sharing a plate of oatmeal cookies on the Danish modern sofa. It was hard to know where to begin. She hadn't spoken to Mrs. Fogarty in what seemed ages, not since she had been fired by Mr. Ko. And so much had happened in the meantime. Did Mrs. Fogarty know she was married now? Perhaps she would be treated with more respect if Mrs. Fogarty was aware of her marital status. The nerve of the woman to look right through her, as if she weren't there.

"My eye," Wanda said as she dabbed at a tear. And then she noticed that the front of her blouse, thanks to the water from the tub, was virtually see-through. She turned sideways, heading for the door. "We had a little accident. Una got some cleanser in my eye, and I was trying to wash it out. You're OK, Una?"

"Stop right there," Mrs. Fogarty called out, as if Wanda had been trying to escape.

"I need to change, Mrs. Fogarty."

Covering her chest with folded arms, Wanda tried to seem at ease while the news vendor surveyed her from head to foot.

"Looks like I arrived in the nick of time. Good thing Mrs. Merton left her door open. In the future, darling," Mrs. Fogarty added to the old woman, giving her a pat on the head, "you keep it locked. No telling what might show up in this city."

"Mrs. Fo—Gladys, I was only trying to help her clean. My husband and I live upstairs, and I try to look in on Una whenever I can. Isn't that right, Una?"

The old woman pretended not to hear as she stroked the Siamese in her lap.

"So we're married, are we?" Mrs. Fogarty said. "How *nice*."

"Oh, there was no ceremony or anything. No party or reception. My own parents didn't come."

Though Mrs. Fogarty's face did not exactly soften, the daggers in her eyes appeared slightly duller. "They weren't invited?"

"No, really, it was sort of a whirlwind thing. You know how most men are, can't stand any sort of fuss. I would have liked to have had a few people over. I was going to call you, but even his own family—none of them were invited. We're really strapped for money anyway. I haven't got a job. Even temp work is hard to find nowadays with the way things are going, you know, the economy and all. And besides, Eric and I aren't spring chickens. He thinks it's silly for middle-aged people to have real weddings."

"Yes, especially middle-aged people engaged to others."

"Arnold and I were never engaged," Wanda calmly replied after subduing a spasm of rage. Why was she trying to appease this hateful woman? she wondered. Just so she wouldn't think she had been abusing Mrs. Merton? "As a matter of fact," she went on, the soul of reason, "Eric and I were hoping you might be able to drop over for dinner one night."

"How about tonight? I'll go right up with you now."

"No!" Wanda cried out as Mrs. Fogarty reached for her purse. "I mean, the apartment's a mess. I'd like to get things fixed up first. And Eric and I have to go out tonight. Some friends," she lied, "a week ago, asked us over."

"I see."

"But we'll do it. I'll give you a call."

"Yes, of course you will. In the meantime, I promised my friend here that you wouldn't come down and bother her anymore."

"What?"

"She's scared to death you're going to take the rest of her cats away."

"But that's crazy. I wouldn't touch Charles or—"

"Whatever, Mrs. Merton's been under a lot of strain lately. She says there's a lot of noise upstairs."

"Eric never plays after ten."

"Cats have real sensitive hearing, you know. They're waking up at two, three in the morning. Isn't that right, doll?"

The old woman sighed. "Charles has been complaining to me."

"It's a shame you can't be a little more considerate, Wanda." Mrs. Fogarty reached for another cookie, which she held between her front teeth while adjusting a pinkish bang. "The idea of causing this poor lady so much grief," she managed to add with the cookie still in her mouth.

"For your information, Una happens to be a dear friend of mine." Her throbbing eye made Wanda protest a little louder than necessary. "I care for her a great deal."

Mrs. Fogarty and the old woman exchanged a look which made Wanda feel bleak. It was almost as if she had forgotten she was the happiest woman on earth.

"Goodbye, Una," Wanda said at the door. "Call me if you need anything"—here she looked boldly at Mrs. Fogarty—"and I'll be right down."

The day after this encounter Wanda was scheduled to have lunch with Kaye Levy. She would have liked to call it off, but since she had already declined two previous dinner invitations from her sister-in-law, Wanda didn't dare. The trouble was, Wanda wanted everything to be just right when she presented herself to Kaye in her new role as Eric's wife. It all seemed too fragile at first, this married bliss, as if Kaye could easily burst the bubbles that hid Wanda's all-too-naked vulnerability. She needed time to get used to being happy. A lifetime of pining, in a resigned way, had not prepared her for the task of dealing with this jackpot. It was all something of a shock to the nervous system—even a little scary.

Kaye had suggested dinner at her apartment, but Wanda thought she would feel more secure on her own turf—for lunch. Lunch would mean a limited amount of time, since Kaye would have to get back to work. And it would also mean Eric wouldn't be there. The two of them together, Eric and his sister, had always made Wanda feel left out before she was married. She had no desire now to see if this would still be the case. There would be plenty of time for that later.

"I'm not sure if she's going senile or what," Wanda found herself saying after Kaye had complimented her on the crab salad. It was real crab, which Eric had made a fuss about when he had come across it in the fridge the night before. Why couldn't she have bought sea legs? he had wanted to know.

"She accused me of wanting to get rid of her cats," Wanda went on, after describing in detail the damage she had suffered to her eye. Why she was saying all this she was not sure. She had instructed herself beforehand to stick to pleasant topics. Carping at other people would only give Kaye a bad impression. Perhaps it was the feeling that Kaye was curious about her still bloodshot eye that had made Wanda bring up Mrs. Merton.

"But I thought you did get rid of them, dear."

"No, she's got three left. Besides, no one got *rid* of them. They were placed in a very nice shelter."

"How you managed to bring that off is beyond me."

"Una called the shelter herself."

"You're kidding."

"We got to be good friends, and then I told her the truth about the smell. See, if someone you hate tells you the truth it's never the truth. I mean . . . more water?" Wanda added as she poured Kaye some Pellegrino. Wine was not offered. There was no need to loosen any tongues.

"I'm sorry your father couldn't make it," Wanda said as she poured vinaigrette sauce over her baby asparagus.

"Make it?"

"To lunch." Wanda had, of course, waited until he had returned to Tallahassee before asking Kaye over. "I hope your father can come too," she had said over the phone, and then acted surprised that he was no longer in New York. Lamar was yet another reason why she had not accepted Kaye's dinner invitations. He had told Eric that if Wanda came to dinner at Kaye's, he would eat out alone. Wanda had cried when Eric relayed this information to her. But she had forbidden Eric to say they would never see him again as long as he lived. She had hopes that someday, after everyone had gotten used to the idea of Eric's being married, they would be able to spend holidays together like a normal family.

"Yes, it would have been nice," Kaye said after an awkward pause. Her eyes roved about the apartment in a way that made Wanda glad she had knocked herself out cleaning that morning.

"What would?"

"Dad coming. I'm sure you and he will be great friends. You seem to have a way with older people." Wanda was about to demur when Kaye added, "Though of course they will be killed, won't they? The cats."

"Not if they're adopted. Here."

"No, I couldn't." Kaye held up a hand, but the crab arrived on her plate nonetheless. "Well, I suppose. . . . Do you have a table?"

Wanda stared blankly at her sister-in-law. They were eating on a table.

"A ping-pong table," Kaye went on. "There's a paddle on the piano bench."

Glancing over at the baby grand, Wanda turned a little red. How could she have not seen it lying there in plain sight when she had spent so much time straightening and cleaning?

"You play, Wanda?"

"Me? No. Must belong to one of Eric's students, I imagine."

Wanda had intended to put the paddle back in the table by their bed. She had used it on Eric the night before when he wouldn't stop practicing. How much easier it was on her hand, using the old paddle that had once belonged to her brother. When she had first stumbled onto Eric's little proclivity for being spanked, she had been truly angry at him for giving her such a scare in the bathroom. And then he had been so ashamed afterward. No girlfriend of his had ever done that to him before. It was a fantasy he had always had, ever since he was a boy, but he had never dared let anyone know about it. She had told him then about the cats, that he was free to go back to his own apartment. "You needn't ever see me again, Eric." But he surprised her. He didn't run away. Instead he resolved never to let it happen again. They would be better off as just plain friends.

But then had come the day she had hidden a pack of his cigarettes. She was worried about his smoking and thought this childish mischief might be more effective than a stern lecture. Usually Eric simmered when he was angry, an all-day crockpot. But when he realized what she had done, the lid had blown off with a violence that had astonished them both. "You bitch, I wouldn't be smoking again if it weren't for you!" Yes, he had actually said this, as if her job at Philip Morris were the sole cause. This was too much for her. She had lashed back at him, calling him a spineless coward, a pampered little brat. And before she knew it, he was over her lap again.

When it was over, Wanda was completely baffled by the lust she had felt. Before, when she had spanked him, the anger and desire had been two entirely separate feelings. But this time they had merged, one exciting the other, so that when Eric, roused to a fever pitch, was ready to turn the tables and mount her, she had put up a struggle, crying out like a tomboy in a wrestling match. It was all so horribly embarrassing to contemplate, the way she tried to fight off his advances and how this would make him bigger, stronger, harder, until he could no longer contain himself and they would both come, victor and vanquished, with a great sigh.

After several more resolves were broken in domestic set-to's, Eric proposed to her. Of course, he had to make it into a joke of sorts. "I've never had such good sex, Wanda. If we get married, I won't have to feel guilty about it anymore." Gee, thanks a lot, she said, trying to disguise her joy with as much sarcasm as she could muster. "I mean, I like you a lot, too. Maybe I even love you, Wanda, in a funny way." Not one to press her luck too far, she had accepted him on the spot. It was only after she was safely and legally married that she dared to ask what he had meant by "in a funny way."

"Oh," he said, "it's not what I expected love to be like. I always imagined it would be like a Carnegie Hall début. That would be the day when everyone would recognize how great you were, what a genius. The applause would be deafening; some ladies would weep. You're more like what happens every day, practicing alone in a deserted settlement house." I'm sorry I asked, Wanda said, more than a little hurt. For he was definitely her Carnegie Hall. "Hold on, let me finish. You're practicing there, see, it's cold and damp and you wonder what in the hell you're doing there, knocking yourself out day after day. Then you listen, you hear. It's the music, the same music. It really doesn't matter where you play it, does it?"

"Well, at least you've weaned him away from that awful Church," Kaye was saying as Wanda brought out the demitasse cups. Kaye had given them an espresso machine as a belated wedding present.

"Oh, we still go."

"How can you? You're divorced, aren't you? And you weren't married by a priest, just some judge or something at City Hall." Kaye hadn't intended this as a dig, which was what Wanda's face registered. She was merely stating the facts.

"Well, Eric likes to go to Mass on Sunday."

"In my day, you had a bite of toast and you couldn't get communion. Now I suppose they'll take what they can get." Kaye smiled to soften the effect of her words. She was sounding like a disagreeable old woman—like her own mother, in fact.

"Actually, there are a lot of divorced people in our parish—remarried, too."

"And they all receive communion?" Kaye went on, wishing she would stop.

"Eric and I have decided we're not letting some frustrated old men in the Vatican tell us whether we're allowed to have communion or not."

"But it's against all the rules, Wanda. What's the sense of a Church if anyone can do as they please? At least Arnold had the courage of his convictions. When he saw how corrupt the Church actually was, what it had done to the Jews—even now, that Polish cardinal, the one defending that convent at Auschwitz—it's too disgraceful for words."

Wanda offered her a twist of lemon. "You've seen Arnold?"

Kaye was thankful her hostess had found a way to change the subject. Kaye herself didn't seem able to. "I had lunch with him not too long ago. He's off in the Philippines now for a couple of months. He's got a lot of vacation time he hasn't taken."

"That's wonderful."

Yes, Kaye thought bitterly, you've driven a good honest man to the ends of the earth, and it's wonderful. This was really the last straw. No remorse at all does she show about the old woman's cats, no apology for snubbing Lamar, and now this.

"I've really got to be going," Kaye said, after taking only a single sip from the Limoges demitasse. "I can't be late again today. My boss will have a conniption."

"But the tart, I have a raspberry tart."

"Crosstown traffic is awful, Wanda. You know that."

At the door Kaye took some of the drama from her abrupt departure by commenting favorably on the apartment. In all honesty, Wanda, heartless as she might be, had done a remarkable job with limited resources. The place really looked like a home, she thought.

"It's very nice," Kaye repeated when Wanda disagreed, saying it still needed a lot of work. "Though I can't imagine," she added, "where you'll fit a ping-pong table."

"Goodbye," Wanda said coldly, almost rudely.

Kaye paused in her search for a token. "We must do this again," she said, with an aggressively polite smile.

"What are you doing?"

"I just wanted to see what the bed looked like over here."

"Why?"

Wanda paused to catch her breath. It was heavier than she had thought, and she was scraping the pine floor.

"Can you give me a hand?"

"No," he said. "I don't want the bed moved."

"But it's right by that vent."

"So?"

She gave the bed another shove. Ever since Mrs. Merton had complained to Mrs. Fogarty, Wanda had been concerned about what the old woman might be hearing through this particular heating vent. After Kaye had left the day before, Wanda had even gone so far as to put her ear to it and listen for a while. She had heard footsteps, and at one point it seemed the old woman was humming to herself.

"Will you stop that, Wanda?"

In a half playful way, he restrained her with a hug.

"But—"

"Don't you think I tried to move it when I was trying to get away from the smell?" He tightened his grip as she squirmed. "There's no room. You move it one way and it blocks the closet. Over there, you won't be able to get the door open."

"All right. Let me go. I'm getting wet."

Eric had just come from the shower and had not finished drying himself. They were going to dinner that evening at Russell's.

"Eric, stop! My dress!"

He had still not let go, and she was so worried about how she was going to look. It was important to her to make a good impression on Russell. She wanted a friend, someone she could complain about the in-laws to. Eric might be sympathetic, at least initially. But some instinct had told her to give him only an edited version of the lunch with Kaye. How easy it would be to start alienating him by going into detail about his sister's rude and condescending behavior. Besides, she was sure Eric was getting the other side of the story from Kaye. There was no telling what that woman might be saying about her. Strange how marriage seemed to be turning everyone into an enemy. But it was a small price to pay. Wanda hadn't the slightest regret.

"We're going to be late!" she protested as he threw her onto the bed.

"Good."

"Stop it, Eric. I'm really getting mad. This dress cost nine dollars to clean, and now it's crushed. I'm going to have to change."

"You're getting mad?"

"I mean it."

The towel fell from his waist as he reached around and yanked open the top drawer of the night table. "Hey, where the hell's that paddle?"

Wanda gave up struggling beneath his knee, which was pressing down on her stomach. "Eric, I'm not joking. I'm really very angry."

"Right, I know." He had opened another drawer. "So where could it be?"

"I threw it out."

"What?"

Wanda got up and surveyed the damage to her dress. Kaye's visit had been too unnerving. Wanda had taken the paddle out into the hall afterward and tossed it into the slot for the incinerator.

"You're the one who said you needed it."

"I know, Eric."

"So you're going to use your hand now, or what?"

"There isn't time," she said with a touch of hysteria. "You're not even dressed yet."

"I am."

"Jeans? You're wearing jeans to Park Avenue?"

"Russell never dresses up. Hey, what are you doing? Calm down. You're messing up all my clothes."

"I'm trying to find a tie," she said from the closet. "I want you to wear a tie."

"Oh, for God's sake."

"Please, Eric. For me. One little favor."

"I wish you'd relax," he said, taking the tie she held out for him. "Russell won't eat you."

Twenty

*I*nez looked sternly at the guests as the praise mounted. Eric declared to the elderly raven-haired cook that he had never eaten such a meal in his entire life. "You are the Alicia de Larrocha of the kitchen."

Wanda concurred. "It's real art, what you do with food. You can't learn something like that. It has to be born inside you. And I should know." She was thinking of Louis, who had spent years at the Culinary Institute but never managed to cook one tasty meal for her after they were married.

Russell looked expectantly at her, but when Wanda didn't go on—she decided it wasn't such a good idea to mention a former husband—he said something in Spanish to Inez.

"*Buenas noches,*" Eric called out as the cook left the study.

"Where was I?" Russell said, apparently unsure where he had left off when Inez had brought in the cognac. "Something about sex."

"I think you were saying there might be something to celibacy," Wanda supplied.

"Right. Christianity ruined the whole concept for me, made it seem priggish. But then I was reading Aldous Huxley. You know that a lot of Eastern religions recommend celibacy as a path to spirituality?"

"Until another Sylvester comes along," Eric said.

Wanda gave her husband a look. It was rude of him to make fun. Couldn't he see that Russell still hadn't recovered from the breakup? He had given them all the details over dinner, how he had tried to remain calm when Sylvester had hung up a poster of Oliver North in the bedroom but how it turned out to be too much for him.

"I have an uncle who's been celibate all his life," Wanda said from the divan draped with Guatemalan shawls. Russell was beside her while Eric tilted against the wall in a Hepplewhite chair.

"You do?" Eric said as the chair squeaked.

"You've heard me talk about Uncle Joe. He was a priest, very devout, used to scourge himself every Friday until the bishop made him retire. Eric, you're going to break that chair. Sit up straight."

"Why retire him?" Russell asked, taking her hand and giving it a friendly squeeze. "They should have made him a saint."

"Well, they—" Wanda was about to explain how there were some alleged difficulties with altar boys. But then she thought better of it. There was no reason to bring up a subject that might stir up an argument between the two men. How nice it was for Russell to take her hand, making her feel right at home. And what a home, grand as could be, with the most marvelous oak wainscoting. If only Eric would be a little more sociable. Why did he have to contradict everything his friend said? And he really was drinking too much. Before dinner there had been two Rob Roys (an odd choice, she thought; she had never seen him drink one before), then the wine, and now cognac.

"So how much vacation do you give Inez?" Eric asked, his chair still tilted against the wall.

"You've just proved my point," Russell said, "what I was saying at dinner; there's no such thing as conversation anymore. People really made an effort in the eighteenth century. They stuck to a subject, discussed it from every angle, and their transitions from one topic to the next were always elegant. Now no one cares, no one makes the slightest effort."

"His attention span is very short," Wanda put in. She had just remembered the dress he had crushed and couldn't resist the dig. Because of him she had had to change into a turquoise shot-silk outfit that really wasn't right for her figure.

Russell stood up and refreshed Eric's drink. "You don't even care what sort of vacation Inez gets. Where did such a stupid question come from anyway?"

"I think I liked you better as a garbageman's boyfriend. This Lady Blessington business is a real drag."

"Eric," Wanda reprimanded, blushing for Russell. But Russell was laughing as he collapsed back onto the sofa.

"And stop fondling my wife," Eric added, causing Russell, still chuckling, to cover Wanda's arm with sarcastic kisses. Wanda pulled away, offended. Both of them, she could see now, were really potted.

"Come on, all this celibacy shit," Eric went on, obviously pleased with the reaction he was getting, "and look at your house. It's a disgrace, not a thing out of place, clean as a museum. Here, I'll—"

"Eric!" Wanda got up and whisked the salver of cheese and cream wafers out of his reach. He had actually broken one of the wafers and scattered the crumbs over what must be a priceless carpet.

"I think maybe I should get him home," she said confidentially to Russell, ignoring her host's dazed grin.

"He's going to play!" Russell clapped his hands like a child as Eric took a bow before the Steinway.

Wanda said something about its being late, the neighbors, while her husband adjusted the bench.

"What's this?" Russell exclaimed. "You're smoking again?"

After cracking his knuckles and positioning his hands above the keys, Eric had reached into his pocket and drawn out a pack of cigarettes. Well, Wanda thought, that explained his irritability. He had not smoked all evening, no doubt trying to hide his lapse from his friend. Now that he was soused it didn't seem to matter.

"So the cat's out of the bag," Eric said, taking an exaggerated puff from the bench.

"You're kidding." Russell sounded sober again. "It's been ages, not since your wedding—the almost wedding, I mean—in Atlanta."

"Yes, and it's all my fault," Wanda said as Eric began to play with his left hand while continuing to smoke with his right. Somehow he was able to make it sound like a two-handed piece with a melody and accompaniment. She had never known it was possible to do all that with one hand.

"Scriabin?" Russell asked quietly.

Eric nodded. The mannered "great artist" look he had assumed gradually relaxed as the ash lengthened. Wanda worried about its falling onto the rug, but when it did, she let it lie there. After all, she was not his maid. Glancing over at Russell to see if he was going to do anything about it, she was disconcerted by the tears in his eyes.

Yes, she suddenly realized, it was a beautiful piece.

"You really shouldn't," Russell murmured when it was over.

Eric regarded the cigarette before taking a final puff. "Yeah, I know. Killed my mom."

Wanda was about to protest. Hadn't he told her that everything his sister had said about his mother's accident was a lie? Hadn't he insisted that his father had made up all the business about cancer of the mouth in order to shift the blame from his own shoulders?

"I thought it was an accident," Russell said for her. "Wasn't she in a wreck?"

"Yeah, but it was cancer. She had cancer."

"But Eric," Wanda began but was silenced by his look.

"I saw the records myself just the other day. Kaye mailed them to me at work, copies of the medical reports."

Wanda's dread was confusing to her. It was almost as if she had just heard it was Eric who had been diagnosed. "Can you play something else?" she suggested, wishing the men would go back to being drunk and silly.

In the morning, suffering from the mixture of cognac and red wine, Wanda left Eric asleep in the bed and padded quietly to the living room. She punched out the numbers on the phone and let it ring twice. Then, remembering it was Sunday and still quite early, she lost her nerve and hung up. It had been underhanded of Kaye to mail those reports to the settlement house, as if she, Wanda, could not be trusted. But what would be accomplished by getting into a wrangle with her? Restless, tired, Wanda found herself unable to go back to bed. Something felt so wrong. She tried reading, but then on impulse she threw on a robe and went out the door.

She must have dreamed the phone had rung, for when she reached for it there was nothing but a dial tone. If only humans could learn the secret chemistry of bears, Kaye thought. She herself would choose to hibernate through spring, when the hope in the air made a mockery of her loneliness. What was there to live for but another week of trying to believe her job was not horribly boring and useless, trying not to smoke, trying not to eat too much, trying not to call Joel. All this had been endurable when Eric had been around to listen to her complaints and laugh at her foolishness. But after he had gotten the medical records, he had called to say he wouldn't be able to make it to dinner. Just the two of them it was going to be, her treat at a two-star bistro not far from the settlement house. Well, she had blown it with her passion for facts. Eric had been polite, had even thanked her for the records. But that civility, she well knew, was the kiss of death with him. How often had she seen him become extremely solicitous about a girl-friend's health and happiness just before throwing her over for good? Oh, if only he could have blown up at her, called her a scheming bitch. But Eric had never learned how to get angry in a healthy, masculine way.

Hunger finally gave her an excuse to get up. As she munched a toasted bialy in her pajamas, she caught a glimpse of her neighbor, Betty Lovejoy, in the areaway. She seemed to be rooting through the cans as if she had lost something. Curious, Kaye approached the window, being careful at the same time not to let herself be seen.

Yes, Betty was going through the garbage, sorting out plastic bottles and stuffing them into a Gucci shopping bag. The matted fake fur of her mules was as greasy as her hair, which was several ill-matched shades of blond. She was talking to herself, keeping up a gentle scolding as she unearthed a soggy *Daily News*. This she added to a pile of newspapers after gazing for a moment at one of the ads.

In the bathroom Kaye fought back tears of self-pity as she applied makeup to her sleep-creased face. A new Liz Claiborne dress, one that she had been saving for a special occasion, a real date, made her feel a little better after she put it on. She considered it from different angles in the mirror and then chose not her best shoes but a good pair she needn't be ashamed of.

Betty was gone by the time Kaye emerged. She hesitated a

moment on the sidewalk, wondering if she wanted to go west to Riverside or east to Central Park. Well, it didn't really matter. Just go. Go.

She had crossed against the light when she came upon the woman, early sixties perhaps, handsome, smartly coiffed, with a homemade sign draped over the front and rear of her linen pants suit like a sandwich board. *Attention residents of 86th St.,* Kaye read from a distance, after she had hurried past the canopy under which the woman stood. *Gareth Wintersit, Esq., raped me and is suing me for libel.*

"I must not come home this way," Kaye said aloud to herself as she crossed Columbus. The pain and rage in the woman's eyes had been too much for her.

Bare-chested, the gorgeous young man in the bus shelter ad writhed in a St. Theresa-like ecstasy over his choice of jeans, while out of his mouth, in crude Marks-A-Lot, came a cartoon balloon of graffiti: HITLER OBEYED THE MASONS. END THE MASONIC NIGHT-MARE. Kaye puzzled over this as she got caught in traffic in the middle of Central Park West. *The Magic Flute,* Eric had once told her, had something to do with the Masons. All their great art, and what did it lead to? The most barbaric slaughter the world has ever known. And yet Joel could listen not only to Mozart but even to Wagner. This Kaye would never understand.

Stop reading, Kaye advised herself as she settled onto a bench in the park. Stop looking for signs everywhere you go. She had even studied the intricate tracery of an oak's foliage, as if it could be read like tea leaves.

Not far from her bench a man was guiding a toy destroyer across the concrete Boat Pond by remote control. Lamar had liked to come here and play with the rented boats. She had scolded him one evening for harassing a mallard with a cigarette racer. And one afternoon he had tormented a black Labrador by squirting it with his fire-fighting boat.

"I'm not hurting anyone."

"You're upsetting the dog, Dad."

"He's having fun."

"No, he's not. Listen to him whine. He's scared."

"For Christ's sake, Kaye, I wish for once in your life you'd butt out."

Remembering this exchange, Kaye smiled in the way well-brought-up children disguise their pain. Her father was still angry at her for telling Eric the truth about their mother's death. He claimed she had ruined Eric's peace of mind and made a mockery of his, Lamar's, sacrifice. For that was what he had considered the lie, a sacrifice for the good of his children, some sort of atonement. As much as this rejection hurt her, Kaye realized that if she had it to do over again, she would not be able to smother the truth. Even if it meant her whole family turning against her, she would rather endure this loneliness than a bad conscience.

Twenty minutes passed, she had timed it, and not a single person had looked at her. A clown on her way to twist balloons into dachshunds by the Alice in Wonderland statue, happy couples, disgruntled couples, men alone with lost looks, women jerked along by their dogs—they all walked by as if the bench were empty. And now it looked as if a gray-haired Japanese with a frozen custard in each hand was about to back right into the bench and sit down on her. She coughed; she cleared her throat. Glancing over his shoulder, the gentleman nodded politely before walking on.

How did Wanda do it? Kaye thought with a surge of anger. How did someone so mousy and blah, someone she had felt sorry for, how did she manage to—

"Wanna fuck?"

Clutching her purse, Kaye jerked to her feet. A grizzled loony had alighted beside her. His rank, filthy T-shirt was emblazoned with a head shot of John Updike, she noticed, as she hurried away.

On the other side of the oval pond, Kaye paused and squinted across the water toward the bench she had just vacated. It occurred to her that the man might have been joking, parodying New York crudeness in an attempt to break the ice. Was he really as disreputable as he had seemed on first impression, out of the corner of her eye? Had he really smelled awful, or did she just assume he must? After all, Updike was on his shirt. And from this distance he seemed to have a nice build, tall and lanky, maybe around fifty-five or so, a good age for a man.

She circled back cautiously, pretending to be fascinated by a schooner. A few yards away she stood with her back to him until it seemed safe. Then with a quick glance she took it all in: the open sores on his legs, the missing teeth, the rose tattoo on his neck. She retreated, thankful he hadn't noticed her giving him a second look.

Her practical, crepe-soled shoes squished as she mounted the slope to the cherry trees above the pond. The earth beneath the limbs was carpeted by blossoms that had fallen, though there were still enough on the trees to make them look glorious from a distance. She sniffed but smelled nothing. If she hadn't been wearing her good dress, she would have plopped right down on the damp petals and given up the ghost, there and then. She had had all she could take of this life. It was enough.

A few drops trickled down her forehead, yet the sky was blue. She looked up and saw a squirrel eyeing her. He had apparently shaken some dew or moisture from the blossoms as he bounded onto a delicate limb.

It was then, as she emerged from the pink canopy of wilting blossoms, that she saw the joggers on the park road, a wave of modern-day penitents scourging themselves with ever greater distances. Her heart gave a leap, for among them she saw someone she knew could not be there. He was halfway around the world, and yet she was sure she had seen him.

"Arnold!" she cried and started to run. If only she had worn her jogging outfit, she was sure she could have caught up with him. But she felt so foolish in her Liz Claiborne and all her makeup; she gave up after a few yards.

Wanda tried to concentrate on *Northanger Abbey*, but she was too worried about how she was going to break the news to Eric. Stretched out beside her on an old army blanket, he was fiddling with the controls of a portable CD. A large ant had crawled inside the new player, and he was worried that damage might have been done.

"I'm sure it will be all right," she said, wishing he wouldn't let it upset him so much. "You want some more coffee?"

"How can you expect me to hear you with headphones on?" he snapped, keeping them on.

She was about to give him a sharp reply when she saw Kaye strolling beside the chain-link fence that bordered the park's Sheep Meadow. Tensing as she put on a smile, Wanda waited for her sister-in-law to greet them. But Kaye seemed in a daze of sorts. If only Eric didn't notice and call out to her, she might pass by.

But Eric had noticed. He was looking right at his sister. And then, to Wanda's surprise, he became preoccupied with the CD player again.

The guilt Wanda felt was neatly balanced by a modest rush of pride. It was a small victory for herself. Feeling generous she let Eric take a cigarette from the soft-pack he had been concealing in his money belt. Such a child. In any case, now was no time to lecture him about his health.

"By the way," she said, after a few puffs that seemed to calm him down and get his mind off the ant, "I've asked someone to dine with us this evening."

"To dine, Miss Austen?"

Wanda hadn't meant to sound ridiculous. To pretend she had done it on purpose, she replied, "My dear, you don't object to having a friend in to sup?"

"Pray tell who this friend might be."

"Mrs. Gladys Fogarty."

"Who the fuck is Mrs. Gladys Fogarty?"

Eric's language had somewhat deteriorated as of late. She couldn't remember his using such words before they had married. And she didn't really remember him being so critical and mean—although this could be, she realized, her memory playing tricks on her. Overall, though, she seemed to recall a kinder, gentler soul.

"She was at your recital, remember, at Mr. Ko's? She's short, real short, with a lot of hair."

"Forget it."

"What?"

"I'm not having that wacko over."

Wanda felt a slight surge of panic. She had already asked the wacko over. "I'm afraid it's something we'll both have to endure. I called her before we left for the park, and she—"

"You can just call her back then. I've got enough to endure as it is. Three more students they're making me take. I hardly have any time as it is."

"Yes, I know. It's terrible." Eric had already complained to her many times about these new students, wealthy socialites who had already made substantial bequests to the settlement house. Three poor students wouldn't have upset him so much.

"And why the hell are you asking her, if it's an endurance contest for you too? What sort of friend is that?"

"She's got her nose out of joint because she didn't come to the wedding. And you see"—Wanda had been hoping she could keep this part to herself, but since Eric was being obstinate, he would have to know—"I went down to Mrs. Merton's this morning before you got up. She wouldn't let me in at first, but I kept on buzzing and—"

"What's this got to do with Fogarty?"

"Hold on. I'll explain." A sudden gust of light, not wind—or so it seemed—restored the sheen to his golden hair, which had been looking a bit dull and thin. She couldn't resist sinking her fingers in it, which he seemed to enjoy, especially when she tugged.

"I got in finally," she went on, forcing herself not to say it aloud, *I love you I love you I love you,* "and now listen, don't fly off the handle and get crazy about it, but Eric, she had—there were two more."

"Huh? No!"

She nodded. "I don't know where they came from. Strays, probably. I didn't recognize them. And she wouldn't let me see in the bedroom. There could've been more in there."

"Great. This is just great."

"You don't want to move down to Tompkins Square, do you?"

"How can we? You gave up your place."

"I know, but it might be cheaper if we looked for something down there. Without my job, we're not going to be able to find anything in Murray Hill—you know what one bedrooms are going for now. And I told you I've called about temp work. I can do word processing, but everything's slow now; they can't use me that much. It's not going to make a big difference, anything I make, until I land another decent job."

"Why is the old bat doing this? I thought you had worked everything out with her."

Just as she had feared, his anger was ricocheting in her direction, as if she were somehow to blame.

"Relax," she said, trying to sound in control, sure of what she was doing. "The whole thing got messed up because of Gladys Fogarty. She's been visiting Una a lot, getting chummy with her."

"She a relative?"

"A friend of a relative. Anyway, ever since Una found out I'm married to you, she's not been all that happy with me, and then with Mrs. Fogarty putting in her two cents, maybe even stirring her up against me—"

"And so you want to cook dinner for her?"

"Mrs. Fogarty is very sensitive to social slights. I don't think it would be hard to get her back on my side. We've got to do this, don't you see? Unless you feel like moving to Alphabet City."

Eric, who had been resting on one elbow, collapsed onto his back with a theatrical sigh.

"So what should we have to eat?"

"You have whatever you like, Wanda. I'll eat out."

"I'm sorry, but it's not going to count unless you're there too."

"What?"

"She'll know you're snubbing her. Now cheer up. It won't be that bad."

Eric had his eyes scrunched shut, his lips compressed, as if he were a kid about to be force-fed beets. She put down her book and began to make a list of the things she would need to pick up at the market.

Twenty-one

*H*is shirt off, though still in his jeans, Eric tossed the spatula back onto the night table. "What's this doing in here?"

Wanda was trying on a new shade of lipstick at the desk next to the bed. She didn't reply, hoping he wouldn't need everything spelled out. There were some things, after all, that were not meant to be discussed. Talking about them seemed in some way more embarrassing and intimate than actually doing them.

"You like this coral on me, Eric?"

"This thing here," he persisted. "You plan to cook in here?"

For a while now Wanda had discouraged Eric's attempts to start a brawl before they had sex. She was hoping it would be possible to ease him into the kind of sex life more appropriate to churchgoing couples, the kind you didn't have to mull over and feel confused and guilty about afterward. But she wasn't sure this was turning out to be a success. Eric's lovemaking was becoming more and more perfunctory, and she herself had begun to fake her climaxes.

"You're not wearing jeans, are you? Mrs. Fogarty is sort of fussy. She likes to get dolled up."

"I already told you I wasn't going to eat with that dame."

"Oh, but Eric, please, you have to."

"Life is too short."

"You don't have to dress up if you don't want to."

"Sorry."

"Just a nice shirt, that's all. Or that work shirt," she amended as he began to put one on. "That will be fine. And afterward, think how nice it will be when she's gone and we can—"

He had been buttoning up the front but paused now. "I can't believe it. You're actually bribing me?"

"What?"

"Christ, Wanda. What a mind." He glanced at the spatula and then, shaking his head, finished buttoning the shirt.

That's so unfair, she wanted to say as he slipped into his running shoes. How could you think that for one minute, she almost said when he buckled on his money belt. But she couldn't tell if he was angry or amused, and she didn't want to exacerbate him by blurting out something inappropriate.

"Where are you going?" she finally managed to say in what she hoped was an offhand, innocent manner.

"To McDonald's."

Mrs. Fogarty arrived early, the buzzer startling Wanda as she drifted from the kitchen to the bedroom in a haze of anxiety, trying to get ready. What must Eric think of her? She simply had to convince him that there was no thought of bribery in her head at all, not the slightest. She wasn't that type of person. She was moral, so moral that for most of her life she hadn't enjoyed sex at all.

"Eric had a last-minute rehearsal," Wanda explained to the news vendor, whose disappointment was all too evident. Mrs. Fogarty's embroidered dress of gold and silver thread, her tiered hair, a delicate oyster pink that matched her nails and beaded purse, meant that she had gone all out. Wanda was glad she herself had chosen one of her nicer outfits, a designer skirt and blouse she used to wear to Philip Morris.

"Caviar?" Wanda had found a jar of orange roe for $1.99 at a deli.

"I usually eat mine with toast," Mrs. Fogarty said as she accepted the generous dab on a saltine. "Chopped-up onions and eggs, that's how Mrs. Monastere would do you. But don't go boiling up eggs for me. A wedge would do."

"Lemon? Oh, of course."

In the kitchen Wanda stood with her hand on the refrigerator door. At first she had feared that Eric might lose interest in her, might actually leave her, if she didn't play along with his games. And now that she had shown she was ready to step up to the batter's box again, he had made her feel like some sort of perverse harlot. There seemed to be no way to win. Damned if you do, damned if you don't.

"You all right?"

Wanda gave a little start. Mrs. Fogarty had appeared at the kitchen door.

"It's lemon, sweetie. You're looking for lemon."

"I know."

Back in the living room, after discovering there was no lemon, Wanda was about to settle into the wing chair when she noticed her feet. She had on a pair of Eric's crew socks, which she used as slippers around the apartment.

"Now what?"

"My shoes," Wanda said as she hurried into the bedroom. "I'm sorry, you must think—I've been running around all day. . . ."

Changing into high heels, Wanda admonished herself to get a grip. She had a duty to salvage the evening as best she could, to turn Mrs. Fogarty into, if not a friend, at least an ally. As for Eric, there was nothing she could do about that for now. There would be plenty of time to explain to him later.

Eric had cleared away her makeup and atomizers and turned the rolltop back into a desk. She would have been glad to type the report for him, a summary of his students' progress for the settlement house's board of directors, but he was stubborn. Still acting moody and withdrawn, he refused to let her explain why she had decided not to use the spatula on him when he returned from McDonald's on Sunday evening. Two fingers hunted and pecked for a while before he finally snapped, "How can I think with you hovering there?"

"Good news."

"Huh?"

"Our worries are over. Mrs. Fogarty just called. Do you want to hear—or are you too busy?"

He stopped typing and for the first time in days looked directly at her. "Go ahead."

Wanda perched on the side of the desk and smoothed her lap

as if she had on a dress, not jeans. It was a moment to savor. "Well, you know when she got here on Sunday, she was pretty upset that you weren't here. I had a big handicap to begin with, thanks to you, sir."

He did not smile, but neither did he seem hostile.

"Anyway, after a couple of glasses of sherry, she was a little less prickly. I think she knew I was lying about your having a rehearsal at the last minute."

"Why did you lie? Why not tell her the truth?"

Wanda let that one pass. *I'm sorry, Gladys, but my husband will not be joining us because he thinks you're a wacko and life is too short.*

"By the way, did you know that Mrs. Fogarty's husband was murdered? She'd never told me this before. It was the same year Martin Luther King was killed, I think. Mrs. Fogarty said something about the union getting mad at her husband. He delivered newspapers, and there was something about an election or a bylaw he was opposing, it was sort of complicated and I could tell it was painful for Mrs. Fogarty, so I didn't ask a lot of questions. A man came to the door of their house when she was out buying a pair of hose and shot her husband point blank. They never did convict anyone, and Eric, listen to this, she's stayed in the same house ever since. It's in Canarsie, I was there myself once. How she stands it, I'll never know. I would have moved out first thing, left New York altogether. But she said she's not afraid and wants whoever did it to know he can't scare her and she'll rip his throat out if he ever shows up again; that's what she said. She's had a lot of chances to get married since then, she said, but her heart belongs to Herman and that's that. Herman was a real gentleman, always opened doors for her, she said, and—"

"Hey, the cats, Wanda, what about the fucking cats?"

His impatience did not have much of an effect on her. She was wondering if Mrs. Fogarty's husband had been as innocent as Mrs. Fogarty liked to think. Surely you don't get gunned down because of a bylaw.

"Wanda, I got work to do."

"All right, hold your horses," she snapped back. "I couldn't bring up the cats right away. If I had, Mrs. Fogarty would have suspected I had asked her over just to see what she could do to help out with Mrs. Merton. She's pretty smart in her own way. You can't really put anything over on her."

Eric poked a key or two. "But you did, right?"

"No, not really. She did it herself after I brought out the brandy."

"Not the good brandy, I hope."

As a wedding present Russell had made them accept a bottle that, Eric feared, might have cost as much as three hundred dollars. Wanda had made sure that Mrs. Fogarty realized what she was drinking.

"Mrs. Fogarty brought up Una Merton herself. She said she's always leaving the gas on, and twice she's gone in the kitchen and seen a saucepan with beans burned to a crisp. Mrs. Merton forgets she's turned the flame on, and that could be very dangerous."

Eric moaned childishly. "My good brandy."

"So Mrs. Fogarty is going to talk to Mrs. Monastere; she's Mrs. Merton's daughter-in-law. There's this real nice retirement home only a few blocks from Mrs. Fogarty in Canarsie, and Mrs. Fogarty knows someone who works there. She's going to see about getting her admitted right away. They have all sorts of activities, arts and crafts and song recitals, and Una won't be so lonely there. She can make a lot of friends. Besides, it'll be easier for Mrs. Fogarty and Mrs. Monastere to visit her. They won't have to trek all the way in from Brooklyn."

"One dinner, and she does all this for you?"

"She's not doing anything for me, Eric. Mrs. Fogarty is doing it for Mrs. Merton, for her safety. I just happened to mention that I was worried too. We could all be gassed or blown up. She's not just forgetful, either. Mrs. Merton is getting a little paranoid. She thinks she's being persecuted. I explained to Mrs. Fogarty about how she burst in on me when I was trying to clean her toilet. Don't sigh. It was very embarrassing and sad, Eric. And then I felt it was my duty to tell Mrs. Fogarty about the time Una went out in her slip."

"Huh?"

"She went to a restaurant with me once—didn't I tell you?—with nothing on."

"Oh, that. Well, I got to hand it to you, kid. I was really starting to go nuts thinking about another invasion of cats. You deserve some sort of medal."

"Forget the medal. Just tell me you're sorry you walked out on me Sunday night."

"Yeah, right."

Realizing that this halfhearted mutter was the best she could do for now, she deftly filched a pack of cigarettes he was inexpertly concealing beneath a draft of the report for the settlement house. He was typing again and didn't even notice as she dropped them into a floral wastebasket.

"What do you want for lunch?" she asked innocently.

"French fries. Make me a nice batch, OK?"

"Sorry, we're having bluefish. It lowers your cholesterol."

Wanda groaned. The pain was killing her; she wanted to die. But Serge would not let up. "Four more!" he barked. "Three, two—and now another ten, my dears. Yes, ten!" How she hated him. He was a liar, a cheat, a sadist. Never again—this would be the last time.

When it was finally over, Wanda lay on her back in a stupor. Beside her Russell, bathed in a curiously pleasant-smelling sweat, propped himself up on one elbow. "Well?"

"I'm never speaking to you again."

Nevertheless, Wanda returned to the studio the following week. It was not far from Worldwide Plaza, where she was doing temp work at an advertising agency. Russell had invited both Eric and her to join the exercise class as his guests, but Eric said he was too busy, so Wanda came alone.

The studio was spartan, a fifth-floor walk-up devoid of chrome, mirrors, and music. Serge Kipps, the instructor, had an unfashionably squat though powerful body. In his early sixties, the bald Englishman pushed the five people in his class to their limit with unorthodox workouts using no equipment at all. Because there was rarely enough hot water in the showers and only bare bulbs in the ceiling, Wanda was shocked to hear—or overhear—how much each session cost. A TV newscaster on a station Wanda rarely watched was grumbling about the price to her boyfriend as they all limped down the stairs one evening after Wanda's fourth or fifth session.

"I'm getting a discount for bringing you in," Russell said when Wanda mentioned her concern about what he was paying for her.

They had walked east to a Broadway diner that featured a California menu—avocado salads, mango chicken, goat cheese with sun-dried tomatoes, all served on paper plates. Wanda and Russell had ordered their usual passionfruit shakes with macadamia nuts on the side.

"Still, Russell, it's so much."

"You can pay for the nuts. Just don't make a fuss about the classes, please. It's annoying and petty, and I don't like to think of you as annoying and petty. Annoying and pretty, maybe—No, not pretty. Pleasing is more like it."

"Oh, shut up."

"I'm not kidding. You've got a strange appeal. Serge asked me if you were available."

"Stop," Wanda said, hoping he would go on.

"He did. And Jordan. I've seen him eyeing you in class."

"That creep?"

"That creep used to date Deborah Kerr. As a matter of fact, you remind me a little of her, the way you do your hair now, and you've got that cool sort of remote air about you, always observing, peering out from the underbrush, a little shy, afraid of being trampled—and yet, somehow beneath it all, tough as nails, a real survivor."

The warmth of his gaze was disconcerting. She couldn't help wondering for a moment just how gay he was.

"Such bullshit, Russell."

"Then why are you blushing?"

"Lies always embarrass me."

"Lies? Do you think if you were as plain and ordinary as you think you are, you would have trapped the idol of millions?"

"Opposites attract."

His look now was more appraising. "I can't figure you out at all."

"I thought I was the Deborah Kerr of the nineties."

"Someone wrote an essay once," he went on before she had finished her sentence, so that they were both talking at once, "about the tiny mammals living their furtive lives in the shadow of the dinosaurs. Who would have ever thought those little, insignificant creatures—"

"Hey, you're supposed to be flattering me."

"Then he compares this to squirrels in the shadow of man. Once we blow ourselves up with our megaton bombs, it'll be the squirrels who will inherit the earth, those little, alert, insignificant creatures we think are so totally useless and cute."

"Now I'm a useless squirrel."

"But cute. So what were you saying about Kaye?"

Wanda wasn't sure, but she thought her feelings might have been hurt. It was a nerve-racking experience, being complimented by Russell. "What?"

"Before you brought up how much Serge cost, you were saying something about Kaye."

"Yes, she's been calling me a lot," Wanda said after a slight hesitation. She decided not to be offended by him, to go on and confide in him—though really, why did he have to be so damn complicated? Why couldn't he just say, *I like your hair* or *I like your new shoes*, and leave it at that? "She's worried about Arnold."

Russell looked politely interested while his eyes roved to the smoked mirror tiles on a column near their table. In them he apparently had a view of other diners out of Wanda's range.

"Arnold is supposed to be in the Philippines, Kaye said, but she saw him in the park a few weeks ago."

"Mmm."

How ordinary Russell looks, Wanda thought as her resentment surfaced. Gray hair, a faded knit shirt with a bleach stain near the collar, just average height, a little overweight, pouches under his eyes. . . . He was jealous of her, of course. That was why he had called her a useless squirrel.

"That's it?" he asked.

"No, it goes on. She tried to call Arnold and found out his phone was disconnected. Then she says she went by his apartment a couple of times—they live near each other—and no one answered when she buzzed. I try to reason with her, say it all makes sense because he's in the Philippines, but she's sure she saw him. And she tried to call him at work—this really got her going—and someone told her he no longer works there and wouldn't give her any more information."

The dried aster on their table got a sniff before Russell asked, "Who's Arnold?"

"Don't you ever listen to me? I was telling you about him before class, the guy Kaye likes."

"Oh, the priest, ex-priest. I get him mixed up with that short guy you were going to marry."

"I never was going to marry him! Where in the world did you—"

Holding up his hands in mock defense, Russell said, "Bark but don't bite."

"Honestly." Riled though she was, Wanda couldn't help smiling. He was so impossible it was almost charming. "I did date him a long time ago, and then Kaye got interested in him and now she's in a swivet. First she thinks he might have tripped or fallen in his apartment, knocked his head or something and can't get help. So what does she do? She says she can't find the super to let her in so she goes to a locksmith and pretends she's locked herself out of her own apartment."

"What?"

"That's right. She gets the locksmith to let her in so she can see if he's lying on the floor unconscious." Kaye had reported to Wanda that there were barbells in the living room and muscle magazines. This puzzled Wanda since she had never known Arnold to lift weights. But then again, here she was working out with a TV anchorwoman, sweating like a pig—and she had always hated gym in school.

"That woman is too much, breaking and entering."

"I know. Arnold wasn't there, of course. Good thing for her, too. He might have killed her. I mean, what if he had a girlfriend over?"

Russell smiled and shook his head. "I love Kaye. She's great."

"Great?"

This was hardly the sympathy and consolation Wanda was looking for. Kaye was making a real nuisance of herself—breaking into people's apartments, phoning up day and night with strange, wild fears—and Russell considered this great?

"It just so happens—" Wanda began, but couldn't go on. The two men at a neighboring table had begun to glance their way. In any case—Russell would probably make a joke of this too—Kaye had told Wanda that, besides barbells, she had seen a gun rack on the wall. Rifles. Now Wanda had been to Arnold's apartment

247

often enough and had never once seen a gun. As a matter of fact, she was almost sure that Arnold gave money to Handgun Control and hated the NRA. Would this be great, too, that Kaye was beginning to see things? Or that she was deliberately lying to stir up trouble?

"What? Tell me. You started to say—"

"It's late, Russell. I have to get back home."

"Can you wait a second? Let me go to the bathroom."

He caught up with her at a bus stop a block away—or what she had thought was a bus stop.

"You can't wait here," he said. Video games in a nearby arcade provided twelve-tone Muzak for the sidewalk vendors. Black Muslims in djellabahs presided over a table of incense sticks and Malcolm X literature, while on the other side of Wanda a West Indian hawked T-shirts to out-of-towners on their way to *Cats.*

"You can't, see?" He pointed up to the sign she was waiting beneath: NO STANDING.

"It's Kaye, right?" he said as she moved on. "She's trying to make you feel guilty."

"Why should I feel guilty?"

"If anything's happened to Arnold, you know it's not your fault, don't you?"

He had put his arm around her, making her ashamed of her earlier impatience with him. What a good friend Eric had, and she too. "Oh, Russell, you get a little happiness in life, and everyone goes nuts. They just can't stand anyone being happy. Now what?"

He was holding out a ten-dollar bill. "Take a cab, will you? I don't want you walking through this neighborhood alone."

"I'll get a 104. Would you put that away?"

"It's your change from the diner. You left way too much."

Kaye listened patiently, though she did glance at her watch from time to time. Outside in the hall of the settlement house Eric could hear the ladder scrape as Omar went about replacing a bulb. He should not be aware of all this, Eric realized as he played. He should be so absorbed in the Prokofiev that he noticed nothing else. Then it happened: In the middle of one of the technically easiest parts of the sonata, he lost his place.

"Wonderful, Eric." Kaye applauded symbolically, not actually touching her hands together.

"It's not over yet."

"Well, why did you stop?"

Why indeed? Why was it that no matter how well prepared he was, he always had a memory slip when playing for someone. By himself he could breeze through his entire repertoire, which was considerable, without a hitch. But even so undemanding a listener as Kaye, who knew almost nothing about music, made him self-conscious and anxious. He had worked so hard that month on mnemonic devices, but now on this test run in front of his sister, who had dropped by unexpectedly, he had failed once again.

"It doesn't matter," Kaye said when he admitted to the memory slip. "They let you use the music anyway, don't they?"

The Mani Light did. But for the next performance he wanted to play without a score, hoping this would build his confidence. A cellist had asked him to perform the Rachmaninoff cello sonata for a Long Island public television program, but the cellist, a sixteen-year-old with nerves of steel, insisted it be done without music. Eric was not sure he could accept.

All this he explained to his sister in great detail, mainly to forestall her own agenda, which was bound to be unpleasant. She was undoubtedly going to bring up Arnold, and he did not want to have to reprimand her for upsetting Wanda with all those phone calls. His conscience was bothering him enough as it was. Surely he could have made more of an effort to see Kaye in the past few weeks. There hadn't been a single lunch or dinner together. He knew she must be lonely. But at the same time, he had his own life. He was trying to make a little more money these days, accepting more students, more accompanying stints, so that Wanda wouldn't have to worry about paying the bills. He had encouraged her to buy good clothes. They really made a difference in the way she looked. And Russell's ex-wife had recommended a hairdresser who had done wonders, giving Wanda's tawny rinse blond highlights and real body. Of course, it cost a fortune, but it was worth it to see how she carried herself with such confidence now, never slouching as she used to. Even her voice had an authority that would have surprised her if she were, or could be, aware of it. Eric sometimes felt the tenderness a father must feel as he watches a gawky daughter blossom after a difficult adolescence. The fact that adolescence could last so long, clear into the forties, did not surprise him in the least. After all, he had a father who still behaved like a juvenile delinquent.

"So it doesn't bother you that all of a sudden he's interested in guns," she said, interrupting him in the middle of a sentence. No preamble, no transition. She didn't even bother to supply the name.

"A lot of people hunt. You want those?" he added as she inspected a flowered tin, cookies from Tiburcia's mother. "You can take them home with you."

"Can't you see how fat I'm getting?" She looked offended. "So what are you going to do about it? I think you should do something."

"About what? Your weight?"

"That's right, joke. Don't you realize, Arnold is very high-strung. He was really upset when he heard Wanda was married."

"How do you know?"

"I had lunch with him right after. He was like a zombie, not himself at all. And Wanda told me he never used to lift weights before. She never saw any dumbbells in his apartment."

Eric resisted making a crack. "You know you're upsetting Wanda with all this nonsense. I don't think it's fair."

The cookie Kaye was about to bite into was set aside, onto his file cabinet. "I'm tired of trying to help people. I give up."

This was an exit line, but she remained where she was. He could only smile and play a note or two.

"So let him go off the deep end," she went on. "Why should I care if Wanda gets harmed? Well, I'm off. You can practice all you want now."

Another exit line that left her solidly in place.

"Look, Kaye, you're getting me steamed. The guy's in the Philippines. You said so yourself."

"I said *he* said he was going there. I saw him plain as day."

"He's a fucking priest."

"Ex-priest. And I'd appreciate it if you wouldn't use such language with me."

Eric was amused at her sudden prudery. Usually it was she who got to aim the four-letter words at him.

"What do we know about that man, after all? Just because he used to be a priest—if anything, that makes him suspect right there. Why would a normal, healthy man want to become a priest in this day and age? It's weird, unnatural."

He did not rise to the bait, so she went on.

"I hate to tell you this, Eric, but I have reason to be worried. The man is something of a sex fiend. Don't look at me like that. I've never slept with him myself, though Lord knows it was through no fault of his. He can't get enough of it, must be some sort of glandular problem. And I might add, I hope Wanda's been careful. He's slept with men as well."

"Oh, come on. He was in love with Wanda."

"What planet did you come from? Here, give me one."

The folding chair squeaked as she rose and plucked a cigarette from the pack he had just reached for, behind an untidy mound of scores.

"Of course he's in love with Wanda," she continued after they had both lit up. "That's the whole problem. But it doesn't mean he might not have fooled around too. Not everyone is as pure as your driven snow."

A surge of panic made him sound childish. "You're making this up."

"It's not just Wanda I'm worried about," she went on, unfazed. "There was no love lost between you and Arnold, after all. Has Wanda ever told you what he really thought about you? I spent a lot of time defending you. He thought you were a real monster."

"Me?"

"Are you really that shocked?"

Actually, he was. He had always assumed that he was the only one who considered himself a monster. Despite his modesty, he did have some faith in the camouflage his good looks and good manners provided. As for Wanda, yes, she knew the worst about him. But her love was so strong, so constant, that, basking in it day after day, he was beginning to feel more kindly toward himself. That was why he had finally made up his mind that he must love her; she was fearless, undaunted by the beast.

"Dad said—Eric, are you listening—Dad said you should be careful. I talked to him last night in Tallahassee, and he thinks Arnold is very unstable."

This was too much for Eric, bringing *him* into it. "What the fuck does Dad—"

"Calm down."

"—know about Arnold? He's never even met him."

Her eyes closed, Kaye took a luxurious drag on the cigarette, like someone in a film noir. "He talked to Arnold at the recital. And he was there when Arnold broke into the apartment."

"What apartment? You mean Tompkins Square? He had his own keys. He didn't break in." The lid of the piano slammed down. "I don't know what you're up to, but goddammit I've had enough!"

She regarded this outburst with maddening composure, a hint of pity in her green eyes. Without haste she gathered her things, adding the cookie tin to her Macy's bag, and went to the door.

"You should hear yourself," she said, pausing on her way out. "You're really not yourself at all. What happened to the kind, considerate brother I used to know? At the very least, I thought we could discuss this like two adults."

It took a moment to recover after she left. He raised the piano lid and stared at the keys, brooding. The way she had smoked, it was not just like a Fifties B movie, it was their mother's unconscious imitation of the way a film star smoked. And that last business—"I thought we could discuss this like two adults"—how many times had his mother leveled that charge at Lamar? But of course this was not Kaye's role at all. *She* was supposed to play Lamar, not him.

Twenty-two

Time and again they assured each other that Kaye couldn't have seen Arnold in the park. Indeed, both Eric and Wanda began to wonder if Kaye was not experiencing some sort of nervous collapse. When Eric told her about Kaye's weird experience with a lamp cord, how she had seen their mother spying on Lamar and her, Wanda could only agree that the poor woman should be getting help from a responsible professional. As for the so-called rifles in Arnold's apartment, Eric remembered how he had once looked in his sister's purse and found a gun.

"A gun?"

"At the hearing last year about the cats, she brought a gun with her. I looked in her purse and—what's wrong? You look so odd."

"Nothing."

"It really bothered me. She's always making everything seem so dramatic. Throw in some rifles now, that ought to get everybody's attention. That's it, you see. She's got to be center stage."

Eric was surprised at how easily one thing led to another, despite the fact that he had never before thought of his sister as desiring center stage. She had always seemed content with a supporting role.

"Besides, if there really were guns there," Eric went on, "why haven't we been shot yet? Or at least threatened. It's been awhile; he's had plenty of time."

"Don't joke. It's not funny."

The idea that their love was forbidden, punishable by death, stirred Eric in a curious way. He had never felt so tender, so protective toward a woman before. It was almost as if he wished then, as his lips worried her nipples, that his sister were not crazy.

"Stop. We can't."

"Come on, Wanda." His hand wedged between her thighs.

"No, not now. What are you doing?"

With his other hand he pulled off the condom he had been using since Kaye's visit to the settlement house. Wanda had assured him Arnold was not bisexual, but he had thought it was better to play it safe. Now he realized how much he trusted Wanda. He was not afraid anymore.

"Put it on, Eric. Maybe it's better if you—"

"What are you saying?"

"I don't mind if you use it, really. Please, get another and—Oh, good morning, Uncle Joe."

Wanda's uncle had opened the bedroom door and stuck his bald head in. "Forgive me. I thought this was the john."

"Down the hall."

Eric gave a feeble wave, the condom still in his hand, as the door closed on the old man's kindly, but baffled, round face.

"Great," he muttered.

"Wonderful," Wanda echoed as she got out of bed.

The uncle was in town on a clerical errand for the Waterbury Knights of Columbus, something to do with stationery, Eric had surmised from his disjointed remarks at dinner the night before. Wanda had prepared him for the visit by telling him about the "nervous breakdown" with the altar boys some thirty years ago. Uncle Joe had never been quite right in the head since then, she explained, and her mother always worried terribly if he tried to go anywhere alone. She had actually forbidden him to visit the city this time, but he had made an upsetting speech about his duty to the Knights and then snuck off, walking all the way to the Waterbury depot.

Hearing this the day before, Eric had been prepared for the worst. But he was pleasantly surprised when Uncle Joe turned out to be rather charming, in a Jainist way. He winced and crossed himself when Eric stomped the life out of a roach hiding beneath their table in the restaurant. And in his bright blue suit, the portly old man seemed so benign that even the most menacing-looking street people would answer him politely as he started up conversations at busy intersections or bus stops.

"I thought you had locked the door," Eric said as he too got out of bed.

Wanda gave him a look. "There *is* no lock on the bedroom door. Don't you know your own house?"

"Well, why didn't you say so? I could have—oh, Uncle Joe."

The head was in the door again as Eric zipped up his trousers.

"Come quick." He motioned impatiently. "Hurry up, kids. There's two birds on the sill, pigeons."

"That's nice, Uncle Joe," Wanda said. "I'll be right out."

"Louis, hurry, you'll miss them."

"His name is Eric, Uncle Joe. We already told you."

"That's right."

"Don't call him Louis anymore, hear? Now shut the door. Let us finish dressing, OK?"

If Uncle Joe hadn't been there that day, Wanda would have taken the L train out to Canarsie to visit Mrs. Merton at the nursing home. The temp agency had told her there would be no work until Wednesday, and the awful humidity of the past couple of weeks had finally let up. Yes, it would have been a nice day to visit.

"Go," Eric urged. "I can fix him lunch."

"Did he say he's coming back for lunch?"

"He's just going to the stationer's. It can't take that long."

"I should be here, then. It would be rude. I haven't seen him in so long."

"You were in Waterbury just last weekend, Wanda. Remember? You got that rug I hate from your mother."

"You don't hate it." Wanda had put the rose-patterned carpet under the piano so that the new tenant, whoever eventually moved into Mrs. Merton's downstairs, would not be annoyed by Eric's playing. "And besides, I didn't see Uncle Joe last weekend. Only my parents, and I thought you were going with him to the stationer's."

"He's a big boy."

"But Mom said we should watch him. Oh, shut the door, will you?"

He was peeing and hadn't bothered to close the door behind him. Wanda did it for him. She was edgy because Eric hadn't seen the necessity of her remaining at home. The truth was, she had been putting off the visit to Canarsie for some time. What if the nursing home turned out to be one of those places that are always being "exposed" on TV docudramas? Of course, Wanda reminded herself, she wasn't the one who had put Mrs. Merton away. Nevertheless, it would be painful and upsetting to discover an unpleasant home. And then again, Wanda was troubled by what Eric had told her about Kaye's gun. She had always assumed that Una Merton had imagined seeing the gun, and now to learn that Una wasn't quite as senile as she had been led to believe. . . . Furthermore, there was the problem of Mrs. Fogarty. If Wanda visited Una, chances were that sooner or later Mrs. Fogarty would hear about it and feel slighted because Wanda hadn't bothered to drop by her house, only a few blocks away from the nursing home.

Of course, Wanda had been meaning to get together with Mrs. Fogarty again. But she was so busy these days. And Mrs. Fogarty was so prickly, always making sarcastic remarks when Wanda turned down an invitation for lunch or dinner in Manhattan. Did the woman really expect her to go traipsing all the way down to lower Broadway for a sandwich? It was unreasonable. And as for Canarsie, Wanda didn't like the idea at all of going to a house where a man had been shot. In fact, the more she thought about it, the more she was sure that it was best to disentangle herself from any further involvement with Mrs. Fogarty. After all, she could very well be mixed up with some criminal element, thanks to her late husband. All those Italians Mrs. Fogarty knew—it made Wanda uneasy to think back to that Sunday she had found herself munching cookies with the Rosary Altar Society ladies. Who knows that someone couldn't have come to the door and gunned them all down? Vendettas, after all, could last for years. Just look at Louis. Wanda had caught a glimpse of her ex-husband at the mall in Waterbury last weekend. His arm was thrust into the maw of a blood-pressure machine at Walgreen's, and she had swerved down another aisle just in time, completely forgetting what she had come to buy.

* * *

When Uncle Joe didn't show up for lunch, his business obviously taking longer than they had expected, Wanda hurried off to 57th Street. A last-minute cancellation at her salon allowed her to be squeezed in. Afterward she walked to a nearby music store to look for a particular edition of Scriabin for Eric. In her handbag was a pair of leotards, just in case she had the energy for an early session with Serge. She decided she didn't but went anyway. Eric had complimented her the night before. Her body seemed so firm and toned, he had said. She was getting such a nice shape, no longer skinny but slender now, svelte. Wanda realized it was worth all the agony. Serge was really making a difference—and at her age, too, when most people seemed to give up.

"What should we have for supper?" she asked when she returned home with a cramp in her side. "Uncle Joe likes pork."

"Did you get the Scriabin? Oh, thanks. What? Thirty-nine dollars? You didn't pay thirty-nine dollars for this, I hope."

"What am I supposed to do, haggle? Move, please. I have to look in the refrigerator."

"I can't afford this. Take it back, will you?"

"There's nothing here. Let's see, I don't have time for a roast. Maybe I'll get some pork sausage. No, don't give that back to me. I'm not taking it back."

"Thirty-nine dollars?"

"Will you eat sausage, Eric? I don't like it either, you know, but I think we should get something nice for him."

Wanda went down to the butcher shop around the corner from their building. They charged too much, but she was afraid there would be a long line at the grocery store. While she waited for another customer's order to be trimmed of fat, she had the distinct feeling that she was being watched. Glancing over her shoulder, she saw no one at the door. But on her way out with the sausages, she noticed a cat dozing on a ledge by the window. It was bluish-gray, like Charles, Mrs. Merton's Siamese, and for a moment Wanda thought how nice it was that Charles had found such a relatively pleasant foster home. But when she went back for a closer look, she saw the eyes were rather dim, not at all the startling blue she remembered.

* * *

"Sausage? You know I can't eat sausage."

"Eric, I asked you just a few minutes ago. Now don't be difficult. It's not going to kill you for one meal. Oh, great," she added, noticing the score on the counter. "You've got ketchup on the Scriabin. Now you can't take it back. What were you doing with ketchup, anyway? Were you sneaking something?"

He looked innocent, which was enough to convict him, even without the dab of ketchup on his chin.

"Bad boy, out of my kitchen," she said, giving his fanny a good pinch. He looked unbearably cute. It was all she could do to keep from spanking him.

"Your mom called," he said from the other room as she got out the skillet. "She's worried about your uncle."

"What?"

"Stop all that clatter and you can hear. She said something about Uncle Joe was supposed to be back in Waterbury by now. It's his bingo night. He never misses it."

"He's eating with us. Didn't he tell us that himself this morning? Eric, call Mom and tell her to stop worrying. She's going to drive me crazy."

"He had our address and phone number, Wanda. I told you."

"You saw it with your own eyes?"

"I wrote it out for him myself in big block letters." Cradling her in his arms, he peered over her shoulder at the TV. "And I saw him put it in his briefcase, right on top of his change of underwear." Uncle Joe's briefcase doubled as a suitcase.

"Then where could he be?" She dabbed a tear away with a handkerchief and then blew her nose. "We should have gone to the stationery store with him. Mom was right. He's not competent enough to handle himself all alone here. This will kill her, I know."

The local news was on, a 9 P.M. edition. Wanda seemed upset by the anchor, a woman she exercised with, and from time to time she would criticize her hair or her grammar. Yet she was the one who had turned the set on, fearing the perky voice might rattle off some item about an elderly man set upon by a gang of vicious youths and shot for the twenty dollars in his wallet. It was childish of her to let her imagination run away with her like that, and Eric told her so. Nevertheless, she had managed to make him a little anxious as well. During commercials they would cross-examine each other about what Uncle Joe had said he would be doing that day. The more they tried to reconstruct his vague replies at breakfast, the more contradictory they seemed.

"Ow!" Eric exclaimed as Wanda suddenly bolted for the phone. Springing from his lap, she had banged her foot into a sensitive area.

"For you."

"Who is it?"

"Hurry, Eric. I don't want the line tied up."

Taking the receiver from her, he heard the voice even before he managed to say hello. "Look in your drawer and see if you come across a tie with whales on it. I've been looking all over hell and creation."

"Dad, I don't keep my ties in a drawer. And I don't have any of yours."

During the "Are you sure?" phase, Eric relaxed a bit as he learned that his father was not at Kaye's, as it sounded, but down in Tallahassee. The connection was alarmingly clear.

"Listen, Dad, I'm sorry, but I've got to get off," he interrupted Lamar as Wanda signaled impatiently to him from across the room. "Wanda is—"

"What? She won't let your own father say a few words after he hasn't had a single call or letter in over a month? I like that."

"I sent you a birthday card, and Wanda spent weeks knitting you a sweater."

"Just what I need. It's ninety-nine degrees out today."

"You know it'll get cold soon enough."

"Eric, will you please get off that phone!"

"I heard that," Lamar said. "She knows it's me. Barely said hello. I thought maybe by now she might be a little less hostile. You try to be nice, see how things are going, and—"

"Please, Dad, listen. There's a little emergency. Wanda's uncle, we've got to keep the line open for him."

"Don't you have call waiting? For a few dollars extra you wouldn't have this problem. But you're always trying to cut corners, aren't you? Save a few pennies and then find yourself up shit creek, that's your philosophy. Well, enough is enough. I'm going to sign you up for it the minute I hang up."

"No, don't. I don't want call waiting, Dad, understand?"

By the time he was able to wrench himself free from this conversation, Wanda had worked herself up into quite a state. "I ask you one simple thing, keep the line open—"

"Calm down, will you? I had to tell him about your uncle, that's what took so long. You said you wanted to be friends with Dad. If I had just hung up without an explanation—"

"Now is a fine time to be friendly."

"Where are you going?"

"Where do you think? I can't just sit around here wondering. I'm going to look for him."

Eric had already spent forty minutes walking around the neighborhood. He reminded her of this and then added, "You're overreacting, you know. This isn't like you, Wanda."

"I just have this gut feeling, it keeps gnawing at me, something's wrong, really wrong. Eric, please, go back inside." He had followed her out into the hall. "Someone should be by the phone."

"You're getting like your mother," he warned as the elevator door opened. "She's the one who set you off tonight with her crazy worries. Who knows, he might be on the train right now back to Connecticut."

Saying, "Is that so?" she got into the elevator with an obscure, almost bitter smile. "Hold the door."

Sticking out a bare foot, he managed to keep the noisy door at bay while she rummaged through her tote bag.

"What's this?" His voice was almost drowned out by the groans and shudders of the door as it protested against his foot. She had handed him a whip, a cat-o'-nine-tails, supple and compact, each thong aged to perfection. Nothing had ever seemed so repulsive to him, so cruel and menacing. Was this what she thought he wanted? How could he be so totally misinterpreted? A spatula, a paddle, a hand, those were essentially playful, domestic games. Granted, they weren't very mature, but they were light-years away from anything like this. He felt tainted by the very feel of the leather, sickened even. And yet he could not help staring at it, against his will.

"I wasn't going to show you, Eric. It's embarrassing."

"But—" His finger palped the handle gingerly. All this time he had felt so guilty for making her play such a role, fun as it might be. Now it dawned on him. He hadn't made her do anything. She was the one who had initiated the spanking. And though she would attempt to dissuade him from time to time, that reluctance was probably as much a part of her game as the actual sex. The paddle, the spatula, they were her ideas, not his. Fine, so maybe he had told her once how his mother had pretended to beat him with her spatula, how his father had come upon them both, he, Eric, with his pants down, laughing so hard the tears made Lamar a blur. "How could you, Wanda? How could you think. . . . And why are you showing this to me *now?*"

"Well, you're so sure I'm overreacting. I had to give you proof."

"Proof of what? I don't want this. How could you think I would like something like this?"

"Like it? Eric, this is Uncle Joe's. I found it under the sofa tonight while you were out looking for him. Why are you acting so weird? *Like* it? This has nothing to do with . . . you." As she said this last word their eyes met. The recognition seemed just as painful to her. They both looked away in confusion and shame.

It was Wanda who was the first to recover. In a calm, matter-of-fact tone, she said, "All right, that's enough, Eric. Enough of this nonsense once and for all. Listen to me: Uncle Joe wouldn't have gone back to Waterbury without his . . . thing. Now if Mom calls, don't mention it to her. He was supposed to have given up this foolishness ages ago. She'll have a fit. So move your foot, please. Let me go."

The door rumbled shut. He remained where he was for a moment, appalled at his own stupidity. Yes, Wanda had mentioned once—was it at Russell's?—something about her uncle's asceticism. In this day and age, though, it was hard to believe someone could have such a primitive mentality. The poor man.

"There's no dog food," someone said in the apartment across from the elevator.

Eric was wearing gym shorts, nothing else, which was his way of keeping the Con Ed bills down, using the air conditioner only when Wanda complained about the heat. Not wanting anyone to see him practically naked with a whip in his hand, he trotted to his apartment.

"No, this isn't happening."

He tried the knob again. The door was locked, which shouldn't have been a surprise. After all, they always had it set so it would lock automatically behind them. If he was going out with the garbage, he would shove the pig doorstop in the way. But hurrying after Wanda, he had forgotten.

It was eight flights down, but if he went all out, he just might beat the elevator, especially if people were getting on and off. Fortunately, the stairwell wasn't used much by the tenants. And besides, if he saw someone, he could pretend he was exercising. Maybe they wouldn't notice he didn't have any shoes on, and, of course, they wouldn't see that he didn't have a jockstrap or underwear, though it was evident enough to himself as he took the stairs two at a time.

As he descended he seemed to age, a mere youth from eight to six, then from five to three came intimations of mortality, twinges, and palpitations that eventually slowed him to a geriatric hobble by the last flight. Smoking had done him a lot of good, he could see.

Peering out into the lobby from the stairwell door, he saw Mrs. Cobb waiting for the elevator with her Labrador. Gently, he closed the door. This was not the person to ask for help. Years ago, when he had first moved in, he had been foolish enough to accept a dinner invitation from her. Single at the time and a good twenty years older than him, she had been mortally insulted when he had politely declined her invitation to go to bed with her after the crème brûlée. "You must be queer" had been her parting shot after he had thanked her profusely for the meal.

He heard the elevator arrive and dared another peek to see if, by some miracle, Wanda might get off. But Mrs. Cobb and the dog breezed right in without having to wait for anyone coming out.

"Quiet, Erica," he heard her reprimand the Lab as the door shut on its halfhearted barks. It was a disturbing name, but Eric had trained himself not to think about it. After all, Mrs. Cobb had gotten the dog years after the dinner. It would be quite vain of him to imagine the name as some sort of revenge, wouldn't it? And she was happily married now to a kindly old gentleman who boasted at every opportunity of his wife's guest appearance on *Sky King*, back when she was Miss Rheingold.

The super had a closet in the basement he called his office. Eric decided to give this a try, even though Neto rarely stayed past nine. There was no doorman to ask for help; the building was not classy enough for that. All Eric needed was a phone, which Neto had in his office. He could call Kaye then and have her run over with her set of keys. Or Neto, if he was there and not in a foul mood, might be persuaded to jimmy the lock. He had done this for Eric once or twice in the past, without damaging the lock, and only charged ten bucks.

Though a machine was running, no one was in the basement's laundry room. He hurried on, past a huge, ungainly furnace to an unmarked metal door. Steam pipes ranging along the low ceiling clanked like bolder echoes to his tentative knocks. As he expected, no answer. "Neto?" he called out vainly before giving the door a sound, final rap.

It budged. Calling the super's name again, he pushed the door open, wincing as the metal grated against the concrete floor. Once he managed to take hold of the string that switched on the bare bulb, he knew he was saved: The phone sat in plain view on a worktable. Now he wouldn't have to venture out to a pay phone on the street and call Kaye collect (if such a thing was possible) or wait huddled in the stairwell for Wanda to return.

But why was there no dial tone? He punished the phone with a good shaking before he noticed there was no cord. Neto must unplug it every night before he left. Advising himself to stay calm, Eric began a methodical search through the shelves above the rickety table. The cord had to be there, somewhere in that mess. Wrenches sat in jars of fuses and drain plugs; jigsaws and rasps leaned against economy rolls of toilet paper; a screwdriver marked the place in a lurid paperback written in what seemed a made-up language but was probably Maltese, the super's native tongue.

The dank, stale air was beginning to have its effect. Eric's heart pounded as he tried to ward off claustrophobia while pawing the shelves. Then he heard a rustle in the corner, by Neto's padded chair. Or had he just imagined the noise? The thought was too horrifying. To be barefoot, nearly naked, with some sort of rodent crawling about (he refused to even think the three-letter word) . . .

"Oh, shit!"

His groin was on fire! But no—take a deep breath—no, it was all right. Relax.

Recovering from the initial shock, he realized what had happened. Alarmed by another rustle, he had knocked his elbow against a can of turpentine or paint thinner, which had splashed onto him. The pain wasn't really as bad as he had imagined. It was manageable. All he needed to do was find something to wipe it off with, a rag or towel. Better yet, the toilet paper.

His gym shorts were damp with the fluid. After pulling them down he dabbed with the toilet paper at the burning itch, raw and red and gorged with blood.

It was then he noticed the shadow, which at first he had assumed was his own, yet the shadow was motionless. Turning toward the half-open door, Eric saw the face, a horribly familiar face that for a moment or two he couldn't identify.

"You?"

"You?" the ruddy, freckled face replied.

Whether his fear was greater than his shame, Eric couldn't tell as he raised the whip in his hand—yes, he had carried it with him all this time, not knowing what else to do with it. Now that the name had occurred to him, he must protect himself. There was no telling what this maniac might do.

"What the fuck are you doing here?" he asked, trying to sound menacing as he tugged at his gym shorts.

"My laundry."

"What?" With the shorts finally up, covering his huge embarrassment, Eric felt less at a disadvantage. Unarmed, Arnold would not stand a chance in a fair fight. But who knew, Eric warned himself, he could be concealing something in his jeans.

"How long have you been following me, Murtaugh?"

Arnold's eyes widened as he took a step back. "You nuts or something? I came down to get my laundry and thought I heard the super. I wanted to ask him—"

"Your laundry? You can't just break into a building and do your fucking laundry. That's the worst excuse—"

"I live here, buddy."

"What?"

"I fucking live here. Now, are you going to put that thing down or what?"

It finally dawned on Eric that what he saw on Arnold's face was not anger but fear, the same fear that was contorting his own face and making him talk like a fool. Somewhat abashed, he tossed the whip onto the table.

A half hour later, when they were still talking, trying as best they could to explain themselves to each other, Eric detected another rustle under the padded chair. His suggestion that they move somewhere more comfortable was seconded by, "Yeah, I better get back to my place. Someone's waiting for me. You might as well come with me till Wanda gets back."

And so Eric followed him out of the super's closet and, after a brief pause to gather the laundry, trudged behind him all the way up to the seventh story, where Arnold had the key to Mrs. Merton's.

Twenty-three

$\mathcal{T}$he apartment that Eric had always considered a cesspool, a mire of filthy waste, looked as tame and ordinary as a living room from a Fifties sitcom. After finishing up in the bathroom, where Eric smelled nothing but Arnold's Hermès cologne, Eric went into the bedroom and selected a Hawaiian shirt that was no doubt baggy on his host but tight enough on himself. Because of Arnold's potbelly, the bikini underwear drooped when Eric put it on. A pair of fashionably outsized shorts, the kind favored by teenage surfers, completed Eric's makeshift decency.

Before going back into the living room, Eric tried to squeeze himself behind the headboard of the bed so he could put his ear to the heating vent. But what would he hear? No one was upstairs.

It was unsettling to think that Arnold had been their neighbor all this time, ever since Mrs. Merton had been forced to leave. Arnold claimed he had no idea when he moved in that Wanda and Eric lived upstairs. That was why it had been such a shock to run into Eric in the basement.

"Fogarty's the one who got me in here," Arnold had told him in the super's closet. "I was paying eighteen hundred a month over on the West Side when I lost my job. The jerkwater outfit I was working for, they weren't getting enough business and had to lay me off. What am I supposed to do? I owe a fortune on my credit cards, you know how it is. So Fogarty, she's this dame that runs a newsstand down in the lobby, a friend of Wanda's who kind of had this mother thing for me—she was all shook up when Wanda got married, almost as bad as me." (Here a spark of resentment, even hatred, had flared up in the pale eyes, but a weary sigh betrayed the toll such malevolence takes when you're over forty.) "So Fogarty comes to the rescue. She tells me I can move into this friend's apartment for only two hundred a month. See, Merton's is rent controlled, and her relatives don't want the landlord to find out she's out of here. They're going to try to keep the place in the family, but no one can move in right now. So I'm keeping an eye on the place, getting her mail and stuff."

"And you didn't know you were right under us?" Eric had asked, still suspicious.

"No, Fogarty didn't say a word about it."

"And you never saw Wanda or me in the lobby or elevator, not once?"

"Hey, Fogarty told me to keep out of the way. I use the stairs mostly, good for the heart, you know. And besides, I haven't been here that long."

Eric had tried his best to believe him. After all, Eric himself sometimes didn't see Mrs. Cobb for weeks, and she lived right down the hall.

"So why did you tell Kaye you were in the Philippines?" Eric had asked just before they had left the super's.

"That was my first impulse: pick up lock, stock, and barrel and get the hell out of here. I mean, first I lose my girl and then my job, what the fuck? But then when Fogarty told me about this apartment, life in New York seemed possible again. I suppose I should have told Kaye about changing my mind, but I was so god-dam pissed at her. She'd made me believe I had a chance with Wanda. Every time I gave up, the woman would give me a pep talk, keeping my hopes up right to the very end. Shit, I'd have a new girlfriend by now, I'd be recovered completely if she hadn't kept opening the wound, saying there was still hope. She sounded so positive all the time, like she knew something I didn't. And I was enough of an asshole to believe her."

Coming out of the bedroom, Eric saw that the old man was still dozing on the Danish modern sofa. The serene look on his pink, round face was too much for Eric. Ignoring Arnold, who was leafing through the classifieds of the *Village Voice*, Eric took a seat by the end table and said, "Uncle Joe."

"Hey, let him sleep," Arnold said in a whisper loud enough to wake any normal human. "He's exhausted."

"Do you know all the trouble he's caused?" Eric asked in a low voice, angling toward Arnold, who was still glancing at the paper. "I want some answers."

Yes, Eric had been vastly relieved to discover Uncle Joe sleeping peacefully when he had come into the apartment. But the relief had had time now to change into irritation and puzzlement. Sure, it made perfect sense that Uncle Joe had left his briefcase behind when he called at the stationer's. Arnold had described the old man's dilemma convincingly enough, how he had tried to find the right stationery store again but had gotten turned around, confusing the East Side with the West. It was all he could do, after hours of wandering, to make his way back to the right apartment building without the address Eric had written out and placed so carefully in the briefcase.

And Eric could believe that once Uncle Joe had found the right building, he had simply begun to ring doorbells on the higher floors (he remembered an elevator ride, not the floor) assuming he would eventually hit the right apartment. What he couldn't understand, though, was why the old man had asked Arnold, when he had answered his door, if he knew where the McNabbs lived.

"Why McNabb?" Eric now asked Arnold. "Where would he get such a name?"

Arnold shrugged. "That's why I didn't know what the hell was going on when you walked in tonight. God, I'm glad he belongs to you. I didn't know what to do with the poor guy."

"Well, it was nice of you to let him stay here and rest. He must have been really worn out."

"And he hadn't eaten since breakfast, he said. I was afraid he might collapse. That's why, when I went down to get the laundry I had started already, I thought I could ask the super where the McNabbs lived. Remember, when you spilled the turpentine on you, that shout, I thought it might be the super."

Eric nodded. It was beginning to make some sort of sense. "But why couldn't he have just called or looked me up in the phone book? I'm listed."

"We did look. I heard him call myself. He called all the Mc-Nabbs in the book. Some of them were getting pretty pissed, too, let me tell you. He said he'd been calling from pay phones all afternoon as well. And you know, down in the lobby, there's no names of the tenants. I always thought that was sort of strange."

"There used to be, by the buzzer. But last year a couple of tenants were robbed by a guy pretending to be from Federal Express. He got in by reading their names off and then—well, we all decided it was safer to just put the apartment numbers downstairs."

"Say, those clothes don't look too bad on you," Arnold commented, going back to his paper.

Eric didn't know how to take this. He knew he must look ludicrous, Arnold being so short, such a different shape. But then again, the guy might be trying his best to be friendly. Maybe it really did take too much effort to hate someone over a long period of time. After all, Eric had forgiven him weeks ago for assuming he was a monster—and gay. At least, he thought he had.

"Where you going?"

"I better leave a note for Wanda, let her know where I am."

A minute later, after running up and down the stairs, he was back in the apartment that was so like his own, the floor plan exactly the same, the plumbing fixtures, the stove and refrigerator, even the built-in toothbrush holder. It was like being in a spatial déjà vu, a not altogether comfortable place to wait, especially since he didn't have on his own clothes. And the old man snoring so peacefully, there was something almost sexless about his face.

"Give him a break," Arnold protested as Eric shook the uncle gently.

"He's got all night to sleep." Eric decided he had to know about this McNabb business. He was tired of being puzzled, suspicious. If Arnold was telling the truth about this, if he really hadn't been holding onto Wanda's uncle just to torment her and make everyone anxious, then maybe it would be possible to go on living with Arnold as a neighbor. Otherwise, something would have to be done.

"So Uncle Joe," Eric began as soon as the man opened his pale blue eyes, "what's going on?"

"Ah, I finally found you." His smile was as serene as it had been in sleep. "Dear boy, if you only knew what I've been through. Where have you been?"

"Mr. Pond, would you like a drink?" Arnold asked, and then with a frown in Eric's direction, added, "Or maybe you'd like to go back to sleep."

"I'm quite refreshed," the old man said, letting Eric help him sit up. "Careful, that arm is sore."

"Sorry. Here, try this." Eric stuffed a throw pillow behind the old man's naturally well-padded back.

"McNabb?" the uncle repeated after Eric finally got around to posing his question. "Why would I call McNabb?"

"Yes, it doesn't make any sense. Do you realize that right now Wanda is out looking for you? She's very upset."

"But that's your name."

"I'm Thorsen, Eric Thorsen."

"You mean to say you're not my niece's husband?"

"I am."

"And Eric is a nickname, right? Wanda told me this morning you enjoyed being called Eric instead of Louis."

Eric and Arnold exchanged a glance.

"McNabb," Eric said as it finally dawned on him. "That's Louis's last name."

Finally there was a ripple in the uncle's placid composure. "*Your* last name, Eric."

"No, not mine, Uncle Joe."

"But I was there, just yesterday, I saw the priest put the Sacred Host on your tongue—and hers, the body of Christ."

It was true. Eric and Wanda had gone to Mass with Uncle Joe and received communion.

"Louis McNabb is dead, is that it?" the old man ventured, his eyes filled with a desperate hope.

"I'm sorry, Uncle Joe. He's alive. Didn't Wanda's mother tell you about me?" As he said this, Eric suddenly understood why Wanda's mother had been so frantic about Uncle Joe's visit. She had forbidden him to come to New York for good reason. Maybe she didn't want the poor, addled man to know the truth about his niece. Such an absurd family, Eric thought with righteous disdain. Yet the pain in the old man's eyes was real.

270

"Look, we're very happy, your niece and I. We love each other."

"But she renounced her sinful divorce and married again."

"Yes, me, not Louis."

"But Our Savior has made it perfectly clear in Scripture and the teaching of the Magisterium that there can be only one." He crossed himself and then rose from the sofa, brushing Eric's helping hand away. "Only one," he muttered as he wandered into the bathroom.

"What's with this Magisterium stuff?" Arnold asked, scratching a freckled arm vigorously, as if he were allergic to the word. "Is he nuts or something?"

"He used to be a priest, or still is. I'm not sure."

"What? Him?"

"I told you down in the basement, the whip and all, remember?"

Arnold smiled, shaking his head. "So that's the guy you were talking about."

"Right, Wanda's uncle. Who did you think?"

"Well, I didn't realize this was her uncle until you came up with me. I just thought you were making him up."

"Making him up? Why would I do a stupid thing like that?"

"Hey, buddy, relax. I just thought you were bullshitting me, trying to blame someone else, say it was his."

"Listen, that goddam whip belongs to him. You heard him yourself. He's a real basket case, used to whip himself every Friday until the bishop threw him out."

"All right already." Arnold held up both hands in an exaggerated gesture of surrender. "I believe you, Thorsen."

Eric didn't see a smirk on the ruddy face, but he certainly felt one. "You don't believe me, do you? Well, maybe you'll believe her."

"Huh?" Arnold said, a little too innocently, as he tugged on his graying mustache.

"Don't you hear?"

The footsteps above were sharp and distinct. Wanda had apparently just returned home. In a moment she would be down to clear up the matter once and for all.

"Say, listen, buddy, I'd just as soon not see her. You can understand that, right?"

271

If the footsteps were so loud, Eric could just imagine how the piano must sound. And yet Arnold could still claim that he didn't know who lived upstairs? Surely he must have heard familiar voices. And what about the mail? He would have seen Merton's name. Wanda was bound to have mentioned the name back when she was dating him. All he had to do was put two and two together.

"Why don't you go up now?" Arnold urged. "I'll send Mr. Pond up soon as he's finished in the bathroom. Come on now, give me a break. I really don't want to see her. I can't."

From the door Eric regarded him coolly. "Why not?"

"Goddammit, get out of here. Go back up to her."

"You're still hoping, aren't you? You haven't given up yet. You've been waiting all this time for her to find out what a monster I am. Then when she makes the awful discovery, she can run back into your arms." Eric would have enjoyed this speech a little more if he had a cigarette. But he would be back in his apartment soon enough. "Well, sorry to disappoint you, Murtaugh, but she already knows who she married. Nothing you can say to her is going to make her change her mind. That's what you don't want to see now, how happy she is, how much she's still in love. So go ahead, ask her about the whip, ask her anything you feel like. Don't be afraid."

He could hear her coming down the hall now. Soon he would open the door, and Arnold would learn the truth, once and for all. But the poor guy looked so miserable that Eric's triumph was soured. Where was all the cockiness, the slick macho bravado that Eric found so distasteful? Why did he have to look so deflated, so human that Eric suddenly felt a perverse urge to protect him?

Nevertheless, he answered the knock on the door.

"What in God's name are you doing *here*?" Kaye demanded as she strode into the apartment. "I've been calling and calling and no one answers and—oh, hello," she inserted, noticing Arnold in the chair by the window. Her face turned a harsh, obvious pink while Arnold's, usually so ruddy, seemed siphoned of all color.

Seeing this, Eric couldn't help coming to the man's rescue by diverting his sister's attention. "This is all I need, you barging in now."

It worked. She seemed to forget Arnold for the moment as her eyes blazed full force upon her brother.

"Barging in, Eric? Thank you very much."

"Well, what are you doing here?"

"Oh, I didn't have anything better to do tonight. You know how it is with us meddling women. I was in the middle of doing my hair when I decided it would be much more fun to spend a fortune on a cab so I could go barge in on my darling brother."

She yanked a loose state-of-the-art curler from her hair and stuffed it in a pocket.

"Dad breaks in on a conversation I was having with a dear friend in Los Angeles," she went on, "a man who seems to care about a woman's feelings, a man who listens, so Dad ruins this for me by telling me I've got to help Wanda find her uncle. I'm forced to hang up on Joel—yes, him—and start calling your apartment and get no answer and then I call Dad back in Tallahassee and he says it's my duty to go over and make sure little brother and his wife are all right because they sounded so upset and so I go out into this wonderful New York soup and nearly gag on the fumes and the cabdriver is trying to stiff me by going way out of the way and what do I get for my trouble but, 'What are you barging in on me for, Kaye?' Yeah, well, all I can say is I'm sorry Mr. Murtaugh here has to see his in-laws behaving like this."

No one—including Kaye, it seemed—knew quite what to make of this last remark. She was evidently a little confused and disoriented. Perhaps it was something of a strain playing the role of an abused grande dame in jeans and a man's wrinkled shirt, a shirt that looked awfully familiar to Eric. And for good reason. It was his, he suddenly realized.

But before he could ask for it back—his wardrobe was meager enough as it was—she had turned on Arnold, perhaps as a way of covering her verbal slip. "And you, sir, you have a lot of nerve telling me you're in the Philippines. All right, you want to hide, that's fine with me. But be a man about it, huh? Be a man. You think all those stupid rifles are going to make you into a man?"

"Uh, Kaye, those guns—"

"Hush, Eric. He has this coming to him. Do you realize, Mr. Murtaugh, that every time you buy a gun you're contributing to the death of innocent children? Don't look at me like that. It's a fact. Those gun manufacturers are the folks keeping the goddam NRA in business, and they're the ones paying off the fucking wimps in Congress who haven't the common decency to ban the automatic weapons that are killing inner-city children. I hope you're proud of yourself. You ask me, you should go back to being a priest. It would suit your politics fine."

"Are you through now?" Eric savored this chance to be so calm and reasonable with her. "It wasn't his apartment, Kaye. You broke into a stranger's apartment. Those weren't Arnold's guns. He moved out, see. He lives here, right here."

She had been looming over Arnold's chair in a menacing fashion. As she retreated a step or two, Eric could now see the ex-priest's eyes, as wide and pleading as those of a mink on an animal rights poster.

"Very nice, boys, very nice. So you've managed to make a fool of me. You should be proud of yourself, Arnold. Good job. You've had my family thinking I'm crazy because I see you in the park. Kaye's losing her marbles, that's what they were saying. And you want to know something, mister? They were right. I must have been out of my mind to wonder if you might be hurt or ill, if you had anyone to get you food or whatever. Yeah, you got to be nuts these days to think about anyone but yourself, a real ass."

The two men didn't dare exchange a look; she was watching them too closely, her eyes narrowed as if she had a bead on first one, then the other.

"Say it, Eric. Say what an ass I am. Because I am, Arnold, aren't I? When a man runs his bare foot up and down my leg, this loony dame here thinks he might find her attractive, that he might even care for her a little. Especially when he calls her day and night and moans and groans about how unhappy he is. Sure, the poor boy's heart is broken. His life is over, right, but at the same time he still manages to run his foot up and down her leg and tell her in detail how good he is in bed, how much he really loves women and is so sensitive to all their needs. Well, you know what you are, Father?" She let the tear run down her cheek without bothering to wipe it away. "You're nothing but a great big phony.

"The two of you," she added a moment later, after adjusting a

274

curler that had drooped down her forehead, "you deserve each other."

Her disgust was so compelling that neither man was aware that someone had been standing in the half-open door until they heard, "I agree."

It was Wanda, and from the look on her face as she went over to comfort her sister-in-law, who had begun to sob outright, she meant what she had said.

They were about to turn the lights off in the bedroom when the door creaked open. Kaye pulled the sheet up over her bare full breasts. "Yes? What do you want?"

It was Mr. Pond, the crazy uncle. He had refused to go back up to Eric and Wanda's for the night. Some nonsense about them not really being married.

"Where is my scourge?"

"Huh?"

"I can't sleep without my scourge."

Kaye looked over at Arnold, who was standing stark naked by the light switch. "Over there," Arnold said, turning instinctively to face the wall.

"Where?" Mr. Pond wandered in a few steps and then said, "Oh," as he spied the scourge sitting on top of a jumble of clothes in the plastic laundry basket.

"Can't he knock?" Kaye said after Mr. Pond had left, going back to the sofa in the living room. "I can't stand people creeping around."

"Shh. Not so loud." Arnold had crawled in bed beside her.

"He can't hear."

"You never know. These walls—"

"They're thick as can be, Arnold. What are you talking about?"

"My, what big tits you have, grandma, mmmm. . . ."

Kaye let herself be kissed, hoping the physical pleasure would help block out some of her resentment. She heard herself groan with pleasure and say, "My love." Except that she hadn't groaned. And she certainly hadn't said, "My love." That had been some other woman's voice.

275

"Shh, honey, not so loud," came a whisper, her brother's. Her eyes closed, Kaye savored the mystery of the body next to hers. For a moment or two it all seemed possible, the misery of separation only an illusion. These voices spoke of a joy unshakable, more profound than the deepest grief.

When it finally occurred to her where these voices were coming from, neither her own mind nor Bernini's heaven, she still found it difficult to separate herself from his embrace. It would have been so nice to go on, in that darkness. . . .

"What are you doing?" Arnold protested as she sat up, untangling herself from his arms, his legs.

"Can't you hear?"

"Believe me, Kaye, I didn't know at first. Fogarty didn't tell me a thing. Anyway, look." Taking his pillow, he wedged it between the headboard and the vent that had tormented her brother for so long, sending up the cries, the stench of the cats. "This cancels out all the sound. I was just about to do it like I do every night, really. I even got ear plugs I put on sometimes."

He was sick, yes, a very sick man. "Arnold, it's crazy, you can't stay here."

"Two hundred a month."

Still turned away from him, she smiled at his pathetic attempt to justify himself. It had been a mistake to want to stay over. She must have been out of her mind.

"You're leaving, Kaye?"

"Of course." So simple, just walk out. Don't get yourself involved with a nut case, she told herself.

"Kaye, I need you. Help me."

"I'm leaving, and that's it," she said, fighting with all the common sense she had against the wave of tenderness and compassion and raw need of her own, the wave that was going to win anyway, engulfing them both sooner or later.

"You're the only one who can understand."

"For God's sake, Arnold I'm leaving. And . . . and you're leaving, too."

"I am?"

"You're coming back to my place with me. I got plenty of room. Two hundred or not, this dump isn't worth it."

* * *

276

In the living room the uncle was hugging the scourge to his chest like a teddy bear. Kaye tried to wake him gently, saying his name, Mr. Pond, Mr. Pond, touching his shoulder. But his breathing continued as serene and undisturbed as a Buddhist monk's in the last stages, close to Nirvana. Becoming impatient, she gave the scourge a tug, the ridiculous plaything that she suspected was all a hoax. The old man had probably given himself a few love taps back in his days as a priest, and everyone had gotten all upset and excited over nothing. Just trying to get attention, that was what it all amounted to as far as she could figure. Wanda had told her the story over a late supper the two women had shared at a diner, without the men, shortly after Wanda had returned from her search.

"Forgive me, forgive. . . ."

"It's all right, Mr. Pond," she said as he clutched the scourge, trying to keep it from getting away. She let him have it when his eyes finally opened.

"I'm sorry I had to wake you, but there's been a change of plans. Are you listening? Good. You see Arnold there?"

From the apartment door Arnold gave a little wave. Beside him were his overnight bag and Mr. Pond's briefcase.

"He's going to take you back up to your niece's, understand? You're going to have to sleep there tonight."

"I'd prefer to stay here, thank you."

"Well, I'm sorry, but Arnold and I don't think it would be a good idea to let you stay here alone. You might get lost again or—well, Wanda told me you left the gas on in their apartment yesterday. Now come on."

"I will go to a hotel then."

Kaye and Arnold exchanged a look as the old man began to unbutton his pajama top.

"Don't be silly," Kaye said. "Hotels cost a fortune. You've got a free room upstairs, perfectly nice and clean. Now don't make me lose patience with you. It's late, and I have no intention of traipsing around all night looking for a hotel that will—my God."

His pajama top off, Kaye got a glimpse of his back. The scars were old but, even so, savage looking, the bas-relief of welts a nacreous pink.

"What is it?" Arnold asked.

"Never mind," she said as Mr. Pond yanked an undershirt over his large round head.

"Look, Mr. Pond," she went on, her voice more natural now, less patronizing. "We're all tired and want to get to bed, right? So why not come with us over to the West Side? You can have your own room. I'd love to have you as my guest."

"What?" Arnold protested.

"Hush, Arnold, or we'll never get out of here."

After some coaxing, the old man agreed to go with them to Kaye's. At the elevator, though, he seemed to be overcome by doubt again. Kaye had to ask him if something was wrong.

"You *are* married, my friends, aren't you? I mean, I just assumed all along you were. Good people like you, you wouldn't live in sin, correct?"

"Sin? Just what do you mean by sin?"

"Oh, Arnold, would you please be quiet?" Turning to Mr. Pond, she added more gently, with only a touch of asperity, "Of course we're married. We just keep two apartments for—well, our work. Yes, that's it. Now come along, Mr. Pond, the elevator's here."